The Children of The Serpent

I

Arden's Crisis

S.T. Mason

This is a work of fiction. All of the characters, organizations, and events portrayed in this novel are either products of the author's imagination or are used fictitiously. Any resemblance to actual persons, living or dead, events, or locales is entirely coincidental.

First Edition: January 2020.

Edited by: Stefanie Molina

Cover design by The Book Cover Whisperer:
ProfessionalBookCoverDesign.com

ISBN: 978-1-7344942-0-4

Published by Mason Press

Learn more about Arden, Mason Press, and S.T. Mason at:

ExploreArden.com

A special thanks to:

Jadiel and Manuel,

Thanks for always being there for me and listening to my crazy rambling. The two of you were my creative team since the beginning.

Becky,

I'm grateful for your insight, wisdom and knowledge that assisted me in bringing this project to life.

Mom,

You've always supported me regardless of the initial outlook. Thank you and much love, now and always.

Also:

Joseph Farley, Logan Snider, Adrienna Barba, Jeremy Thomas, Alan Mendez.

The Grey Waste
North Sea
Viden
Ilvion
West Spire
Hearthelm
Tovand
Stonewell
Bastille
Blud
The Unknown
Tulfius Hall
Carvalel
Ornian Ruins
Torkus Lands
Masterstown
Barrington
Sunrise Sea
New London
Arden City
Von Isla
Sohn
Garshinian Sea
Somerta
Emerald Island
Lunsera
Arden, 243 A.O.A

Arden's Crisis

Prologue

A thousand voices uttered his name from the abyss below. "William." they called in unison.

His body ached as he limped along the sky bridge looming over the feverish waves of the sea. Salty gusts of wind threatened to throw him over the railing. He paused to catch his breath, impeded by the bloodstained chest plate he wore. Behind him, another cannon fired off in the city engulfed by war.

Fires raged along the eastern wall of the city, spewing warm light into the night. The Duke of Barrington laid siege to his prize as his army thundered with muskets and engines of war. The defending forces of the city garrisoned not only the stone wall and It's gate, but as well as several of the towers and bastions nearby, turning an entire civilian district into a militarized zone. Amidst the cacophony of battle, a new chant reached the knight on the sky bridge.

"Lionheart! Lionheart! Lionheart!" Hundreds of men chanted the name with palpable excitement, conjuring chill bumps along the dark skin of William's arms. The knight squinted at the fray, where a man soared through the night sky above the tallest building in the city, cutting through the mist of sulfur that hovered over the battle like a bird through a cloud. Alighting beyond the invading army, the Lionheart threw the enemy's cannons into the air. One by one they splashed into the sea.

The tide of the battle would now sway in the defender's favor thanks to the actions of the man from the Otherworld. The American.

"William," the symphony of voices uttered again. The knight shook his head, remembering his purpose and yet questioning his actions all the same. Since he had awoken that morning, the sea had called to him; his body felt anew, as if it were not his own. The bridge led him to the stairs of the spire standing alone above the waves. The stone steps passed beneath him in rapid succession as he raced to the top of the structure. Upon reaching it, he was knocked to the ground by a strong gust of wind. Groaning, he rose and crawled to the edge of the stone structure, looking out.

The ocean heaved beneath the stars. Waves thrashed wildly against the base of the spire. Further out, scattered cyclones formed in the water, growing in size and strength until dozens of whirlpools appeared.

Suddenly, the surface of the water adjacent to him began to stir. A new vortex began to form before his eyes. The whirlpool grew wider and deeper, spraying the knight with salty mist.

"William," the thousand voices said from the base of the vortex. He peered further over the edge and saw it.

A glowing sphere of light at the bottom of the sea.

He had never witnessed such an element, but his heart and soul recognized it as if from some distant dream. The glowing orb shined brighter and his armor began to scrape against the stone as he was pulled forward by some unseen force. The nostalgic daydream was swept away as panic engulfed him. He flailed in the air, his ears filled with his own screams and the sound of the raging water. Mist stung his eyes as he descended, falling toward the sphere as it grew even brighter.

The instant his right hand touched the orb, light enveloped him. His body felt numb, yet he ached with overwhelming pressure, robbed of air by a rush of cold water. Propelled by an unseen force, he spiraled through the cold water until he felt land beneath him.

He hugged the wet sand and took a few welcome breaths as his nerves calmed. His muscles and joints ached as unseen weight pushed down on every inch of his body, threatening to shatter his bones even as he lay still on the beach. Struggling, he turned to his side, toward the sea. No whirlpools could be seen. The vast ocean lay still and serene beneath the full moon. He groaned as he turned toward the beach.

His breath escaped him.

Beyond the beach, tall buildings stood clustered together, dominated by an overwhelming display of artificial lights.

It was a city, he realized. A city that was not his own.

Chapter 1

The Boy From Virginia

Rain fell onto Peter Loneheart's blond hair and into his sapphire-blue eyes already filled with tears. He glanced upward at his grandmother as they walked side by side toward the black canopy at the center of the cemetery. Her old hands trembled holding the umbrella and her shoulders heaved as they had all morning. She was crying so much, he thought. He looked around to the crowd in black that converged behind them. There were so many people, and most of them were crying too. As he looked around at the ocean of black under the scattered clouds of umbrellas, Peter decided that the entire city of Norfolk must be at his uncle Jack's funeral.

Upon entering the dry clearing underneath the canopy, Peter's eyes darted back and forth between two men who stood facing one another, the casket between them covered by the red and white stripes of the flag. Their uniforms were so cool, he thought. He remembered seeing his uncle's uniforms on several occasions.

His eyes settled on the covered casket and he grew confused. What was in it? he wondered. In the wake of the storms at sea, Jack's body had not been found off the coast. Only rubble remained of the pier he had always stood upon in the evenings.

But before he could inquire about the contents of the casket, he was guided to one of the three chairs that stood facing it. He sat in the center with his grandmother on his left. Peter's mother gave him a water smile before speaking from behind the podium. "Good morning"

Even though she had been sad since Jack's death, Peter thought his mother still looked pretty. Though she dressed like all the others in attendance and her blond hair was fixed in an ordinary fashion, a gentle radiance emanated from her, making Peter thankful that she was his mother.

". . .My brother was Jack Garrick Loneheart. He was known and loved by many. He did much and never asked for anything in return. His motivation was simple. It was love. Love—and compassion—are what motivated my brother to—" Her face briefly contorted with grief. She cleared her throat and continued.

". . .Love and compassion motivated my brother to do such great things with his life. It was his love for his country that motivated him to enlist in the army. My mother and I were heartbroken when he left home, and more so when he left for Afghanistan. We were so angry, but that was the thing about Jack: you just couldn't stay mad at him.

"You can imagine how pleased we all were when he finally came back home for good. He was relieved, too; he didn't have to worry about us being so angry anymore." She laughed gently, prompting chuckles from the crowd.

"But this time—" She cleared her throat as her blue eyes began to gleam with tears. "He is gone forever, and I can't be angry at him. The only anger I feel is for the storm that took him from us. . ."

Peter stirred in his chair as his mother's tears painted a black trail along her cheeks and down to her jawline. Her display of emotion proved infectious, and more tearful sobs came from the crowd behind Peter and from his grandmother beside him.

He had never witnessed so much emotion before and certainly not from his mother. He hated it and never wanted to see her cry again.

". . .However, we can rest easy knowing he is in God's kingdom. He devoted his life to his country, to his family, and to God. Compassion was at the forefront of his faith."

His mother smiled tearfully and stepped away from the podium. Walking over to sit on Peter's right, she gently kissed his head and put her arm around him as the pastor stepped forward and began to speak.

Peter's attention wavered during the older man's oration. He preferred to gaze upon the neat uniforms of the two servicemen who stood in place like two statues overlooking a tomb. He grew restless in his chair and was relieved when the pastor finally concluded his speech and the stationary servicemen finally moved into action.

The uniformed duo gently removed the flag from the casket, holding onto the corners as they folded it slowly and methodically into a triangle shape until only blue and white stars showed upon the folded flag. After a crisp salute, one man in uniform departed and the other slowly approached Peter and his family, kneeling down to present the folded American flag to his grandmother.

* * * * * * *

One Year Later

The morning sun shined through the window of seven-year-old Peter's bedroom. As he stretched, he took a deep breath to yawn, and detected one of his favorite scents lingering in the air: breakfast!

He raced downstairs without changing out of his shorts and t-shirt. At the bottom of the stairs, he paused at the sight of the closed door to his left. Uncle Jack's office, he thought. Typically on a Saturday morning, his mentor would have been the first person awake, often working alone while listening to rock or metal. But for the past year, the hallway had remained silent. No music had been heard since Jack's disappearance and the funeral that had followed.

The sizzling of his favorite breakfast food distracted him and Peter continued down the hall to enter the kitchen. On the far side of the breakfast table, his grandmother looked up from the newspaper she was reading.

"Good morning, handsome."

"Good morning, Gran."

The bacon popped to his left where his mother stood in front of the stove. She turned and smiled, wiping her hands on the stained apron she wore. "Good morning, bedhead."

"Good morning." He yawned again as he sat in the chair across from his grandmother. The stove clicked as his mother twisted the knob to turn off the heat. He felt her kiss the top of his head as she set down his plateful of scrambled eggs, a biscuit with grape jelly, and of course, bacon. The sight of his favorite food filled him with a desire to devour every last crumb on his plate and a frenzy ensued.

"Someone's hungry this morning," his grandmother noted as he finished off his bacon and moved on to the eggs.

His mother sat in the chair between them to his left. "He needs his strength for the big game. Slow down, Peter! You're going to have a bellyache if you eat so quickly."

He slowed his bites as he finished off the eggs but disregarded his mother's suggestion entirely when he got to the sweet, buttery biscuit.

"Done!" he declared after he savored the last bite. His grandmother chuckled. He sipped his orange juice and looked at his mother examining the tips of her long blond hair.

"I swear I have more gray hairs this morning," she sighed.

"Serves you right, Laura," his grandmother said. "You and your brother stressed me to the point that I only had a few strands of blond left by the time you left for college."

Peter's mother chuckled. "But my son isn't even ten and I'm already graying! One of these days I'm going to wake up an old relic, just like you." The two women laughed in unison as Peter finished off his orange juice. He didn't understand why they were so concerned about gray hairs and stress; after all, his only concern today was winning the last game of this season.

After breakfast, he rushed upstairs and washed up before putting on his blue jersey, the number seven on its back. A surge of excitement grew within him as it always did when he put on his shin guards and cleats. He raced downstairs and began to dribble his soccer ball around the living room, tapping it left and right across the carpet, eventually growing bored as he waited for his grandmother and mother to finish up their beauty routine.

Why do girls need so much time to get ready? he thought to himself.

His grandmother came downstairs just before his mother, who immediately drew his attention. She looked different. Prettier than usual. His nose stung slightly when she came close enough for him to smell her perfume.

"Who are you trying to impress?" he asked her. His grandmother laughed as his mother's eyes widened and her cheeks grew red.

"Peter Jason Loneheart!" she exclaimed.

What's she embarrassed about? he thought. *She's not the one playing in a game today.*

* * * * * * *

The parking lot of the civic center was packed, as was the green field next to it. A herd of people walked about on the sidelines and in the bleachers. Peter scanned the field for his friend and looked to the nearby goal where several other kids practiced their shots.

As he approached the entrance to the field with the two women, a tall man whom he did not recognize approached. The eyes of several nearby women followed him as he walked up to Peter's mother.

"Laura," the man said in a deep voice. Her face turned a shade of red again.

What's with her?

"Everett," she said sweetly. "This is my mother, Sarah."

"Ma'am." He gently shook her hand. The man's gaze shifted to Peter but the boy ignored him and continued to look for his friend.

"This is my son, Peter." He felt his mother's hands on his shoulders.

The man extended his hand to him. "Peter, nice to meet you."

Peter ignored him, noticing his friend standing behind the kids at the goal. "Hi!" Peter said, running past him. "Bye!"

"Peter!" he heard his mother exhale as he dashed through the crowd and onto the field, where his friend spotted him coming.

"Hey, Tyler," Peter called out. Tyler's jersey was blue like Peter's, bearing the number two. He stood a little taller and his skin was a few shades darker than Peter's. They were the forwards on their team. Together, they stayed near the opposing team's defenders, focusing on taking shot after shot at the other team's goal.

"Hey, Pete!" Tyler smiled and kicked the ball across the grass to him. Peter lightly tapped the ball forward and slowly made his way over to his friend.

"Ready to win?" he asked.

"Yeah. . ." Tyler said, shifting his eyes from Peter to the fence behind the goal. Peter followed his friend's gaze.

In an old gray robe, standing alone and leaning heavily on the fence, was a tall peculiar man. His skin was dark and he had no hair. The man appeared exhausted but continued to stare at the two boys.

Suddenly, a whistle blew loudly and they jumped. It was time to play.

* * * * * * *

The score was tied at two when Peter's coach called for a timeout. Peter sipped his water as he panted in the huddle and looked up to the bleachers, where his grandmother and mother both smiled and waved at him. The tall man named Everett sat next to his mother. He wished his uncle Jack could be there to watch and cheer like he usually did.

The timeout ended and another ten minutes of play passed with the tie unbroken despite strenuous effort. Dread filled him as he feared the long whistle blast that would signal the end of the game—or overtime. Neither was acceptable to the seven-year-old.

To his delight, one of his teammates intercepted a poor pass by the other team and now ran up the center of the field. The cheers grew louder as the player passed to Tyler. Peter ran forward toward the goal, bypassing a defender and opening himself up for a pass. Tyler kicked, and the ball met Peter's cleats.

His reception was flawless. He turned and faked left as the final defender in red challenged him. The defender made a move, and Peter rushed to the right, sprinting forward toward the goal in a blur of blue. He was close enough, he thought. He eyed the goalkeeper in black, wound his right leg back, and kicked hard, sending the ball sailing through the air and into the corner of the net.

Cheers thundered from the bleachers. He leapt with excitement, thrusting his fist into the air as Tyler met him with the same palpable joy. With the rush of the goal still in his mind, he ran toward the bleachers and pointed to his cheering mother. “That was for you, mom!” he yelled over the commotion. He heard several women whimper and gasp as his mother placed her hands over her heart with gleaming eyes.

The referees blew their whistles and the game was over. As he darted toward the center of the field, his teammates swarmed him, forming a huddle of youth and victory.

After shaking hands with the other team and finding his mother in the crowd near the entrance of the field, he embraced her as she showered him with kisses. “You're the sweetest boy who ever lived,” she assured him.

He laughed. “I know. Since I made a goal for you, can we go get pizza with Tyler’s family?”

“We can if your grandmother wants to,” she told him. He looked up to his grandmother, who smiled and nodded.

“We certainly can. You played so well. Your grandfather and uncle would be proud,” his grandmother told him. He knew it to be true and wrapped his arms around the older woman.

Most of the crowd departed as Peter waited at the entrance with his grandmother. He dribbled his soccer ball around her while his mother talked and laughed with Everett near the concessions stand. As he tried to perform a quick movement, he botched his touch on the ball and it rolled away across the concrete, stopping at a nearby bench.

He chased after the runaway ball but halted when he saw the strange man slouched on the bench. It was the same man who had watched him and his friend before the game.

"I. . ." the man said through heavy gasps. "I witnessed your bout. Well struck!"

He spoke in an unusual way, Peter thought. He watched the man as he shifted around, grimacing and sweating profusely. Amber eyes looked up to Peter, gleaming with a gentle radiance that reminded him of Jack's.

"Thanks," Peter said.

"You. . .move well, with the grace. . .of a lion."

He didn't understand what the comment meant, but admitted that it sounded cool, and the way the man said it made it seem even cooler.

"Your name is Peter?" He paused. "Peter. . .Loneheart?"

"Yes, sir."

Despite the man's apparent pain, he smiled. "Always bear in mind, Peter...be humble. . .even in victory. . .and love God with all your heart for he will always love you."

Before the boy could exchange another word with the man, his grandmother walked up to steer him away and back to his mother.

"Peter!" his grandmother said as she guided him. "What have your mother and I told you about talking to strangers?!"

"But that man looked like he was hurting," he told her. She stopped and glanced back to the bench with a concerned expression. The man slowly rose from where he sat with the help of a pastor Peter recognized from one of the city's churches.

* * * * * * *

The years passed like the wind and the boy from Virginia now stood in his bedroom, contemplating everything that could possibly go wrong during the planned evening.

There was a knock at his bedroom door.

"What is it?" he asked. His voice had grown deeper.

"Selena's dad is on the phone," his mother answered through the door.

Peter's heart stopped. *I've never even met him,* he thought. *Why would he want to talk to me?*

"He wants to know why his daughter is crying!"

"What?!" he exclaimed. He lurched forward and quickly opened the door. His mother stood in the doorway with crossed arms and no phone in hand, bearing a mischievous grin.

He playfully pushed her face away. "You think you're so funny, don't you?"

She laughed. "You need to relax." Reaching up, she adjusted the black tie around the collar of his navy-blue dress shirt. He had grown taller than she was and she had grown so proud of him. She had cried incessantly during his high school graduation just a few days ago.

"I don't know about this," he confessed. "Why am I so nervous? Why do I always get so nervous?"

"Because you care about how good you do, no matter what. And if it works out with Selena, and I know it will, then you will have your first girlfriend."

"But what if it doesn't?"

"Then she is the dumbest girl who ever lived if she doesn't see how big of a heart you have. . .or how handsome you are. Though I'm positive she knows that."

The mirror on his wall displayed how much he had matured. The strands of blond were a menace that he frequently had to push from his eyes.

She nudged him aside and gazed at her own image. "Good genetics."

Peter pointed to her head. "Except for the gray hairs."

She gasped. "Peter Jason Loneheart!"

He laughed and ran out of his room, taking flight down the stairs. At the bottom, the eerie silence in the hallway stopped him as it sometimes did. He looked at the closed door to the left. Stepping forward, he twisted the knob, opening the door ever so slightly so that he could peek inside.

Across the office, the sun shined through the window and onto the desk where books, electrical components, and a soldering iron sat. To the right, a large American flag took up the entire wall, and underneath it, several pictures and medals had been arranged in ceremony on a table. It was so quiet. Peaceful and yet so somber.

* * * * * * *

Upon his mother's request, he reluctantly agreed to drive to the beach where the event was being hosted. Although he had his license, he despised driving. He had enough confidence in his own skills; it was the others on the road that often frightened him. When he finally parked his mother's car in the parking lot adjacent to the beach, he relaxed.

His relief was short-lived: when he gazed at the large crowd of graduates and parents that bustled about beneath the canopies, he grew nervous again. A small sense of comfort washed over him when he caught sight of his friend Tyler jogging over to him. Like himself, Tyler had grown and their friendship had endured.

“What’s up, man?” Tyler greeted before looking to the two women next to him. “Hello, Mrs. Loneheart and Mrs. Loneheart.”

“Hello, Tyler.” Peter’s mother smiled. “We'll leave you boys to it.” She and his grandmother walked over to where most of the parents congregated with drinks in hand. Peter continued to glance around the crowd.

“Looking for somebody?” Tyler asked.

“Er...you could say that.”

As if his friend knew what was on his mind, Tyler pointed toward the furthest canopy, near the ocean. “Selena was over there. Better move quick though.”

The comment concerned him. "Move quick? What's the deal?"

"Something's in the air. She gets approached literally every five minutes. Make your move now or hold your peace, kid."

Peter groaned and his heart fluttered as his palms grew sticky. He focused on taking deep and controlled breaths, accepting his anxiety and working with it rather than against it. "Alright," he said. "Thanks, man. Wish me luck."

His anxiety grew with each step toward the solitary canopy. His eyes remained fixed on the few small groups of his classmates mingling beneath the black overhead. As he stepped under the small dome, he stopped and glanced around, alone.

"Hey!" a sweet voice said as a girl gently punched his shoulder. He turned to meet her gaze.

"Woah! You're like a ninja," he said, looking her up and down to admire the fitted oriental-style dress she wore. Her dark hair was fixed into one braid that fell past her neck and onto her chest.

She chuckled. "Fashionably late." She cocked an eyebrow at him. "But your tie is a mess."

"My mom helped me fix it."

"Did she?" she laughed. Selena stepped forward and began to adjust the fabric around his collar. He felt the blood rush to his face. "This might be weird to say," she began, "but I told my dad about you."

"You what?!"

"He's old-fashioned and he wants to meet you."

"But why? Is he here?"

"Of course he's here. Like I said, he's old-fashioned." She stroked her dark braid. "He would really appreciate it if you spoke with him before. . .you know..." She suddenly seemed nervous. After a moment Peter began to suspect what she was going to say, but she said nothing and stared at him as if expecting him to take the initiative.

He sighed. "Okay. Let's go see your dad."

“Great!” She kissed his cheek. “And so I was thinking that. . .maybe tomorrow we could go to the mall? If you aren't doing anything.”

A rush of excitement filled him. “That's perfect.”

“And it might be best if you ask him if you can take me tomorrow. He would really like that.”

“Sure. Let's go.”

They had started forward when she suddenly stopped. “Wait! I almost forgot your gift from Philly.”

“A gift? Selena, you didn't have to,” he told her as she looked around the crowd. She glanced in the direction of the pier further down the beach, straining her eyes.

She gasped. “I think that guy has your gift!”

Peter turned to stare in the same direction. The figure of a man in gray walked slowly toward the pier, leaving footprints in the sand. By his side, he held the poster meant for Peter.

“Ugh! He does.” She frowned.

“I'll get it,” Peter assured her as he started forward. He stopped and turned, kissing her on the cheek. “And thanks for the gift, Selena. I bet it's a copy of the Declaration of Independence.”

“Could be!” she teased after him as he ran across the beach.

Sand flew into the air with each step as Peter ran after the man. He was catching up just as the man made it to the entrance of the abandoned pier. The figure grunted as he heaved his body with great strain across the wooden planks. Peter made his way up the steps, following after the stalking gray robe and the man that wore it as he arrived at the end of the pier.

Peter stopped short, watching the man’s body tremble as he held himself up against the wooden railing. “That doesn't belong to you!” Peter told him.

The gray hood fell back, revealing the sweaty face of the dark-skinned man he had seen before. Though he bore the same pained expression, he was older.

"Apologies," the old man wheezed. "I assumed. . .the young lady would present this to you." He shakily extended the rolled-up piece of parchment in plastic.

Peter took it. "I know you. I've seen you before, around the city since I was a kid. At one of my soccer games and around a church downtown." The man nodded and grunted as he quickly glanced out to sea and then back to Peter.

"The community has graced me with much thought and care," he said with what Peter decided was a British accent. "I will forever be grateful. . .for all that they have done to assist me. . .in my quest." He looked back to the sea again before resting his eyes on Peter.

He's still in pain, after all this time? It's like he's constantly being pushed down by something, Peter thought. "Are you alright?"

The man glanced at the sea once again. "All will be well soon enough." He turned back to Peter with a smile on his face. "I do regret that I cannot explain what will happen, for I do not yet understand it myself."

"What?"

"Do not fret, Peter." He spoke softly as the sound of moving water grew louder. "I have made this trip before. I was fearful, but you will do well."

The noise from below drew his attention, and Peter finally looked away from the man and watched, startled, as the water from the sea receded from underneath the pier, revealing moss, seaweed, and sand. His eyes followed the flowing water further beyond the pier, where the waves heaved. Suddenly, they converged and began to flow in a circular motion until a small cyclone formed. Dark clouds appeared overhead. Further down the beach where the party continued, there were screams as all witnessed the cyclone grow in size to form a massive vortex.

A tremor shook the pier, its wooden planks creaking, until Peter heard the sudden snap of a large beam that reminded him of a rifle firing off. The railing the old man clung to broke apart and flew into the air, carrying him with the debris.

"No!" Peter jumped forward to grab him but instead fell onto what remained of the planks underneath him as gravity pushed down on him as never before. He looked up to see the body of the man flailing in the air like a rag doll as he soared away and over the surface of the water before disappearing into the dark center of the vortex.

A sudden gust of wind struck and the pier completely shattered as he was pulled up and through the air, spinning wildly across the surface of the water. He screamed and flailed as he was thrown over the water and into the twisting mass. Mist splattered against his face. The ferocity of the ever-churning water screamed in his ears like a jet as he fell over the edge and toward the darkness of the abyss in the center of the cyclone.

As terror rushed through his being and he considered accepting death, he spotted a gleaming light in the darkness below. And when he finally came close enough to the sphere of warm light in the depths, it swallowed him.

A sudden, bone-shattering heaviness descended upon him as he was plunged into darkness.

But as quickly as it had settled, the heaviness subsided and water again surrounded his body. He spiraled through the water until he was thrown onto a sandy beach.

He coughed up seawater and his body trembled with terror as he clutched the wet sand and hugged the solid ground beneath him. Seagulls called out above him as he took a breath of air and felt the warm sunshine on his skin. He was dizzy; his body felt so light.

After another welcome breath, he lifted his head. His jaw dropped when he rested his eyes on what lay before him. He had expected to see the canopies of the graduation party, his friends and family, with his city in the distance. Instead he was greeted by the sight of over a dozen tall stone structures surrounded by a giant wall on a pearl-white cliff.

Is that a castle? he thought. *Am I dead?*

Regardless, the castle and white cliffs did not belong in Norfolk, nor did the three men that came riding on horseback toward him.

Chapter 2

The Lady Of Lunsera

Each gallop of the horses sent sand into the air to be dispersed by the breeze that rolled in from the sea. As the three figures approached, Peter was able to distinguish what appeared to be leather armor that the three men wore over their chests. They each wore the same blue jacket. A small black cloak covered the left arm of the man in the center, who carried no weapon, unlike the two spear-wielding men riding at his flanks.

Peter stood up, sinking in the wet sand. His head and body felt light, so he took a deep breath. The three men came to an abrupt stop before him, their horses towering over the boy from Virginia.

"Oi!" said the man in the center with the small dark cloak.

"Er. . .hi!" Peter greeted nervously.

"What are you doing near the sea at this hour?" he said. His accent seemed British, like the man from the pier, but different, as if from another region.

The old man, he remembered. He turned back to the sea for any sight of the man's body, but there was only the ocean stretching for endless miles in all directions.

"The sheriff asked you a question!" one of the other men said.

He hesitated, speechless until the prominent question rolled off his tongue. "Where am I?"

The two underlings exchanged apprehensive glances while the sheriff stirred in his saddle. He shifted the dark cloak that veiled his left arm and the two spearmen clutched their weapons tightly.

"Your accent," the sheriff noted with a cocked eyebrow, "and your garments. Most unusual."

One of the spearmen beside him dismounted. His eyes remained fixed on Peter's hands, hanging by his sides. "What province do you hail from?"

Peter shifted his gaze from the sheriff to the spearman on foot who was slowly walking toward him. "Province? I'm from Norfolk," he said with sincerity, taking a step back as the three men inched closer.

"*That* is likely," the sheriff said sarcastically. Suddenly, he whipped the dark cloak concealing half his body to the side, revealing his left arm and the archaic-looking pistol he held, which he then aimed directly at Peter's head. "You are an assassin! And you are here to kill the Lady Helen before the parliament can convene."

Startled, Peter took a step back faster than he meant to. "What?! I'm not an assassin. I don't even know who Helen is or where I am." His eyes rested on the pistol. *Is that a musket?*

"Seize him!" the sheriff roared. The spearmen on foot lurched forward with open arms as if to tackle Peter to the ground, but only managed to entrap the boy's arm. Peter instinctively flexed the captured arm to pull away from the man, and in an instant sent the spearman flying into the air. He landed at least thirty feet away with a splash.

The sheriff and the remaining underling exchanged wide-eyed glances of terror and astonishment. “He's a bloody monster!” the underling on horseback exclaimed.

The sheriff's finger pulled the trigger and the fuse at the end of the musket ignited, followed by a percussive bang that sent the shot through the air into Peter’s shoulder.

Peter grimaced and held his fresh wound tightly as the warm blood soaked into his navy-blue dress shirt. The adrenaline coursing through him voided the pain and propelled him to move as the remaining spearman charged Peter in a cloud of dust and sand. Peter moved to the side clumsily and with intense speed to avoid the oncoming attack, falling face-first into the sand.

The sheriff drew a gleaming saber from its sheath and charged past the confused underling. The sand muffled his horse’s hooves as Peter hurried to his feet with a mouthful of blood and sand. The saber sliced through the air toward his head and again Peter leapt to the side. Propelled by his force, he flew at least twenty feet, crashing into the sand again.

The spearman on horseback turned and came charging at him again, the sheriff following behind. But the two men pulled back on their steeds, and Peter instinctively flinched as a new musket was fired off, the sound ringing in his ears. He and the two horsemen looked up the beach where two columns of riders dressed in the same attire as the spearmen raced toward him. At the front of the formation, rode a fit woman in the same attire. All of her hair was tied into a long black braid that flowed behind her in the wind as her horse galloped.

The woman stopped short of Peter as the dozen riders that followed her encircled him. One by one, all the new riders leveled their muskets at the boy from Virginia.

“What is the meaning of this?” she demanded. “Quickly! I do not want to be away from the Lady Helen any longer than I need to be.”

“An assassin,” the sheriff answered from atop his horse, saber still in hand. All eyes looked to Peter, who shrugged hopelessly.

“I'm not an assassin!” he insisted. “I don't want to hurt anyone, I. . .”

But before he could continue, the spearmen he had thrown finally emerged from the water.

"He's a monster!" the spearmen yelled to them.

The woman warrior turned back to Peter with a raised eyebrow. "Put him in chains."

* * * * * * *

The black iron chains rattled with each step as he trudged up the stone staircase that led up the cliffs. His escort consisted of the dozen guards that had arrived late on the beach with the woman that had led them. Ascending the stairs ahead of Peter and his armed escort were the woman herself and the sheriff Peter had fought with earlier, who now followed closely behind her.

"This is a mistake, Barda!" the sheriff exclaimed to her back. "Assassin or not, he should be executed on the spot."

"That is not for you to decide." she calmly but sternly replied. "You had your opportunity to take his life."

"You did not see what that villain did on the beach! He threw one of my men into the ocean as one could throw a stone."

What's going on? Where am I? And where's the man from the pier? He glanced back toward the sea. Nothing. *Still, did that really happen? Did I really throw him like that? What's going on here?*

As Peter contemplated, he took a link of iron between his thumb and index finger and applied some pressure. He gasped as the old iron began to bend and break. Looking casually at the guards who flanked him to see if any had noticed, he held the broken restraints together in his grasp, remaining silent and compliant.

For the remainder of the journey up the stone steps, the sheriff was relentless in his complaints to the woman called Barda. When they reached the top, Peter was able to finally take in the fortress he had seen when he washed ashore. The dirt road they came to at the top of the steps led to a large gatehouse made of the same stone as the numerous bastions and four high towers, from which hung long blue streamers, as well as the wall that surrounded the erected stone buildings. The party came to a halt before the gatehouse, giving Peter enough time to assess the size and condition of the large wooden doors that began to creep open.

The gatehouse was like a tunnel, filled with the sound of Peter's chains and the footsteps of the dozen guards around him. Slowly the echo of what seemed like dozens of voices and other clamor began to grow louder until the group came out of the other side of the gatehouse, revealing the origin of the noise.

Various buildings of stone and wood aligned the interior of the great stone wall. The vast cobblestone courtyard that lay between the buildings featured wooden stalls that the chattering people walked to and from. The people's clothes seemed like a cross between eighteenth- and nineteenth-century garments to Peter. The women staring at Peter with intrigued expressions wore dresses, while the men wore an assortment of knee-high boots, vests, tunics, and pristine jackets. In the center of the courtyard stood four cherry trees in a line that led straight to the ostentatious building at the center of the walled community. Long blue banners draped from the top of the two tallest points of the center building. Both featured a single silver crescent moon against the rich blue fabric.

The gossiping crowd followed the chained seventeen-year-old and his armed escort until they proceeded through the grand oak doors of the keep. The entry hall was lit by sunlight that radiated through the windows above the entrance.

The heavy doors closed with a thud, echoing against the marble floor and stone walls.

Barda turned to the escort. "Take him to the great hall," she commanded, and departed through a door in the corner of the empty room. The sheriff nodded to his men and the escort made their way through a pair of doors that led down a hall and up a flight of stairs, where they entered through another pair of wooden doors.

Sunlight shined through the large windows on the left side of the large room as they entered the great hall. Peter gazed around the crowd of well-dressed people that stood in small groups throughout the room. To his right, where several stone columns lined the wall,

Peter heard the giggling and whispering of a group of attractive women around his age. He felt renewed anxiety as all eyes in the room watched him As he was marched forward across the marble floor, his chains rattling with each step.

At the end of the great hall, a large bench of dark wood overlooked the room and its occupants, reminding Peter of a judge's bench in a courtroom. He was halted forcefully a few feet away from the bench by the guards that escorted him. The men each stepped back from the boy from Virginia and watched him as they clutched their weapons.

Peter released a relieved sigh and looked around toward the windows. The view outside offered Peter a revitalizing image of the ocean and allowed him to collect his thoughts. He studied the restless waves, recalling the cyclone, the man on the pier, and the weightlessness he had felt, as if gravity itself had sucked him into the center of the vortex. His throat began to feel tight as he thought of his mother and grandmother, his friend Tyler and Selena. Were they all safe? Were they searching the beach for him? He struggled to hold in tears.

His introspection was cut short and the urge to cry subsided when the door next to the tall bench before him swiftly opened. Barda entered the room and stepped to the far side of the stand. The chatter in the room quieted and Peter's stomach began to stir with anticipation.

The door opened again, gently, as a beautiful woman in a navy-blue dress emerged. Peter forgot about his own sadness and longing for home as he watched the woman walk gracefully to sit behind the center of the bench. He looked up to her and met her alluring yet fierce gaze. The sunlight swept across the creamy skin of her delicate face, lending a shine to her hazel eyes. And though she kept her honey-brown hair neatly kept and tied up behind her, Peter could tell it was long.

Every well-dressed person who had been waiting and chattering politely bowed to the woman at the bench. She nodded in return and stared around the room before her eyes fell on Peter. An awkward silence followed as she looked him up and down.

"State your name, sir," the woman finally said. Her voice was soft and melodic, but firm.

"Peter," he muttered.

"Louder, please." Her face remained devoid of emotion as she stared at him. He could feel the blood rush to his face.

"Peter," he said loud enough for all to hear.

The woman cocked an eyebrow expectantly. "Is there nothing further to add to your name?" she asked. Peter could hear several laughs and giggles from the men and women throughout the room behind him. "Do you not possess a surname or title?"

"Loneheart. Peter Loneheart," he told her. Though her gaze remained focused, for a brief moment, a flicker of emotion flashed across her face as Peter stated his last name.

"And where do you hail from, Mr. Loneheart?"

"Norfolk. Norfolk, Virginia," he announced, and noticed her lush red lips form a faint grin that quickly disappeared.

"I have been informed that you attacked several of the guards that defend this province. Have—"

"That's not true. I—" he began, but she raised her right index finger.

"Do *not* interrupt me again, Mr. Loneheart!" she warned him coldly. He swallowed and feared that all in the room could hear how intense his heart was beating. *What's going on? Who is she?*

"Now, if you are so eager to prove yourself innocent of the claims made, then please explain to us all what occurred." She leaned back in her seat and crossed her arms. He again felt his blood rush to his face as he became the center of attention in the room.

"I...er. . .washed up on the beach and three guys on horses came up to me. They thought I was an assassin and one tried to grab me so I pulled away and the guy went...well, flying," he sighed hopelessly.

"Threw him into the ocean like he was a small stone, Lady Helen," the sheriff said from behind his men.

So she's Helen. The one that they were talking about at the beach.

"Continue, Mr. Loneheart," she said.

"Well, the two other guys came charging at me and I dodged them."

"You dodged them?"

"Yes," he said. "Ma'am."

"Specifically how did you dodge?"

"I tried to run and I just tripped over myself and fell into the sand."

"You moved at a greater speed than you anticipated?" she proposed for him.

"Yes, ma'am."

"Have you ever moved as quickly as you did on the beach?"

"Er. . .no, ma'am," he said. He watched as her lips formed another grin that soon disappeared before she straightened in her seat.

"I will grant you a short respite to confirm your story, Mr. Loneheart, as I do have a number of appointments that are more pressing at the moment," she concluded.

Why was she dismissing him? Had he said the wrong thing? He tried to remember what he had told her and felt a new anxiety emerge within him.

"Sheriff," Lady Helen said. "Please escort Mr. Loneheart out of the chamber."

"The dungeons, Lady?" he asked to Peter's dismay.

"That will not be necessary. Have your men escort him to the Lunar Courtyard where they will maintain a watchful eye over him."

"Of course, my lady." He bowed. A sudden force hit Peter on his shoulder where he had been shot. He grimaced as a guard shoved him again and then took hold of his chains. Peter looked back over his shoulder to Helen. She maintained her stoic expression even as he was finally escorted out of the room.

* * * * * * *

The Lunar Courtyard was a garden of shrubs and trees divided by white stone walkways and bordered by the tall gray stone wall that encircled the small Eden. A welcome sea breeze brushed Peter's face as he was escorted outside and into the courtyard. He heard the sound of a few horses galloping in the distance, hooves against the stone; they echoed throughout the stone walls and structures of the castle.

The twelve guards forced him to the edge of the largest stone walkway in the courtyard, which led toward open gates on the left and right side of the stone wall. He was then pushed onto one of the many marble benches that could be found throughout the courtyard and the dozen guards spread out around him.

He glanced around the courtyard under the sun before looking at the guards around him. Some had muskets that could be used to shoot him if he tried to run, so he relaxed his muscles and sighed, relieved to be out of the great hall and away from the woman Helen's intimidating gaze, even if for a little while.

Suddenly, the sounds of hooves grew louder. Three of the animals emerged from the open gate to the left. Two women and a man, all about Peter's age, rode toward them.

Peter jumped to his feet as the brown horse at the front of the trio stopped in the center of the walkway and stood over him, breathing in his face. The animal pushed Peter with its nose. The young woman that sat atop it looked down at him with intrigued hazel eyes and a mischievous grin. Her honey-brown hair was long and fell over the right side of her leather jacket. She looked much like the woman Helen, but younger, and yet there was something about her that put his nerves at ease.

"What is this?" the young woman smiled. She looked around to the guards surrounding Peter and then to himself. "Who is this and why is he in chains with an escort of this size?"

On the stairs overlooking the courtyard, the sheriff spoke. "Lady Helen commanded that he be given a respite."

"A respite?" the woman questioned as she reached down and tucked her black trousers back into her riding boots.

"For the prisoner to reevaluate his story."

"Reevaluate," she muttered to herself as she looked at Peter. "I do hope you did not tell a lie to Helen. If that is so, then you should pray to Fyraen at this very moment."

Peter agreed. He didn't know who Fyraen or this young woman before him were but evidently she knew about Helen.

"Aurora," the young man on horseback behind her said, "perhaps we may leave this cretin behind and continue?"

Aurora sighed. "Well, whether you attempted to deceive her or not, do not let her bully you, and most importantly do not let her deceive you in turn. She can be clever, but her personality is as plain as the desert of Sohn is dry."

She laughed and then kicked her heels into her horse. The three animals raced off down the stone walkway and departed through the open gate.

Aurora, he thought. For the first time since he had washed ashore, he felt some degree of joy as he recalled the way she had talked and how she had laughed when she rode away.

He sat back down on the marble bench and let his mind wander. For the next hour his thoughts shifted between his home, the place he was now, the dread he felt when he thought of the woman Helen, and the relief he felt when he remembered the woman Aurora. Finally, he was led back inside through the numerous hallways and up the familiar staircase that led to the great hall.

To his surprise, the great hall was void of the crowd that had occupied it before. Helen stood at the far end, and behind her, Barda bore a watchful gaze.

Peter was marched forward once again and halted just short of the stand. Helen dismissed the guards with a wave of her hand, leaving Peter alone before the bench, the two women staring at him intently.

Helen looked him up and down again and then her eyes rested on his chains. He continued to clutch the broken links of rusted iron in his hands.

“You may release your restraints.” She spoke softly, unlike when they had spoken before. “I surmise that you shattered them some time ago.”

But...how did she know? He hesitated before releasing the shards. The shattered pieces of iron clanked against the marble floor. He looked back up to Helen and saw her smile.

“Now, I am certain that you are curious as to why we are speaking alone,” she proposed. Uncertain, he simply shrugged. “I wanted to confirm what I and many in the province are beginning to suspect: the Lionheart has been found.”

“The what?” Peter asked.

She ignored his question. “May I ask of your immediate family?”

“My family? Er. . .Well, my mother's name is Laura. My grandmother's name is Sara.”

“And what of the men in your family? Your father?”

The topic ignited his fury. “I didn't know him,” he hissed.

“My apologies,” Helen said gently, to Peter’s surprise. “Perhaps any other family?”

“I had a grandfather who passed away after I was born, and an uncle, but he died when I was seven.”

“And how old are you now? You appear no more than eighteen years of age.”

“Seventeen,” he confirmed.

“Seventeen,” she said to herself. “And you hail from Norfolk, is it?”

“Norfolk, Virginia,” he said, and watched as she traced her index finger along her lips. *I want to kiss those lips,* he thought. *Wait. . .what?* He shook his head, regaining his focus. “Ma'am, where am I?”

“You are in the province of Lunsera, Mr. Loneheart, in this two-hundred and forty-third year of the age of Arden. The season of Carraas is upon us.”

“Lun...sera?”

“Indeed, Mr. Loneheart. This is the ancestral province of the Moonwey family. My family. And from what I can reveal to you, your family and my own bear a history together.”

“What do you mean?”

“Ten years ago, when I was but thirteen, I met a man with similar talents to your own. Though he had black hair rather than blond such as yours, he spoke with the same unusual accent, which he informed me was American.”

“You know Jack!” Peter concluded, his mind racing. His uncle that had been lost at sea ten years ago had come to Lunsera and now the same thing had happened to him.

“I knew Jack Loneheart,” she said solemnly. For a moment Peter felt as if they shared the same sadness. “But while he was in Arden, he went by a different name. He was simply referred to as the Lionheart.”

“But where is he? If you know him, then you have to know where he is!” Peter swallowed. His head felt light. Helen hesitated and her gaze fell on Peter’s injured shoulder.

“You are wounded and in need of rest,” she concluded before turning to Barda. “Have him taken to the physician, bathed, and then taken to the tower where he will sleep,” she ordered. Barda waved for the guards.

As they escorted him toward the door, he looked over his shoulder to Helen. “Please. Where is Jack? You have to tell me!” he tried, his words slurring. But Helen just stared out the large windows, appearing perplexed.

* * * * * * *

The small chamber was heavy with the smell of old books and dimly lit by a dozen candles on mounds of paper. Numerous medical instruments lay on the adjacent dusty tables. An old man shuffled toward Peter, who lay on the wooden table in the center of the chamber.

The physician cleared his throat. "You have remarkable physical qualities," he said behind his white beard before adding, "in regards to your anatomy and physiology."

"What do you mean?" Peter asked.

The physician grew excited. "Your bones and muscular tissue are far denser than any one person I have ever studied. I surmise it is because the world you hail from possesses gravity greater in intensity than our own."

"So...this is a different world?"

"Of course, boy. Now lie still." He patted Peter's chest gently and finished the last of the stitches. Peter grimaced as the sharp needle stung the tender skin of his shoulder.

"What do you know of the worlds?" the old man asked as he worked.

"Er. . .like Mars and Venus?"

"Are those planets near the Otherworld?"

"The Otherworld?" Peter asked.

"The name that the people of Arden assigned to the world that the twelve and the Lionheart hail from."

"The twelve?"

The physician sighed. "Do you know anything, Boy?"

Peter suddenly felt ashamed. Sullenly, he muttered, "Apparently I don't know anything at all."

The old man paused his work. "I sympathize with you, young man. Losing your home and finding yourself in a different place than before.

But it is during these times of uncertainty when you must use your strength to maintain your bearing."

Peter stared at the stone of the dark ceiling and mulled over the physician's words. "Now!" the old man continued. "One final stitch."

Peter felt the last pinch before the physician applied ointment to the freshly stitched wound.

"Thanks," he said as he sat up and put on his bloodied shirt.

"Now before you depart to the tower for the night, for I do assume that is where the Lady Helen will have you kept, I must urge caution regarding your abilities." The physician pointed to Peter's wounded shoulder. "You are NOT impervious to injury and therefore death itself! Also, your bones are indeed remarkably dense and because of this, I strongly suggest to you that you avoid bodies of water at all cost!"

"But I was in the water when I first came here."

"And it is fortunate you did not sink into the abyss like a stone. You may jump mountains and throw boulders if you must, but do stay far away from the water, Mr. Loneheart! Lions do not swim well in this world," he warned. "Two of your predecessors learned of this fact quite practically long ago."

Following the appointment with the physician, Peter was escorted down the hall to a dark chamber that was warm and humid like a hot summer day after rain. He was beckoned to wash in the warm mineral water baths there.

Afterward, Peter was escorted again down a series of halls and stairs that took him to the highest level of the castle. Finally, as he reached the end of another hallway with his guards closed in around him, the door of his chamber was opened before him. He looked around the modest-sized circular room, where a small round table and single chair sat near the door and a small bed awaited him near the open window.

The guards pushed him into the room and slammed the wooden door behind him. The sound of the door locking was oddly reassuring. Finally alone to collect his thoughts, he walked across the stone floor and made his way over to the window, where the view provided the ultimate solace. The sun was beginning to brush the horizon of the ocean. At least a dozen ships remained out at sea, sporting variously colored sails. The surface of the water shimmered in the warm dusky light. The seagulls called out, unseen, and there was little chatter to be heard from the street far below.

He hoped his mother and grandmother were alright, and soon, thoughts of Tyler and Selena came to his mind, too. He hoped they were all safe and wondered if they were looking for him.

"Arden," Peter said to himself, "Lunsera. Helen. Aurora. Lionheart." So much had happened so quickly. Was he really in a different world? How was it even possible?

Regardless, the long and eventful day had taken its toll on the boy from Virginia. He stepped over to the modest-sized bed and flopped down upon it. Easing onto his back, he sighed and closed his eyes as the waves of the sea sang their lullaby and put him to sleep.

Chapter 3

Sharp Knives, Sharper Words

For a moment when Peter first awoke he felt as if he was in his bed back home in Norfolk. He imagined the softness of the freshly cleaned sheets that smelled of detergent.

But as he slept in the smaller bed of his chamber, he heard movement outside the door. He opened his eyes to the early morning light, not yet bright enough to wake the castle. The seagulls called out as waves crashed against distant cliffs he could not see.

Peter listened for further sound and heard what seemed like small footsteps outside the door. He sat up and then stood, his bare feet cold against the stone floor. He debated whether he should sit or stand and decided to remain standing in the center of the cool chamber. He continued to watch the wooden door as the mechanical sounds of the lock clicked repeatedly. As his anticipation grew, the door finally opened.

A small head poked out from behind the wood. It was a little boy.

"Morning, Lord." The boy smiled. His hair was unruly and black, like the long tunic that appeared to be two sizes too big for him.

"Er. . .good morning," Peter greeted awkwardly. He watched as the boy opened the door with his entire body and revealed a large plate in his hands. "Lady Helen sent me with your breakfast."

Peter liked the sound of breakfast, but what was Helen playing at by sending this little boy alone to bring it to him? Did she trust Peter that much?

Nevertheless, his eyes followed the tray of thick-sliced ham and eggs sitting beside a bowl of a pale, thick-looking liquid. The boy placed the tray on the small round table and politely pulled back the exclusive wooden chair. "Allow me," the boy said with shining brown eyes. "My name is Thomas, Lord. But most call to me as Tom."

"I'm Peter," he told the boy as he sat down at the table.

"Please, Lord Peter. Eat!" the boy beckoned with glee.

"It's just Peter," he gently assured the boy, who stepped back and watched as he took his first bite of ham. The thick slice of meat and fat was packed with a salty taste; it was smoked. He quickly finished off the ham and moved onto the two fried eggs. Wiping the grease from his lips, he timidly took a small taste of the pale liquid in the bowl. It was surprisingly coarse and thick, but also sweet and creamy.

"Tasty wheat, Lord," the boy told him from the doorway. "It's my favorite."

"It's great," he admitted after a mouthful that turned into several more.

When the bowl was empty, Tom said, "I also have a message from the Lady Helen that I was instructed to relay when you finished your meal."

Peter sipped on the cup of water. "What is it?" he asked.

". . .the food was poisoned."

"*What?*" Peter gasped. His stomach churned and growled.

Thomas smiled. “My apologies, Lord. The food is not poisoned, I promise. And Lady Helen said no such thing. The Lady Aurora told me to say it and that Lady Helen was the one who poisoned it.”

Peter sighed with relief. “Why?”

“Lady Aurora is fond of playing jokes on anyone she can, and it would not be wise to refuse her if she requests that you assist her in her schemes,” Tom said.

Peter sat back in his chair and rubbed his face as he recalled the name. *Aurora. She's the one from yesterday. On the horse. She looked almost exactly like Helen.* “Helen and Aurora are sisters?”

“Yes, Lord. Lady Helen is the elder; she is the leader of the province.”

“Lunsera.”

“Aye. Lunsera is one of the eldest provinces in Arden, consisting of four islands. Our province possesses the largest fleet in the world!”

“So this is an island?”

“Yes. Lunar Rock is the name. The capital island of the province. Home of the Moonwey's.”

“Arden. So...what is it? I mean, what is Arden?”

The boy hesitated before answering, “Arden is the world, as well as the alliance of the twelve provinces.”

“So it's not a country?”

“At times. . .” Thomas looked around and twiddled his thumbs as his face grew a shade of red.

He's nervous, Peter noted. *Does he not know? Is it really that complicated here or does he just not know his own history?* “So Arden is an alliance between twelve. . .states?”

“Provinces. Well. . .there *were* twelve.”

"Were? There isn't anymore? What happened?" The question lingered in the silent room before Thomas walked forward and took up the remnants of the breakfast served.

"I will return shortly with your garments, Lord," the boy said, and exited the room. The door closed and was locked again, leaving Peter alone to ponder the obscurity the boy had displayed toward the end of their conversation. There had been twelve provinces that made up Arden. What had happened?

Peter stood and walked to the window. A cool morning breeze carried the scent of fish and smoke into his chambers. Hesitant, he poked his head out of the large open window, grasping the frame to avoid falling out. Glancing down to the cobblestone street below, he saw a brown horse galloping along the empty road. The young woman riding the animal munched on an apple with her free hand as the other held the reins of her steed.

Shuffling footsteps echoed from the hall behind him. He heard running and then the mechanical clanking of the lock.

The door opened slowly and Thomas reappeared.

"That was fast," Peter told him.

The young boy closed the door. "I can move quickly. And my family provides the services for the castle. I know every corridor and passageway," he said proudly as he ran over to the bed and dropped the clothes he held in his hands onto the ruffled blanket.

Peter ran his fingers along the soft fabric. "These look expensive."

"Lady Helen requested that you wear them."

"They're beautiful." Turning the tunic Tom had brought around, he marveled at the silver crescent moon on its back.

He put on fresh-scented fitted black trousers and a long-sleeve tunic that reached mid-thigh, securing the tunic with a leather belt around his waist. As he sat on the bed and began to step into what appeared to be riding boots, Tom asked, "May I ask you questions, Lord?"

"Sure."

"Is the Lionheart really your uncle?"

"Helen said that's what everyone here called Jack. So I guess so."

"Jack Lionheart," the boy said to himself. "Peter Lionheart, The Lion of Lunsera."

Though Peter had no interest in being the Lion of Lunsera, he had to admit that the title did sound intriguing. "Do you know anything about Jack? I mean, where he is?"

Thomas shrugged. "I can tell you about some stories I've been told!"

"Stories about Jack?"

"Aye, Lord. The battles in Sohn! Or the battle of Blud, it was the biggest battle of the war of reclamation!"

"War of reclamation?"

"The war for Arden City. When the Duke of Barrington went to war for it. The heroes who fought during the battles are my favorite!" he said excitedly. "There was the Lionheart, Sir William of Bastille, Sir Henry Fife, The Baron of Hearthelm! The fallen knight—"

"Tom!" an older woman yelled from the hallway. The boy inhaled sharply with wide eyes before running to the door and pulling it open enough so his head could fit through.

"Yes, Mum?" he called out beyond the other side of the door where Peter could not see. "I'm helping Lord Lionheart!"

"Lady Helen has summoned you!" his mother called.

Thomas turned back to Peter. "Apologies, Lord," he said before he exited and closed the door behind him. Peter listened as the door was locked on the other side. He continued to hear the boy and his mother.

"Wash your face before you go! And make haste!" the woman ordered.

"Yes, Mum!" Tom said from beyond the door before both voices disappeared and only silence remained in the hallway.

He walked back to the window as he could hear several men talking in the street below. Three older men walked with a horse and wagon. Peter listened intently as they walked along the street.

"Lady Helen and the second Lionheart," one of them said.

"Wager she will finally marry?"

The third man spat onto the cobblestone. "Be a fine match, I'd say. Now how much you wager she's going to take him to Arden City?"

"How much? For the Parliament or the plague?"

"I wager both!" the first man concluded. "*Now*! How much you wager he disappears like the others?"

The third man nodded. "I take that wager! That kind from the Otherworld never stay long. The twelve didn't, the Lionheart didn't. I say this one won't either."

The three men disappeared further down the street and their conversation became distant mumbling. He turned from the window and sat on the bed as more and more people began to walk along the street outside to begin their day.

His head began to ache as he considered what the men had said as well as what Helen had told him yesterday and how vague she had been. Jack disappeared? How? When? The twelve...were they talking about the provinces? *Just what is going on?* He buried his face in his hands. What was he going to do? How would he find Jack if he had disappeared? How could he go back home to Norfolk?

He paced back and forth in his small chamber for what must have been hours. Occasionally, he would stop and listen to the orchestra of noise outside his window. Hooves thundered against the cobblestones. A hammer beat against hot iron. Seagulls continued to call out in the distance as the hundreds of people outside talked and laughed and sang.

He grew lonelier and more frustrated the longer he listened to the lively commotion outside. Without thinking, he moved over to the window and peered down at the busy street below. Suddenly a figure caught his eye across the cobblestone freeway. It was a woman in a slim, navy-blue dress.

It's her! Helen! The woman who has the answers.

His heart fluttered when she looked up the tall tower and met his gaze before sitting on a stone bench nearby, crossing her legs and maintaining a watchful eye on him.

Suddenly, Peter heard commotion in the hallway beyond his chamber. The door opened and Thomas reappeared. The boy swallowed as he panted.

"My apologies, Lord," he managed between breaths.

"For what?"

Toms' eyes remained fixed on the stone floor as he twiddled his fingers. "Er. . .Lord. Lady Helen commands that you...that you jump out the window."

"What?!" Peter asked in disbelief. *Jump out the window? Has she lost her mind?*

Thomas pushed the door completely open, revealing the narrow hallway behind him and the dozen guards there, all with muskets in hand. "Lady Helen said that you will be shot if you do not."

This has to be a joke! Peter thought before recalling the musket shot that hit his shoulder just yesterday. It still felt tender and painful. He looked out the window and saw her looking up at him. Casually, she waved.

"This is crazy!" Peter said to Thomas before the boy was pulled out of the chamber by a guard.

"Use your powers, Lord!" the boy called from the end of the hallway.

"What? I don't have powers!"

"Make ready!" the captain ordered his men. The dozen guards readied their rifles.

"I can't do this!" Peter deemed through gritted teeth as he paced between the window and door.

"Take aim!" the captain ordered. The dozen muskets pointed toward him.

"Jump, Lord!" the boy yelled.

Peter looked to the captain. He was going to give the order.

With a desperate groan, Peter turned and stepped out the window, falling through the air. His stomach felt higher as he plummeted and he was filled with both terror and excitement. Faster than he had anticipated, his boots met the cobblestone, and he was on solid ground again. A two-hundred-foot drop had felt as if it were only two feet to him.

He looked across the street as Helen made her way over to him.

"Good morning, Mr. Loneheart." She grinned. "Walk with me."

"You're insane!" he told her as she started forward.

She turned to him. "Other than the injury you received the day prior, are you hurt? Did the fall cripple you so?"

"No! But you were going to have me shot!"

"May I ask how it felt when you landed?"

He paused and considered it. "Like I had just jumped a few feet."

Helen nodded. "And as for the muskets—merely gunpowder. I ordered for no projectile to be loaded."

"So if I didn't jump..."

"You would have dirtied the beautiful tunic you wear. And I might say that you wear our colors well, Mr. Loneheart." She took his arm in her own. "Now please, walk with me."

The two walked together slowly along the street. A breeze brought her scent across his face. She smelled of honey.

“I imagine you have questions,” she said.

So many came to his mind, he didn't know which to ask first. “Jack. You know him. How?”

“As I said yesterday, I met Jack Loneheart when I was thirteen. Ten years ago I attended a ball in the capital with my father. The ball was to celebrate the end of a plague that had ravaged the mainland. It was known as the black touch to some and grullens fever to others. When my father and I were departing the capital, we discovered a man who had washed ashore. He was strange and spoke with a most unusual accent. What was more intriguing than what he said was what he was capable of. He ran faster than any animal and was capable of tearing cannons asunder with merely his hands.”

“Did you request him to jump from a tall tower too?”

She grinned. “Yes. And he obliged.

“Shortly after my father brought Jack Loneheart to Lunsera, a war began on the mainland.”

“The war of reclamation.”

She looked at him with raised eyebrows. “Correct, Mr. Loneheart. The peaceful and ancient province of Sohn had been invaded by the Duke of Barrington. My father enlisted your uncle to help him liberate the province and bring the war to an end.”

“But. . .why? I mean. . .why didn't he try to find a way home instead?”

“Because your predecessor was compassionate and cared deeply for his fellow man. He understood that he possessed abilities that could be utilized to bring the war to a quick end before further lives were lost. Is that so foreign of Jack Loneheart?”

He hesitated, knowing it to be true. “It does sound like him. Jack fought in a war in my world too.”

"Afghanistan, was it? Am I correct?"

He was surprised. "Yeah. He told you?"

"He told me many things. It was surreal and overwhelming to hear his stories, and he told them with such passion." As she spoke, he noticed her pale cheeks grow light red. "He possessed a certain boldness, quite boyish; he was surprisingly brilliant, and yet he was so gentle and compassionate."

He felt as if she knew more about his uncle than he did. "So what happened to Jack?"

"There was a final and decisive battle that took place when the Duke of Barrington finally laid siege to Arden City. Your uncle and Sir William of Bastille led the defenses. The siege lasted throughout the night, and when morning came, the Duke had been slain, along with his army. Jack and Sir William both disappeared that night. Neither has been seen since."

The news stopped Peter in his tracks. "So Jack's dead? I just...don't believe it! I can't!" A lump formed in his throat.

"Nor can I, Mr. Loneheart. He certainly seemed indestructible, did he not?"

"Yeah," he muttered sullenly. "He always did."

The sound of commotion ahead of them grasped their attention. The citizens further along the street parted as a brown horse galloped toward the two of them, carrying Aurora. The horse halted in front of them and once again poked at Peter with its large nose.

"You certainly have a way of treating a man," the woman said from the saddle. "You wrap him in chains one day and then embrace him the next."

Helen tightened her grip on his arm. "Mr. Loneheart, may I introduce my sister, Aurora Moonwey. Aurora, this is—"

"Peter Loneheart," the younger sister said with a smile.

"Aurora," he greeted in return, unable to look away from her. The two women looked so similar. Both were beautiful and yet they seemed as day and night. "The poison tasted fantastic this morning," he told her. The young woman suddenly busted out laughing as Helen shook her head and sighed.

"I hope you bear no ill will toward me," she said as she reached down, stroking the neck of the horse. "It was just a bit of fun."

Helen chimed in, "I wonder if I will have the pleasure of your company at court this afternoon, sister."

"I thought you would have given up that cause by now, Helen. I'm not interested, and I have no reason to be as long as you are around as the Lady of the Rock. I am perfectly content."

"Quite right, and as the Lady of Lunsera, I am obligated to marry you to whomever I please. Perhaps to Lord Turner. He has long desired to marry into the Moonwey family." Helen then looked at Peter. "What are your thoughts, Mr. Loneheart?"

His pulse quickened beneath the gaze of both women. "I. . .er. . .that's not my call. But shouldn't she be able to choose who she marries?"

"If she were the leader of a family, then yes. However, she is not and thus the decision falls to me."

The woman on horseback remained silent for a moment. Though she grinned, there was irritation that could plainly be seen on her face. "Do be cautious, Peter Loneheart. Helen is far more devious than she may seem now. She's quite the manipulator and views others as no more than pawns in her schemes." With a sigh, she kicked her heels into the sides of the horse and it raced forward, knocking Helen into Peter's arms.

"Are you alright?" he asked her. *She's so soft and vulnerable,* he thought as he held her.

She paused. Her chest rose as she took a deep breath. "As well as can be, although I am contrite to be sure."

“Contrite? Are you really planning on marrying her to some random guy? Can you do that here?”

“An idle threat of little consequence. I would never subject my only sister to such an archaic practice.” She regained her balance and they began to walk again. “Allow me to clear any uncertainty. I do not view others as pawns. My father instructed me from an early age to lead the province. At times I must. . .motivate others if necessary.”

“Like with me jumping from the tower.”

She smiled. “Correct, Mr. Loneheart. It was to your benefit. And I love my sister to be sure; however, she is. . .spirited at times. She has not had to lead our people since the age of fourteen. That task fell to me.”

The street they followed opened to the large courtyard in front of the keep, filled with merchant stalls and over a hundred people milling about. As he and Helen walked through the center of the courtyard, several people at a time would notice the pair and then bow to them.

“I imagine there are several more questions that you desire to ask,” she noted.

“Yeah. Do you know how I can get home?”

She took his arm in hers again. “Are you truly so tired of our province, Mr. Loneheart? Is our hospitality insufficient? Or do I repulse you so?”

“No,” he tried to reassure her. “I appreciate everything you've done for me. I just. . .I just need to get home.”

“Without Jack?” she asked. “Have you abandoned your quest to find him so soon?”

He paused and considered her words. Was he abandoning Jack? Was he being selfish? What would his uncle do if their roles were reversed?

But Jack hadn't been seen for ten years, he thought. Helen herself had admitted that. Was she trying to manipulate him somehow? Was Aurora right about her sister?

"Well, Mr. Loneheart?" she asked him.

"I'm not abandoning Jack."

"No? But you desire to return to Norfolk. With or without him?"

"With him! If I can. My grandmother would do a backflip if I brought him home."

She stopped and turned to face him. He looked down at her. *She's so unreal. Gorgeous.* "Then perhaps you and I can work together to solve the mystery of his disappearance."

"But—"

"The legacy of your uncle lives through you. He accomplished much in Arden during the brief time he was here. Jack has done great deeds for many in this world, including myself, and even yourself from what I gather. I may be so bold as to say that perhaps you are indebted to him, as am I. Does he not deserve your loyalty?"

He couldn't find the words, so he instinctively nodded.

"Then work with me, Mr. Loneheart. Pledge yourself to me."

"Pledge myself?

"Yes! Swear to serve me. Fight for me. Use your strength to fight for Arden and for Lunsera. Take up the mantle of Lionheart; it is what Jack would have desired for you."

He backed away from her. "And not go back home? You weren't there when my mom and grandmother cried for months when they couldn't find Jack! I was! I'm not going to put them through that again with me."

She sighed and crossed her arms as her expression suddenly turned neutral. Her voice grew cold. "It is evident that you have made your decision. So be it."

She began to walk away toward the keep before halting and turning back to him. "I see now that you are more a boy than a man. Either you will assist Arden or you may walk into the sea to find your city." She inclined her head. "Good day, Mr. Loneheart."

She turned and walked toward the doors of the keep. Out of the corner of Peter's eye he saw the woman Barda quickly follow after her. Had she been following them the entire time?

Helen's mood had changed so quickly. One moment she spoke so softly and with sweet words and the next, after he had refused her request, she was without a doubt cold and intimidating. He felt insecure as a result of her words, questioning whether he had made the right decision.

* * * * * * *

Peter's gaze fixed upon the same place in the wet sand where he had washed ashore the day before, contemplating Helen's words and the physician's warning to avoid the water. A few tears slipped from his eyes. He was alone, homesick, and as Helen had observed, not yet a man able to endure the hardships that fate had presented.

He turned his head, looking over the field of sand to where a squad of guards awaited him at the base of the steps he had climbed yesterday. His escort of six musket men stood idly, cross-armed and exchanging few words. They all roused suddenly, alert as the sound of muffled galloping caused Peter's ears to twitch. He looked to his right and saw her. Aurora rode toward him from the island's rim.

As he stood, her horse slowed its pace. "Sulking?" she asked. The horse trotted up to him, nuzzling at his shoulder and breathing into his face again. Clearing his throat, he turned away to quickly dry the tears.

"Just thinking."

The six musket men trotted over to them, clutching their muskets. Aurora looked over to them. "You're the escort?"

The leading man nodded. "Yes, Lady Aurora."

She nodded in turn, looking down at Peter. "May I join you?"

"My lady," the guardsmen chimed in as she dismounted. "Are you—"

The reigns of the horse were thrown into his hands. Aurora walked to Peter and sank onto the sand where he had been sitting. With her horse, the escort turned and departed, leaving the two alone with the seagulls that soared above them as their only company.

After watching the men recede across the beach, he turned and met her gaze.

"Sit," she said. He obeyed, easing down near her and her eyes followed.

After a few moments, he asked, "What?"

"What?" she shot back.

"Why are you staring?"

"Merely observing. It would seem as if your stroll with Helen was an unpleasant one."

His answer came in the form of a scoff.

"Fair response." She giggled. "Might I inquire what she said?"

"It doesn't matter."

"Please. Tell me. I find your accent. . .intriguing."

He shook his head before resting his chin on his folded arms. "I don't understand your sister. She forced me to jump from the window of the room I was staying in, then she kept bringing up Jack to make me feel like I was abandoning him. And then she tried to make me swear myself to her. What does that even mean—"

Her eyes widened. "Did you?"

"What?"

"Did you swear yourself to Helen?"

"No. I don't know what that even means. I don't know what's going on and I don't belong here. I'm still not convinced this is real."

A sudden stinging pain radiated from his shoulder and he flinched, looking over at the young woman who had poked at the injury he had received yesterday.

"Does that feel real to you?" she asked. He avoided answering, inching a few inches away from her to avoid being poked again. "But I suppose it is fortunate that you declined her service. I would truly pity you if you had, so do not be disheartened, Peter Loneheart. You managed to deny the great Helen Moonwey, something few have done before. Take pride in it." She paused. "However, I am curious. . .why did she ask for your fealty? After all, she met you just yesterday. We do depart for the parliament in two days' time. Perhaps she desires to have you attend by her side. Or perhaps it is the plague that compelled her to seek your services."

"Plague?"

She turned to him with a grave expression. "Yes, Peter. The plague that currently ravages the mainland. Several provinces have already been destroyed by it. The entire western region is gone, consumed by it."

"What kind of plague?"

"There is nothing that it can be compared to. Imagine a person, Peter. Imagine a human that contracts a sickness and then dies of it, and in just a short time after their death, they arise with eyes black as pitch. Rabid, mindless, and famished with an incessant appetite for the flesh of those not infected. Imagine it, Peter, for there are thousands of infected as such in what remains of the west."

A chill ran along his spine and he swallowed dryly. "Zombies?"

"While I am not familiar with the term, I assume you understand the severity of the situation at hand or can at least imagine it. No province has ever faced a threat such as this. It is likely that our world will soon come to an end. That is the purpose of the parliament which will convene in some days in the capital itself. The remaining provinces will band together to fight the plague."

"But Lunar Rock is an island. Why doesn't Helen just decide to stay here? And I heard that Lunsera has the best navy in the world."

"Helen would never abandon Arden. She is honor-bound to protect and serve the capital. Our father would curse her from his grave if she chose to refrain from the fight."

"So that's why she wanted me to pledge myself to her," he concluded.

"Certainly. Perhaps she also had other motives for wanting you. Perhaps she sees her great love within you."

"What?"

Aurora laughed. "It is rather obvious, is it not? She has been in love with Jack Loneheart ever since she first met him as a little girl."

Peter stopped and considered. *It kind of makes sense. It did look like she was blushing when she was talking about Jack, and women always liked him wherever he went and no matter what he was doing.*

"I guess you're right."

She rolled her eyes. "Helen may display a facade of power that commands respect, but behind that mask is a young maiden still waiting for a romance so great and memorable that it will be written in the stars for centuries to come. She has an entire library of romances, you know."

"Really? I find that hard to believe." He sighed. "So, what am I supposed to do? Do I swear myself or—"

"No! Have you lost your mind?" She looked away from him and back toward the sea. "Aside from your assistance with the plague, I wonder what more she requires of you." She turned to the cliffs behind them and her gaze caught. "I do wonder indeed."

He followed her stare, over the beach and to the rocky wall beyond it. At the top of the cliff stood a lone figure. It was Helen, peering down at them both.

* * * * * * *

With his escort behind him, he strolled through the gate and into the courtyard at the center of the community. Aurora had continued her ride after their conversation had left him with more to consider.

There was a plague within Arden. A plague of rabid humans that numbered in the thousands, slowly consuming more and more people every day. As if he needed any more reason to find a way back home to Norfolk.

He paused as he came upon what looked to be a live-action play within the center of the courtyard, surrounded by vendors and a crowd of citizens. Standing in the crowd of dozens of onlookers, he watched as two men dressed in tribal-like clothes reenacted a fight. "The legend of Arkus and Tobius," an older man told him after he inquired about the play. After the actor portraying Tobius pretended to slay his compatriot, Peter departed for the keep with his armed escort.

Upon entering the capitol building, he was escorted back to his small chamber. The door was shut behind him and he stood alone again in the center of the room, listening to the sounds that echoed from outside. A few hours passed. He watched through the window as the sky grew dimmer. Lanterns were lit along the streets and candles illuminated within the windows of homes. He was envious of the people sleeping in their own homes tonight with their families close by. The small bed beneath him felt more comfortable than the night before, and it gave him rest.

He jumped when he awoke in the middle of the night. The milky light of the moon radiating through the open window was his only source of sight. *I fell asleep so quickly*, he thought, and now he felt strangely agitated. A ruffle of movement sounded from beyond the entrance of his chamber and he stared at the wooden door in the dim lunar light.

The latch on the other side of the door was pulled with a gentle metallic clank. The door opened slowly and then stopped, leaving a small opening of darkness where Peter could not see. An eerie stillness came over him as he watched the small opening. Someone was beyond the door in the hallway, watching him from the darkness. Was it Thomas? Or had Helen sent someone to test him again? Was it Helen or Aurora? His heart fluttered at the thought of either beautiful woman meeting him late in the night. He remained still, knowing that whomever it was could see him perfectly.

Slowly, he grew annoyed and decided to find out who it was. He jumped out of his bed.

At once, the door burst open and a dark figure moved rapidly toward him. Amidst the darkness, a silver gleam caught his eye. A sharp looking dagger was thrust toward him. He stumbled backward and caught himself before he could fall out the window.

The intruder in black rushed at him again and lunged forward with the dagger, the tip of the blade aimed at his throat. He had no time to think. Instinctively, he brought his right leg up and pushed the bottom of his boot into the attacker's chest.

He heard numerous snaps as the kick sent the person in black flying back across the room. They crashed into the stone wall before falling to the floor.

Peter saw stars for a moment. His heart was racing as never before. His legs shook uncontrollably beneath him. He kept his gaze fixed on the attacker and watched as the body that lay on the floor slowly curled...and then ceased all movement.

Did that really just happen? he wondered. *Was it another of Helen's tests?* He stared at the dagger that lay on the floor between himself and the motionless person in black clothing. Was it real? He kicked the silver blade. It shimmered and skipped along the floor, clanking against the stone. *It's real!* he realized with dread before looking to the lifeless body.

The person that had attacked him was dead. He had killed someone. He had taken the life of another person.

A man shrieked from the hallway and Peter heard what he thought was the sound of a body falling onto the stone. Quick footsteps came again, growing louder until another figure in black appeared in the open doorway. Not a single glimpse of flesh could be seen beneath the black clothing until the shimmer of another dagger was revealed.

The new attacker rushed at him, faster than the first. He reached forward with both hands as the dagger came at him.

He caught the wrist that held the sharp piece of metal and squeezed. To his surprise, the bones broke with little pressure and the tendons completely tore. The dagger fell to the ground and the man in black howled in agony as he fell to his knees. Peter maintained his grip around the flesh of the wounded attacker and could feel the shattered bones shift around under his fingers.

Movement echoed again from the hallway and two castle guards appeared in the doorway with fresh blood dripping from their drawn sabers, which they pointed at the trapped attacker.

"Well done, Lord!" one of the guards panted. "You captured one alive. Lady Helen will be pleased."

Chapter 4

The Choice

It was early morning. The faint glimpse of the sun's first light peeked over the distant horizon of the sea as Peter glared out of the window of the great hall where he had first met Helen. He heard several yawns erupt throughout the large room from the thirty castle guards that surrounded the wounded and chained attacker. He remained on his knees, clutching his shattered wrist, often looking over to where Peter stood near the large window. The boy from Virginia glared back at the exhausted face of the man who had attacked him in the night. The pain the man felt was evident.

The door behind the tall bench opened. The Lady of Lunsera emerged with Barda following closer behind her than usual. Aurora followed after, yawning and leaning up against the wall behind the bench as Helen sat down. Peter stiffened when the two sisters each cast a quick glance at him. Aurora's eyes lingered for a moment longer than her older sister's.

Silence filled the room as Helen glared coldly at the wounded man in chains. Peter did not envy the man's position. The heavy silence continued until she finally spoke.

“There has been a common suspicion shared by many province leaders regarding the existence of a group of assassins. Now, our suspicions are confirmed. Now, we possess the evidence before us wrapped in chains, defeated and captured by the courageous defenders of this province!”

An explosion of cheers erupted throughout the great hall from the many guards standing around the wounded captive. The captured man grimaced again. No doubt the man was berating himself for getting captured and cursing the one that had shattered his wrist and subdued him.

Helen raised her index finger, silencing the cheers. “Several assailants including yourself entered the castle during the night in an attempt to take my life. You failed. However, you may take solace if you can, knowing that you are not alone in your failure and captivity.”

Peter was suddenly intrigued. Had she captured another assassin? The man in chains traded his defiant look for one more befitting of a prisoner, bearing his concern on his face for all to see. Peter found himself wishing that things could have gone differently in the night—both for the men that attacked him and himself.

A thud echoed from the entrance of the great hall, and a series of rattling chains and yelling soon erupted. Every head in the chamber turned toward the closed entrance.

It's true. She captured another assassin.

Helen stood, maintaining her composure as she stepped toward the restrained assassin. Barda followed close behind and Aurora looked on, concerned. Every guard in the room clutched their weapons tightly and prepared themselves to leap into action if the captive man decided to try to attack her. She stopped in front of him, peering down as the judge about to sentence a criminal.

“We will have justice!” Helen declared. Her right hand swept across his face. Peter and several other guards winced from the firm impact of the slap. “THAT was for the lives of those taken during the night, for the men that defend this province!”

She slapped the man again, harder than before. “And THAT is for their families!” She turned to the captain on her left. “Take him to the dungeons. Do not let him near the other captive for I desire him brought here at once so that I may question him.”

Peter watched the wounded man as the guards grabbed him and hoisted him to his feet. The fear in the man's eyes was obvious and his mouth opened slightly as if to speak. He was dragged from the great hall, followed by the entirety of the guards.

Peter was left with a feeling of apprehension as he continued to stare at the double doors in anticipation of the second captive. But the doors remained closed and the room silent.

Aurora whispered in his ear, “There is no other captive.”

He looked at her. “But I thought Helen said—”

“It was merely a deception she devised. Helen will force the man to believe there is another that has been captured and has spoken against him. She plans to threaten him with a false confession that does not exist in hopes that he will reveal anything he can regarding the assassin group.”

“He did look worried. Like he was about to talk. But what if he doesn’t?”

She grinned. “Perhaps we may send you to his dungeon cell. After all, you were the one who shattered the bones in his wrist.”

He sighed and rubbed his face.

She chuckled. “A jest, Peter Loneheart.”

“Mr. Loneheart,” Helen said behind them. They both turned to where the elder sister stood in the center of the chamber with Barda behind her. “Aurora. Barda. Please excuse Mr. Loneheart and I.”

He looked at Aurora who smirked at him and shrugged before following Barda through the single door behind the bench.

Silence remained in the large chamber as he stood alone with Helen. He took a deep breath as she slowly walked over to the window where he stood. “The red dawn,” she noted, watching the bright red sunrise over the distant waves of the ocean. Silence followed her words and he felt greater pressure to speak but questioned what would be appropriate.

“I'm sorry,” he quickly told her. “About your guards who didn't make it during the attack.”

Her lips formed a faint smile. “As am I, and I must express my gratitude to you, Mr. Loneheart. For if you had not intervened as you did, more of my men would be dead for certain and we would also not have a captive.” She spoke again before he could form words. “I also must offer you an apology. I was quite. . .harsh toward you yesterday.”

“Er. . .it's okay,” he said. *She's being so sincere and sweet again. Is this a trick?*

“No, it was unacceptable. I was so fixated on my own desires that I was inconsiderate of how you must have felt, being taken from your home and your life, only to be cast into a world you do not know. It was severely delusional of me to thrust any burdens upon you. It was cruel. Forgive me.”

“It's alright. I promise.”

“I would also like to take this opportunity to display how grateful I am that you were not harmed in the night.” She glanced at him alluringly. “. . .Were you?”

“I'm alright. I was terrified, but I'm alright.”

She chuckled. “I am pleased to hear of it. And are you. . .well?”

He somehow knew what she meant. Was he fine that he killed a man? He replayed the scenario in his mind and had done so a number of times that morning since the attack happened.

“I had never killed anyone until last night. To be honest, I never thought I would have to. I didn't expect him to move like that. The way his body curled up, or the sound he made when he. . .”

She placed a hand on his shoulder gently and spoke softly. “You were defending yourself. You have no reason to feel shame or regret. It was justified the moment he attempted to take your life. You were right in what you did and because of your efforts we may be able to save more lives, depending on the one captured and if he reveals anything of note."

"So there really is a group of assassins? And they were after you?"

"All will be revealed in time." She sighed. "I am aware that my sister informed you of Arden's crisis?"

He cocked an eyebrow in confusion. Arden's crisis?

"Aurora told you of the plague on the mainland?" she proposed for him.

"Yeah. She told me."

"And what are your thoughts on the matter, Mr. Loneheart?"

"I can't say. I honestly don't know enough about the situation. But it does sound pretty bad. I wish I could—"

"You wish to help?" she proposed quickly.

"I wish there was something I could do. I don't like suffering any more than anyone else does."

"Your actions during the attack in the night prove otherwise, Mr. Loneheart. I will take care not to overstep any boundaries as I did yesterday. However, tomorrow morning, Aurora and I will depart for Emerald Island. It is my wish that you will accompany us."

"You're leaving tomorrow? Both of you?"

"And the entire fleet of Lunsera, along with most of our fighting men. We will sail for Emerald Island and then to Arden City itself. I understand it may seem sudden to you and thus I will give you the choice to remain here if you wish, or to depart with us."

There's so much happening so fast

"Can I have time to think it over?" he asked her.

She smiled, revealing her beauty to its fullest in the morning light. His gaze remained fixed on her smiling hazel eyes.

My God, he lamented. *How could anyone say no to her?*

“Of course. As I said, we will depart at dawn tomorrow. You have until then to decide. Good day, Mr. Loneheart.”

* * * * * * *

He stood in the hallway, staring at the partially open door of his small bedchamber. Sunlight beamed from the window in the small room and a breeze followed after. He didn't want to go inside just yet. It felt too soon for whatever reason. The snapping the man's bones had made when Peter had kicked his chest seemed to linger in the hallway, echoing against the stone as he stood still and remembered. His kick had thrown the man across the room.

He felt so light, just like the man that grabbed me at the beach. As he imagined the fractured bones of the man's ribcage and the way his body curled up, his stomach churned. *I have to get away from this room.* He turned and departed the keep.

He found joy in the sun as it warmed his skin. As he walked through the courtyard, the crowd of citizens talked with new ferocity about the attack on the castle in the night. To his surprise, many began to bow to him as he passed by and they simply referred to him as “Lionheart.” Evidently many were discovering that he was the one who had captured one of the assassins alive. The polite and humble greetings continued until he finally exited through the front gate of the castle. He halted beyond the walls, where two roads lay before him.

He recognized the road that split off to his left, leading to the stone stairs and eventually to the familiar beach. The straight road ahead led along the top of the cliffs and past several burial mounds and a few apple trees. The road seemed long enough and he saw not a single person.

A good sprint! he thought. *It's what I need to clear my head.*

After a deep breath, he widened his stance and lurched forward, pushing the dirt beneath him away. The air rushed past him and roared in his ears as his legs propelled him along the road faster than he had anticipated and faster than he had ever run before in his life. The burial mounds and apple trees blurred past him like streetlights at night. Deciding to stop, he braced his legs underneath him. His boots dug up fresh dirt as he slowed.

Spinning around to survey how far he had traveled, he saw that the gatehouse stood nearly four hundred meters away. A faint blue trail lingered in the air after him.

He widened his stance and dashed forward toward the township and castle. Again, the burial mounds and apple trees blurred past him on both sides as the silhouettes of the castle and gatehouse grew rapidly larger. By the time he stopped, the stone structure of the wall and the wooden gate towered over him, just a few feet away from where he stood.

Not only was he strong, but fast, just as Jack must have been. He turned back to the open road and sprinted again, leaving another blue trail behind in the air. Stopping, he turned and sprinted again toward the gatehouse, halting in time to see a growing crowd of spectators forming along the walls and within the open gate.

The people gasped and cheered as he turned and sprinted back along the road, performing the circuit another three times before stopping in front of the crowded wall to catch his breath.

His gaze trailed along the wall where men cheered and women giggled. He caught Aurora watching him. She looked down at him with an intrigued expression accompanied by a wide grin. She nodded a single time.

The salty air of the rushing coastal breeze entered his lungs as he widened his stance and the crowd of spectators grew quiet in anticipation. He dug his boots into the driven dirt and dashed forward with even greater intensity than before. He felt powerful and free.

Deciding to stop, he dug his boots into the ground, throwing dirt and small debris into the air.

He looked around to both sides of the road and beyond, where the waves crashed against the rocks below the cliffs. He turned and dashed forward with the same intensity toward the castle and town. The silhouette of the castle quickly grew in size as he raced forward. The gatehouse appeared before him and as he came to a stop, the people erupted in cheers. It sounded as if the entire population of the island was there.

Panting heavily, Peter looked up to the wall where Aurora stood. Her honey-brown hair flowed in the wind as she smiled and applauded along with the citizens of Lunar Rock.

* * * * * * *

Peter stood in the hallway, staring once again at the half-open door of his chamber. His legs ached from the sprints and hours of walking around the township and castle. The numerous foods he had eaten at the incessant requests of the citizens throughout the day were also taking their toll on him, and now, as the sun was setting in the western sky, he craved sleep.

He took a deep breath and gently pushed open the wooden door, revealing the small bedchamber, faintly illuminated by the warm light of the setting sun. As he began to walk into the chamber, he paused to enjoy the view his window provided. The way that the sky shifted in warm colors during sunset had always had a way of soothing his soul.

He sat on the bed and looked over to the corner of the room near the door, where the first assassin that had attacked him had died. He wondered who the man was and whether he had a family waiting for him to come home.

The waves of the sea grabbed his attention. *They're so soothing,* he thought as he eased himself onto his back. He closed his eyes, and soon the combination of exercise, food, a warm bath, and the lullaby of the sea finally sent him to sleep.

* * * * * * *

"Lord," a voice said as he slept, rolling onto his left side. "Lord!" the boy's voice said again.

Peter's eyes opened slightly and the boy Thomas appeared, standing in the center of his chamber with a worried gaze illuminated by gentle morning light.

Thomas jumped up and down, waving his arms at his sides. "Lord! The ships are departing!"

The ships, Peter thought. *What ships?*

"Damn!" he exclaimed as he jumped out of his bed. He paused after standing. Why was he worried? Helen had given him the choice to stay or go with her. It was his decision to make; he could stay in Lunsera and try to find a way back to Norfolk. But something bothered him. Something in his heart pulled and screamed at him to go to the ship.

He looked down at Thomas. The boy was distraught and wore an expression that threatened tears. "Lady Helen's ship is going to depart from the dock soon," the boy said. A horn blew in the distance. "The last boat is leaving!"

Peter started for the door and stopped as he thought of Helen. *The window*. Maybe if he jumped, he could get to the docks in time. After all, he had jumped before. He went to the open window and looked down to the street below, then back to the boy in his chambers, whose face now displayed a wide smile and expectant, gleaming eyes.

"Thanks for everything, Tom."

The boy bowed. "An honor to serve you, Lord...make left down the street!"

Peter turned and stepped out the window, allowing gravity to take full effect. He landed gracefully on his feet in the middle of the empty cobblestone street.

"Cool," he told himself. *And easier without guns pointed at me.*

The sudden ringing of a bell echoed along the corridor of stone buildings leading up from the port, and he discerned the sounds of a crowd further along the road. There was no time to waste, he knew. The strange yearning in his heart that propelled him aided his steps and he dashed down the cobblestone street toward the south gate, dodging and weaving through the crowds.

Once at the gate, he saw that the road led over a few small green hills until the grass met the sand of the beach. A crowd of at least two hundred people bustled about the wooden structures of the many docks.

He looked out to sea, where at least a dozen large ships remained afloat, teetering ever so slightly with each wave that struck their dark wood. One by one, large sails of navy blue appeared above each ship. As they began to catch the wind, the sails enlarged, displaying the silver crescent moon of Lunsera.

Between the ships at sea and the farthest dock at the port, a trail of longboats cut through the waves toward the larger vessels. At the nearest pier, Peter saw the last longboat. He jumped forward, skipping down the hill and over another with his new strength until he landed in front of a crowd that stood outside of the entrance to the port.

"Hey! Wait for me!" he called out to the last boat as he sped through the crowd, taking care not to knock anyone over. When he came to the edge of the dock, he was pleasantly surprised by the sight of four guards and four oarsmen awaiting him in the longboat.

"Lady Helen instructed that this boat would remain for you, Lord," one of the oarsmen said. Peter sighed with relief as two guards stepped aside to make room for him.

"Thanks, guys," he said before taking his first step down into the boat. The small vessel wobbled violently from side to side as he sat down and he instantly recalled what the physician had told him about the density of his bones and the water.

The oarsmen pushed off from the chipped posts of the docks and propelled their small vessel farther out to sea with each oar stroke. The port, walls, and castle of Lunar Rock receded little by little. Peter avoided the edges of the longboat, instead gazing toward the island as the waves heaved them back and forth.

The boat ride came to its end, to Peter's delight, when the longboat reached the largest of all the ships, which bore silver engravings along the entirety of the vessel. A ladder of rope and sturdy wood fell from the top of the ship for him to climb. It creaked with each step as he ascended. Climbing over the damp railing, he looked around as sailors rushed about in a flurry of movement.

Standing in the center of the deck, Helen looked at him and grinned triumphantly as she spoke. "Welcome aboard, Mr. Loneheart."

Chapter 5

Plague

A rush of wind carried the salty scent and cool mist of the sea over the railing of the ship, enlarging the enormous blue sails and propelling the vessel with greater intensity through the waves. Though the frequent teetering of the ship upset his stomach, Peter basked in the warm sunlight, watching as sailors busied themselves on the various levels of the ship. To his right, the double doors of the main cabin opened, and Helen emerged in discussion with the captain of the vessel. Barda followed the two as they walked about the ship.

"Well," a familiar voice said. Aurora descended the stairs from the aft deck to stand next to him. "You conceded after all. Ill-advised. . ."

They both looked over the railing to where the water frothed.

"It was either come along or stay behind. I felt like I was better off going with you guys if it meant finding a way back home."

"Do you truly think you will leave Arden?" she chuckled.

"Why wouldn't I think that?"

“You are rather optimistic, Peter Loneheart. From what I gather, your uncle never discovered a way to return to his world and neither did the twelve. They spent their entire lives in Arden.”

Whether it was her words of discouragement or his churning stomach, his head began to feel light. He groaned. “Why are you saying this?”

Out of the corner of his eye, he noticed her shoulders raise as she shrugged.

“Would you prefer I lie to you?”

“Whatever.” He decided to change the subject. “And who are the twelve? I keep hearing about them.”

“The twelve from the Otherworld. The twelve who founded Arden.”

“Founded Arden?”

“Must I give you a history lesson?” she groaned, looked around the main deck and then sighed. “Well, I suppose if there is nothing more for me to do on this wretched ship.”

Peter listened intently as he watched the sun’s warming light shine onto the creamy skin of her face and neck. A gust of wind tossed her shimmering honey-brown hair over her left shoulder toward him, bringing a fragrance of salt and lavender into his nostrils.

She took a deep breath. “It has been said that at the end of the age of calamities, the greater civilizations and lesser tribes of Arden continued to wage war on the monsters of old and each other.”

“Monsters?!”

“Hush, Peter. I am telling a story.”

“Sorry.”

“But yes, the monsters of the old world. The great beasts that fell from the sky or arrived from unknown worlds through the sea, much like yourself. They say some were birds larger than castles that would breakfast by consuming the largest of horses. Others were great beasts of unspeakable horror that roamed the world eating entire villages in a single night. There were even colossal squids that devoured whole ships and continue to swim within these waters at this very moment."

". . .You're kidding."

"No. But none grew so terrible and wretched in fame as the black morning. They say it was a meteor that fell from the heavens one morning, turning the sky black as pitch. They say it was a heap of rock bound together by the venom of Norvok."

"But what is Nor—"

"I am aware you do not know of Norvok or Alvasar. I will explain shortly; please let me continue." She cleared her throat. "The black morning fell onto the kingdom of Du'Vhan, destroying half the kingdom. The other survived, but for little time. The survivors of the destroyed half had changed. The meteor had cursed them, made them into monsters of the night that stalked about the land, consuming all tribes and kingdoms regardless of culture or race. It spread rapidly."

"Like a plague," Peter concluded.

Aurora smiled and nudged his shoulder. "Much so, yes. However, there is no historical proof that such a monstrous plague did exist. I digress. As the curse of the black morning spread and infected more and more tribes, our extinction was assured, until the final calamity arrived to mark the end of that age: the twelve from the Otherworld.

"The twelve washed ashore on the mainland and soon discovered their remarkable abilities. They encountered the remnants of the Du'Vhani kingdom and formed an alliance. After bringing more tribes into the fold, an alliance led by the twelve destroyed the curse of the black morning. Legend says that the twelve then went in search for the source of the curse and never found it. In its wake, many tribes began to regard the twelve as gods. To many they were, for of all the calamities during the past age, none had brought what the twelve had: hope."

Peter yawned. "Hope?"

"Hope. It was an age of monsters, Peter. Hope was necessary. And along with hope, of course, the twelve established the first of the new cities and gave it the name of Arden. With the city, the twelve brought their culture to our world. Their skills, history, language and—"

"—English!" Peter concluded. Whether it was the fact that his stomach had started to settle or that he had discovered the origin of the twelve founders of Arden, he began to laugh.

Aurora smiled awkwardly. "Why are you laughing? Have you gone mad?"

"I don't know, but I think I needed it," he said as his laughs slowly subsided. "The twelve were British?"

"I suppose as much. Helen knows far more about the details than I. After all, our father always favored her and thus dedicated more time to educate her." Aurora sighed and rested her head on her arms, folded over the wooden railing of the ship. "You know, by the time she was thirteen, our father received more marriage proposals for Helen than any woman had in history."

Peter's jaw dropped. "Marriage proposals? At thirteen?"

She nodded. "Of course father accepted no offers. Helen was a priceless gem and everyone knew it. She was beautiful and brilliant and destined for greatness. Even the Duke of Barrington proposed that she and his own bastard son marry. Of course, this was before the war of reclamation."

Peter glanced around to the front deck, meeting Helen's gaze from a distance. The Lady of Lunsera smiled gently as the captain of the ship continued to speak to her. She waved and then turned her attention away.

"And it would seem you have also fallen for her charm," Aurora sighed. Peter turned back to the younger Moonwey sister, who chuckled.

"I'm not falling for anyone's charm," he stated.

"Truly?"

“I'm going to find a way home.”

“Oh?”

“And I’m going to find Jack if I can.”

“Certainly.” She chuckled again. “You know, when your uncle was brought to Lunsera, Helen washed his feet.”

“What? How is that relevant?”

She shrugged and slowly began to chuckle again. As her laughs grew louder, he shook his head and slowly he began to laugh too until they joined together in a hysterical culmination, attracting the attention of Helen, Barda, the captain, and the crew.

As their laughter died down, he looked at her. “You're so strange.”

“Am I?”

“Not in a bad way! I mean, you're unique and random.”

“And is that unpleasant for you?”

“No. I guess it's just. . .different. You and Helen are just so different. She seems so much more serious and you're just. . .you.”

“Should I feel insulted? I'm uncertain.”

“I'm not trying to offend you.”

Resting her head on her hand, she watched him. “How are we different?”

“Er. . .well. . .it's like you're day and she's night. You seem more social and open. Extroverted, I guess. I get the feeling she's the opposite.”

“Fair observation. What more?”

He hesitated, and guided by his instincts, said, “You're different, but the same. I get the feeling that you want the same thing.”

Her eyes narrowed. “And what do I desire, Peter Loneheart?”

Before the answer could depart his lips, he cleared his throat and decided to change the subject. "So. What's Norlok and Alvabar?"

The young woman chuckled. "Norvok and Alvasar," she corrected. "It's the eldest story in history. Despite cultural differences, every tribe and civilization tells the same tale. At the beginning of time. . .it was but darkness and Fyraen, the first and last, and the father of all. He snapped his fingers and brought forth countless living diamonds within that darkness.

"He created the stars and countless worlds in between, but the first world he crafted was Arden, before it was dubbed thus. After all worlds were created, he rested and looked upon his creation with glee, but his peace was disturbed, for out of the infinite darkness between the worlds and stars, the serpent that devours worlds came. Norvok."

"Norvok," he repeated, conjuring a chill up his spine.

"Norvok, the serpent of old, devoured one world after the next until it came upon our own. To prevent the coming destruction, Fyraen breathed life into a new being, the great lion, Alvasar."

"Alvasar," he repeated. The name rolled off of his tongue and ignited within him a sense of justice.

"The great lion clashed with the serpent and they fought above the world itself, swaying the entire cosmos and scarring the sky. Finally, Alvasar struck a killing blow, bruising the serpents head, but not before the lion himself was bitten on his heel. Norvok had been slain and at a price, for the venom killed the great lion upon the serpent's death. Further, the remains of Norvok fell onto Arden, bringing death and suffering as its venom pervaded the world.

"Seeing what had transpired, Fyraen spoke from the heavens in which he dwells, promising to the world that the great Lion would be reborn as a man and that he would be the one to destroy the remnants of Norvok, finally restoring order and bringing peace. His name would be. . ." She hesitated as she watched him.

"Well? What's his name?" Peter demanded. Rather than answer, she simply grinned and shook her head.

“That is sufficient storytelling for one day, I think.”

“What? You can't do that! I was really getting into it.”

She turned and ascended back up the stairs, laughing. “I can see that.”

* * * * * * *

There were stars all around him. Countless living diamonds amidst the ever-expanding darkness. From the shadows, it slithered forward. The serpent's scales were gray, its eyes a glowing red as if bathed in blood.

It was beautiful yet terrifying. The rhythm of its movement was oddly tantalizing until suddenly it lurched forward like lightning, consuming a hovering sphere that he knew to be a world. The serpent gulped and continued after another, striking again and again. It was horrible, an injustice that had gnawed at him for all eternity. He felt such sadness for the lives that had been extinguished.

Suddenly, every light vibrated and every world shook as a thundering roar echoed. The serpent halted for the first time as its crimson gaze narrowed at the golden Lion that had emerged from an abrupt light of creation. The divine feline emanated justice and righteousness as it strolled forward and confronted the snake.

The two beings faced one another, the entire cosmos as their witness. The tongue of the serpent flickered and the lion again roared. And the two beings collided in a bout of everlasting struggle for the fate of life and light. The cosmos shifted and stars were hurled out of place as the universe itself shook with great anticipation.

A blow was struck. The vile fangs of the serpent plunged into the golden fur of its enemy's heel. A majestic roar escaped the lion as it countered, thrusting its claws into the head of the snake that had bitten him. The crimson-eyed serpent retracted its fangs and coiled, withering as it died.

Though victorious, the great lion had paid a price. Slowly but surely, its own life faded as a result of its sacrifice. Venom coursed through its body, pervading and destroying what was good and righteous. Another roar escaped the divine being, its final howl to its creator: a call of desperation and love. The lion faded, and new darkness emerged from the hovering sphere of light below.

As a drop of water on the surface of a pond, the serpent's venom struck the world, and with it came death.

"Peter!" someone hissed, and he woke with a jump. Collapsing onto the deck of the ship, the remnants of his hammock beneath him, he groaned as his heart continued to beat wildly. His tunic stuck to his skin with cold sweat, and he heard a woman laugh.

Opening his eyes, he saw Aurora's head hovering over him.

"What. . .are you doing?" he asked.

"I couldn't sleep, so I decided to walk about and I found you here."

He arose. "So you decided to wake me up? Wait! Let me guess. . .it was. . ." he attempted his best impression of her accent, "just a bit of fun?"

The young woman burst into a fit of laughing as she applauded him. He retreated, collapsing onto the railing of the ship near the bow. She followed. "I assume you were having an unpleasant dream?"

His heart mellowed as he took deep and slow breaths. "Something like that."

"They say Fyraen grants dreams to all but permits terrors of the night only unto the guilty. What crimes have you committed, Peter Loneheart?" she jested.

He ignored her question, whether serious or not, and rubbed his head, stroking his hair away from his face.

"Golden hair," she noted. "You know, a shade such as yours is a rarity in Arden."

"It's blond."

"So you say." Her lips curled into the familiar devious grin she often bore.

“What? I get the feeling you're scheming. You really are like Helen. Oh!” He paused as his eyes rested on her hair. Among the long locks of honey-brown, there were a few strands that seemed a bright gray beneath the moon's light. “And you have gray hairs!”

“What?” She jumped and quickly began to examine a handful of her locks.

“I mean, my mom has them too,” he attempted to reassure her.

She suddenly began to laugh before extending her hand with hair in her grasp toward him. “I am quite certain she does, having to endure your brash nature. And mine is not gray but silver. See?”

He bent over and examined the hairs before taking them into his hand, admiring the smooth touch. What he had considered gray now appeared as a glowing silver. “Woah. . .you weren't lying. Silver hair.”

“May I have my hair returned to me?”

“Oh! Sorry.” He released his grip on the monochrome-looking band of hair. “But...how? I mean, how is it silver?”

“Well. . . the Moonwey’s are descendants of Lady Lunsera. As you may surmise, our province is named in her honor.”

“Okay. So who is she? And what does that have to do with having gray hair?”

“Well to begin—” She paused and gave him a stout glare. “My hair is not gray, Peter Loneheart!”

“Sorry.” He chuckled.

“The tale of Lady Lunsera is one of the fabled legends of Arden. It is even regarded as a romance by some. It took place shortly after the age of Arden began, so your twelve predecessors had already arrived. While many civilizations began to adopt their customs one after the other, some held true to their old ways for however brief a time. Our ancestor, Envar, the chieftain of Lunar Rock, held a celebration after a successful season of pillaging the mainland. My ancestors were great sea raiders, you see.”

“Congrats?”

“Hush.” She rolled her eyes and continued. “Well, during the great celebration, the entire island tribe had gathered. During the night, as the fires blazed, a woman appeared to Envar from the sea. A beautiful woman with long silver hair, she strolled forth from the very waves, singing a tune as she walked onto the beach in the midst of their celebration. Her name was Lunsera. It was said that she hailed from the planet Carraas. But, as she sang, her melody put all into a deep slumber one after the next until only Envar remained unaffected by her power.

“Lunsera was impressed that her power had been resisted by this strange bearded man, for she knew men not. Her world had no men, only women, it was said. Envar and Lunsera embraced one another, there next to the sea beneath the moon's light, and they married shortly after.” A longing sigh escaped Aurora before she continued. “They Sird a daughter named Luna. After her father and mother's deaths, Luna became the first woman chieftain, and over time she united the four islands of the south sea, dubbing the new kingdom Lunsera in honor of her mother. During such a time, many prominent families began to create surnames throughout Arden as a result of the twelve's influence. Inspired by this, Luna decided upon Moonwey in honor of both her father and mother.”

“Woah. Aurora, that's incredible. So that's why you have gray. . .silver hair?”

“Indeed. Our family's origin is well known. Of course, there are other families of greater relevance with lineage far more interesting as well.”

“Like who?”

“Well. There are the Turners of Barrington, the first family of Sohn, and even the Ornian’s, though they are now extinct.”

“Barrington? You mean. . .”

“Indeed. The Duke of Barrington, George Turner, the one who waged a war for Arden City. He belonged to the Turner family. They still rule over the eastern spire of Barrington, one of the largest cities in Arden. Aside from the Turners, I spoke of the first family of Sohn. You know, your uncle led the attack to liberate their province during the war of reclamation. They say that he won every battle without killing a single man.

"But enough of Arden and its families. I must know more about Peter Loneheart and his esteemed family."

"Well...not much to tell. It's just my mom, Laura, my grandmother, Sara, and me."

"Of course. What more? I know of your uncle already. . .tell me of your father."

The request ignited irritation. "No. There's nothing to talk about."

She tilted her head. "What do you mean?"

"He's not worth talking about."

"Please?"

He shook his head. "Trust me, he's not worth knowing. And I'm not talking about it anymore."

She sighed. "So you say."

"What about your dad?"

"Why should I reveal anything further of my family to you? After all, you will say nothing more of your own father." She pushed off from the railing and walked away. "Goodnight."

* * * * * * *

Morning came in fragments. The seagulls cried out and waves thrashed against the vessel, tossing it ever so slightly. The air felt sticky as a mist set in. He opened his eyes, yawning and standing from the hammock he had repaired in the night. A few sailors were about as the orange and pink sky grew brighter over the eastern horizon, dipping low to touch the sea. Peter shivered in the morning chill. He reclined against the wooden railing and watched as the scarce pockets of mist slowly evaporated before the sun's rays.

"Good morning," Aurora greeted, strolling over to join him. In her hand was a basket, which he hoped contained food to satisfy his growling stomach. "Did you truly sleep about here all night? Why?"

"It wasn't all bad. I had the moon and stars to keep me company."

"Growing fond of the open sea, are you?"

"Maybe a little. It's more relaxing since my stomach settled. Thank you." He took one of the pink apples from the basket she presented. The juice exploded into his mouth with a crunch.

"Well, you can remain at sea until your heart is content. I, for one, am weary of this drudgery," she groaned. "I should be on land, surrounded by horses in a green field. Emerald Island has a lovely pasture of casidians that surrounds the city there."

"Is it called the Emerald City?"

"Yes."

"Oh...really?"

"No."

He shook his head. "How long till we're there?"

"Do I look like the captain to you?"

He looked her up and down.

"Shortly, I think. Be patient, Peter. Did you know that every emerald in the world comes from Emerald Island?"

"Nope. Sure didn't."

She scoffed and the same devious grin formed on her face. "Are you familiar with the Garshin family?"

He shook his head with a mouth full of apple.

"The Garshin family are the ruling family of the Emerald Isle. They were once pirates that roamed the seas. Direct descendants of the Carnal King in fact. He was the king of pirates, or so they say. Others claim that the Garshins are descendants of an unknown tribe that also came from another world."

"Like the Moonwey's and Lady Lunsera?"

"Quite right, Peter, very good. Regardless of their exact origin, they had a long history of collecting scalps."

"Scalps?" His face grew warm as her hand gently glided through his hair, ticking his scalp.

"Yes, Peter. They collected scalps. Some say they possessed an affinity for rare colors such as yours. I'm certain Lady Lorena will simply adore you. . .or rather, your particular shade?" She giggled.

"I assure you, Mr. Loneheart," Helen said from behind them. "The Garshin family renounced such tribal practices well over a century ago."

The Lady of Lunsera strolled over to join them. From the basket near Aurora, she reached down and took an apple with her delicate fingers.

"Er...good morning, Helen," he told her.

"And good morning to you." Her gaze shifted from the hammock back to where he stood. "You slept outside during the night?"

"Yeah. It was kind of nice actually."

She smiled, as radiant as usual. "I'm certain. The night sky is lovely, is it not? So silent and serene, unlike the day." A sigh escaped her as she looked to her sister. "Aurora, would you excuse Mr. Loneheart and I?"

"Certainly," Aurora said, turning to Peter. "Enjoy your hair whilst you still have it!" Laughing, she walked away.

"Pay no attention, Mr. Loneheart. By now I am sure you see that my sister is quite the jester."

"She's. . .colorful, I guess."

"I desired to speak with you before we arrive. I must inquire: what do you hope to find on Emerald Island?"

What's that supposed to mean? "Is there something I should be looking for?"

"You chose not to remain in Lunsera and to accompany my sister and me. I surmise that you still hold to your quest of discovering a way back to your Norfolk, correct?"

"Yes, ma'am."

"Is it your hope to find a means to do so upon Emerald Island?"

"If I can. Are...are you going to help me?"

She had raised the apple to her lips but did not take a bite. Her eyes narrowed. "It is possible that Lady Lorena possesses some knowledge that could assist you, though I cannot say for certain as I have not seen her in years. However, she may not deem you worthy of such information if she does indeed know of it, due to the fact you are not of particular relevance nor a friend of her family's."

"So what are you saying?"

"If you were to enter my service, you would be privy to such information and you would receive copious benefits that—"

"You want me to swear myself to you," he said flatly.

"I do, Mr. Loneheart. I feel as if a union between you and I is inevitable and it is fate."

"No."

Her eyes closed as she sighed. She extended the uneaten apple toward him. "Fruit remains so ripe for such little time. . ."

He took the apple and she walked away.

For the next hour, he stood alone, mulling over what she had said.

When he was informed that they would arrive at the island soon, he spied the mass of land that had appeared. As the port came into view, he saw hundreds of sails of various colors hovering above the water. The capital ship of the fleet from Lunsera slowed as its royal blue fabrics were hoisted up, and from the port, a series of large longboats inched toward them across the water.

He stood with Aurora in the center of the main deck as they waited for the smaller vessel that would take them to the port. His gaze often turned to the back of Helen's head as she stood in front of him. *What is she thinking right now?* he wondered. *How many schemes can she possibly be thinking about all at once?*

The longboats arrived, and they stepped onto a smaller vessel via a series of planks that formed a bridge between the ship and boat. Oars shot out from the sides of the longboat and the men that operated them pulled and heaved them toward the port. When they arrived, Helen and Barda were the first to step onto the large pier. As Peter and Aurora stepped up behind them, he noticed the other five piers were as large as the one they were standing upon.

"You seem to be sulking again.," Aurora said next to him as they walked across the bridge of planks.

"Just thinking."

"Of course."

They reached the end of the pier and suddenly what he had thought to be simple talking from the crowd turned to screams. The entire party halted as the screams grew louder. Peter's gaze followed those of the others toward the nearby pier surrounded by vessels. A column of smoke ascended there and mobs of people ran toward the beach in utter disarray. Before any could ask what was happening, the answer came to them in screams: "Plague!"

Ahead of them, Barda ushered Helen forward as her guards parted the crowd with force and she was placed on a horse.

"Peter, run!" Aurora told him as she started forward. The Moonwey guardsmen made a pathway through the frantic crowd for the younger sister and she followed it, looking back at Peter. He rushed forward, glancing to the nearby pier as chaos ensued. He saw several people tackled onto the wooden planks as others were knocked into the water. Horrid snarls and primal growls grew louder and greater in number.

Before he could reach her, Aurora's eyes widened at something behind him. "Peter!" she called again. He turned and a powerful force struck his head. He heard her yelling his name one last time before losing consciousness.

Chapter 6

Emerald Island

The morning sun shined through his bedroom window. He stretched beneath the sheets. The classic rock song he heard was one of many that Jack liked to listen to on repeat. The words echoed from the hallway and into his bedroom.

Slowly, the boy opened his eyes. Yawning as he stood, he took a deep breath and detected a familiar scent. A whiff of fried bacon! He quickly tapped his soccer ball on the way out into the hallway, taking a shot into the open doorway near the staircase. The ball soared into the darkness of the room as he descended the steps, bypassing the silent family room.

He stopped as he entered the hallway at the base of the stairs and peeked inside his uncle Jack's office. From the desk in front of the open window a few stacks of papers took flight and scattered in a gust of wind. In the left corner of the room, a black record rotated and the music continued. To the right, a large American flag took up the entire wall, hovering over a table that featured dozens of awards, medals, and photographs.

“Peter!” his mother called from the kitchen. Her plea and the bacon she cooked grasped his attention. Turning, he completed his journey down the hallway, entering the kitchen. As his feet met the tiles of the room, he halted in his tracks.

At the kitchen table ahead of him, his grandmother sat on the far side, facing him. She nearly dropped her coffee mug as she laughed. The woman to her left finished telling a joke before turning to Peter. “Good morning, Mr. Loneheart.”

Helen smiled as radiantly as ever. In her slim blue dress, she sat with one leg over the other, holding a cup of coffee with both hands.

Peter shook his head in disbelief. How was Helen there with his Grandmother? He turned to his left as grease popped from the stove. His mother turned to greet him with her usual smile. “Good morning, handsome. Your friend has been keeping us company. Go sit down.”

He looked back to the table, hesitant to walk toward it with Helen there.

“You neglected to mention that there were such beauties in your family, Mr. Loneheart.” The comment spurred giggles from the two women. “Come.” Helen motioned toward the seat next to her. “Sit with me.”

Reluctantly, he obeyed, easing into the chair. His feet barely touched the floor.

“So, Helen,” his mother said softly, sitting across from the woman she addressed, “now that Peter is here, would you tell us how he has behaved?”

“Certainly,” she smiled. “I have come to understand that he is without purpose or meaning, seeking himself above all else, despite the fact that he does not yet know who he truly is. He is an utter failure with nothing to offer anyone, nor any woman for that matter. He is a boy, that much is certain.”

The words cut him deep like a searing hot knife. His mother and grandmother exchanged a series of glances, nodding in agreement as if they had known all along.

"Furthermore, I have deduced in our interactions that he lacks confidence. He is weak and incompetent."

He stared at the tiled floor as the three women looked down upon him. It was the worst feeling. To not be adequate or to be less than worthy of any woman.

Before despair could consume him entirely, Helen spoke again. "But. Despite his current state, I see potential. If he were to be forged, perhaps by another man or even himself, he could be great. He could be what is needed. To bring order from chaos. An embodiment of strength and sacrifice." She looked to the two women. "I am curious. . .the boy's father. Who is he?"

With tears in his eyes, he looked to his mother, hoping that she would not discuss the man. To his displeasure, she said, "He's. . .different from Peter. Powerful is the best word to describe him."

"Indeed. What is his name?"

Desperate, Peter tried to scream but was unable to muster a sound. To escape the cold reality of hearing her utter the name he despised, he cupped his hands around his ears, clamping his head tightly as her lips moved, forming words. He closed his eyes. Without sight or sound, he thought only of Jack. His uncle, his mentor, was the only father figure he needed. A strong man of compassion, wisdom, and righteousness.

But he was gone.

* * * * * * *

A ruffle of fabric that woke him. His eyes opened and the light from the sun briefly blinded him from the window of the bedchamber. In the far corner of the room, a teenaged girl folded garments and hummed a beautiful tune. Peter stretched and then rubbed his fingers over the cloth wrapped around his forehead where he had been struck. As he sat up in the bed the humming stopped.

The young maiden frantically cast aside a piece of cloth and nodded toward him. "G-g-good morning, My Lord."

“Good morning.” He grimaced as his head throbbed with a dull pain.

“Your pardon, Lord,” she said and quickly moved toward the chamber door. “I will ensure Lady Helen knows that you have awoken.” The girl smiled before exiting the room.

He stood and walked over to the window. Rather than an ocean, he saw a sea of green grass, hedges, and exotic trees under the warmth of the shining sun. Several birds hovered beyond the glass of the window, fluttering like hummingbirds before flying off in different directions. The door to the room opened behind him and a boy in an emerald green tunic appeared. He looked only a few years older than the boy named Thomas on Lunar Rock, Peter thought.

The boy in green bowed. “Good morning, Lord.”

“Morning.”

“Welcome to Emerald Island. Did you sleep well?”

Peter rubbed his aching head. “Yeah. . . I. . .What happened?”

“You do not recall the events at the port?”

“I. . .No. I don't remember what happened.”

The boy nodded. “Well...whenever you are dressed I will show you to Lady Helen.”

“Where. . .” He hesitated as he remembered Aurora's terrified expression when she had called his name at the port. “Aurora! Where is she? Is she alright? What about Helen?”

“Lady Helen is breaking fast with Our Lady of the Island in the western gardens. They await you, Lord. As for Lady Aurora, she came to your chamber just before sunrise; currently, she is occupied at the stables outside the city.”

He exhaled and smiled. “That sounds about right.” The boy from Virginia washed his face and dressed in his freshly cleaned clothes.

"And my name is Elgen, Lord," the boy told him after they exited the room.

"I'm Peter," he replied as they continued along the hallway and through a series of corridors. As the two descended a flight of stone stairs, a trio of teenaged girls giggled and starred at the Lionheart in passing.

"News of your heroics is quickly spreading, Lord," Elgen said.

"Heroics?"

"Your actions during the attack at the port. The plague."

The plague? There had been smoke and screams. People snarling and growling like wild animals as they tackled others on the pier. His palms became sweaty, his throat dry.

"Are you well, Lord?"

"Yeah," he lied. *Heroics? I didn't do anything but run away when Aurora told me to.*

"Come. They await you."

Elgen guided Peter through the halls of the villa and the double doors that led outside to the garden. The two followed a path through a labyrinth of green hedges to a meadow with a gazebo, surrounded by a variety of exotic trees. Several servants stood outside the gazebo, along with Barda, who watched Peter as he entered the wooden structure.

"Good morning, Mr. Loneheart," Helen said to him from across the table. The Lady of Lunsera sat straight in her chair and turned to the woman in the emerald green dress on her left. The woman appeared a few years older than Helen and bore a darker complexion and jet-black hair. "Lady Lorena, this is—"

"—the American!" she answered excitedly. "How wonderful."

Helen quickly shot an expectant glance at Peter.

"Ma'am." He bowed awkwardly.

"A hero and a gentleman. Please join us." Lorena indicated the empty chair near him. As he sat down, the Lady of Emerald Island watched him with a fierce, intrigued gaze. "Tell me, Mr. Loneheart..."

A few moments of silence followed.

"Tell you what?"

"All that you can tell me! I am rather curious about your. . .capabilities."

"Er...well. I. . ." He looked to Helen, who took pity on him.

"Mr. Loneheart is modest to be sure. I have learned that he is not fond of speaking of himself."

"Humble." Lorena grinned as she looked him up and down. Peter's stomach growled loud enough to be heard by the servants outside the gazebo. "And evidently famished." Lorena laughed. "Please eat."

After a moment of hesitation, he took a bite of a nearby pastry. A combination of butter and honey excited his taste buds and put a smile on his face. As he continued to eat, a servant poured red juice into his glass goblet.

"What news have you heard from the capital?" Helen asked Lorena.

"The commanders of the coalition army have been appointed by the city council."

"Who?" Helen asked eagerly.

"Sir Hector of New London will command the cavalry forces with some notable lieutenants to serve under him. As for the army itself, Lord Rulfin of the city council will be the commander. From what I have gathered, three vice-commanders will serve under him."

"Any of note?"

"Lord Carlon from Stonewell, and another whose name I have forgotten. However, the choice of Lord Alvar Blackheart has become the topic of much discussion."

Helen stopped before taking a sip of juice from her goblet. For the first time, she looked concerned. "Alvar Blackheart? Truly? His skill is well known, but why choose someone so. . .arrogant? A deal must have been made."

"I assume so. After the rumors that he had slain a beast in the north, the council seems to view him as their golden defender in black. Though regardless of his pride and blessed abilities," Lady Lorena said, looking to Peter as he continued to eat, "there is a rather boyish charm about him."

Helen sighed. "His fixation with the fabled five is his motivation no doubt. I had thought many would reconsider entering the tournament when it was learned he would compete."

"His entry alone was enough to dissuade many but not all. Jadiel of Sohn will debut and represent his province in the tournament. Though I wonder—will Mr. Loneheart compete on behalf of Lunsera?"

Peter and Helen looked at one another before she answered. "Certainly not. Mr. Loneheart has other ambitions."

"Oh? Pardon my surprise. Many will expect the Lionheart to compete, though I expect it would not be a lengthy competition if you chose to partake. Might I inquire as to what your intentions are?" The Lady of Emerald Island gazed at him.

He looked pointedly at Helen and cleared his throat.

"He seeks to return to his own world," Helen said flatly, earning a gasp from the older woman next to her.

Lorena stared at him in disbelief. "Surely you will seek to assist us during this time of crisis, just as your predecessor did."

He searched for the right words and once again looked to Helen for help, but the Lady of Lunsera sat back in her chair, sipped her juice, and watched him in a way that reminded him of a cat watching a mouse.

"What of the plague?" Lorena asked him. The question and the silent stares of both women bore down upon him and sent his heart racing. His face grew warm and he wiped his hands on his trousers.

"I. . ." He cleared his throat. "I'm just trying to get home, ma'am. I can't do anything about a plague."

Lorena's black eyebrows furrowed. Peter's ears twitched as he picked up on a sudden whispering between the servants outside the gazebo, followed by a loud scoff from Barda.

"You are certain?"

"Yes, ma'am."

Lorena looked away and sighed before turning back to him, presenting a fake smile. "Mr. Loneheart, would you excuse Lady Helen and I?"

"Yeah." He lingered for a moment. "Would you know how I can get home?"

Lorena tilted her head. "I am confused, Mr. Loneheart. Do you not recall how to return to your world?"

"I was hoping you would know."

"I'm afraid I possess no knowledge of links between the worlds. I can assure you that none in Arden do. It has been a mystery that many have endeavored to discover to no avail. Surely Lady Helen has informed you of this."

"It has been broached between us," Helen confirmed.

The news from Lorena and Helen's cold stare robbed him of words and he remained standing, uncertain. "Thanks, I guess," he muttered. Slowly, he departed the gazebo and followed Elgen through the labyrinth of hedges. *What just happened? Why did Helen act like that? I don't remember her telling me that there was no way back. Did. . .did she lie? Was Aurora right about her all along?*

His confusion remained and became frustration by the time he and Elgen reached the main gate of the city. The streets of the city were just as narrow as the ones in Lunar Rock, but the green pastures outside the gate before him were a new and welcomed sight. The road that led from the gate to the forest in the distance was flanked on both sides by vast green fields, where several people rode horses.

Elgen squinted as he looked off to the field to their right. "I believe that may be the Lady Aurora."

Peter followed the boy's gaze to a brown horse galloping with great intensity toward the two. The rider's long honey-brown hair flowed behind her as grass and chunks of dirt were kicked into the air with each fierce stride of the animal. The young woman kicked her heels into the horse, spurring the steed to race faster, directly toward them.

"Will she stop, Lord?"

"I hope," he said truthfully. She kicked her heels again. The horse raced faster toward them. "She's not stopping," Peter realized.

Just before the racing horse could run the two over, Peter grabbed the boy and stepped out of the way. Again he moved faster than he had anticipated and landed in the grass just as the horse trampled the spot in which they had been standing. As he stood and dusted off his tunic, the sound of Aurora's laughter caught his attention as she turned and briskly trotted back over to him. After hoisting Elgen up from the grass where he had landed, he looked up to the woman.

"Why did you do that?" Peter asked.

Aurora wiped sweat from her brow. "Just a bit of fun. And I was curious."

"And what if we didn't move out of the way?"

She shrugged. "It would have been unfortunate."

He crossed his arms and sighed loudly, resulting in the young woman raising an eyebrow and watching him with a neutral expression.

"What vexes you, Peter Loneheart?"

"You! And your sister!"

"Your pardon?"

He scoffed. "I don't get what you and your sister are playing at. You like playing cruel jokes on people, like running them over with a horse, and she likes to torture people with her mood swings."

Aurora suddenly grinned. "I see. What atrocity has she committed as of late?"

A tempest of emotions churned within him but no words came to mind. As he searched for the right words to explain she released a sigh, increasing his frustration.

"I...she just. . ." He struggled to explain, fists clenched. Suddenly, his heart began to race and his legs grew restless. Aurora's horse bobbed its head and began to step backward.

Elgen stepped away from him timidly. "Lord?"

"Peter!" Aurora called to him as she steadied her horse. He looked at Elgen, taking note of the boy's concerned expression before meeting Auroras focused gaze. "Race me!" she commanded before digging her heels into her steed. Peter's body trembled as he watched the horse race across the vast green field. Without a second thought, he jolted forward and began his sprint after the galloping animal.

The wind howled against his ears as each powerful stride brought him closer to the young woman ahead of him. Out of the corner of his eye, he noticed several other riders halt their horses and point toward him, gasping with awe and admiration as he sprinted across the field. He caught up to Aurora faster than he had anticipated, running next to the horse and looking up at her, low over the saddle.

She looked over to him and grinned. "Ru'vai!" she called out and the horse pressed forward with new energy, forcing Peter to exert himself as never before to catch back up. His strides grew and gained more ground as his toes touched the grass and pushed off. The wall that surrounded the city began to blur past him as he caught back up with the young woman. Aurora looked to him with a surprised smile and shook her head. Before she could utter another word, Peter exceeded his limits and sprinted harder, leaving behind the charging horse.

To his surprise, his speed increased further and the towers along the walls of the city disappeared one after the other. Directly ahead of him a rock formation stretched across the field from the walls of the city to the forest. Before he could even consider stopping, the rock formation grew too close, towering over him. Instinctively, he jumped and lunged upward toward the top of the rock formation, leading with his right leg outstretched. His momentum carried him through the air and clear over the formation, which must have been fifty feet high.

With grace, he landed on the other side and carried his momentum onward, continuing his sprint along the entirety of the walled city, eventually passing the road where Elgen still stood and finally slowing and coming to a complete stop as Aurora rode toward him from where he had passed her. Panting, he eased himself onto the grass and sprawled out on his back as the sun beamed down on his sweaty skin.

"Peter!" Aurora exclaimed excitedly, stepping down from her fatigued horse with reins still in hand. "That was marvelous! How do you feel now?"

"Tired. And. . .better." He smiled and took a deep breath, taking in the heavy scent of grass and horse.

"As I suspected you would!" She turned to her horse and gently stroked its large neck, saying affectionately, "Well done, Vrollo. Now. What of this catastrophe with Helen?"

He paused to think and to his surprise, his thoughts seemed clearer and more organized after his workout. "I just don't understand her. Over the last few days, she's been so nice, saying that she would help me find a way home, but this morning during breakfast. . .she just seemed completely different. I don't get her, Aurora."

The young woman looked off into the distance thoughtfully as she continued to pet the brown horse. "I must be honest with you, Peter. I do not envy my sister. Since the age of fourteen, she has been responsible for the well-being of our entire province. Nearly ten thousand men, women, and children." She turned to look at him seriously. "Do you have any notion of the stress that can conjure?"

He shook his head.

“Helen dedicates nearly every waking moment of her life to our people. She didn't have a choice whether she wanted to or not. I admire her, Peter, as I love her. You may perceive her as wicked in her ways, and she may, in fact, be manipulative, but I assure you that my sister is ruled by compassion and seeks only to protect our people by any means at her disposal.”

“Like me? I'm just a tool at her disposal?”

She stared at him thoughtfully. “If Fyraen deems it so. Though I am certain that Helen views you as more than a tool. After all, you are the Lionheart, are you not? Who else in Arden can outrun Vrollo?” She patted the horse's large neck. “Who else can run around an entire city within mere moments? Or leap over a rubble of stone without effort?”

“Aurora. I know what she wants. But I can't.”

“And why can you not?”

“I just want—”

“—to return home? Peter, I understand this is not what you desire to hear but it is what you need to hear: you will never leave Arden. I do not know what forces carried you here; perhaps it was Fyraen himself. But even your predecessors never returned to their homeworld. They remained in Arden and died in Arden.”

“But Jack—”

“Your uncle has not been seen for ten years in this world or your own. And he didn't hesitate to assist during the war of reclamation. Your uncle witnessed our suffering and decided to use his blessed abilities to end it. Why do you not do the same when confronted with the same dire circumstances?”

“What? But you saw how I just ran at the port. I can't help anyone!”

Aurora rolled her eyes and hoisted herself into the saddle. “You are not made of glass, Peter. You are stronger than you think. Whether you linger on your inadequacies or decide to rise and conquer your fears is your choice. I cannot help you with it. I pray you will know what is right. Good day.”

Her gaze softened and lingered on him before she kicked her heels and Vrollo raced away.

* * * * * * *

"I advise against this, Lord. I do not think it wise," Elgen told him as they continued along the corridors of the villa. Peter walked with purpose and the boy followed.

"I've had all day to think about this," he told the boy as they passed an open window through which a cool evening breeze rolled.

"If I may, what will you say to Lady Helen?"

"What I need to," Peter stated as they turned a corner. The door to the chamber stood open and a young handmaiden lingered, speaking and bowing as she exited the chamber and closed the door. The girl jumped in surprise when she set eyes on Peter and Elgen.

"Lady Helen is retiring for the evening," she said as she bowed to him.

Peter took a deep breath. "I need to see her now."

"Lord, I do not think it would be wise to intrude upon the lady at this hour."

He shook his head and walked past the handmaiden, pausing before knocking on the door. His hands felt sticky again, and he thought he could hear his racing heart beating aloud.

After speaking with Aurora, he had spent the day rehearsing how he would confront Helen. Now that the moment had come, his nerves attacked what fragile confidence he had constructed. He took another deep breath and knocked three times.

"Yes?" Helen asked from the other side of the door.

"It's Peter," he said to the wood. A moment of silence followed.

"Mr. Loneheart?"

"Yeah. Look, Helen, I need to—"

“This is hardly appropriate. Surely this matter can wait to be discussed until a more appropriate time.”

“But I need—”

“Please return in the morning, Mr. Loneheart.” A moment of silence once again followed.

“No.” He gritted his teeth and pushed the door open, revealing a candle-lit chamber of rich furniture and a single large bed. On the far side of the large room, Helen gasped and jumped out of her chair, dropping the book she had been reading. He paused and stood transfixed by the rare, fearful expression that her face displayed. She seemed so vulnerable, dressed in a nightgown with her hair tied back in a tousled manner.

Then fury filled her eyes. “This is *not appropriate*!”

He could hear Elgen and the handmaiden scurry away down the hallway as he swallowed dryly and prepared himself for what was to come.

“I know. I just need—”

“Mr. Loneheart! Leave this instant!”

“No,” he said.

Helen shook her head in disbelief. “Your pardon?”

“No!” He crossed his arms and stared at her with a hard gaze of his own while his heart raced and his legs wavered. Would she see through his bold facade? “You and I need to talk,” he told her.

“The only discussion of relevance is courtesy and your lack of it!”

“I've been courteous enough! Can you say the same?”

Suddenly, an arm wrapped around his throat and pulled him back against a lean body in armor.

“You will die for your insolence!” Barda hissed into his ear. The cold edge of her blade rested on the exposed skin of this throat.

His body naturally tensed and he leaned forward. Barda growled as she tightened her hold on him. She struggled to keep her hold as he took a step forward and carried her with little effort, picking her up off of the ground. With the adrenaline coursing through him, he reached for her arm and prepared to throw her across the room.

“Enough!” Helen commanded. “Barda, release him. Mr. Loneheart, calm yourself!” As his fingertips brushed against the flesh of her arm, she released her hold on him and stepped back, panting as she eyed him while maintaining a ready stance. They both looked to Helen who closed her eyes and took a deep breath. “Barda, please excuse us; evidently we have a number of things to discuss.”

“Lady He—” Barda tried before the Lady of Lunsera raised her index finger and silenced her protector. The amazon bowed and eyed him once last time before she departed the chamber and closed the door behind her, leaving the two alone in silence.

“Sit,” Helen said sternly, indicating a pair of chairs and a small table in front of an open window. He obeyed, glancing out the window, admiring the milky light of the moon that shined onto the vast field surrounding the city. He turned his attention back to the woman as she sat down next to him.

“Speak,” she said.

“You lied to me,” he said flatly.

“Pardon?”

“You lied to me about Lorena. You told me she would know a way to get me home.”

“You are mistaken. I merely implied.”

“But did you know?” he asked.

She hesitated. “Yes.”

“Why didn't you tell me the truth then?”

“Had I told you the truth, would it have mattered? Would you have decided to swear yourself to me if I had?”

“Probably not.”

“Certainly not, it would seem.” She crossed her legs and her naked foot appeared briefly before slipping back underneath her robe.

He hesitated as his thoughts briefly escaped him and shook his head to focus. “So that means you lied about everything. You could have just told me the truth from the beginning, that I wouldn't. . .that I wouldn't find a way back home.”

“You draw conclusions in a most unusual manner, Mr. Loneheart.”

“Aurora told me the truth and she didn't try to manipulate me like you did.”

Her index finger tapped her lower lip pensively. She shifted in her chair and her lower leg revealed itself for a moment, catching his attention. She spoke but he heard little of what she said.

“What?” he asked. She cocked an eyebrow and her lips briefly formed a faint grin. *What's she smirking about?* “Listen, I know what you want from me, but I—” She shifted in her chair once again, allowing her foot to slip from the veil of her robes. The pale skin of her shin seemed to shine with smoothness under the pale light of the moon.

“And what do I desire from you?” she asked. His eyes darted from her exposed leg to her gleaming hazel eyes. From the bundle of her hair that was tied back, some strands shined with the same silver light as her sister’s.

“Er. . .I. . .” He struggled to find the words and he rubbed his temples. What was I going to say? Why can't I focus?!

“Hmm?” her sweet voice hummed, conjuring excited chills all along his body.

“Give me a second.”

“Certainly.” A few moments of silence passed and her robe veiled the exposed leg. “What do you propose is the reason why I sought your services?”

"I'm fast."

"Eloquently spoken. Indeed, your abilities are certainly unparalleled and would be of great service to the suffering people of Arden. Your mere presence projects power that few have witnessed. I happen to be among the few who have, which is why I move to motivate you even against your own will and selfish desires."

"Trying to go home is selfish?"

"Depending upon the point of view, yes. Permit me: when you witnessed the desolation the plague caused at the port, what did you feel?"

"I was terrified."

"Any sane person would be. Can you envision what all the plague victims felt before they were killed? And what of the men who fought the day before? They did not possess your blessings and yet they ran toward the chaos as others ran away from it."

"Like me."

"Indeed. I can see that the decision continues to vex you. You know you could have made a difference. If you had chosen to stand with the men-at-arms, perhaps more would still be alive to see their families, and you would not continually chide yourself for your cowardice." The brutal honesty of her words forced him to bury his head in his sweaty hands.

"I can't do anything right," he confessed. A cool and gentle breeze moved through the window and caressed the skin of his neck. Warmth rushed throughout his entire body as both of her hands wrapped up one of his own.

"I do not believe that to be true," she told him. "Look into your heart and discern the noble intentions it holds." He looked up and marveled at her enchanting gaze. A look that could inspire any man.

"So what do I do?"

“That is your quandary. I will no longer attempt to deceive you. I swear for the sake of Jack Loneheart. Instead, I will offer you the opportunity to freely join my guard.”

“Your guard? Like Barda?”

“Essentially, yes. I will not demand an oath of fealty from you, only that you protect my sister and I, and remain at my side as we travel for the capital. As I said before, the mere sight of you projects power and that is a tribute I will use to full effect. To see the Lionheart walking beside the Lady of Lunsera will provide great inspiration to others during this time of crisis.”

“I get it.” He took a deep breath. “I'll do it,” he said to her delight, putting a genuine smile on her face that kindled a flame of passion within him. *How can someone be so beautiful?*

“Wonderful.” She stood and he followed. “We will depart in two days' time. Until then I request that you remain with Aurora. She is smitten with Vrollo and I suspect she will remain preoccupied with him until we depart. As I have been informed, his speed failed against you.” Her comment filled him with pride.

“I didn't know I could go that fast.”

“I wonder, Mr. Loneheart. What more will you discover about yourself?”

Chapter 7

A New Dawn

A rooster crowed and there was a knock at the door. Peter shifted in his bed. He nestled his head deeper into the pillow, unwilling to awaken from his peaceful slumber. Another knock, louder than the first, finally roused him and his eyes opened to the darkness of his chamber.

Another knock and a small voice followed. "Lord."

"Elgen?" The chamber door eased open and the boy's head poked inside.

"Apologies, Lord. I was bid to inform you that Lady Aurora is awaiting you."

"Already? What time is it?" he yawned. "The sun isn't even up yet."

"Soon, Lord. She and Vrollo await you in the courtyard of the villa."

"Naturally," he mused, and put on his clothes from Lunsera. After slipping on his boots, he followed the boy through the corridors, down the stairs, and through the front doors of the villa, where Aurora raced the great horse in large circles around the courtyard.

"Morning, my protector!" she japed, tugging on the reins and guiding the steed over to him.

“Good morning,” he yawned. The horse nuzzled his shoulder. “Good morning, Vrollo.”

“Well?” Aurora asked expectantly.

“Well, what?”

“How do you feel?” He paused and considered it.

“Better,” he confessed, “and I slept great too.”

“I am relieved to hear it. Now come. This island yearns to be explored.” She twisted in the saddle and reached into one of the two saddlebags.

“Explore? Right now? I'm starving.”

She retracted her hand from the leather satchel and tossed him a wheel of tightly bound parchment. He peeled back the paper, revealing a wheel of sweet-smelling bread.

“A sufficient meal for a Lion I hope?”

“Sure.” He took a bite and chewed with delight as the creamy bread tickled his taste buds. “Ah! It's amazing.”

She smiled. “I'm pleased you enjoy it. Now, can you ride?”

“Er. . .ride?” He shook his head. “I've never...”

Aurora groaned. “You are truly frustrating.” She stroked the waves of her hair as she thought. “I suppose we may contribute a few hours of the morning to train you to ride. It would benefit you to learn since Arden is your new home.”

Her words struck him like a cold winter wind. Though he felt her words were true, a part of him still couldn't fully accept it.

The next hour was filled with Aurora’s stern instructions. He admired her passion. Aurora guided Vrollo around the courtyard on foot as Peter sat in the saddle, occasionally reminding him of his errors. “Easy on the reins! Don't grip so tightly with your legs! Keep your feet in the stirrups! Stand, don't sit!” Elgen sat on the steps before the doors of the villa, watching with enthusiasm and occasionally laughing whenever Peter was corrected. The boy darted for the stables when Aurora told him to prepare a horse for Peter.

"Good form, Peter!" She began to say, standing in the middle of the courtyard and watching as he rode the champion steed on his own, gently tapping his heels into the sides of the animal and bringing it to a brisk gallop, then gently pulling back on the reins to slow its pace.

Finally, Elgen returned, guiding a saddled gray horse through the open gate of the courtyard. Peter relinquished Vrollo to Aurora and strolled over to the other steed, gently stroking its soft hair as it gently poked at him with its nose.

"Her name is Mary, Lord," Elgen told him, and handed him the reins. Peter looked into the eyes of the animal and felt a profound aura of gentleness radiating from it. It reminded him of his grandmother.

"She's beautiful." He lingered for a moment to continue petting it before mounting the way Aurora had shown him.

"Shall we?" the young woman asked from the saddle of Vrollo.

"We shall!"

* * * * * * *

The city was dwarfed in their view from the hilltop where they took their respite. Peter looked around at the forest.

"Beautiful," he breathed.

"Average," Aurora said before she sunk her teeth into a vibrant red apple. She looked at him. "I'm impressed. You rode through the paths so well. Mary truly suits you."

He combed his fingers through the pale line of hair along the back of the horse's neck. "She did all the work," he mused. "She's perfect. My mom would love her and she would have the time of her life if she were here."

"Oh? Your mother has a fondness for the greatest of beasts as well?"

“I don't know about the greatest, but yeah, she loves horses. I prefer dogs.”

“Ah. . .a lover of the wolf I see.” She swallowed the last bite of apple and tossed the core over her shoulder. “You know. . .there are legends of a giant wolf in the west. They say it roams about the northern roads between Hearthelm and Ilvion. Not even the infected dare trifle with the beast.” She chuckled. “Perhaps it will be your steed.”

“I meant just regular dogs. Not wolves, let alone giant ones.”

“As you wish, wolf-lover.” She playfully tossed a twig from a nearby tree at him. “Now, tell me more of your mother.”

“Er. . .well. . .she loves horses.”

“Indeed.”

“She's really supportive, always pushing me to be better. And she likes to joke around.” He smiled, though his eyes stung. “She's the perfect mom.” he concluded. “I really miss her.”

A few moments of silence followed. A breeze flowed through the trees, rustling the leaves.

“I am sorry, Peter,” she told him softly. “I. . .”

He looked to her and stared at her perplexed expression.

“You inquired once before about my own parents. If it brings you some solace, I will tell you of them.”

He was surprised but nevertheless curious. “Yeah. If you want to, but you don't have to.”

“I'm aware. Regardless. . .I feel as if you deserve to know.” Her brows furrowed as if she were unsure.

“Yeah. Okay.” He leaned onto the pommel of the saddle, listening intently.

“Sometime before our father's death, there was a ship that—” she hesitated and shook her head. “Perhaps another time. It was ridiculous of me to even consider. . .”

"No. It' s okay. Really," he assured her.

She sighed and straightened in the saddle. "Never mind that. Let us continue. I believe the respite should be sufficient." She kicked her heels and Vrollo darted toward a nearby dirt path leading down the hill into the woods. Peter kicked his heels and Mary followed after.

The two took a path that snaked through dense shrubbery and various sorts of trees. Sunlight scarcely found its way to the forest floor, leaving pockets of beaming radiance. The chirps of various birds echoed throughout the trees and occasionally Peter heard the roar of what he assumed was a mountain lion. Aurora ignored the sounds and pressed forward, finally slowing Vrollo as they came into a clearing of grass flanked by stone and trees.

A wall of rock nearly forty feet high stood before them, extending in both directions toward the trees. He thought it was an ideal place for an avid rock climber. Aurora circled around in the clearing and stared at him with lively eyes and a gleaming smile.

"Do you think you can jump it?" she asked. He detected both excitement and mischief in her voice.

"What? That?"

She nodded enthusiastically and grasped the reins of his horse when she came close enough. "I will stand guard over your beloved Mary."

"Thanks so much." He rolled his eyes.

Stepping down, he shuffled through the tall grass toward the high wall of stone, gazing at the top. After a deep breath and a widened stance, he pushed off against the ground, leaping into the air. He ascended faster than he had anticipated and quickly cleared the top, landing on the grass of the cliff. A cool and constant breeze flowed above the tops of the trees below and kissed the skin of his face as he looked around from his vantage point. Bellow, Aurora clapped.

His adrenaline spiked as he eyed the ground far below where he had jumped. He remembered the window of his chamber in Lunsera and the motivation that Helen had given him. He stuck out his right foot and plummeted to the forest clearing.

"Well done!" Aurora exclaimed and applauded once again. "You have defeated the fastest horse in Arden in a trial of speed and now you have mastered the ability to jump." She laughed. "What more can you do?"

He shrugged. "I don't know. What do you think?"

"They say your uncle could tear apart cannons. I heard on one occasion that the Lionheart smashed his way through an entire mountain."

"You have to be kidding."

"Certainly not." She grinned wolfishly. He sighed and strolled over to the wall of rock he had jumped. He placed his hands on the cold and grainy stone with outstretched fingers. Flexing, his fingertips pressed into the hard surface. He grimaced and flexed his hands as if he aimed to squeeze a rubber ball. Slowly the stone beneath his fingertips chipped and shifted out of place. He gasped in astonishment and squeezed harder, digging his fingers into the splitting stone until he could go no further.

He retracted his hands and studied his bruised fingertips, plastered with dust. "Woah!"

"Not quite on par with your predecessor in terms of strength, but it is a start I suppose."

"Yeah. Jack was really strong in my world too, but to think that he could rip apart giant rocks here? Incredible."

"Then we shall endeavor to increase your strength so that perhaps one day you will rival your hero." She chuckled and turned her horse toward the forest.

Hours passed like the blurring trees as the two raced through the paths in the woods. Often, they took breaks to water the horses and to sit on the grass rather than a saddle. Slowly throughout the day, each became privy to the others past in brief bouts of storytelling between snacks of bread, salted beef, and apples. Though he continued to long for home, Peter felt distracted when he was with her, even telling her the story of his childhood puppy being killed by a snake, nearly bringing her to tears. She told him the tale of Barda, Helen's personal guard. The young warrior's father had been Royce of First Fire island. He had been the greatest warrior to ever come out of Lunsera. During the war of reclamation, he had led a detachment of Lunsera's troops, but was ambushed and slain after making his final stand, killing one hundred men by himself. Barda had only been fifteen when she heard about her father's death. She trained for years, becoming a warrior to honor her father. Finally, during a tournament held on Lunar Rock by Helen's counselors on her eighteenth birthday, Barda entered despite being a woman. Though she lost in the first round, Helen took personal interest in her and after months of friendship, she had taken the warrior into her personal guard.

The sun's light was receding over the western sky and bats fluttered about the fields outside the city as they finally made their way back. Though the day had been long, it had also been fun and informative for Peter. He looked over to the woman riding next to him as the last of the sun's light caressed her face. Though Aurora enjoyed playing her jokes on him, he enjoyed her presence. For the first time since he had arrived in the new world, he felt as if he had a friend.

* * * * * * *

Another night of peaceful sleep passed and he awoke with the sun filled with vigor and new purpose. He quickly donned his garments from Lunsera, taking some time to primp in front of a mirror. Over the last few days, he had grown to like his blue tunic and the embroidered crescent moon of silver on his back. The thought came across his mind to take the tunic with him as a souvenir back to Norfolk if he could.

After slipping on his boots, he departed his chamber and greeted Elgen. The two made their way to a small dining room, where a banquet table stood with breakfast prepared. Peter indulged in a series of pastries and sausages, surprising Aurora when she entered the room.

“Awake already,” she noted before taking the pastry he held in his hand and biting into it with a crunch. “Ready to see the capital?”

“Yeah, I—” he jolted to his feet as Helen entered the room with Barda close behind.

“I am positively famished,” the Lady of Lunsera stated, darting for the banquet table. He studied her face as she chewed in a less elegant manner than he had expected. She had bags under her eyes and strands of her hair poked out in different directions.

“You look atrocious,” Aurora stated flatly, earning a wide-eyed glance from Peter. The elder sister ignored the comment and continued to eat, merely extending her hand with an envelope in her grasp.

“What is this?” Aurora asked, taking the yellow piece of parchment and reading it as she paced back and forth.

Suddenly Helen’s tired gaze fell on Peter and his pulse quickened. “Good morning, Mr. Loneheart.”

“Er. . .good morning.”

“Did you sleep well?”

“Yeah. You?”

She cocked an eyebrow. “Not as well as I would have preferred.”

“Infected sighted outside Arden City!” Aurora exclaimed. “Are they certain of this?”

Helen continued to chew as her gaze remained on Peter. “It would appear so. But it is rumored, nothing more.”

The younger sister groaned and flopped into a nearby chair. “Can you imagine the amount of security throughout the city if it's true? Will the horse race and tournament be canceled?”

“Nothing can be said for certain until the parliament convenes,” Helen sighed. “I pray that I may receive some rest before the drudgery commences.”

Elgen reentered the room and politely bowed. “The detail is prepared for you, Lady Helen. Also, Lady Lorena will depart shortly with her own escort.”

“Wonderful. Thank you, Elgen.” She turned to Barda. “What of the port?”

“Purges have continued since the incident, by both Lady Lorena's men and our own. Nothing of note to report.”

Helen sighed. “Excellent. Then let us depart.”

The party gathered in the courtyard where Aurora had trained Peter the day before. Over two dozen guards from Lunsera stood ready on horseback. Helen and Barda sat in the protection of the lone carriage while Peter and the younger Moonwey sister rode separate horses and followed after. Flanked by the guards in leather armor, the party departed the villa, following the main road through the city and out the front gate.

After an hour-long ride, the party came to the end of the forest road, and Peter heard the ocean. The endless body of water appeared before them as they passed over a hill. Over a dozen ships hovered in the distance. Soon the beach came into view, and Peter’s breath escaped him. Half of the entire port was gone, either sunken into the waves or charred and broken, protruding from the surface of the water. Along the beach, piles of debris burned, sending up spires of black smoke. A foul odor lingered in the air that instantly made Peter think of rotten smoked ham.

“Behold,” Aurora breathed next to him. “The desolation of the plague.”

Upon arriving at the port, the party ferried to the flagship via longboats. The captain welcomed back the Lady of Lunsera and eventually Lady Lorena and her own party. Finally, when all were accounted for, the ship set its course for the capital and departed Emerald island.

The day at sea went by quickly. Peter napped when he didn't feel sick, and to his surprise felt a yearning to ride horses again. Finally, as the sun began to set on the western horizon and transmute the sky into shades of orange and pink, lanterns were lit along the main deck of the ship and a celebration commenced. A small crew played jovial music with their string instruments, inspiring dancing as peoples of the two provinces drank wine and mingled. Peter watched from the railing as Aurora danced with a small group in the center of the celebration. On her toes, she pranced with rhythm, synchronized with the others around her. When she locked eyes with Peter, his heart skipped a beat.

Bringing his fears to life, she darted for him and grasped his hands. "Dance with me!"

"I can't dance!"

"Then prance. Like a lion!" She pulled him into the rotating circle of movement. She was stronger than she looked. He stumbled to keep up with the flurry of movement. From the onlookers on the deck, he heard laughs and applause, even looking over to witness Helen apparently laughing as she sat with Lorena.

Each time he stumbled and berated himself, Aurora would hold his hands tighter and guide him. Just as he found his rhythm and pranced on his toes, the music abruptly ceased and not a murmur was heard from any on the deck. He looked around to see several faces of horror looking in the same direction. He followed their eyes over the railing of the ship to see an island.

On the mound of earth there lay piles of rubble taller than trees. Once-tall stone structures smoldered. A few continued to stand as silhouettes against the sunset behind the ruined city.

"The rumors are true," Aurora muttered next to him.

"What?"

"Somerta. It was a city and a trading hub. A fortress from the former age. There were rumors that it had been destroyed some weeks ago. . .destroyed in a single night." Her grave words sent a chill down his spine.

"Was it the plague?"

She shook her head, her eyes transfixed on the horrific ruins. "The plague cannot destroy stone. Not all the cannons in Lunsera could have done this."

"What could have?"

She turned to him. "You."

Chapter 8

Arden City

Morning mist hovered above the vibrant green grass of the open field. Peter looked around at what reminded him of a golf course, with no one in sight, only the animal across the green that watched him. With fur as white as snow, the lamb stood atop the grass and took a step toward him. From it he felt a warm presence, as if the lamb was projecting some measure of goodwill.

The lamb began to nod its head toward him. Unsure of the animal's message at first, he slowly turned upon the realization that it was signaling him to turn around. He turned and halted, paralyzed by fear.

From where the grass was tallest in the field, the beast slithered through the sea of green. It was a snake with black scales and eyes bathed in blood, hungry and sinister. Its body was thick like the base of a cedar, its head large enough to swallow him four times over. Slowly, it crept toward him, inch by inch, and prepared to strike. Its tongue flickered and his heart raced as he remained unable to move. The snake hissed, victorious, and lunged forward as quick as lightning with fangs as long as his arm.

“Good morning!” Aurora's voice exclaimed, waking him from his nightmare. He jumped, tearing his hammock out from underneath him again. He fell onto the wooden deck of the ship. Groaning, he rested his head on the wooden planks beneath him.

“Unfavorable dream?” she asked.

“You guessed it. Nightmare,” he sighed, finally calming himself. He wiped away his cold sweat and stood, looking around the ship as the crew began to move about in the gentle light of the morning.

“You seem to have them so often. You recall what I told you before about terrors of the night. What have you done to disappoint Fyraen?”

He ignored her inquiry and leaned against the railing of the ship, basking in the cool morning breeze and feeling grateful for wakeful solace.

“Finally our three-day journey at sea will come to its end.” She stared into the distant horizon as she joined him. “I hope the capital will bring you some peace, Peter. It truly is a wondrous place.”

“If you say so.”

“Hmm? Do I detect uncertainty?”

The deep metallic gong of a bell tolled in the distance. He turned to gaze in wonder upon the mass of land that had appeared. Standing high above the waves, the distant green wall of earth extended in both directions, never-ending. In the center, Arden City stood above the sea and below the mountains behind it. He discerned tall towers of gray stone numbering in the hundreds and eventually thousands as the ship came closer.

“They look like skyscrapers...” he muttered in disbelief.

“How does it compare to your Norfolk?”

“We're still far away but. . .it's bigger than my city. . .a lot bigger!”

They stood in silence for the next half hour, watching as the city grew in both size and detail. As the ship came close enough that the full scope of the city could be seen, Aurora frequently pointed out notable buildings.

"The citadel!" She pointed at a tall and gleaming spire toward the center of the city. "Where the city council sits and does nothing." She shifted her arm to the only dome-like structure in the metropolis, which stood closer to the sea. "The arena! Where the tournament will be held." Her finger pointed to the far right of the city. "You cannot see it, but the palace lies beyond those pesky buildings there." Finally, her finger lowered toward what he assumed was the port where the city met the ocean. Two marble men standing as tall as some of the buildings faced one another above the piers. "Adam and Edmund. Two of the twelve. They were the last of the founders to die."

"How did they?"

"Die? They killed one another over the fate of Arden City. Adam thought the city should be governed by a council of elected officials whilst Edmund believed a king should rule, that either himself or Adam should be chosen by the people. They could not come to a compromise, so they fought one another, throwing each other throughout the city and into the mountains above it until their fight took them into the sea and they sank into the abyss below. Thus concluded the time of the twelve."

Peter looked to the snowy peaks of the distant mountains, hovering above the city, and then to the waves of the sea.

"So I guess Adam got what he wanted."

"I suppose they both did. Edmund's son was the first Duke of Barrington and his son became known as the brat prince. He launched a conquest for the city. He succeeded and became the first and only monarch to rule over Arden City, fulfilling the dying wish of his grandfather Edmund. Of course, his rule did not last long as he was dethroned by the order of Bastille."

"The order of. . .Bastille?"

"Indeed. The legendary knights."

"Knights? Like the kind that slays dragons?"

“They aren’t that old. But they are the first order of knights in history. Founded by the first John, one of the twelve. There are many guilds of knights within Arden but none are so revered as those of Bastille. Our cousin is a member, you know.”

“Really? So they're fighting the plague too?”

“Apparently not. Aaron wrote to us some time ago, divulging that the order has no interest in fighting the plague.”

For a reason he did not know, the news irritated Peter. “Why don't they help?”

“No one knows for certain. It's been years since they have had proper leadership. Sir William was said to have been the greatest leader in their history. His legend supplied many young boys with notions of honor and glory, even our cousin.”

She yawned and turned. “Oh! It's time, Peter!” She grabbed his sleeve and pulled him over to the center of the deck as two groups of people began to gather in formation.

Vassals gossiped from behind the personal guard of both provinces. At the head of the green and blue formation, Helen and Lorena stood together and exchanged a series of inaudible whispers. Darting between two of the guards in formation, Aurora took her place behind her sister and beside Barda. Several pairs of eyes watched Peter as he stood awkwardly, not knowing where to go. Helen peered back and noticed his plight.

“Mr. Loneheart,” she said with a smile. “Here.” He followed her instructions. Lorena and Helen both stood aside, allowing him to stand between them, seemingly at the head of the entire formation.

He stiffened as Lorena slipped her hand through his right arm and held it. “Delightful to see you again, Mr. Loneheart. Your hair looks positively radiant this morning.”

He laughed nervously. “Thanks.” His heart fluttered as Helen’s hand slipped through his left arm and gently grasped his bicep.

“Stand straight,” she said softly. He obeyed and hoped that he wasn't blushing. Suddenly, a bell began to toll from the city and a dozen more joined in a concussive display that made Peter’s ears ring.

The symphony of bells ceased as the ship glided up to one of the stone piers. Though he could not see beyond the railing, the sounds of what sounded like dozens of people roused him and he rounded his shoulders. The gate of the railing opened, revealing the wooden bridge that had been fastened to the ship from the pier, where a horde of people stood and began to cheer. Various wind and string instruments began to play throughout the crowd as drums joined along.

Lorena and Helen tugged on his arms and they started forward, exiting the ship toward the crowd of cheering citizens. As they stepped onto the stone, one man in a silver jacket with rich golden embroideries met them. His neatly tied gray hair shimmered in the sunlight as he approached with opened arms.

“Welcome, Lady Helen Moonwey of the Lunsera province, and Lady Lorena Garshin of Emerald Island.” The elder gentlemen then saw Peter. “And of course welcome to you, Lord Lionheart the second. If I may permit myself, I am Lord Edward Bracken, member of the city council and magistrate of the Edrics district. On behalf of the council, I welcome you to Arden City.” The crowd erupted into cheers and music for a few moments until Lord Bracken smiled and raised his hand for silence.

Lady Lorena smiled brightly and spoke clearly for all to hear, “It is of the greatest pleasure to return to Arden City.”

Helen added, “And we are honored to have none other than Lord Edward Bracken at the forefront of our greeting party.” The man smiled with satisfaction and bowed again as the crowd once again erupted into cheers. Lord Bracken showed the two parties to a series of carriages surrounded by scores of city guards on horseback, all armed with sabers at their hips and muskets slung over their shoulders. Helen and Barda climbed into the carriage first. Just as Aurora stepped into it, a sharp pain emanated from his stomach and Peter fell to his knees. An eerie feeling of dread seemed to invade every fiber of his being as his stomach churned and he gasped as he knelt on the stone.

"Peter!" Aurora's head shot out of the carriage. "What is it? What's wrong?"

He gasped for air against the sudden unpleasant sensation. Finally, it abated and he could freely breathe. He shook his head and stood, leaning against the carriage.

"Are you well, Mr. Loneheart?" Helen asked from the inside. He nodded but remained unsure.

After climbing inside, he looked out the window to marvel at the wonder of the city as the procession began. He counted twelve massive stone piers making up the city port. His eyes were drawn to an enormous spire that stood alone above the waves of the sea, connected to the city by a skybridge.

"A storm spire," Aurora told him, "or I suppose the last of the spires." He turned his attention from the lonely structure to the two hulking marble figures that formed an archway and entry from the port into the city.

"Adam and Edmund," he said, earning an intrigued glance from Helen beside him.

"You have been studying your history, Mr. Loneheart," she observed.

He looked across to Aurora. "I've had a good teacher."

"Perhaps I will test your knowledge soon," Helen teased.

He looked back to the statues of the former British soldiers. They were well crafted, he thought as he studied the detailed facial features of both. Even as he gazed upon them in their immortal forms of stone, he felt akin to both men.

After passing through the archway, the detail quickly moved through a series of streets, shadowed by the countless tall towers that loomed overhead.

It's really a city! It has to be three times bigger than Norfolk and with a lot more people to boot. The multiracial array of citizens wore a vast assortment of clothing and spoke various languages. As the carriage was pulled along a street, Peter's mouth watered and his stomach growled as the enticing culmination of scents filled his nostrils.

"I'm famished." Aurora breathed.

"Indeed." Helen said. "I am certain there will be a banquet when we arrive at the palace."

The four stomachs in the carriage growled incessantly after passing the aromatic street. Half an hour passed quickly as the detail continued through the labyrinth of a city. At last, the palace came into view, surrounded by a wall of stone.

"Is that it?" he asked.

"Indeed," Helen answered. "The prince's palace. It was built during the brief rule of Henry Turner, the brat prince. Constructed within a year, can you believe? Utterly magnificent."

"It looks like the white house," Peter muttered. "It was really built within a year?"

"Certainly. The only deed of reverence to result from the prince's rule."

The detail stopped briefly before entering the main gate of the palace grounds, continuing along the road flanked by two gardens until they came to a stop in the palace courtyard.

Peter's heart jumped when Helen leaned against him to look out the window. The honey-like scent of her neck filled his nose "The entire city council is here to greet us," she noted before whispering to him, "Ensure you step out first and then assist me as I exit. It will surely delight the council to see a display of chivalry from you."

"Yes, ma'am," he said before opening the door and stepping outside. He turned back and extended his hand, gently taking hers into his own to assist her as she exited the carriage. He assisted Aurora as Barda exited on her own.

"Well done," Helen told him, slipping her hand into his arm again.

The city council stood in full force. All twelve members applauded as Lady Lorena approached along with Helen and Peter. Each was dressed in rich garments that rivaled those of Helen and Lorena. He recognized Lord Bracken, who had greeted them at the port. He stood between an elder woman and a smaller gentleman who reminded Peter of some tycoon from a board game in both dress and physical appearance.

The monopoly man stepped forward and bowed to the two province leaders and the Lionheart. "Welcome! Welcome! And welcome! A truly joyous day is upon us. It brings tears to these old eyes." He wiped at them. "Lady Lorena! And of course Lady Helen! And what more. . ." He paused and looked to the sky, muttering a few words as if to pray before looking back to Peter. "And. . .a Lion of the Otherworld! Fyraen smiles upon us!" he exclaimed before prancing over to Peter and grasping his hand. "Remarkable! My friend, permit me. I am Lord Roland Ornwell. Come!" The man wrapped his arm around Peter's back and began to escort him toward the council away from Helen.

"Roland," an elder woman said from the group of council members. Lord Ornwell halted and turned. "Perhaps our guests first deserve a respite." The council members began to laugh.

"Ah!" Lord Ornwell exclaimed, releasing Peter. "Of course. Of course. Take your reprieve." His brown eyes looked Peter up and down one last time with disturbing enthusiasm. "Magnificent!"

He turned to the Lady of Emerald Island. "Lady Lorena Garshin, would you accompany me or is a respite necessary?"

"A respite is not necessary. It would be a pleasure to accompany you, Lord Ornwell," she said, and the two departed up the stairs toward the entrance.

The female council member stepped forward and curtsied. "Lady Helen."

"Lady Vera." Helen nodded. "To see you again warms my heart." The two women walked together up the stairs toward the palace. The council disbanded and followed after.

Aurora dashed up to Peter, snickering, "You were nearly abducted! This trip is already proving entertaining."

"No kidding," he stated, looking around. "This place is incredible though. The palace and the city."

"Indeed." Her stomach growled loudly and she took his hand, straining to pull him up the steps. "Come! Helen said there would be food inside!"

They made their way up the steps. As they entered the front doors, Peter inhaled sharply as the eerie feeling from the port set in once again. A sharp pain radiated from his stomach as if he were being stabbed.

What is this? Something isn't right. . .

"What is it, Peter?" Aurora asked.

He shook his head. "Nothing," he mouthed without air. A few moments passed and the pain subsided.

"Peter, you are not well. What—"

"It's fine," he told her. "I guess I'm just hungry."

Her brows remained furrowed as she watched him and she nodded. "Very well. Then let us eat."

They continued through the entrance and fell short of words at its beauty. The bright tiled floor shined from the sunlight that beamed through the high ceiling of stained glass. Across from the entrance, a massive staircase led to the second and third floors of the palace. The council stepped through the open archway to the right of the entrance as Lady Vera led Helen into the archway on the left. A few staff members escorted Peter and Aurora to the western wing of the palace, where their party would stay. The common room of their assigned quarters was decorated with lush, vibrant furniture and ostentatious tapestries. Two fully stocked bookshelves stood next to the hallways that led to the bedchambers on both sides of the large common area. *I bet those are for Helen.*

He took the hallway to the right and entered his own chamber. The window that allowed light into the room also offered a balcony overlooking the gardens and entryway to the palace. The city lay beyond.

Peter looked around his bedchamber with enthusiasm. A small table stood in the corner of the room with two wooden chairs nearby. A wardrobe stood across from the large and enticing bed that was flanked by two nightstands. After a moment of standing in silence, alone for the first time in what felt like an eternity, Peter leapt into the air and crashed onto the soft bedding with a deafened thud. He closed his eyes and sleep followed.

* * * * * * *

A knock at the door awoke him from his nap. He ignored it and snuggled deeper into the soft fabrics of his new bed. Another knock at his chamber door and a familiar voice followed.

"Peter," Aurora said through the door. "Peter, are you asleep?"

"Not anymore," he muttered under his breath.

"There will be a preliminary race in the city shortly. If we leave now we should arrive in time for the start. It's arguably the best part of the race save for the finish." She paused and scratched the wood like a cat. "And we can scavenge for food!"

He yawned and leapt out of bed, rushing to the door and opening it with a ferocity that caused the shingles to screech. Aurora stood in the hallway, examining the door with a smile. "I suspected the prospect of food would motivate you. Come." She took his hand and led him to the common area.

"Didn't you eat while I was asleep? I thought there was a banquet."

"Hardly a banquet. Besides, aren't you feeling adventurous?"

"Awful food. Got it," he concluded.

As he stood in the center of the common room, Aurora retrieved a black tunic and leather jacket like her own. She extended her hand with the clothes.

"Put these on."

"Why?"

"You cannot go waltzing into the city dressed like royalty without security, even if you are the Lionheart. Do you desire to have the entire population of Arden City crowding around us everywhere we go? I thought not. Remove that tunic and put these on." She handed him the clothes and he began to take off his Lunsera tunic before pausing.

"Aren't you going to turn around?"

She crossed her arms and shrugged. "No. Is that an issue?"

"Okay," he conceded, and removed the tunic. Goosebumps formed along his naked arms and the pale skin of his chest.

"Cold?" she grinned. He retorted by playfully tossing the Lunsera tunic at her face, earning a few chuckles from the Moonwey sister. He put on the black tunic and fitted leather jacket.

"Alright. Let's go," he said. She nodded in agreement and they departed the western wing of the palace.

They made their way to the stables, where Aurora swindled two horses from the stable keep. She eyed the boy from Virginia as he carefully mounted the palace horse as she had taught him how to. He thanked the stable keep and they departed the palace grounds, entering the city through a main street full of shops, merchants, and customers.

Aurora rode ahead and he followed through the twisting labyrinth of narrow streets and alleys. Though he felt lost, he trusted that she knew where they were going. The city noises raged discordantly. Hammers beat against heated metal and merchants bartered with one another in loud verbal exchanges.

A series of bells rang in the distance, atop one of the many great towers. As they progressed down an alleyway, the bustling sound of people seemed to echo louder and louder. Finally, as they followed the flow of traffic out of the narrow alley, a restless crowd gathered around a compound of buildings adjacent to the enormous stone wall that encircled the city. A single tower stood high above the two others like an air traffic control tower. Parting the crowd was a dirt road that extended in both directions, following after the stone wall of the city. *The track.*

Without delay, Aurora darted toward the stables, where a few beautiful horses stood. He followed after and they rode across the track and through the crowd, which parted for them unwillingly. They tied off their own horses and Aurora dashed over to the nearest steed and began to speak with enthusiasm with the woman that brushed it. He stood nearby outside the stables, often glancing over to the Moonwey sister he was supposed to protect and then to the track and crowd surrounding it, where suddenly an argument broke out between a group of men.

"Despicable lot," spat a man that stood nearby, leaning against the stables in the shade. Peter glanced over to the man, clad in slick black attire. Like Helen, the man appeared only a few years older than Peter. His fit jacket, impeccable hat, and black mustache made Peter think of a musketeer from some film he had seen as a child. He walked with grace toward Peter and tapped on the pommel of a rapier that hung from his hip. "Gambling is a despicable act. No man that considers himself a worthy man in life would partake."

"I. . .agree." Peter said.

Stroking his mustache, the man stood next to him, keeping his head tilted at an angle so that his eyes remained veiled by the brim of his hat.

"Hopefully there won't be a fight or anything," Peter added.

The man simply indicated with his leather glove toward the crowd, where the argument turned physical and three men began to brawl.

"Still, entertaining, hmm?" he mused like a purring cat.

"Not really. I don't like fighting," Peter stated honestly.

"Oh? No talent for it? Or perhaps you do have talent and have grown weary of conflict. Not uncommon in those with great potential for destruction."

A few moments of silence followed as Peter thought back to the assassin he had killed in Lunsera.

The man in black crossed his arms. "It would seem as if I spoke some truth. My apologies."

"Er. . .it's okay."

The man nodded and then turned back to him. "May I ask where you hail from? I have traveled extensively in my twenty-three years but I do not recognize your accent. Are you one of the refugees from Somerta?"

"Yeah, you could say that."

"As I suspected." He grinned and stroked his mustache. "Did you happen to see what it was?"

"See what?" Peter asked. The brim of the man's hat raised, showing a pair of fierce dark eyes.

His voice deepened with both seriousness and enthusiasm. "What it was that destroyed Somerta? Something powerful, they say. Beyond the capabilities of the plague. What was it?" he demanded. "You must know."

"I'm sorry. I don't."

"Useless," he scoffed. "The mystery remains. Perhaps, with the help of the second Lionheart in Arden, this unknown force will be unveiled and I will obtain some measure of satisfaction. I have heard rumors that the new one fled from a fight during the outbreak on Emerald Isle. Can you believe it?"

The man's words bore down on Peter and again he cursed himself for running. "Yeah. Who would have thought?"

"Lies!" the man spat. "The Lionheart would never flee from a fight. His predecessor was the greatest warrior in history. Surely the current holder of the title knows something of honor. Regardless, I intend to meet the new one and I relish the opportunity to duel him. Shall make for a fine legend, Hmm?" He looked at Peter expectantly.

“Lord,” a voice called from behind, causing both men to turn. A hefty stable worker stood there, scratching his beard. “She's ready.”

“Lovely,” the man in black stated, following after the sweating stable worker without another word to Peter. As he watched the man in black walk away, Aurora pranced over with palpable excitement.

“I have wonderful news!” she exclaimed. “The preliminary race is canceled, which is unfortunate; however, the game's commissioner happened to be in the stables. I informed him who I was and I made a simple request.”

“Oh, no...”

“Oh yes!” She grinned mischievously. “You and I are going to race.”

* * * * * * *

Hundreds of eyes watched the two as they sat atop their palace horses in the middle of the track.

Peter sighed. “Is this necessary?” he asked her. She circled her horse around his, strutting confidently.

“At least I am not having you run on your own two legs. Think of the attention we would garner then.”

He groaned. “I still can't believe we're doing this. Everyone's watching us.”

“Then let them watch.” She halted. Her finger tapped her lower lip as she thought. “I know what will entice you.”

“What?”

“If you win. . .I'll let you kiss me.” She winked and his heart fluttered.

“What?”

The two crowds on both sides of the track suddenly cheered and whistled.

"You heard me, Peter Loneheart. I won't tell Helen if you don't. Are you...are you blushing?"

He turned away from her and cleared his throat. As a rider on the track came toward them with the white banner hovering above him to signal a clear track, Peter's stomach fluttered with anxiety.

They guided their horses to the starting line drawn on the ground. The official took his place on Aurora's side of the track, where the compound was. He raised his white flag and Peter looked over to her, resting his gaze on her lips. *I'm winning this!*

A gunshot rang out from above and Peter tapped his heels into the horse's flanks. Both animals surged forward, tossing dust behind them as they darted along the track. They remained neck and neck, with Aurora staying within his field of vision on his right side.

The straightaway of the track followed the enormous stone wall of the city on its right side. As the two raced along, spectators on both sides cheered. The buildings on his left side seemed to vanish one after another as he stood within the stirrups as she had told him.

He glanced over at her. She hovered above the saddle, gazing at the path ahead with determination in her eyes and a wry smile. As they rounded the corner of the city and followed the western wall toward the sea, she finally glanced over at him. She winked and uttered "Ru'vai!" The steed beneath her suddenly thundered against the ground as it began to race ahead of Peter.

"No!" he gritted his teeth as she surged ahead. For the remainder of the race, she maintained her lead on him as they entered the final stretch. The track ended as they ascended a ramp onto the walls of the city itself. As Aurora crossed the finish line, she extended her fist into the air, claiming victory. Peter followed after, slowing his horse as she turned around to meet him. They both panted and smiled, maintaining a silent stare.

"Pity," she finally said before dismounting. He did the same and they both relinquished their steeds to one of the game wardens. Atop the large bastion, they walked over to the edge, peering down at the waves of the sea. "You raced as if you wanted to win," she noted.

"The thought occurred to me."

"More than once?"

"Maybe." He turned and she followed. From the bastion above the sea, they gained the top of the stone wall of the city. To their left, a vast forest stretched from the coast to the foot of the mountains. Far across the tops of the trees, a lone mountain stood with the sun beginning to set behind it. They both stopped to gaze upon the western horizon.

"Magnificent," she said, resting on the edge of the wall. "I hope the west will one day regain its former glory and be rid of the plague. I've been told the sunsets there are a true spectacle."

"You haven't been there? I'm surprised."

"Merely New London. Hardly the west. And I was a little girl when I stayed there. But could you imagine it. . .riding a horse across the vast plains all the way to the western sea to watch the sunset? I would feel as if I were on the edge of the world."

He imagined her proposal. "You know what. . .I do like the sound of that actually."

She turned toward him for a brief moment before something below the wall caught her attention and she gasped, standing straight. "What is it?" Peter asked, peering down at the tree line below.

"I saw one of them, I think!" She pointed toward one of the many trees.

"Saw what?"

"Infected!"

"The plague?" He scanned all along the tree line, seeing nothing but the leafy branches swaying in the coastal wind, until something caught his eye. From the wall on which they stood, someone in black attire strolled forward toward the tree line. "Hey!" Peter instinctively yelled to warn them. The man turned toward them, looking up at them and removing the brimmed hat he wore, revealing his raven-black hair. *It's the man I saw earlier at the stables. The one that looks like a musketeer.*

The man tapped above his eyebrow with his index and middle fingers before gesturing toward the two of them in an unusual salute. He placed his hat upon his head and turned, walking into the forest alone.

What is he doing? Where is he going? Who is he?

Chapter 9

The Prancing Lion

He awoke slowly and well-rested. Twisting beneath the thick blanket, Peter snuggled with his pillows and yawned as he looked out the window of his chamber. Rain fell in heaps, splashing against the window and balcony. Further beyond the gardens and walls of the palace, he watched as gray clouds hovered low above the tallest towers of the city. It was hard to believe he was there, in Arden City, a different world from his own. His mother came to mind and in the solitary silence of his room, he allowed himself to sulk.

But his sadness passed as an eerie feeling crept over him again, stealing his breath. What was this dark feeling? Regardless, he rose and leapt out of bed, taking time to bathe before putting on his Lunsera tunic and trousers.

His stomach growled as he departed his room and made his way down the hall into the common area where three women awaited. Sitting at the table in the center of the large room, Helen and Lady Lorena looked up to him as he entered. Aurora stood with her head against the window, staring at the storm outside with a bored expression.

“Good morning, ladies,”

Lorena inclined her head. “Good morning, Mr. Loneheart. Despite the deluge at hand and dull atmosphere, you seem so radiant.”

“I slept really well, I guess.”

“Of course,” the Lady of Emerald Island smiled.

Helen looked at him thoughtfully. “Was the city to your liking yesterday, Mr. Loneheart?”

“It was fun, yeah.”

“And how fared your race?”

He stiffened. “Er...the race was good.”

“Was it? Are you disappointed that you did not win?”

“I let her win,” he lied.

“Chivalrous of you. So the notion of winning did not cross your mind?”

“He raced as if he desired to.” Aurora grinned. He couldn't deny it; he had wanted to win.

“Did he?” The elder sister's gaze lingered on him before shifting to the lady next to her. “Lord Ornwell inquired about the events of the port?”

“Indeed. A surprisingly vigorous fellow despite his age. His inquisition was so sudden and incessant. He requested a detailed report on the incident.”

“No doubt he will desire to have the information given to the appointed commanders of the coalition army. The more they know, the better.”

From the window, Aurora groaned loudly, catching Helen's attention. “Bored? Have you no excitement for the event this evening?”

The younger sister tapped her lower lip with her finger. “To some degree, I suppose.” She looked to the boy from Virginia as he sat on a nearby sofa. “Will Peter be your escort to the celebration?”

“Perhaps. The council will expect an ostentatious display of Mr. Loneheart. There was some disappointment yesterday because he did not remain in the palace to properly introduce himself to each member of the council; however, they did not press the matter knowing how special he was. I place the blame upon myself.”

“Hear that, Peter? You're adored more than Helen.”

Lorena chimed in, “Furthermore, there is much talk from the other leaders. They too await with great anticipation the official reveal of the Lionheart. I do urge caution as it is rumored and I suspect that a number of prominent individuals seek to bring Mr. Loneheart into the political fold.”

Helen glanced over to Peter and then back to the Lady of Emerald Island. “Whom?”

“Lord Ian Turner.”

“The Lord of Barrington,” Helen noted. Peter remembered the name Barrington and its significance during the war of reclamation.

Peter cleared his throat, “I thought he was the *Duke* of Barrington?”

“His late father was the Duke,” Lorena corrected. “An exclusive title now lost due to their foolish antics.”

“Peter,” Aurora said. “Tell us of Lord Barrington's lineage.” The three women watched him expectantly.

She's quizzing me. “So. . .the brat prince is an ancestor.”

“Correct,” Helen said.

“And his grandfather was Edmund, one of the twelve.”

“Well done, Mr. Loneheart.” Lorena gently applauded. “What more do you know of their line?”

“That's about it.”

"Well, it is important for you to know more before this evening's events. The Turners of Barrington are one of two surviving families that can trace their origin to the twelve. Lord Ian Turner may attempt to use that to bring you to his cause, and I do suspect he has one. They are schemers, Mr. Loneheart. Since the start of the new age, they have schemed to take this city as their own. They believe it to be their divine right, granted to them by the first Edmund."

He considered her warning. "I'll be on my guard tonight."

"Wonderful. I am certain Helen will keep you close during the night."

"Got it. So. . .you said the Turner family is one of two remaining families. What is the other?"

"The first family of Sohn, of course. They trace their lineage to the first Sebastian, the founder of the province of Sohn. The current ruler of the province is Lady Isabella. She will be succeeded by her son Jadiel upon his coronation as the first son of Sohn. Like Lord Turner of Barrington and yourself, they too possess blood of the Otherworld."

"So are they strong, like I am?"

Lady Garshin chuckled. "Of course not. The blood's potency is known to dilute with each passing generation. The brat prince did possess some great strength, but not to the extent of his grandfather. The current generations are quite normal, I assure you. But remember you are a true spectacle like your predecessor before you. Many will try to befriend you this evening; others will attempt to sway you to perhaps marry into their family. Regardless, be polite and stay close to the Moonwey's."

"Yes, ma'am."

* * * * * * *

His stomach fluttered throughout the day. He ate little as a result and spent most of the day learning about geography and history. Lady Lorena and Aurora alternated in divulging locations of importance on the map of Arden's mainland. To the far east, nestled along the coastline, Barrington was the major eastern city, rivaled in size only by

Arden City itself and another city called Ilvion in the far northwest. A single road stood out to Peter. The Prince's Road, as they called it, traveled from Barrington through Arden City and the Ornian ruins, forking after passing the vast Ornian plains in the heart of the western region. The western region was enormous, twice as large as the remainder of the mainland. The two were divided by the Ornian river, which ran vertically across the map.

After his lessons, it was time to prepare for the festivities. Lady Lorena departed to her own quarters. Assisted by handmaidens, Helen and Aurora spent seemingly hours preparing in their own bedchambers while Peter quickly put on his new clothes for the occasion. Bearing the same royal blue colors of Lunsera, he admired his new jacket, once again finding himself enjoying the sight of the large silver crescent moon embroidered on the back. He put on his black trousers and struggled with new boots that reached his knees. After adjusting the large collars of his jacket, he primped in his mirror for a few moments before halting.

Mom. Gran. I wonder how they would react if they saw me dressed like this.

He awaited the Moonwey sisters in the common area, pacing as he reflected upon the day's lessons. He walked over to the window and gazed into the night. The storms had cleared, leaving behind a starry sky and a bustling city below. Rustling fabric caught his attention and he turned to see Helen enter the common area.

He had become so accustomed to seeing her wear dresses, but the elegant design of the one that now hugged her surprisingly fit figure robbed him of any words that could justly describe her beauty. Her fingers twirled one of the two strands of hair that hung over her face, the rest tied back.

She looked at him and smiled. "Proper. You look dashing."

"You don't look so bad yourself." The words rolled off his tongue without thought. She walked over to him and tugged on his collar. He gazed at her: her long eyelashes, high cheekbones, and full lips.

"There." She finished and looked into his eyes. As she continued to linger, her eyes darted to his lips.

The silence was interrupted by one of the handmaidens. "Apologies, Lady Helen. Lady Aurora requests that you depart without her and relays that she will join you shortly." Helen crossed her arms and sighed, a faint growl rumbling in her throat. He found it oddly attractive.

"Very well. Are you prepared, Mr. Loneheart?"

He raised his arm, allowing her to take it within her own. "Yes, ma'am." he said to her delight, and they departed.

They walked slowly through the decadent halls of the palace. He enjoyed walking with her and occasionally looked at her to marvel at her beauty. An instant passed when she noticed his glance.

"Do I appear so repulsive that you must continually leer?"

"Er...no. I just. . .you look phenomenal."

She grinned faintly. "So you ogle, then?"

"I guess..." He paused. "What does that mean?" The woman chuckled and pulled him along.

As they approached the stairs that would lead to the second floor, he heard voices echoing from below. When they reached the top and began their descent, he looked around the open floor below, where several other people stood dressed for the occasion as well. Near the large pair of doors, a few staff members in service to the palace huddled around the man Peter recognized as Lord Ornwell, the city council member who had greeted him yesterday. The smaller man turned and jumped as Peter and Helen stepped off the last stair.

"Lady Helen." He smiled, moving with grace toward them.

"Lord Ornwell," she replied, nodding her head.

"And of course. . .Lord Lionheart. My apologies for the lack of courtesy on my own part yesterday. I was overcome by the sheer joy your presence inspired." He took a step back and looked the two up and down. “The most beautiful pair that my eyes have spotted this evening, and I daresay the most anticipated.”

He pointed to the large set of double doors. “On every occasion those doors have opened, every eye has searched for that silver crescent moon. Needless to say, the populace grows frustrated as they await the Lionheart.”

Helen gripped Peter's bicep. “Then Mr. Loneheart and I shall endeavor to renew the life of the celebration.”

“Very well. I shall enter first as your herald.” He started for the door. Helen’s body seemed to shake and her chest arose as she took a deep breath.

“Are you nervous?” Peter asked.

“I suppose.”

He noticed his own sweating palms. “Me too.”

Lord Ornwell pushed open the large doors, revealing the enormous ballroom. Directly ahead on the far side, the symphony that played ceased their movement and every head in the room turned to face the new additions to the celebration. Peter looked around as they entered. Curtains of various colors dangled along the many lengthy windows. Columns of marble circled the grand room. Between two, a table was filled with appealing cuisines. In the center of the room, the dancers stopped to stare at the two as they entered.

Lord Ornwell knocked his cane against the marble floor and cleared his throat before announcing, “The Lord Lionheart and the Lady Helen Moonwey, of the Lunsera province.” Peter liked the sound of it and the crowd, which must have numbered to about a hundred, applauded. Helen initiated a bow, pulling on his arm, and he followed. After a moment of being the victims of incessant stares, she tugged on his arm and guided him to the right corner of the room. Standing in a small group, a familiar woman spoke with two men in unusual jackets. All three held glasses of wine as they turned toward Peter and Helen.

“Helen.” said the elder woman. She was the female council member from the day before, he knew.

"Lady Vera. May I introduce—"

"Peter Loneheart," chimed in the slender gentleman standing next to Lady Vera. His complexion was dark, reminding him of his friend Tyler from Norfolk. The man took a sip of wine and spoke with a smooth and melodic voice, "The Lionheart of our time."

"How did you know my name?" Peter asked.

"Ah. . .the wind, my friend. It hears much. It mutters its incantations to me and I listen intently. Apologies. Where are my manners. . .Elgen Stormtrope." He bowed, extending his long arms. "A Castillian of Ilvion, or should I say the last Castillian of the great city of old."

"A tragedy."

"Indeed, Lady Helen. Our wondrous city was the eldest in all the world. Full of splendor and rich in culture before that vile infection. Come. Let us sit." He indicated the nearby round table and they all took their seats, with Helen between Peter and Lady Vera while the two men sat opposite.

Elgen Stormtrope sat straight, dwarfing his paler companion next to him. "Did you ever travel to Ilvion, Lady Helen?" he asked.

"Unfortunately, I was never granted the opportunity to venture so far into the west, Highest Elgen."

"Indeed. Unfortunate." His slender face turned to Peter. "And you, Lord Lionheart? I wonder if you will remain long enough to visit our fabled city when it is redeemed after the coming conquest." All eyes turned to the boy from Virginia.

"Yeah. I look forward it." He smiled and glanced at Helen. "Arden is a. . .wondrous place."

"Truly. I am certain that the great provinces of both Lunsera and the Emerald Isle have made notable impressions? But are you familiar with the western region?"

"Er...yeah. Aurora told me about it. Apparently, it's the wild west." He laughed nervously. The two men chuckled.

“The wild west, you say? Clever.” Elgen raised his glass to Helen. “He's clever.”

“Notably,” she retorted. “Oh, Mr. Loneheart, my apologies,” she said, turning to Peter. “May I introduce Lady Vera, a senior member of the city council. She was also a tutor of my father.”

“Hardly,” the woman chuckled. “Your father was in need of little instruction. A truly brilliant and blessed man. His political instincts and ability to forge friendships with noteworthy individuals served him well during the war.” She looked to Peter and then back to the Lady of Lunsera. “A trait he seemingly passed on to you.”

Helen’s cheeks turned a shade of pink. “Noteworthy praise; however, I could never hope to rival his accomplishments.”

“Oh? Your father befriended the Lionheart, bringing him into the fold of the war at the time, and now you have done the same. Your modesty is admirable but hardly necessary, dear.”

“Surely,” Elgen added. “As the topic is broached, what are your thoughts on the current crisis, Lord Lionheart?”

“On the plague?”

“Indeed.” Again, all looked to Peter.

“You're from the west, right?” he asked, trying to shift the pressure from himself.

The man nodded. “Of course.”

“So you've seen the plague firsthand? What do you think?”

Elgen's slender fingers stroked his bald chin. “The world has experienced many illnesses, but the one at hand is vastly different than any other in history.”

“Save for the black morning.” said a man’s voice over Peter’s head. He looked up to see a dark set of eyes under the brim of a hat and a grin beneath a black mustache. The man that had reminded him of a musketeer leaned against Peter’s chair, staring down at him.

"You," Peter said.

"And you," he retorted. Every person that sat at the table seemed to stiffen.

"Lord Alvar." Helen's brow furrowed. "The two of you have already been acquainted?"

"Hardly," he answered, maintaining his bearing and continuing to glare down at Peter. "If I had known that I was speaking with the Lionheart, then perhaps. . ." He fell silent and watched Peter. Growing frustrated with the silence as Alvar continued to stare down at him, Peter stood and extended his hand toward the man.

"Peter Loneheart."

Alvar grinned and glanced down at his open hand before turning and walking around the table to the open chair between Lady Vera and Elgen Stormtrope. The man in black flopped into the chair, reclining to prop his boots onto the table. Peter eased back into his chair.

"Now. . .what was the discussion at hand?" Alvar asked. "Ah! You lot deeming the current infection the pinnacle of destruction. It would do you well to recollect the legends of old."

"Children's stories," Helen said coldly.

"Perhaps, Helen of the Moon Rock. Or perhaps you deem the great legends as stories for children because your own family origin is merely a love story and nothing more, hmm?" Peter thought he heard her teeth grind.

"And your family origin, Alvar Blackheart?" Helen asked.

A flicker of irritation flashed in his eyes. "Irrelevant. My destiny is not decided by where I started." Lady Vera leaned forward to speak but was silenced as Alvar simply lifted his finger and looked to Peter. "So! I must admit to you, Little Lion, I'm impatient to see what you are capable of. Will you be entering the tournament?" His eyes grew bright.

"Mr. Loneheart will not—"

“I inquire from the man himself, not you, Lady Helen.”

“No,” Peter said.

“Quite right. You cannot sully your reputation by brawling with the pathetic drudges who think themselves warriors. No! You deserve a proper contest, therefore I offer you the opportunity to duel.”

“With you?”

“Quite right. A friendly exhibition. What say you, hmm?” he purred, staring at Peter as if he were food. Peter’s pulse quickened and his hands grew thick with sweat.

“He will not,” Helen stated flatly. “Dueling is beneath the Lionheart. His predecessor did not, therefore he will not!”

“As you say. What of the guard in your personal service? Barda the Bold they call her. The failure that fancies herself a fighter?”

“Her skill is proficient and her loyalty is without question. As for a duel with you, I would prefer that she live to remain in my service.”

“Very well,” he replied with a satisfied expression. A few moments of silence passed between them before Alvar stood abruptly, causing Helen to jump. “I shall take my leave,” he said, clasping Elgen’s shoulder. “My fellow countrymen shall endeavor to. . .discuss the niceties of art and music and the like with you all, I am certain. Good evening.”

He walked away with purpose. Peter watched as Alvar made his way past a few nearby groups of people to Lord Ornwell and struck up a conversation.

For the next hour, Peter sat silently, listening as those at the table spoke at length about topics he did not know and didn't care to. He would occasionally glance over at the door to the room when the herald knocked his cane against the floor and announced who was entering the festivities. Elgen Stormtrope happened to be telling the others about a recent failed assassination attempt on the Lord of Barrington when Peter looked to the doors as they opened and Aurora entered the room.

The herald knocked the cane against the marble and announced, "Lady Aurora Moonwey of the Lunsera Province." Peter shook his head in disbelief. Her hair, usually flowing freely down her back, had been styled in a methodical and beautiful fashion like her sister's. Instead of wearing trousers and a leather jacket, she wore a fitted blue dress bearing silver embroideries. *Could that really be her?*

She stood alone, the center of unwanted attention, twiddling her fingers. Overcome by a desire to rescue her, Peter rose and walked with purpose of his own toward her. Her anxious expression abated as she set eyes on him.

"Oh my God," Peter murmured as he stopped short to look her over. "You're..."

Her eyebrows raised with concern. "Don't be cruel," she said.

"No." He could feel his face grow warm. "You just look amazing. Different. But amazing."

"Thank you. And look at you. Quite dashing." She took his arm into her own and leaned in to whisper. "I'm certain that you wish you had won that race now."

"Oh?" He playfully nudged her. "Like I said, I let you win."

"Of course you did. So what is the situation at hand?"

They scanned the room together. He pointed to the man in the hat, now speaking with a husky man in a rich coat of red and gold, bearing a black cape over his left arm.

"Do you remember him?" he asked her.

She inhaled sharply. "The Lord of Barrington!"

"What?"

"The plump man in the crimson garments with that ghastly cape. That's Ian Turner, the Lord of Barrington."

"That's him?"

"Yes! Who were you. . .oh! He survived the forest?"

“His name is Alvar Blackheart.”

“That's Alvar Blackheart? The greatest duelist of our time?” she scoffed. “I hear he is fixated with your uncle's legend.”

“You should have heard the way he talked to Helen. He's a real son of a —”

“Peter!” She stared at him in awe. “What is this renewed energy? Lord Blackheart seems to have aroused a boldness from you.” She was right, he knew. The way that Alvar had spoken to Helen and the overconfidence he displayed irritated Peter.

“Sorry.”

“You should be,” she jested. They both turned to greet Helen and Vera, who were accompanied by a middle-aged woman and a young man who appeared to be the same age as he and Aurora. They both watched Peter with lively dark eyes befitting of their tanned skin.

“Sister,” Helen sighed. “I suppose we should be grateful that you decided to appear at all.” Aurora eyed her sister expectantly before the elder added, “However, you are a true vision. Beautiful. Father would be proud.”

“Most radiant,” Lady Vera added. Peter looked to the young man who watched him with obvious excitement. His athletic build was displayed by the copper and black jacket he wore, which bore an oddly feminine design. He feared the boy would explode soon if he did not speak.

Before Helen could introduce the woman and the young man with her, Peter stepped forward and outstretched his hand to him. “I'm Peter.”

With alarming speed, the young man grasped his hand. “Jadiel, the fir...ah!” he winced as Peter applied a little pressure.

The four women gasped and Peter retracted his hand. “I'm sorry! I didn't mean to—”

“No, no, no. It’s quite alright.” Jadiel flexed his hand to display it still functioned. “You possess a powerful grip, truly fitting for the Lionheart!”

Helen turned to the woman in the copper dress. “Lady Isabella, my apologies to you and your son. Mr. Loneheart’s abilities still yet remain a mystery to us all.” She turned to Peter with a hard gaze. “He does not yet understand the true scope of his strength.”

Lady Isabella placed a hand on her son's shoulders. “No harm, therefore, no concern,” her motherly voice seemed to sing. She extended her hand to Peter. “Lionheart.” They all watched Peter with palpable anticipation.

“Oh,” he realized after a moment. He gently took her fingers into his hand. Bowing, he gifted the skin of her knuckles with a kiss.

“There,” she said. “A proper gentleman. Pay attention, Jadiel.” She giggled.

“You're the first family of Sohn,” Peter realized.

“Indeed, my Lord.” Isabella nodded. “Lady Isabella. And my son, Jadiel, soon-to-be first son upon his eighteenth name-day.”

Peter thought back to the lessons of Lorena and Aurora. The first family of Sohn were descendants of Sebastian, one of the twelve, and a man from Peter’s own world.

Jadiel smiled brightly. “A title I intend to honor. I will claim victory over the combatants of the tournament!” His head slowly turned toward Peter. “Unless. . .you decide to enter.”

Peter smiled politely and shook his head.

“Then it would appear I have a fighting chance.”

“We were informed of your entry, Jadiel,” Helen said. “You must have practiced a great deal to desire such a hazardous undertaking. Though I am certain you will dazzle us all with your skill, I shall pray to Fyraen for your safety.”

“A notion well received, Lady Helen.” Isabella smiled. “Though with legends supplied by the actions of heroes such as the Lionheart and Sir William of Bastille, it is inevitable that boys will long to be as the men they worship.”

Jadiel cocked an eyebrow as he asked, “Would you prefer we not aspire to such ambitions?”

“I would prefer—” his mother’s words fell short and she stiffened along with the others as the Lord of Barrington joined them. A ghostly silence loomed over the group. Tension lingered so palpably it drew attention from others in the room.

The husky man in the rich red coat bowed. “Greetings,” he said with a deep voice, reminding Peter of an opera vocalist. “I beg your pardon for my intrusion.”

Helen broke the silence, politely saying, “You are most welcome to join us, Lord Ian.”

Lady Vera added, “We were informed of your trouble along the road from the eastern spire. We are all thankful you escaped unharmed.”

“Truly.” Helen smiled.

“Your warm words are welcomed, fair ladies. Assassins. Scores, it seemed.”

“So many?” Helen inquired.

“Aye. I understand you have also survived an encounter with the lot, Lady Helen.”

“Indeed. A failed attempt on my own life.”

“Thanks to the Lionheart,” Aurora interjected, “one was also captured. Alive.”

The Lord of Barrington stroked his thin brown goatee and his blue eyes found Peter. “Aye. Lady Helen is blessed to have you at her side during this crisis, my Lord. Every citizen of this world is blessed to have you. I have brought what forces I could muster to assist in the endeavor to combat the growing horde. Unfortunately, I was forced to leave a portion of my own forces garrisoned within my city for fear of further attacks against my people."

"Most noble of you," Lady Vera stated. "The city council is grateful for the large support you have already given."

"I am hardly worth any praise. I do what I must for the good of Arden and its posterity." Peter looked to Helen and Vera who bore seemingly sympathetic expressions. Isabella and Jadiel both stared at Lord Ian neutrally, masking the obvious cynicism they both felt.

There was a moment of silence before the Lord of Barrington spoke again. "I shall take my leave. Again, apologies for my intrusion. I wish you all a lovely evening. May Arden endure." He bowed and departed.

Before anyone else could speak, Jadiel's face contorted with discomfort as he hissed. "Ese gordo malparido de Barrington!"

"Jadiel!" his mother exclaimed. "No maldigas en la presencia de las damas!"

"No pueden entender lo que digo."

Helen and Vera watched the two intently, obviously listening closely as Isabella spoke. "No importa. Tu eres el hijo de Sohn y lo vas a demonstrar de igual forma."

A few moments passed as Jadiel simmered. Finally, he said, "Si, madre. Perdoname." His expression softened and he bowed to the group. "My Lord and ladies, my deepest apologies for my outburst."

Helen smiled. "You need not be ashamed, Jadiel. Those of us here understand your plight. And might I add. . .the secret tongue of Sohn is truly mesmerizing to hear."

"Spanish," Peter muttered louder than he had intended.

"Your pardon, Mr. Loneheart?"

"Er. . .Mi nombre es...Peter Loneheart. Mi comida favorita es pizza." To his amazement, Helen's jaw dropped and a hint of admiration flashed within her eyes.

“Tu entiendes el sagrado y secreto idioma de Sebastian?” Jadiel asked.

“I don't know that much.”

“Nonsense! You understood and you spoke. Mother, he understands our language!”

Isabella placed a hand on her son's shoulders to calm his robust enthusiasm. “You are most impressive, my Lord,” she told Peter. “Never once in our long history has any come to understand our secret tongue, though there have been many attempts to. It remains a private jewel of sorts for our family. A true heirloom you could say. May I ask: how is it you come to know of it? Is it common in the Otherworld?”

“Well. . .it's one of the most common languages in the U.S. right after English. My mom made me take a foreign language elective in high school, so I chose Spanish. I took it for three years, And I dated a girl for a few months who was fluent, so she taught me some too.”

Jadiel’s grin remained while his mother stared at Peter with thoughtful eyes. Aurora crossed her arms and watched him expectantly as he mentioned the girlfriend.

The Lady of Sohn smiled faintly. “You have made quite the impression, my Lord, and you have provided my son and I with much to consider.” She took her son’s hand and they both bowed. “Good evening to you all. May Arden endure.”

“Good evening,” they all said as the pair departed. The three women that remained stared at him and grinned. Lady Vera was the first to break the silence.

“You are as a stone thrown into the water, My Lord, forming ripples as you go.”

“Eloquently spoken,” Helen said as she crossed her arms. Her eyes blazed with admiration. “You have truly impressed me, Mr. Loneheart.”

Her comment filled him with just pride and he stood a little straighter for the remainder of the night.

* * * * * * *

Another hour passed, which Peter spent tasting the countless decadent finger foods that Aurora pressed upon him one after another. The flavors varied. He would hardly be finished savoring the sweetness of a pastry before she yet had another in hand.

"Are you trying to fatten me up?" he asked her after swallowing a forced bite.

"You scarcely have any fat at all!"

"I want to keep it that way."

When the symphony began to play a new series of movements, all in the ostentatious room circled around the center of the celebration as several people began to dance and were soon joined by others. Peter and Aurora watched the dazzling display from a stone column against which Alvar Blackheart leaned as he sipped from a glass of wine. His expression displayed no sign of joy, Peter assumed as a result of what he had observed earlier as an argument between the Blackheart Lord and Lord Ornwell, the head of the city council.

Aurora looked to the man in black. "Do you dance, Lord Blackheart?"

He upturned his glass goblet and gulped the remainder of wine. "I am not a prancing jester." Alvar placed the glass firmly onto a nearby table and departed the room.

She turned back to Peter. "A simple no would have sufficed. And you?" He had suspected she would ask at some point.

"No. He had a good point. I'm not. . .prancing tonight."

"Perhaps not as a jester, but as a Lion, you shall prance. And you did quite well on the ship." She tugged on his arm.

"Aurora, please. I really don't want to."

She crossed her arms. "Oh? Perhaps I shall seek a partner that will prance with me."

A standoff ensued, neither conceding. After a few moments she began to walk away.

He grabbed her arm. “Okay!”

“Wonderful!” She smiled and took his hand, leading him through the crowd of spectators. As they came to an opening, every person looked to him with obvious anticipation. He groaned as his nerves attacked his stomach. Those that danced did so in pairs, as man and woman, spiraling around one another in circular patterns like a flower aided by the jovial tempo of the music.

“Oh God,” Peter muttered under his breath before he was pulled into the fray. She twisted to face him and he took her hands as they inserted themselves into the circulation. She laughed and moved with grace. He stayed on his toes like the others that danced. The onlookers began to clap in unison as the pace quickened.

He glanced around the room when he could. Jadiel stood with his mother, both seeming eager to join the dance, while Helen smiled and clapped along to the rhythm at hand. But his eyes always reverted back to Aurora’s joyful expression.

The symphony played faster and the tempo of the dance followed. He could feel the conclusion at hand. Just as the final notes were played, he called upon the memory of those old lessons his grandmother gave him. With Aurora's hands in his, he spun her around and pulled her into the air, catching her as the movement ceased. A thunder of applause followed and she stared starry-eyed at him.

“You don't prance?” she said. Her face was so close to his that their warm breath mingled.

“Sometimes.” He grinned. “Again?”

“Again?” She paused and then nodded enthusiastically. He eased her onto her feet and they prepared for another go.

“Pardon, sister,” Helen drew nearby. “May I appropriate Mr. Loneheart for a moment?”

"To dance?" he asked.

She chuckled. "I possess no gift for the like. I merely desire to speak with you in private." She indicated the door that led to the balcony.

"I'll be back," he told his dancing partner before he and Helen exited onto the balcony. She closed the doors behind them, leaving them under the pale hue of a moon that looked larger than usual and bore strange smudges of green and blue. Peter stared at the milky sphere in the night sky, trying to discern why it looked so different. "What's with the moon tonight?"

Helen chuckled. "Your eyes do not deceive you, Mr. Loneheart. That is not the moon before you; it is the planet Carraas. It appears vividly this evening. It marks the end of summer and the start of the new season—the season of Carraas."

"Incredible." His breath escaped him as he stared at the planet. He turned to her. "So, what is it?"

The fingers of her hands intertwined with one another as she thought. They stood at the railing overlooking the front gardens of the palace. "First, I wanted to thank you for your presentation this evening. Many are smitten with you, while others are not quite certain what to make of you, Lady Isabella being among them. The political setting of Arden is. . .fickle, especially when plagues and Lionheart's are inserted into that setting. This evening you have demonstrated that you are a priceless asset to Lunsera." She stared off into the sea of dark grass below. "On behalf of the province, I thank you, Mr. Loneheart. You have reminded all the great leaders of Arden that Lunsera is a province to be revered and respected. My father would be so thankful for what you have done."

"Helen. I'm flattered. Thank you."

"No. I thank you. My father worked tirelessly his entire life to maintain peace and ensure the prosperity of both Lunsera and Arden."

"Helen. . .can I ask..."

"Ask?"

“I know that your dad and my uncle became best friends. It’s been on my mind. Can I ask what happened to your father?”

She paused. He suddenly felt ashamed for asking.

“Our father, Lord Edward Moonwey, was assassinated as he was returning from the western theater during the war of reclamation. He was overseeing the official end to the conflict in the west during the final meeting in the Ornian ruins, where the treaty was signed. On his return to Arden City, he was passing though Masterstown when he was killed by an assassin. One lone assassin bypassed twelve elite guards and murdered my father with a single stroke.” Anger radiated from her voice. “For years I was fixated with finding his killer. Obsessed, I should say. Nothing was ever discovered about the assassin. Disappeared. . .as if a ghost.”

“I'm so sorry, Helen.”

She forced a smile. “No. You deserved to know. But if you do feel so apologetic...would you care to divulge why it is you seem so frustrated with your own father?”

He paused and felt trapped, as if he were obligated at that point to tell her.

He sighed. “Like I told you before, I never knew him. But my mom did tell me about him and where I could find him.”

“And when you were in the Otherworld, you never felt the desire to seek him out?”

“When I found out who he was, I decided right then and there that I didn't want to know him. After all, he would rather sit in Seattle playing king than know me. . .so why would I want to know him?”

“Fair to say. So your father is royalty. Or does he simply imitate the role?

“I don't care. He can do whatever he wants and I’ll never be like him.”

She chuckled. “Apologies.”

Suddenly the eerie feeling returned. His stomach cramped and he doubled over with a groan. “What is it? What's wrong?” She tried to steady him.

“I don't. . .” *Why does this keep happening? It feels like everything is just. . .wrong.* After a moment, the feeling subsided and his stomach relaxed.

“Are you well?”

He took a deep breath. “I'll be fine.”

“Are you certain? I cannot have you falling ill so soon, and just before the tournament tomorrow. And more...” She paused, and despite the lack of light, he could tell that she was blushing. “I was curious. . .if you would care to instruct me in the secret tongue of Sohn?”

Whether it was the way she asked or the very fact that she asked at all, he smiled. “Yes, ma'am. I would love to.”

Chapter 10

The Tournament

The carriage bobbed from side to side as the palace horses pulled it along the misty road. The shops flanking the busy street remained dark, save for the reflections cast by the security procession surrounding the province leaders. The Arden City security force numbered nearly one hundred, each on horseback with a saber hanging from the hip and a musket slung over the shoulder. The guard adjacent to Peter's window glanced over to him and inclined his iron helm. The boy from Virginia nodded back to the man on horseback.

Aurora yawned, catching his attention. She wore her typical leather jacket and black trousers. "Who do you expect to win the competition?"

"I possess no expectations regarding the outcome of the tournament," Helen replied.

"So the prospect of Alvar Blackheart being humbled through defeat does not intrigue you?"

"I suppose it does. Regardless, I make no prediction regarding the matches, to avoid disappointment, of course. But I am certain that Alvar is as impetuous as he is arrogant. He will ensure his own demise, I promise you."

Aurora shrugged and twirled the brown locks of her hair in her hands.

"And you, Lord Lionheart?" she chuckled. "Whom do you desire to prevail?"

He considered. "Well, I only know about Alvar and Jadiel, so I think I'm going to go with Jadiel. He just seems more down to earth, I guess."

Helen looked to him alluringly. "A fair choice, Mr. Loneheart. He is notably more humble than Lord Alvar." She leaned closer to him. "I am curious—would you be willing to begin our lessons today?"

Aurora raised an eyebrow. "Lessons?"

"Oh. . .sure. Whenever you want to," he told Helen.

"Wonderful. And as a token of my appreciation, I will personally instruct you in return."

"Instruct me?"

"What lessons?" Aurora asked again.

"Mr. Loneheart, I shall bestow upon you the prestigious knowledge accumulated through generations of Moonwey's. I shall instruct you in Arden's complete history and I will act as your private tutor in the language of Du'Vhani." Aurora and Barda both raised their eyebrows.

Barda finally spoke. "Lady Helen, such an endeavor would require so much of your finite time."

"He is a representative of our province, Barda. It is of great importance that he bear an understanding of the world that is now his own."

Peter winced at that.

“To demonstrate. . .during the celebration the night past, Mr. Loneheart.” She looked to him. “Do you understand why there was such tension between the Lord of Barrington and the first family of Sohn?”

“Not really, but I did notice it.”

“As you should. There is a bloody history between the two families. What do you know of the war of reclamation?”

“The Lord. . .Duke of Barrington started a war for Arden City. I think there was also a plague that had to do with it.”

“To some degree. Grullens fever was one of the major factors that attributed to the initiation of the conflict. The fever began in a village within the province of Sohn before ravaging the entire continent. The Duke blamed the first family of Sohn for the destruction it wrought. Furthermore, Lady Isabella was once betrothed to the Duke; however, her father disregarded the arrangement when it was learned the first son of Sohn, Lord Sebastian the fifth, had become interested in Isabella.”

“So I take it they got married and the duke wasn't too happy about it.”

“Indeed. It was one of the first slights against the proud leader of the most powerful province. Again, that happened some years before the fever struck Arden.”

“Okay. So that's why Isabella and Jadiel don't like the Duke's son?” Helen leaned back, her finger tapping her lower lip.

“There is more, much more. Arden had been at peace for nearly a century without a single war until the Duke invaded Sohn, and thus the war of reclamation began. Jadiel's father, the first son of Sohn at the time, Lord Sebastian the fifth, assembled what men he could to defend his province. However, his army was too few in number, and when he met the invading forces from Barrington, the defending army was destroyed, Sebastian was slain, and his body stripped naked to be held high as a trophy while the Duke laid siege to the city of Sohn itself."

A surge of anger rushed through Peter as he imagined how Jadiel must have felt as a little boy seeing his father's corpse being held in the air like a trophy. "That's terrible."

"Yes," Helen murmured as she stared somberly out her window. Suddenly, she looked up and grinned. "Ah! We've arrived."

The carriage came to a stop and Peter stepped out first into the cool morning mist that lingered. He took Helen's hand as she stepped down onto the cobblestone, doing the same with Aurora. He looked the younger sister up and down before she noticed and crossed her arms.

"What are you gawking at?"

He shrugged. "Nothing. I just miss seeing you in a dress."

"Oh? Perhaps I shall don another soon."

"Really?"

"If a situation should occur that warrants such attire." Her lips formed a devious grin. "Such as dancing. The thought plagues me: will you ever prance again?"

"It could happen. How badly do you want me to?"

Her fingers twirled curls of her hair as she shifted her weight, striking a more feminine pose. "Depends on how badly you desire to see me in another dress." Grinning, she walked away, following Helen and Barda toward the enormous stone archway that had appeared. The pale entrance to the stadium remained shrouded by the mist, leaving its true height a mystery.

He followed the Moonwey's as they were escorted up the stairs and through the halls to the spectator's booth that had been appointed to them. Peter marveled at the sight the private booth granted. With two luxurious sofas present, the box was surrounded by windows that provided a clear view over the many rows of seats outside and below. Dozens of other spectator's boxes were evenly spaced around the entire arena, all offering the same brilliant birds-eye-view of the field.

Helen sat on the sofa to the left upon entering, and Aurora sat on the right. Barda crossed her arms and remained watchful behind the Lady of Lunsera. After a few moments of deliberation, Peter eased into the spot next to the younger sister. The four watched as the stands slowly filled with the citizens of Arden City. Golden rays of sunlight pierced the cloud of mist that hovered above the field, finally dispelling its shroud and allowing the blue sky overhead to display its glory.

The opening ceremony filled Peter with mixed feelings. The orchestra that played for the first half of the ceremony enamored him. The meticulously composed pieces of music resonated within him even after they were played. Alone in doing so, Peter gave the orchestra a standing ovation, earning a perplexed expression from Helen and a bout of laughing from Aurora. Following the orchestra, Lord Ornwell gave a haunting speech about the current crisis and how Arden would endure no matter what.

Finally, as the field was cleared, two dozen drummers surrounded the circle of flattened dirt at the center, beating on their percussive instruments. The heralds came forth and announced their respective fighters, earning a series of cheers from the thousands in attendance. One man in full plate armor waved his broadsword in circles around his body, thumping his pale chest plate with his free fist. The smaller man who faced him unsheathed his thin sword and pointed it to one of the spectator's boxes before redirecting the tip toward his opponent.

"A rapier," Barda said. "I assume he hails from the western region where such a style of fighting is more common. Either New London or Ilvion, perhaps. His speed may very well prevail against the one he faces."

A musket shot rang out and the two rushed toward one another, throwing up sand and dust. The man in armor brought his broadsword over his head to strike.

The smaller fighter faked his frontal advance and spun around with grace, swiping a single stoke that merely bounced off the old armor as the man in it brought his larger sword into the dirt. In the brief moments it took for the larger man to remove the sword lodged within the earth, the slimmer fighter lunged the tip of the rapier at the back of the armor to no avail.

Spinning to face the smaller fighter, the man in armor slashed his broadsword wildly, only to cut through the air, the thousands of spectators roaring with excitement with each arbitrary strike. The smaller fighter's grace was displayed as he danced backward and from side to side to avoid the strokes, countering with lunges whenever the opportunity arose.

The armored man's frustration became evident and grew with each missed stroke of his sword. Finally reaching for his smaller opponent and grasping his wrist, he tossed him off balance before bringing his broadsword once again over his head with all his strength and swinging it into the man's collarbone, lodging the blade halfway through his chest.

"Oh, God!" Peter gasped as blood spewed, covering the smaller man's leather armor with a crimson hue in the sunlight. Barda and the two Moonwey sisters all grimaced as they turned from the carnage. Peter's breath escaped him as he buried his head in his hands. The image of the assassin that had attacked him in Lunsera came to his mind. He recalled the assailant's ribs cracking as he kicked him away into the darkness of the small chamber.

His stomach churned. "Jadiel and Alvar are really going to fight. . .like that?"

Barda turned back to the field but her grimace remained. "It is evident that this match was to the death. Most bouts of the tournament are ended upon first blood or by yielding. These two agreed to the terms."

Reluctant to see any further suffering, Peter watched the next few matches throughout the day, all ending with first blood. After the second to final match of the day had been concluded, Peter exhaled and reclined back into the soft sofa. All the fighting throughout the day had left him tense but thankful that no one else had been killed.

As the sun's light began to dim, torches were set ablaze around the stadium. The floor beneath Peter's feet trembled as the crowd cheered louder than ever before. After the dirt, thickened by blood, was raked and flattened, the final match of the day began.

A herald stepped onto the pitch, announcing the first fighter. A bearded man waved to the encircling crowd from the pitch, twirling his two sabers with apparent ease. Another herald stepped forth bearing a flag. The cloth of solid gray flapped in the breeze that rolled over the field. The copper sun in the center of the flag seemed to shine from the combination of torchlight and topaz radiance from the sun above. The herald uttered something that Peter could not discern, but the crowd could, and they erupted into cheers. A few girls screamed loudly from the front rows of the stadium as Jadiel of Sohn stepped onto the pitch in light armor. He waved his halberd into the air, twirling it with grace.

Peter and Aurora both inched onto the edge of the sofa cushions as they watched the two men bow to one another. A musket shot rang out and the competitor lurched forward after Jadiel, slashing with his two sabers. Jadiel deflected them with the poled weapon. After blocking a few flurries of strikes, Jadiel pivoted his body and swung the pole end of his weapon at his opponent. The sudden counterattack caught the bearded man off guard. The saber in his right hand was struck and thrown across the field.

The bearded fighter reached forward, grasping the halberd in the space between Jadiel's hands. He yanked one good time to disarm the younger fighter, only to be knocked back as Jadiel pushed the polished wood into his chest, knocking the wind out of him. He lunged forward with his remaining saber. Jadiel twirled his halberd in front of his body, parrying the thrust to the side and countering with a swipe across the man's face, using the pole end of his weapon. The crowd groaned in unison as the bearded fighter thudded onto the ground. He slowly rose, dirt smeared across his face and beard, fresh blood trickling from his nose.

The thousands of spectators roared with chants and cheers. Peter clapped along with the Moonwey sisters. On the field, the bearded man stumbled onto his feet, aided by Jadiel, who embraced the man and patted his back. And thus the first day of the tournament was concluded.

A celebration followed. The event took place in a large chamber of the stadium that had been decorated with historical tapestries and banners of the provinces. Province leaders, city councilmembers, magistrates, and numerous other city officials mingled around tables bearing wine and food, speaking with the tournament fighters that had been invited to the prestigious event.

Peter stood with the Moonwey sisters as they spoke with the Lady of Emerald Island. Lorena revealed that Lord Alvar Blackheart had been seeded and thus only needed to win one match to enter the final round of the tournament. The chamber suddenly erupted with cheers and applause as Jadiel entered with his mother Isabella by his side. The young warrior no long wore his copper armor, but a tunic like Peter's, only copper with an orange sun rather than a crescent moon. The two respectfully greeted many in passing as they made their way over to the Lady of Lunsera and her party.

"That was awesome!" Peter told Jadiel before any could speak. His dark eyes gleamed in the torchlight and he grinned from ear to ear.

"I am most grateful for your praise! Did you enjoy the competition? Did you all enjoy it?"

Helen's voice sang, "You were marvelous, Jadiel. You displayed honor and courtesy worthy of recognition by Sir William himself."

The young warrior blushed. "The praise of your province is overwhelming, my lady. Your words and the Lionheart's will remain in my heart until I draw my final breathe."

Lady Isabella placed a gentle hand on the shoulder of her son's copper jacket. "Indeed. I can think of no greater gift in this world than the goodwill of Lunsera."

Helen inclined her head. "You are most kind, Lady Isabella."

There was a moment of silence as Jadiel's mother took a deep breath and smiled before proudly stating, "My son and I have spoken at length. My Lord Lionheart, we have agreed to invite you, personally, to visit our fine province whenever you see fit." Helen and Lorena both gasped. Jadiel proudly nodded his head as his hands rested on his hips. "Jadiel's name-day will soon be upon us and within the same fortnight, his coronation will take place. My Lord Lionheart, we would be grateful if you decided to attend the memorable event that will instate my boy as the first son of Sohn. Of course, Lady Helen and Lady Aurora, you will both be welcomed to accompany his Lordship. Lady Lorena, we also wish to personally invite you."

Helen and Lorena both bowed and graciously accepted the offer. All eyes rested on Peter with palpable anticipation.

Go to Sohn? I've already agreed to help protect Aurora and I still want to find a way back home, despite what Helen's told me. And Jack. . .what about Jack? Is it a good idea to agree to all this?

As time passed, he settled on an answer.

He smiled. "Sure. I would be honored."

Jadiel nodded in approval. The four women lightly applauded and smiled. Isabella wiped her tearing eyes with a handkerchief as Peter and Jadiel shook hands. Out of the corner of his eye, Peter noticed a series of intrigued gazes on them from various people throughout the room.

He glanced back to Helen, who looked at him in a way she hadn't before. She did not smile, but her eyes watched him with an alluring gaze that sent his heart racing. She appeared as both predator and prey. As she turned back to Isabella, he found himself wishing that she would look at him with that same desire every day of his life.

The three province leaders spoke eagerly with each other for the next hour. At one point, Alvar Blackheart greeted him in passing. "Enjoying the competition, Lionheart?" he asked.

Peter spun around to answer, but Blackheart had already walked away, leaving him feeling annoyed. "Jerk," he muttered.

* * * * * * *

The second day of the tournament was far more pleasing to him than the first. After the first match, Peter had a few moments alone with Helen during which he instructed her in basic Spanish. She learned quickly, he noted, and she possessed an incessant desire to keep learning. On one occasion, he began to blush at the way she rolled her tongue during certain pronunciations, as if she had spoken the language her entire life.

She learns so fast. Just. . .how can someone be so perfect.

"You're going to speak it better than me in no time," he told her. To his delight, she giggled coyly at the compliment before graciously accepting it.

"I am merely gifted with a wonderful tutor. And I have not forgotten, Mr. Loneheart—you will be instructed in our own mother tongue."

"Yes, ma'am," he replied. He relished any moment he could spend with her.

The day went by quickly; these matches would decide who would be in the semifinals. With each match, the stadium's excitement grew. Finally, when the pitch had been repaired from the penultimate fight, the time had come for the final match.

The crowd roared as never before. "ALVAR! BLACKHEART!"

Peter turned to Helen. "Is Alvar really this popular?"

Helen sighed. "So it would seem. I have been informed on several occasions that his skill is truly remarkable."

"How remarkable?"

"They say that the likes of his abilities have never before been witnessed, not since the age of warring tribes. He appeared from the west some years ago, seemingly out of nowhere, and quickly gained favor with the city council after completing a few quests that had been deemed impossible. They granted him the title of Lord, and he gained the love of the people."

Before he could ask another question, the heralds stepped onto the pitch.

Clad in his rich black jacket, Alvar Blackheart wore no armor. The crowd cheered his name as he was announced. His opponent clashed the tips of his two sabers together as his name was called. He faced the Blackheart Lord and inclined his bald head. His archaic leather armor heaved as he shrugged to loosen his muscles. Alvar barely nodded his head in return as he slowly unsheathed his thin blade of a dark-gray iron.

The musket shot rang out. The bald man rushed forward at first, but gasped in surprise and faltered as Alvar advanced toward him with alarming speed. Thrusting a saber forward, the bald fighter raised his second blade in anticipation.

Alvar's sword arm swiped upward. His dark blade sliced through the outstretched steel.

The crowd gasped as one as the edge of the silver blade fell into the dirt. The bald fighter jumped back as he brought his remaining saber down on his opponent. Alvar twisted his body toward the incoming blade, swiping upward, and once again sliced through the metal like a knife through warm butter. He pivoted again and halted when the tip of his rapier touched the sweating flesh of the bald fighter, who dropped what remained of his swords.

The stadium surged and rumbled with excitement.

"What sorcery," Helen muttered under her breath, her eyes squinting in deep thought.

Barda stared too as she said, "His movements. So fluid and precise." She gulped and a yawn escaped Aurora from her sofa. "His blade. So thin yet so powerful."

Peter looked at Helen. "Is it magic or something?"

"Perhaps, Mr. Loneheart. It may very well be."

The display of Alvar's skills continued to occupy Peter's thoughts all day. As the celebration following the second day proceeded, he stared into the fine stone of the floor, standing again with the three province leaders of Lunsera, Sohn, and Emerald Island.

In reverie, he jumped in surprise as Jadiel spoke with enthusiastically next to him. "It must be enchanted! Never before have I heard of any such blade bearing such an attribute. To cut through the steel of a saber..."

"Indeed," the Lady of Emerald Island said. "As if the sword were enchanted with the same magic as the Lionheart himself."

He felt every pair of eyes upon him.

Before he could speak, Helen chimed in. "Perhaps we may inquire from the wielder." She nodded to the entrance of the chamber as the prestigious partygoers began to applaud. Removing his impeccable hat, Alvar's head inclined as he bowed and presented himself to the finest citizens of Arden City. As he rose, his eyes found Peter from across the room and he grinned before he started toward him.

Don't come over here! Please don't. Peter cursed as he watched Alvar bypass several attempted pleasantries, snaking through the crowd toward them. Out of the corner of his eye, Aurora looked up at him with a concerned expression. She leaned close to whisper, but before she could utter a word, the Blackheart Lord arrived.

"Greetings, Lords and ladies!" he proclaimed with a victorious ring. The three province leaders nodded respectfully as they greeted him. Jadiel and Aurora did the same. Peter faked a smile to match the prideful grin the man wore.

"Lionheart," Alvar greeted.

"Alvar," he replied. Helen grunted next to him. "Lord Alvar," he amended.

"Did you enjoy the events today?"

"Seemed a little boring. Jadiel's match was hands down my favorite."

"Oh?" Alvar stroked his finely groomed mustache, turning to the warrior from Sohn. "I was informed you had proved victorious in your own match, Jadiel of Sohn. My congratulations."

"Did you not care to witness Jadiel's match, Lord Alvar?" Helen asked to Peter's delight.

"If I am inquiring about it now, then it is possible I did not witness it, Lady Helen." His words and tone made Peter clench his fists.

Don't talk to her like that, he wanted to say.

"Indeed, Lord Blackheart." She smiled brightly. "I am certain that you had matters of paramount importance to attend to."

The Blackheart Lord faked a smile of his own. His dark eyes searched her face.

Lady Lorena spoke. "Lord Alvar."

"Yes, Lady Garshin?"

Her eyes fell to the rapier that hung at his hip. "We have been positively enamored by the power of your sword. Would you be willing to divulge its precise nature to us?"

To Peter's amazement, Alvar grinned as widely as a young boy on Christmas day. He chuckled as he tapped on the smooth black pommel of the sheathed sword. Looking at Peter, he uttered proudly, "A remnant of the twelve. The sacred metal."

Lorena and Isabella gasped as one. Jadiel's eyes widened.

"Of course," Helen concluded. Peter looked at Aurora, questioning. The Moonwey sister simply nodded back toward him, further confusing him. As he returned his attention to the group, all eyes were on him.

"Do you have a name for your weapon, Lord Alvar?" Jadiel asked.

"Indeed. Quickfury, I have deemed it. A worthy name."

"Marvelous," Isabella said. "Jadiel and I are most interested in how you acquired it. A story I long to hear, if you would be willing, my Lord?"

"In time. But for now, I must mingle. My Lords and ladies." He bowed to the group and glanced at Peter one last time before turning on his heels and strutting through the crowd with feline grace.

The remainder of the celebration passed quickly, as did the carriage ride back to the palace. Peter's thoughts were full of Alvar Blackheart.

When they entered the common room of their quarters, Helen stopped him before he was able to return to his bedroom. In the silence of the dimly lit chamber, she said, "Mr. Loneheart, there is something dire that you and I must discuss."

What is it this time? More lessons? Or is she trying to get me to swear another oath?

He turned to her. "Yeah?"

She spoke softly but firmly. "What are your thoughts on Alvar Blackheart, if I may inquire?"

"I don't think about him at all," he lied.

Her head tilted as she grinned, knowing better. "I think not. Come now. Indulge me."

After a deep breath he spoke. "He seems arrogant, like you said before. And—"

"Dangerous?"

"Yeah."

"Indeed. From what we witnessed today, he is worthy of his reputation, which is why I desired to speak with you alone. I want you to avoid him. Do not ever even consider fighting him, for I fear that you will lose even with all your blessings."

His damaged pride spoke for him. "What? But I—"

"When Alvar spoke this evening, he revealed how deadly his weapon truly is."

"So it is magic?"

"Yes and no. The rapier he wields is one of the last remaining remnants of the twelve, Mr. Loneheart. Do you understand?"

"It's from my world?"

She nodded. "Indeed. And I fear that it is your greatest threat. I surmise that it could cut through you as a sword from this world could cut through myself. Alvar is fixated with the legends of this world; his skills are truly something to behold, and from what we have witnessed today his sword is possibly the deadliest weapon in Arden. My instincts tell me that he will attempt to provoke you, but I beseech you, do not fight him! You are far too precious to Lunsera, to Arden, and to me."

His heart fluttered and he looked into her soft eyes, the light from the torches in the room caressing the delicate features of her face.

"I'm precious to you?"

Her lips formed a faint grin. "In a certain regard, yes. The Lord of Barrington has his armies, the first family of Sohn their secret language, Bastille their knights, and Alvar his Quickfury. As for Lunsera. . .we have you.

"But I believe that is enough dour discussion for one evening. I will retire. Good evening." She smiled and inclined her head before turning in the direction of her own bedchamber.

"Helen," Peter said, halting her.

She turned to him. "Yes?"

"If Alvar is so arrogant and vain. . .why do the people love him so much? It's been on my mind for a while now."

"Well. I suppose it is in his name."

"His name? Blackheart?"

She smiled and shook her head. "His surname is of little consequence. He is the first to bear it, I am certain. I surmise he hails from Hearthelm or the surrounding area, but that is of little importance. It is the name Alvar."

“Alvar? What's so important about it?”

“My sister told you of the great lion and the serpent?”

It took a moment, but he recalled the oldest legend of their world. “I remember. Alvasar and Norvok,” he assured her.

“And you also know that it was prophesied Alvasar would be reborn as a man, who would destroy what remained of Norvok's venom that had fallen onto Arden. It was said that his name would be Alvar, meaning ‘savior of the world.’”

“Do you think he is?”

She smiled. “Rest, Mr. Loneheart. The semifinals commence tomorrow.”

“Goodnight, Helen,” he said, watching her disappear into the darkness of the hallway leading to her chamber.

Alone, he pondered what he had learned today. *Alvar really thinks he's the savior of Arden, and his sword is my kryptonite, apparently. But still...Helen really seems to care about me enough to warn me about him. She actually cares.*

* * * * * * *

The first match of the semifinals didn't start until well into the afternoon. Peter and the Moonwey sisters took their time departing the palace and arriving at the stadium. From their private spectator's booth, they watched a series of exhibition matches during the morning as the stadium began to fill with the citizens of the city in preparation for the two semifinal matches of the day.

Finally, as the sun's shrouded light peeked over the dark clouds above for a few moments, the pitch was cleared and torches were lit around the stadium as the heralds came forth. One wielded the gray banner of Sohn, distinguishable by an orange sun on the flowing fabric. Peter and Aurora both moved onto the edge of their seats, leaning forward with mutual anticipation as the heir of Sohn was announced.

Jadiel, clad in his copper gilded armor, strolled onto the pitch and waved his halberd at the crowd. A few excited shrieks echoed throughout the stadium from the young women who adored the warrior.

The opposing herald made his own announcement and a tall man stepped onto the pitch. His tanned and aged leather armor was nearly as dark as his ebony skin. With his lanky weapon arm outstretched, he pointed his spear at Jadiel, who simply bowed.

The decisive musket shot rang out and both warriors remained where they stood, eyeing each other as they loosened up and alternated their grips on their poled weapons. The crowd chanted, demanding action. The taller fighter twirled his spear in mesmerizing rotations as he slowly inched toward Jadiel, who did the same with his halberd. Both were obviously wary of the other.

As both fighters continued to whirl their weapons, the taller warrior struck at the ground, tossing dirt and sand into Jadiel's face.

Cheap shot.

Jadiel grimaced and shook his head, swiping his halberd horizontally in front of him in time to counter his opponent's sudden thrust. The spearhead was knocked upward and the tall warrior twisted the weapon around, delivering another thrust and then another.

The warrior from Sohn skipped backward on the tips of his toes as he parried each lunge, his halberd spinning in front of him. Suddenly, his left shoulder jerked backward as the tip of the spear met the copper surface of his armor. He skipped backward again, gaining distance as the spear-wielding warrior stood and watched to see if blood had been spilled.

Jadiel rotated the arm of the shoulder that had been struck. No blood. Together, Peter and Aurora released their withheld breath as the crowd cheered and the warrior from Sohn dashed forward with ferocious and sudden speed. His body pivoted as he swung like a batter for a home run. The full length of the halberd proved true as it sliced through the center of the spear and sent the two fragmented ends flying through the air.

Allowing the momentum from the swing to carry him, Jadiel twisted and spun his halberd, thrusting forward with a sudden burst of energy. The taller warrior howled loudly enough for Peter to hear as the tip of the steel jabbed into his left quadriceps. Jadiel detached his halberd with one sharp movement and blood oozed down his opponent's leg. The stadium thundered with booming cheers of men and the shrieks of young women as the match ended.

Peter sighed with relief as he sank into his seat, thankful the match had ended and that the stress it had brought had abated with Jadiel's victory. He looked over to Aurora, who had had the same reaction, and the two laughed together. During the time it took to prepare the pitch for the final match of the day, he and the younger Moonwey sister discussed the match that had occurred.

When the field was prepared, two new heralds stepped forth. The first made his inaudible announcement and a muscular man with tanned skin stepped forward, leaving footprints in the dirt with his bare feet. An array of crimson tattoos wove along the skin of his chest, up his neck, and along his face, meeting a line salt-and-pepper hair that hung down his back. With his right hand, he patted the strange-looking weapon in his left. Shaped like a tennis racket, it appeared as two pieces of wood bound together, sandwiching a series of razor-sharp rocks that protruded all along the edges of the weapon.

Aurora leaned forward, her eyes squinting as she studied the strange man. "Could it be? Helen, is that—?"

Her older sister bore the same expression. "It would appear so. . .A remnant of the Torkus tribe."

"The Torkus tribe?" Peter asked Aurora.

"One of the first tribes known in history. Archaic. . .ancient even. It's a tribe that hails from a vast forest in the far west, just north of New London. You know that the western regions are unruly and feral to an extent. Of all the states, guilds, and tribes of the west, none are so wild as the Torkus. Are you familiar with the tale of Arkus and Tobius?"

"I think I saw a play of it when I first came to Lunar Rock. They were two demigods that fought in a river?"

“So they say, the Ornian river, centuries before it was even named thus, so centuries before the twelve arrived in Arden. Arkus was the father of the entire Torkus tribe. . .before he was slain by Tobius, the river guardian and founder of the river tribes.”

“I see. So do you think they are still alive after the plague?”

Helen was the one to answer. “It is a wonder that they have survived this long as it stands. After the plague's devastation of the west. . .he may very well be the last of his people.”

Peter turned his attention back to the field, where Alvar Blackheart stepped onto the pitch, resting his right hand on the pommel of his rapier as he waved to the cheering crowds with his left.

Behind Alvar, a third man stood between the two warriors and waved a crimson flag back and forth. The floor beneath Peter's feet trembled as the crowd cheered louder than ever before.

Helen inhaled sharply.

“A death match!” Aurora exclaimed.

“Of course,” Helen muttered. “I have suspected that Alvar hails from Hearthelm. If that is true...”

“—he is a descendant of the river tribes,” Barda said. “They have both agreed to a fight to the death. There is great significance here; the crowds recognize it as well.”

“Indeed,” Helen said bitterly. “It is as if they desire to reenact that confounded legend of their ancestral tribes. I will never understand why men must associate the notions of honor and glory with butchering one another.”

Catching Peter by surprise, the musket shot rang out, followed by a roar from the tribesman. While many in the front row of the stadium flinched from the man’s wild scream, Alvar remained still and focused, retorting by slowly unsheathing Quickfury. Alvar raised his sword arm, pointing his blade at the tribesman, who rolled his shoulders as he started toward his opponent.

Peter's heart raced and he perched on the edge of the sofa as the two men met in the center of the pitch. Alvar struck blood with a rapid thrust across the tribesman's shoulder. He in turn swung wildly with his unusual but deadly weapon. The Blackheart Lord dodged some incoming strokes and parried others with Quickfury. As if the dirt had risen against him, Alvar's boot was caught and he fell back onto the ground.

Get up! Peter thought. Though he disliked the man, he didn't want to see him die, nor anyone for that matter.

The tribesman swung his racket-shaped weapon, but missed as Alvar rolled away, finally spinning back onto his feet and tossing a cloud of dirt and sand into his opponent's face.

Undeterred by the cheap attack, the tribesman continued his assault of arbitrary strikes, grunting with frustration from each miss, slicing through the dust cloud. Suddenly, the tribesman reached forward with his free hand and grasped his opponent's black jacket. After winding his upper body back, he thrust the front crown of his head into Alvar's face. Peter winced as the crowd groaned and gasped as one. Alvar stumbled backward, apparently dazed.

The tribesman slashed again at the dazed Lord. In a flurry of unexpected movement, Alvar lurched forward at the man and his sword arm blurred. A few women shrieked as the tribesman's two arms fell onto the dirt. With an expression of pure horror, he looked to the stubs of his shoulders, spewing warm blood onto the dirt around him.

Aurora and Helen both gagged as they turned away, pale. The tribesman looked back at Alvar, who simply raised his sword arm in front of his face as if to salute the man.

With a simple flick of Alvar's wrist, Quickfury sliced through the tribesman's neck and his head fell to the blood-soaked dirt. The tattooed body followed after and twitched until it moved no more.

As the crowd cheered, Helen rose. “Despicable,” she stated flatly before storming out of the box with Barda.

Helen refused to attend the celebration following the event, so they returned to the palace. After arriving in their quarters, Helen paced back and forth at the center of the common room, hissing in both English and Du'Vhani.

"Are you well?" Aurora yawned from the sofa across from Peter.

"Hardly!" Helen hissed. "Aren't you the least bit infuriated by that barbaric display?"

"I was at first. . ."

Helen finally halted and crossed her arms as she thought in silence, staring at the night sky beyond the window.

Aurora stood. "Alvar and Jadiel face each other tomorrow in the final. I pray it will not be a death match. Goodnight." She glanced at Peter one last time before she departed down the hall to her chamber.

As the silence continued, Peter looked back at Helen, who twisted to face him.

"Well? What are your thoughts?" she asked.

"About the match?"

"Obviously."

"I'm willing to say that I feel the same as you. If anything, I'm just more worried about Jadiel now." His words seemed to resonate within her as she nodded in agreement.

"My apologies for my tirade," she said softly.

That beautiful smile. He adored the sight.

Suddenly she dashed over to where he sat and joined him on the open seat of the sofa. "May we continue with the lessons? I imagine it will be a welcome distraction from the recent bloodshed."

"Er. . .yeah."

Time passed quickly as they reviewed all that he had taught her over the course of the last few days. At one point during the lesson, she corrected his own pronunciation. “Well,” he said, “I think you now officially speak Spanish better than I do, and after only a few days of learning.”

She blushed. Following the review, she somehow talked him into telling her stories of his life, including his childhood memories of Jack. As he explained soccer and his love for the sport, she began to ask question upon question in rapid succession.

“You scored the goal? For your mother?”

“Yeah.” His face grew warm as she smiled and her eyes shined.

“You must have been the most pleasant of boys.”

He laughed. “I think my mom said something similar. She let me choose where we ate that night after the game. Pizza.” His words grew soft as sadness swelled within him and a longing for home arose as never before. He felt her hand touch his.

“I have not forgotten,” she said softly. “I will help you return to your Norfolk, if I can.”

No words came to his mind as his eyes searched her face in the gentle light of the secluded chamber. Her soft gaze radiated with the same allure as her lips.

In a rush of emotions he couldn't comprehend, and compelled by the moment at hand, he leaned forward and his lips met hers. For a second the softness of her lips caressed his own before a gasp emerged and she pulled back. Her soft gaze lingered before it was replaced by a fierce glare. Her hand swept across his cheek with a slap that echoed loudly in the common room.

She grimaced and stood, massaging her hand. “How dare you?!” she hissed before storming away.

Burying his head in his hands, he cursed himself.

What have I done?

Chapter 11

Resurgence

What have I done? he thought to himself repeatedly. Lying in bed, he pulled the pillow in his embrace closer to him, wishing it was her. *Stop! Don't think about her. I've done enough!*

He rolled onto his left side to stare out the window of his chamber. The city awaited him beneath the morning sun, gleaming scarcely through a few clouds that lingered from the night. *The final match is today and I'll be around her all day. How am I supposed to apologize?*

He lingered on the question for what seemed like hours, lying in bed, expecting Barda to bust through the door at any moment to extract vengeance for the Lady of Lunsera.

A knock at the door alerted him. He sighed as he rose and stared at the wooden door of the chamber with dread brewing within him.

Another knock.

"Who is it?" He was answered by what he assumed was a cat scratching the wood on the other side. He deepened his voice and demanded, "Who is it!"

"Peter, open the door," Aurora said flatly.

Oh no. Does she know? What will we she think? I'm so stupid.

He took a deep breath and strolled over to the door with only his trousers on. Raising the latch, he opened the door and the light from the window shined into the hallway. Aurora looked him up and down.

"Why are you not dressed? Are you sulking again?" She crossed her arms with a puzzled expression.

"Sulking?"

"About the match yesterday? It seems to have had an insalubrious effect on Helen as well. She spoke little this morning, as if she were furious."

"Wait. . .is she still here?"

"No. She and Barda departed a short while ago. She didn't say where..."

He planted his fist in the wall, creating a fist-sized crater and sending a crack up the length. "Oh. . ." He turned and began to put on his tunic and boots.

Aurora stepped into the room and examined the destruction along the wall. "Are you so concerned about the match today?"

He paused. "Yeah." *But not as much for as I am about Helen.*

"As am I. I hope Jadiel wins." She spun around and looked to him with a wide grin. "Could you imagine it? Jadiel winning the tournament, the plague being destroyed, the assassin group being discovered and thwarted, and the lot of us going to Sohn for Jadiel's coronation. It sounds like a wondrous future, do you agree?"

"It sounds great," he muttered. *Not as great as going back home or fixing things with Helen.*

"Although it must be horrid for his mother to have to witness the match today."

"It's not going to be a death match, is it?" he demanded with genuine concern.

She shrugged. "I suppose we shall learn of that when you finish dressing."

He rolled his eyes and finished putting on his clothes before washing his face.

The pair acquired two palace horses and made their way through the labyrinth that was Arden City. The crowded streets delayed their arrival at the stadium by around an hour. As they entered the stairs and continued along the corridors of the stadium, his nerves attacked his stomach in growing anticipation of being in Helen's presence again.

Aurora stepped past the two guards at the door and he followed her into the private spectator's booth overlooking the field, pausing as the door closed behind him. Barda cast a quick glance at them both before turning back to the field. In front of the bodyguard, Helen sat silent and still, watching the exhibitions below. Aurora walked around to the empty sofa and dropped onto it.

"Excited?" she asked her sister.

"Notably," Helen replied flatly. Slowly, he made his way over to the sofa where the younger sister sat and joined her. He cast a quick glance at Helen, whose face remained fixed.

She's never going to talk to me again. I'm so stupid. What was I thinking?

The exhibitions lasted for an hour, and not a single word was uttered by any in the box. At last, the time for the final match arrived, and a dozen men strolled out onto the field, surrounding the circular pitch of dirt. Each man bore a large bass drum strapped to his body. One of the drummers began beating his percussive instrument. A second drummer joined in the same rhythm. Another joined and another after until all twelve played the same rhythm in unison.

Jadiel's herald walked onto the pitch, bearing the flag of Sohn, and made his announcement. The warrior from Sohn strolled onto the pitch. His copper armor gleamed beneath the sun's rays as he waved to the crowds and twirled his halberd.

The foundations of the stadium seemed to tremble as the second herald called out his fighter.

With his chin held high, Alvar strutted onto the pitch. His left hand rested on his sheathed rapier. He turned to face Jadiel, removing the black hat that matched his jacket and tossing it to the side. The drums stopped and the heralds ran from the circle of dirt.

"No bloody flag," Aurora noted.

Peter exhaled with relief. Watching the two men square off, his body tensed. The musket shot rang out and the crowd bellowed with thunderous excitement.

The Blackheart Lord dashed forward, drawing Quickfury from its scabbard. His sword arm was a blur of black movement as he repeatedly lunged after Jadiel.

The halberd twirled in a blinding movement of its own as the warrior from Sohn defended against the barrage of attacks. An incoming thrust from the rapier was knocked aside by the poled weapon and Jadiel reached forward with his left hand to punch his opponent.

Alvar sidestepped and the incoming punch grazed his shoulder. He retracted his sword arm from his parried lunge and swiped up at Jadiel's outstretched arm, cutting into the armor of his forearm. The warrior from Sohn skipped backward with haste and examined his arm before extending his fist to the sky. No blood. The Blackheart Lord brought his sword arm in front of his face, saluting. Jadiel did the same, twirling his halberd vertically along his body.

The two men spun their weapons as they advanced toward one another. Quickfury reminded Peter of a helicopter as Alvar twirled it with blinding speed. Alvar's advance was halted as Jadiel thrust forward with his halberd, following up with a series of calculated lunges imitating the Blackheart Lord's initial attack.

Peter analyzed how the length of Jadiel's pole weapon gave Alvar no opportunity to strike back at him. *He's using the distance. Keep it up!*

Alvar continued to rotate his body and jump from side to side to avoid each thrust. On one occasion he attempted to counter but was met with a well-timed and sudden swipe from his opponent, barely blocking it. With obvious frustration, Alvar backed off entirely, pacing back and forth as he stared at his opponent.

Jadiel remained low and ready with his halberd clutched tightly in clear anticipation of what was to come. His opponent ceased his pacing and began to jog around him in a circle as he twirled his rapier. The Blackheart Lord faked an advance, causing Jadiel to flinch. He faked another advance. And again, he darted forward—but did not pull back to fake. Instead, he swung his rapier over his head and sliced through the middle of Jadiel's halberd as it was raised to block.

To Peter's dismay, the pike end of the weapon plunged into the dirt. The warrior from Sohn retreated backward, swinging the fragmented pole in his hands as Alvar pursued him, wild with bloodlust. Grasping the pole with both hands on both sides, he parried an incoming thrust of the rapier and followed through by pushing the staff across Alvar's body and into his chest.

Quickfury fell to the ground as its wielder was pushed back. Alvar narrowly dodged the incoming swings from the staff as he retreated. Bringing his forearms together, he blocked a baseball bat swing from his opponent, quickly reaching after the staff. He grasped the pole weapon and yanked it free, but instead of using it, he tossed it to the side as he dove for his rapier.

Jadiel dashed past Alvar, who swung upward from the ground after him as he passed but only managed to cut through air. The Blackheart Lord gave chase as Jadiel rolled onto the dirt and rose with the pike end of his fragmented weapon. Alvar reached across his body, winding up as the halberd was thrust forward. Quickfury blurred like a bat flying in the night sky and sliced through the steel of the pike.

Alvar followed the momentum and his sword swiped horizontally with full force toward Jadiel's neck.

Aurora shrieked as Peter gasped, expecting their friend's head to fall onto the ground. The Blackheart Lord's sword arm stopped suddenly as it met his opponent's neck and the entire stadium released a withheld breath before erupting into cheers.

The match was over, Peter realized. Alvar must have cut Jadiel's neck. Peter sighed with disappointment as he watched Alvar embrace Jadiel.

Helen stood and, without a word, walked out of the spectator's box with Barda following behind.

"Man..." he groaned, leaning back into the cushions of the sofa.

"Indeed," Aurora chuckled.

Among the tremors the cheering crowds caused in the stadium, a sudden thud rocked the spectator's box.

Peter jumped to his feet in surprise. "Fireworks?"

She yawned, "Perhaps. Something to commemorate the conclusion of the tournament."

Across the stadium, a spectator's box burst into flames and a hideous blast echoed louder than the crowds that now screamed in horror.

"Oh my God..." Peter muttered.

To the right of their view, another spectator's box burst into flames. The floor beneath them trembled. Another ball of fire appeared to their left. Peter grasped one of the hands that Aurora held over her mouth. Ignoring her horrified expression, he pulled her toward the door as another explosion rocked the stadium.

* * * * * * *

What's going on? Is Helen alright? He kicked one of the doors of the spectator's box, sending it spiraling into the air. The heavy door thudded against the stone floor of the corridor. Daylight radiated through the windows along the still and silent hallway. He pulled Aurora along behind him, taking care not to hurt her.

“Peter, what's happening?” she asked in a shaking voice. A series of pops echoed throughout the labyrinth of stone. “Muskets,” she told him as they continued along the passageway.

As they passed the entrance to a hallway to their left, a blur of movement caught him by surprise.

“Peter!” Aurora shrieked as he caught a glimpse of shining steel out of the corner of his eye. He instinctively raised his left arm in time to meet the saber, grimacing as the sword stuck his forearm and rebounded with a soft thud.

A gasp of terror escaped through the black mask of the attacker, who stepped back and examined his clean saber. He wound his sword arm back for another try and Peter lurched forward, punching him in the face. With a series of cracks, the attacker in black flew back and skidded along the floor of the hallway like a flat rock thrown over the surface of water. The body halted its movement about twenty feet away in front of a door and remained motionless.

Peter examined his arm where he had been struck. The blue fabric of his tunic had been sliced and the skin beneath harbored an apparent paper cut.

Aurora gasped and clutched at Peter's chest. Her words falling short in her attempts to warn him. Three figures in black emerged from the door, standing over their fallen comrade. The sight of their raised pistols spurred Peter to twist and hold his friend into his chest.

The shots rang out in rapid succession, popping loudly within the funnel of stone. A sharp pain radiated from his left hamstring, followed by a pelting sting in his right shoulder blade. The third shot whizzed past his left ear, shattering the glass of the window across from him and the woman he protected.

The three men began to reload their pistols as the closed door further along the main corridor suddenly burst open and three more figures in black emerged, trapping them.

“The window!” she told him.

“What?!”

"Hold me and jump. I trust you."

He glanced back at the new trio of attackers to his left and then to the three with pistols behind him. As he had when they had danced, he scooped her into his arms. *Light as a pillow.*

He advanced toward the window, looking down into the courtyard below. Holding Aurora close to his chest, he stepped out into the air and plummeted to the ground. His boots crunched upon the shards of glass from the broken window.

The stone buildings surrounding the courtyard rebounded and amplified the cries of the crowd that rushed around Peter and Aurora.

"The security force!" she exclaimed, pointing at the group of men that ran toward the commotion in gleaming silver armor, bearing muskets and sabers. He flagged one of the men down. A small wave of relief washed over him upon learning the man was a captain with nearly thirty men under his command. Still in his arms, Aurora looked at him with palpable concern. "Peter, we need to find Helen and Barda."

He looked around, thinking about where the older sister could have gone.

The captain's silver helm gleamed as he stepped forward and spoke. "Lord, I can have a squad of my own men accompany you if you wish to reenter the stadium."

His heart began to race as he finally recognized the severity of the chaos. He looked at the young woman in his arms. She looked back and with a faint grin said, "Go. I will be fine with the security force."

He nodded and set her down. Seven men in silver armor stepped forward toward him.

Peter looked at the captain. "Take her to the palace. Now!"

The silver helm inclined. "I will see to it myself, Lord Lionheart."

Peter turned back to the stadium, jogging toward the chaos with seven men under his own command as Aurora sped away, surrounded by her own security detail.

What am I doing? he thought as he ran toward the incoming crowd as they panicked and fled from the chaos behind them. The seven men in armor sprinted to keep up with him. Like a stream of water around a rock, the fleeing crowd parted as he raced forward under the stone archway of the stadium. *Helen, where are you?*

"Helen!" he called out. His only replies were the countless screams and more musket shots. As he stopped under an archway, a figure in black caught his attention to his left. A gleaming saber jabbed at him, but before he could react, the enemy's advance was thwarted as one of the defenders in silver rushed forward and plunged his own saber through the dark fabric. As the saber was dislodged, the attacker fell to the ground in a growing puddle of blood.

He was going straight for me. They must know who I am.

As he and his squad of defenders turned into a corridor, they stopped short as a group of heavily armored warriors trotted toward them, their steel plates clanking with each step. At the center of the formation was a hefty man in a rich crimson jacket and a black cape.

The Lord of Barrington.

The horrified expression on the Lord's face abated as he set eyes on Peter, halting his security detail.

"My Lord Lionheart. Thank Fyraen. This is madness! Assassins everywhere!"

"Helen!" Peter exclaimed. "Have you seen her?"

"Aye." His gaze shifted to the direction from whence he came and then back to the boy from Virginia. "A glimpse, but there were assassins after her as well. I barely escaped with my life. My frie—"

His words faded as Peter sprinted along the corridor, leaving his seven defenders behind, leaving a trail of vaporous teal where he ran. As he raced forward, he recognized the sound of steel on steel echoing from the stairwell to the right. He turned and ascended the stairs, seeking the source of the commotion.

When he reached the top of a flight of stairs, he paused to listen and discern where the sound of fighting came from. Like an animal on the hunt, his right ear twitched as a woman shrieked and he followed after, turning right and sprinting down the corridor. The hall ended in a fork. A group of men in black raced toward him from the left. How many there were, he didn't care to count as he turned to the right and saw Helen.

At the end of the hall, two assassins lay in pools of their own blood and Barda struggled with a third, their blades sparking. Another assassin approached her from the side. In the far corner, Helen shrank against the stone walls. Her horrified face ignited a sudden and potent fury within Peter. He threw himself at the assassin who approached Barda unchallenged. Both men accelerated into the stone wall that cracked open in fragments.

Sunlight protruded through the broken wall. Peter stepped back as dust and pieces of broken stone fell off of him. The mangled body of the assassin remained lodged within the fractured wall. Scarlet blood gathered along a piece of fractured bone and dripped onto the stone floor. He turned away from his handiwork and faced the Lady of Lunsera. Her relieved gaze searched his face before something caught her attention.

“Barda!” she warned. He whirled around and dashed forward at the assassin overpowering the bodyguard. With his momentum behind him, he plunged his fist into the side of the man’s head. The dark figure sailed through the air along the hallway toward more assassins running toward them. The body fell onto the stone floor and the band of attackers stepped over it, racing past the entryway Peter had come through.

He prepared himself. Before he could rush forward, something caught his eye beyond the gang of assassins. In a blur of rapid movement, a tall figure in a gray robe emerged from the hallway the assassins had just run past. With a staff in hand, the tall figure attacked the trailing men in black. One after the other, each assassin was knocked aside with a precise and mighty swipe of the staff. Within a few moments, the group of incoming assassins had been beaten and were writhing on the floor, in pain, but alive.

The hooded staff-wielder stepped over the bodies and walked toward Peter and the two women. As the figure stopped, Peter looked up at the hood, but saw only darkness.

The man beneath the hood finally spoke. “Come, Peter. Follow me.”

I know that voice!

* * * * * * *

The robed man moved faster than the average person from Arden. It was apparent as they followed him along a hidden corridor and down an old staircase. He poked his head out of the door that led outside. The gray hood turned left and right before the man waved them after him and they all proceeded outside to a compact alleyway. A few wooden barrels and crates lay there. They were alone.

“Return to the palace,” the strong voice told them as he began to walk away. As Helen and Barda stared at the back of the robed man, Peter stepped forward toward him.

“Stop!” he commanded. The robed man halted but did not turn. “I know you! Don't I?” The wind howled as it rushed through the alley. “Turn around.”

Slowly, he turned.

“Take off your hood.”

The man’s arms raised and his dark fingers clutched the gray fabric. The hood slid back, revealing a familiar face.

A pair of soft brown eyes stared back at Peter, appearing auburn in the sunlight that also shined off his bald ebony head. Peter’s gaze hardened as he finally remembered who the man was.

It's the man from the beach! The one who stole Selena’s poster she got for me.

“You!” Peter growled.

Behind him, the two women gasped and inclined their heads. "Sir William!" they exclaimed.

"Lady Moonwey." William nodded.

Helen took a step forward and said, "Sir William, where have you been? We thought you dead." Before he could speak, she asked another question with sudden enthusiasm. "Jack Loneheart. Does he also live?"

Although he wanted to ask the same question, Peter flinched as she asked it instead, and with so much enthusiasm.

William raised his hand and spoke softly. "All will be revealed in time, my lady." His gaze shifted. "Peter, take them to the palace. I will find you there."

"No," Peter growled before the man could turn to leave. He walked forward. "This is your fault. I'm in a world I don't belong in. That day at the beach when you stole the poster—you knew I would follow you. You knew!" He stopped and stared up into the man's unflinching gaze.

"I suspect—" His sentence fell short as Peter pushed his chest, sending him flying back at least fifteen feet into a wooden crate. The box shattered as the man crashed into it.

"Mr. Loneheart!" Helen yelled. Barda started toward him with her sword at the ready. Peter held his ground and pointed at the female warrior.

"Try me! I dare you! I bet I can throw you over the stadium like a Frisbee." She halted in her tracks and a flicker of fear flashed across her face. Helen looked to him with a pained expression, but he didn't care.

I'm not playing around today, not with anyone. I want answers.

He turned back to William, who groaned as he stood, dusting himself off.

"Your uncle tossed me once before as well, before we knew to trust one another."

Peter crossed his arms and stared at the older man. "I don't care. This is your fault. I don't belong here. How do I get home?"

The man looked at him with a disappointed expression as he sighed. "Peter. Please under—" Another explosion from the stadium shook the buildings around them, sending dust showering onto the cobblestone.

Peter hardened his gaze on the older man. "Oh, no. You aren't going anywhere! Not until I get answers."

The older man looked over Peter's shoulder. "The safety of a lady should come before the truth. I will tell all that I know, Peter. I promise you. But I beseech you to take her to the safety of the palace."

"I swear I'll hunt you down if you don't," Peter threatened.

The old man smiled faintly and nodded. "You have my word."

William donned his hood and sped forward, leaping over a nearby fence and disappearing. Peter's gaze remained fixed on the shattered crate. The Lady of Lunsera walked up and glared at him, muttering a few words that he didn't care to listen to as he simmered and thought.

William. Finally, for the first time, there's a possibility that I can go home.

Chapter 12

Call To Arms

The province leaders and appointed commanders of the coalition army formed a circle in the middle of the large chamber. Between their chairs, a map of Arden was illustrated on the carpet in the center of the room.

Peter stood behind the Lady of Lunsera as she sat. He looked down at her again. Two days had passed since the attack at the stadium and she had not spoken a single word to him. And William had not delivered on his promise.

"This confounded group of terrorists have dealt a fatal blow!" bellowed the commander of the coalition army. His black jacket gleamed with golden embroideries. Behind him stood his three vice-commanders. Alvar Blackheart was one of them.

"Indeed, Lord Rulfin," the Lord of Barrington agreed to the right of Helen. "So few province leaders remain after the attack. I fear our union will see its end before we defeat the plague in the west. With Sohn in question. . ."

One of the vice-commanders spoke. "The pup licks his wounds still?"

Helen spoke for the first time with icy words, "That pup is Jadiel and he recently lost his mother. . .as I lost my friend."

"Lady Lorena will be missed by us all," the Lord of Barrington said somberly. "As will all of our fallen comrades after these cowardly attacks."

Lord Rulfin, the commander of the army, stood. "My sincerest of apologies. But we must remember why we gathered here. We must look to the west." He pointed to the enormous drawing on the floor. "Scouts have reported that a horde of infected travel from Ilvion toward the Ornian ruins."

"A horde?" the Lord of Barrington asked. "How many?"

"The scouts lost exact count. But they are certain it numbers over ten thousand."

Helen gasped, "Ten thousand?"

"Indeed, my lady," Rulfin continued. "While we have few garrisons that remain in the western regions, including the ruins themselves, we cannot hope to defeat this infection if the army remains here, regardless of our depleted strength. If we do not halt the advance of this horde that proceeds toward the ruins, then we may very well relinquish any hope of retaking the west. If the garrison at the river is overrun, we will be forced to destroy the bridges and pray the infected do not learn to swim across the Ornian.

"Sir Hector departed yesterday with fifteen hundred riders behind him. The cavalry forces will conduct a series of rapid attacks in an attempt to dwindle the large number of the horde. With this council's blessing, I will depart in the morning with what forces we have. I have already given the orders to prepare our advance westward. This council need only will us forth. What say you?"

Silence followed the commander's words until the first affirmative was received and all in the room confirmed, "Aye."

Lord Ornwell, the head of the city council, rose from his chair and spoke for the first and last time. “It is decided. The army will depart as the sun rises. This meeting is adjourned.” He bowed and departed the chamber, followed by several others.

As Helen stood, the commander spoke. “My Lady and my Lord Lionheart. Though we march for war as the sun rises, we have little hope for victory with so few to fight.”

“What do you ask, My Lord?” she inquired flatly.

His gaze shifted from her to Peter. “If you were to fight with us, my Lord, the army could march forth with renewed zeal. Rumors have spread of your power during the attack at the stadium and how you defeated your foes so easily. The men would fight with greater intensity if you fought beside them.”

Silence followed as the commander and his three subordinates watched Peter.

“I...I’ll have to think about it.”

“We shall eagerly await your reply, my Lord.” He inclined his head and Peter followed Helen out of the chamber. She marched ahead through the hallways of the palace.

Is today the day? Will she finally speak to me?

He took a deep breath as he stared at her back. Her black dress rustled with each step.

“Helen,” he said. She kept her back to him, walking forward. “Helen, please talk to me. I'm sorry about Lorena,” he continued. “And I know you expect me to say it, but I’m not sorry about kissing you.”

Finally, she stopped and his heart fluttered. She turned and walked toward him with purpose in her steps and fire in her eyes, stopping short of his face.

“What you feel is irrelevant to me, Mr. Loneheart. I pray that you will depart with the army. Perhaps in the west, you will truly find yourself.”

Without another word, she walked away and left him alone in the silent corridor.

* * * * * * *

After walking through the halls of the palace and into the empty common room of their quarters, he decided to go to his own chamber and ponder what to do. From the darkness of the hallway, he raised the latch on the door and stepped inside the chamber. He jumped when he caught sight of the man that sat in the corner of the room.

William stood from behind the table adjacent to the window, where a blanket of clouds loomed over the city. "Peter," he said, indicating the empty chair across from him. "Please sit."

He closed the door behind him and walked over to the chair. Sitting, he scoffed, "Took you long enough." *Finally! I'm going to get answers.*

William sat back down. "You have many questions."

"Oh yeah. For starters. . .who the hell are you? Really?"

"I am, or rather I was, a knight. I led the order of Bastille for many years."

"You're *the* William of Bastille?" he asked. The man nodded. "I've heard that you're the greatest knight in Arden's history."

He smiled faintly. "Perhaps. Now, I am but an old man."

Peter crossed his arms and reclined. "So. Sir William. How did you know?"

"Know?"

"About that vortex at the beach or whatever it was! How did you know it was going to happen and that I would follow you to it?"

The old knight stared thoughtfully at his own clasped hands. "Did you hear anything when it happened? Or that day leading up to it?"

"I heard water. And my own screams."

William leaned across the table toward him. "Your name was not called out to you?"

"No! Stop being vague."

The old knight reclined in his chair, rubbing his temples. "I und—"

Suddenly, Peter's stomach seized with pain as the strange eerie feeling returned. The hairs on his neck raised and he collapsed onto the wooden table. He glanced across at the old knight leaning against the wood, grimacing with obvious discomfort.

The feeling subsided. He looked again at William, who began taking regular breaths of relief.

"You felt that too, didn't you?"

The man nodded. A vein bulged along his forehead.

"William, what is going on here? Ever since I stepped foot in the city, I've felt that!"

He shook his head. "I have been considering that myself. Ever since I returned from your world I have felt it repeatedly. I recall Jack feeling the same sensation when he first arrived so long ago. He could not explain it then, nor could I, however, I know for certain upon my return. . .this world is not right, Peter. There is something wrong here."

His words sent a chill down Peter's spine. "William, I need to go home. How do I?"

"I do not know."

Fueled by anger, Peter stood abruptly, sending his chair flying backward. He glowered at the old knight. "That's not good enough! I don't belong here, William! Jack must have felt the same. Please, I just want to go home."

"I will grant you the solace of knowing that your uncle did desire to return to you and your family. However. . ." His soft fatherly gaze turned fierce as he stared up at the boy from Virginia. "Jack did not cower when the war began after he arrived. He fought for the people to bring peace and end the suffering. If he were to here to witness your lesser behavior, I daresay he would be ashamed of you."

The words cut into him like a blazing hot knife. He stopped himself before he could reply out of impulse. *He's right. Jack would be disappointed.*

"Where is he?"

"I suspect that you know as much I do. From what I have gathered, he disappeared during the siege shortly after myself."

Peter stepped back and flopped onto the foot of his bed, staring at the floor. "I was hoping I would be able to find him and then go back home to be with mom and gran."

The man sighed. "There is much work for me to do from the shadows, Peter. Arden cannot yet know that I live. When the time comes, I shall assist you in discovering Jack's fate. Until that time, what will you do?"

"I don't know. Helen hates me. The army wants me to go with them."

"Perhaps it would be wise for you to assist the army in their endeavor. I fear the worst for the men that will fight. They will need you."

"Why, William? Why me?"

"You have a great destiny ahead of you, Peter. It is time for you to cease thinking as a boy and begin acting as a man." He stood. "I have faith in you. The decisions you make in the coming days will not only decide your fate but also the fate of Arden."

William stepped over to the window and opened the glass door to the balcony. The evening air rushed into the room. "I will see you again. May the Lord watch over you, Peter."

With that, the old knight stepped onto the balcony and leapt over the railing.

* * * * * * *

The tempest of emotions conjured by the events of the past few days spurred his steps along the corridor. With each stride, flashes of Helen, William, Jack, and Aurora came to mind. The old knight's words resonated perpetually, thwarting any hint of cowardice as he searched for the commander and his subordinates.

Further along the hallway, a man in a black jacket turned the corner and started toward him. *Alvar.*

Though he desired to find one of the men with authority, once again he considered turning around and walking back to his room as he recognized the Blackheart Lord.

"Lionheart," Alvar greeted with a neutral expression.

"Alvar. I..."

"You have decided, hmm?"

"I..." *What am I doing?* He debated what answer to give. Alvar's boot tapped the stone floor as he waited.

After a few moments, the Blackheart Lord sighed. "I see. The Moonwey sisters have weaved their womanly magic upon you, have they not? Disappointing." He strolled past.

"I'm going!" Peter blurted to Alvar's back.

The Blackheart Lord halted and turned toward him. "Did I hear correctly?"

"I said I'm going."

The corner of Alvar's black mustache lifted as he grinned. "Where we go is no place for a woman. Your beloved—"

"Just me. I'll go to the west." The words lingered in the air and a few moments of silence followed before a triumphant laugh escaped Alvar and he clasped Peter's shoulders.

"A wise decision! A wise decision indeed. I have waited for you to display some manner of honor. Let us forsake the folly of this city and depart to the front together. You and I shall create legends of our own, I am certain, hmm?"

"We leave tomorrow?"

"Indeed, upon completion of accountability in the morning. All officers and staff of the command will gather in the palace courtyard to bid farewell to the council and leaders of the provinces."

"Got it. I'll meet you there."

"And I shall relay your decision to Lord Rulfin. Sleep well, Lionheart." He inclined his head and strutted away.

Peter stared at the floor. *Well. There's no turning back now.*

He made his way back to the western wing of the palace, stopping just outside the door to the common room. Two voices spoke over one another, muttering inaudible words beyond the wood. He pulled on the latch and entered. Helen and Aurora stood in the center of the room, each bearing a hard expression.

Aurora crossed her arms and planted her riding boot firmly into the carpet. "And where have you been?" she demanded.

"Busy," he replied.

"Busy? What could you possibly be occupied with?"

"Telling Alvar Blackheart that I'm going into the west."

"...Is that a jest?"

He sighed and shook his head, starting toward the hallway to his chamber.

"You are serious!" she realized. "Peter, why?"

He stopped at the entrance to the dark hallway and turned to face them. Aurora's thin eyebrows furrowed in a pained expression.

His addressed them both. "To be honest, it's been on my mind a lot lately. I really just don't know who or what I really am. Even back home, I. . .I just...always felt like a part of me was missing, something that no one could give to me, something I had to find myself. I don't know what it is, but I know I have to find it and I feel in my heart that leaving is the best thing for me."

The younger Moonwey sister took a step forward, clasping her hands. "Peter, I don't understand. What are you saying?"

"I'm saying goodbye, Aurora." His gaze lingered on her concerned face before shifting to Helen, whose eyes narrowed as she listened with interest. "Everything that's happened. Ending up in Arden, meeting the two of you, the plague, the attack at the stadium, and. . .other things." He faltered as he looked to Helen. "I think there's just too much going on for me here, too much to handle right now and as I am. I think going where I can do some real good would be best for me. . .and everyone else."

"Peter, you can still do good here. You don't have any obligation to fight."

"It's done, Aurora. I'm leaving in the morning. I'm sure I'll see you both when I leave with Alvar."

Without giving her another opportunity for rebuttal, he turned back toward the hallway.

"Mr. Loneheart," Helen said. "You are making the right decision."

Without turning to face her, he continued into the darkness of the hallway, listening to the sisters' voices as they faded with each step.

"Helen, what have you said to him?"

"What was necessary. Do not daunt him, Aurora. And why are you so concerned with what he chooses?"

He closed his chamber door and stood alone in silent darkness.

I hope I'm right.

Chapter 13

The Prince's Road

A cool morning breeze rushed in from the eastern sky. The gust of wind filled his nose with the scent of the many horses that stood around in the palace courtyard. Aurora's delicate hands brushed over the neck of the horse beneath him. She looked up to him and grinned.

"You appear quite dashing in armor."

"Thanks. Alvar gave it to me."

"The leather goes well with your clothes. . .and cape. Our province is well represented, I should say."

He looked around at the city council members and province leaders as they bid farewell to the leadership of the army. Lord Rulfin and his staff members wore pristine jackets that seemed to shine brighter than the armor the captains near Peter wore. The only person on horseback who did not wear armor nor uniform was Alvar. The Blackheart Lord wore his typical black attire. He glanced over at the commander of the army impatiently.

As Peter turned back to Aurora, Helen appeared and looked up at him. Her beauty pained him.

"I will pray for your safety, Mr. Loneheart," Helen said. "Go forth bearing the goodwill of Lunsera. The people of our province hope for your triumphant return."

He simply nodded, turning back to Aurora.

Finally, Lord Rulfin said his final goodbyes and his horse trotted forth.

"Peter," Aurora said. "Bring me a gift from the west, will you?"

He smiled. "I will. I promise."

She stepped away from his steed as Alvar and the two other vice-commanders followed after the leading staff party. Peter glanced at the two sisters one last time before he tapped the flanks of the horse and left them behind. A faint but potent longing arose within him as his horse trotted along with the steeds of the captains. Ever since he had arrived in Arden he had relied on the Moonwey sisters, but now the order of their familiarity disappeared with each step of his horse.

Peter and the party of riders trotted along the road from the palace. The citizens of the city cheered from the sides of the roads they took along their route to the citadel where the army awaited. The tall structure of stone stood in a clearing of its own, vacant of any other buildings. Columns of soldiers on horseback stood waiting. *There must be thousands*, Peter thought. As Lord Rulfin and his party rode past the first line of men along the road, their lieutenant waved his arm and one by one the columns followed behind Peter and the officers he rode with.

The army snaked along the main roads through the city from the citadel. The western gate passed over them as Peter looked forward at the road ahead, flanked by dense forest on both sides. The clanking of metal, chiseling of stone, and array of voices disappeared behind him as they proceeded through the forest. A gust of wind rustled the countless leaves around them and flocks of birds soared over the road ahead, chirping in pleasant discord against the steady trotting of thousands of horses.

He took a deep breath and glanced over the tops of the trees along the left side of the road. In the distance, a lone mountain protruded above the surface of the woods, stretching toward the morning sky. The solitary peak. And beyond it, the ocean.

* * * * * * *

"Masterstown," Captain Gideon said next to him. The officer wiped the sweat from his dark brow and pointed toward the walled town in the distance, surrounded by the forest. The multistory buildings of wood, stone, and thatch protruded above the stone wall, the sun low on the horizon beyond.

"Seems peaceful," Peter said. He looked over to the captain, who stroked his black beard. The man's eyes gleamed like sapphires in the sunlight.

"Aye. Lived here for a time myself. Where I met my wife."

"Kara," Peter concluded. He and the captain had briefly exchanged some information about one another during the long ride from the city.

The man smiled. "My Kara. After we were married, we decided to go east, to Barrington; that's where her family hails from. We remained there for a while and I trained with the eastern guard. Good training, I might say. After she gave birth to our first daughter, we went to the capital. My request to be commissioned was approved by the citadel."

"So you became an officer for the security force?"

"Aye. Busy work. The city is large and with it comes much work and great strain. There was a time when I found solace in the bottom of a wineskin to assist with the strife my duties had brought." His black hair waved from side to side as he shook his head. "I should have been looking to my wife for the support I required. Eventually, I did so. Through her, I saw the error of my ways and we departed back to Barrington, where I acquired a new commission. Life was easier." He sighed. “Then a plague arrived and I was recalled to the citadel during the initial outbreaks.”

“I'm sorry to hear it.”

“As am I, my Lord. I long to return to my darling girls.”

Wish I could say the same, he found himself thinking.

The courtyard opened up as they passed through the front gate. Immediately upon entering, a statue standing roughly twelve feet tall attracted Peter’s attention. The pale marble man stood alone in the center of the courtyard. Pasty hands rested on the pommel of a large sword that must have been at least six feet tall.

“Toven Ornian,” Captain Gideon told him. They both stepped down from their horses and walked over to the towering statue.

“Who is he?”

“One of the sons of the first Oscar. He is a hero in these parts.”

“Ornian? Oscar?”

“Aye. Oscar Ornian was one of the twelve.” He nodded toward Peter. “Founded his own city, built it on a few islands in the center of a river. From that city he started his own kingdom, the Ornian Kingdom, and the river was also given the name. At the height of its power, the kingdom was said to have been as strong as Barrington, Ilvion, and modern-day Arden City itself—combined.”

“Combined?”

The captain nodded. “But that mattered little when the first Oscar died of a strange illness before setting his affairs in order. You see, he Sird two sons that were born on the same day.”

“Twins.”

“Aye. Daniel and Toven. The two brothers were strong, nearly as strong as their father. But ever since the boys were young they had been at each others throats, more so than most brothers. It was said that they truly hated one another and none knew why. After the first

Oscar departed this life, his sons fought a war with one another over who would succeed. Many noble families pledged themselves to one brother or the other. Incidentally, a strange illness struck the kingdom during their war to decide the successor."

"An illness?"

"Not much is known about it, Lord, but they say it killed quickly. Tens of thousands died from the war and the sickness. A final battle was fought and Daniel sank to the bottom of the river. Toven saw that his city and kingdom was doomed, so he took what people he could and fled westward, where he founded a few small towns and led them all to prosperity." Gideon stroked his beard. "And they say he wrestled bears to amuse himself."

Peter looked up to the statue of the man and scoffed, "That's why he has a statue?"

The captain shrugged. "Evidently, Lord. I often find myself wishing I could wrestle bears."

As Peter turned, a small man appeared in front of him, causing he and the captain to jump in surprise.

"The Bard. . ." Gideon sighed. The small man inclined his head of tousled brown hair. His sandy trousers and tunic appeared to have been cut and embroidered to mimic the pristine clothes of any province leader or person of nobility.

"Yes! Bard, I be." His yellow teeth formed an uneven smile. "MY Lord LIONHEART!" he suddenly bellowed, earning the three men a score of glances from all in the courtyard. The Bard reached behind his back and unveiled a lute.

"Oh no..." Gideon breathed.

"Shall I serenade you, Lord Lionheart?" He danced awkwardly as he began to strum the lute that echoed throughout the courtyard.

"No! You shall not," the captain said as he inserted himself between the singing fool and Peter, ushering him toward the adjacent three-story building. The bard continued to dance behind them and play his lute, narrating in a singing tone what he observed about the two men as they walked away. Peter couldn't help but laugh.

As the army itself camped outside the city walls, Lord Rulfin, his staff, and his vice-commanders stayed in the town hall for the night. Peter and the captains were each given their own room on the third floor of the inn. After eating dinner with Gideon and two other captains, he went back to his small room, taking off his armor and staring out the window toward the eastern road they had ridden on that day.

He thought about Helen and Aurora and wondered if they thought about him. The kiss came to mind. He shook his head and cleared his mind before lying down in the small bed.

* * * * * * *

A rooster crowed as he awoke. He rose from the bed and yawned, staring out the open window. The eastern sky was a blanket of pink clouds above the sage forest. He bathed quickly and put on his armor before going downstairs, where a few captains had already gathered, and were eating breakfast. After the remaining officers had arrived and eaten, they departed the inn and rallied in the courtyard with Lord Rulfin and his staff.

As the officers muttered to one another and a few more roosters crowed, the Bard appeared again and began to strum his lute. The acoustic vibrations echoed against the buildings in the early morning hours, waking the citizens of the town. As Peter hoisted himself into his saddle, the bard danced awkwardly toward him, singing his uncle's legacy.

"Lionheart. Oh, Lionheart. . ." The words slowly died behind him as the party passed through the gate and met with the readied army. They continued along the prince's road, west.

* * * * * * *

Six days of riding passed relativity quickly to Peter. As the caravan proceeded west, the forest grew slim into few pockets of trees, and grassy hills became abundant. Each night, they set camp, and the officers would cordon off their own area to sleep, where Peter also stayed. As the campfire died down and the captains fell asleep in their own bedrolls on the ground, he would listen to the serenity of the night. An orchestra of crickets, crackling fires, and steady breathing of the sleeping men near him would serenade him as he gazed upon the night sky with wonder. As if millions of diamonds had been thrown into the infinite darkness, the countless stars smiled at him from above, filling him with gratitude.

I wish I had someone to share this with, he often thought to himself as he looked to the sky with both pleasure and sadness. *I wonder what Helen and Aurora are doing. I bet Aurora is bored out of her mind. What should I get her? What can I get her? I'll have to ask Gideon what a good gift from the west would be.*

"Depends, Lord," the captain replied when he asked the question during the ride the next day. "If I may inquire, who is this gift for?"

"My friend. Aurora."

"Aurora." He stroked his beard. "Lady Helen Moonwey's sister?"

"Yeah. She asked me to bring her something back but I don't know what."

The captain's blue eyes rested on him thoughtfully. "If I may inquire, how close is your friendship? Are you. . .are the two of you. . .betrothed?"

"Betrothed?"

"Will the two of you marry?"

"What? No," Peter chuckled. "Just friends. Well, she's my first friend that I've made here so I want to get her something special if I can."

Gideon laughed. "Aye, Lord. I will assist you in this endeavor if I can, but only if you promise me here and now that you will ensure I return safely to my own ladies if we are to fight together."

The severity of the request weighed heavily on him as he stared at the man. "I promise."

The captain smiled and nodded. “Gratitude, Lord. Then my wife is certain to suffer me for the remainder of our long lives together.”

The hours passed quickly as the afternoon rolled by with the numerous hills. From the muttering of the captains around him, Peter learned that they would soon arrive at the Ornian ruins he had heard so much about. Excitement brewed within him.

The dirt road snaked through a few more hills and passed over another that was larger than any mound of earth yet. As they passed over the large hill, he saw it.

In the distance, miles away, a city of tall towers, bastions, and countless stone structures lay at the center of a wide body of water that ran in both directions, dividing the two plains of flat land that flanked it. Beyond the ruined city and the river, the western region of Arden lay, vast and wide underneath a brewing storm of gray clouds.

Chapter 14

High Tower

Peter couldn't take his eyes off of the ruins. It was a city on the river. Thousands of stone structures of various shapes seemed to compete for the prize of tallest building. The road taking them closer to the ruins was flanked by vast fields that allowed gusts of wind to send his hair flailing like ribbons. Flowing water echoed in the distance.

As they came closer to the city, its damage was made obvious. Chunks of rubble remained buried in the ground outside the fractured walls of the city, slowly being overtaken by nature and time. Many towers and bastions displayed cracks and holes that allowed sunlight to shine through.

It really is a bunch of ruins. It's beautiful in a way. But it's eerie too. The only sounds he heard were the water of the river ahead of them and the sound of trotting horses around him.

The gatehouse they passed through was about the same size as the archway at the stadium. Once within the walls of the city, the buildings towered over them like skyscrapers. They followed along the dusty streets, void of life and movement. The road they followed took them over a bridge of gray stone. The river passed beneath them, spewing a cool mist into his face as he rode. The bridge ended on an island in the center of the wide river. The buildings on the island encircled a clearing where a few tents stood, and soldiers in an array of armors and clothing hurried about the established camp.

A soldier ran toward the group as they entered the camp. Dirt was smeared along his face and dyed within the fabrics of his old uniform.

"Lord Rulfin!" the soldier greeted as they stopped their horses. The commander of the army and his staff stepped down from their saddles, gathering around the panting soldier who spoke to them frantically.

"What do you think that could be about?" Peter asked Gideon.

He scratched his beard. "Nothing good for the cause."

Suddenly one of the vice-commanders spun around and jogged over to Peter and the captains.

"We require two captains," he said to them.

Gideon asked, "What's the situation?"

"I need one more captain." the vice-commander said, earning a few laughs from the officers.

"Damn."

Peter hesitantly raised his hand. "I could do it."

"You will be deploying tonight, Lord. Are you certain?"

He winced. "Tonight? What's going on?"

"Our garrison at Tulfius Hall was overrun this morning. Sir Hector and his cavalry forces departed the ruins to assist, but they arrived too late. The defenses of the city had been overrun by the horde from Ilvion, and the men there infected. Now our last remaining garrisoned city lies in the path of the same horde. Carvalel. Sir Hector and his men are positioned to ambush the enemy when they fall on the city; however, there remains the threat of a smaller horde approaching the city from either the west or the south."

"Observation posts?" Gideon asked.

"Indeed. Low Tower has been garrisoned west of the city. South, High Tower still requires more men and the presence of an officer."

Captain Gideon grinned and nodded, turning to the boy from Virginia. "Shall we, Lord?"

* * * * * * *

What was I thinking? he thought as he and Gideon rode along the road with twenty men behind. The Ornian ruins grew smaller as they ventured farther into the west. He scanned the distant slopes of darkened grass in every direction, searching for infected. Ahead of them, the last of the sun's light receded over the wall of western clouds, leaving behind a dim blue color in the air around them.

Before long, night descended. Darkness surrounded the troop like the armies of crickets that flanked them as they rode, galloping faster to arrive at the safety of the garrison. Peter guessed an hour had passed since they had departed the ruins.

He looked to the south, across the plains, where the planet Carraas rose and slowly drifted across the starry night sky.

Suddenly, a woman shrieked in the distance, sending a chill down his spine.

A woman! Out here? he thought. Before he could say anything to Gideon or any of the men behind him, the unseen woman shrieked again. The primal scream changed into a strange growl. Another voice growled along with the woman. Another joined and then another until dozens of horrifying shrieks, growls, and gurgles called out into the night sky.

Infected, he realized. *I never imagined they would sound like this.* He looked to Gideon, who nodded in turn.

Their horses slowed as Carraas hovered directly overhead like the sun at midday. When the dark gray silhouette of a fort appeared on a hilltop ahead, some relief washed over Peter like cool water over burned skin. The walled fortress featured four towers, with one standing taller than the others, providing an ideal vantage point.

As they approached the gate, he noticed there was none of the torchlight he had grown so accustomed to. The fortress lingered in complete darkness. The unseen men stationed atop the gatehouse and nearby tower hissed commands. One of the wooden doors creaked inwards and the troop of twenty-two men rode inside. The gate closed behind them with a minor thud and they found themselves surrounded by the darkened stone of the inner walls and towers. From a group of dark figures behind the gate, one man in armor walked over to Peter and the captain.

"These are our reinforcements?" he whispered.

"Aye," Gideon said softly. "Did you expect the Lionheart himself?"

The soldier shrugged in the darkness. "Would have been a welcome addition."

The captain chuckled. "Where is your lieutenant?"

"All about the grounds outside the fort. Ripped apart in the first skirmish."

"Ah. . .you're the first sergeant then? His second-in-command?"

"Aye, Captain."

Gideon nodded toward Peter. "His Lordship and I will require a report on the current situation of the fort and the men, our arms and ammunitions, and food and water."

“Aye, Captain. I'll summon my sergeants.” His shrouded face turned toward Peter and he bowed. “My Lord. Forgive me; we were not told that someone of your nobility would be taking command.”

“I'm not taking command,” Peter replied.

“Your pardon, Lord?”

Gideon chuckled as he added, “The Lord Lionheart is not here to command but to observe.”

The first sergeant stared up at them, remaining silent for a few moments. “Lord. . .Lionheart? Forgive my lack of manners, Lord.”

“Er. . .it's okay.”

Gideon's turned toward him. “I think we may dispense with the pleasantries, Lord. First sergeant, rally the other sergeants. We must discuss a number of things before this night is through.”

“Aye, Captain. If I might say, it is fortunate that your Lordship has arrived. The morale has waned with each passing day since the lieutenant’s death. The men will awaken with new vigor in the morning.”

* * * * * * *

His growling stomach woke him as the morning light shined over the walls of the encampment. Yawning, he rose from his cot and walked out of the stone hut to the balcony that overlooked the muddy courtyard below.

Over the top of the gatehouse, where a pair of soldiers slept back to back, the road they had taken last night snaked between the hills of the lowlands and disappeared on the horizon, meeting a wall of pink and orange clouds that veiled the morning sun.

It's quiet, he noted, enjoying the silence until his stomach growled again. He looked to his right as an orange-bearded soldier walked over to him.

“Morning, Lord.” His orange-and-gray head of hair inclined.

The first sergeant from last night, he noted upon recognizing the voice. The man stood next to him, leaning against the wooden railing.

"How did you sleep, Lord? Apologies for the poor accommodations."

"It was fine. Is there any food around here?"

"Aye, Lord. Salted beef and aged bread. We may dep. . .Gah!" he exclaimed as he looked to the gatehouse. He sighed as he bent down and picked up a few pebbles, throwing them toward the two sleeping guards and missing every pitch. He dropped his fist onto the railing, turning to Peter. "My apologies, Lord. I'll see they are dealt with." He walked away, nodding to Captain Gideon in passing.

"Morning, Lord," Gideon said, taking the first sergeant's place.

"Morning. Oh! Thanks," Peter said, taking a strip of dried meat from the man. He took a bite, struggling to chew what reminded him of beef jerky that had been left out to dry for a week.

After both men ate their fill of the beef, the captain ripped in half a small wheel of bread. Peter ate the flavorless wheat, watching as a new sergeant kicked the two sleeping guards. The sentries were forced to hold their muskets over their heads as they performed a variety of exercises.

From behind Peter and the captain, a soldier rushed over to them, speaking quickly to Gideon.

"No. . ." the captain breathed as he raced up the adjacent stairs. Peter followed to the top of the tallest tower in the fortress. The view provided a complete panoramic view of the lowlands, allowing a sentry to monitor all avenues of approach.

The current sentry looked gravely at Peter and the captain, his finger pointing through the gap in the stone toward a few moving specks amidst the green in the distance.

That's south, Peter knew.

Captain Gideon turned to the soldier that had alerted him. “Send two riders. One to Lord Rulfin in the ruins and another to the garrison at Carvalel. Tell them High Tower is under attack.”

Chapter 15

Defender

"I say over a hundred infected. Maybe two," Captain Gideon observed.

"Aye," the first sergeant agreed.

They stood on the highest tower, watching as a few crowds of people ran over a far-off hill and disappeared behind another.

"What are your orders, Captain?"

The captain's narrow gaze remained fixed on the hills. "Why? In all the vastness of the lowlands, they arrive here. Do they smell us? Or is it instinct that they discovered us?"

". . .Orders, Captain?"

"Aside from the main gate, is there another entrance?" The sergeant shook his head. "Bar the gate then. Three riflemen in each tower. One squad of men will remain on standby as reserves. The rest go to the walls with muskets, pikes, and spears. Throw stones if you have to."

"Aye, Captain." The red-bearded sergeant raced off to relay the orders.

"How long till they get here?" Peter asked.

"Difficult to say, Lord. But soon for certain."

From the balcony of the stone hut overlooking the courtyard, Peter and the captain watched as the men strapped on their armor, slung muskets over their shoulders, and fastened their sabers to their belts. A sergeant barked orders at a squad of men struggling to push a carriage through the mud.

I need to do something to help. Anything, he thought, and he jumped over the railing, landing in the mud of the courtyard twenty feet below.

"I think I can get this, guys." He inserted himself between the five soldiers pushing the cart. They all took a step back and the cart rolled forward with ease as he pushed it up against the pair of wooden doors. He assisted in moving a few barrels onto the walls and into the towers, jumping onto the stone foundations from the ground, carrying two wooden containers at a time. The soldiers often watched him with wonder and applause would echo within the fortress after he jumped or lifted something heavy.

After the battlements had been prepped, everyone took their positions. Peter stood with the captain on the balcony, looking beyond the top of the gatehouse ahead. A few people appeared, sprinting toward the fortress along the road. He swallowed dryly as group after group followed the road toward them. Snarls began to fill the air.

Oh God. This is it. It's all been leading to this, ever since the outbreak at Emerald Island. But there are so many. There's definitely over a hundred.

Like a mob, the infected swarmed toward them in disarray, smashing against the gate and outside wall. The growls and groans piqued his curiosity and sent a chill down his spine. Musket shots began to blast one after another as the men on the walls and towers aimed their rifles at the small army outside.

Peter grimaced as he spectated. *I feel so useless.*

Atop the wall to the left of the gatehouse, a soldier wound up his arm, ready to throw a spear.

He fell onto the stone and slid off the other side as if pulled by something.

To Peter's horror, an infected climbed onto the wall in the man's place, another following. Captain Gideon yelled and pointed toward the section of the wall that had been breached. The men nearby turned their attention toward the two infected.

How did they climb? he wondered. His stomach knotted and his legs grew restless as he watched two soldiers draw their swords and begin hacking at the monsters atop the stone. More plague victims climbed onto the same section of the wall, darting straight for the men nearby and finally overwhelming the two swordsmen. Horrifying screams echoed from the wall as the two soldiers were torn apart by the pack of vile monsters.

Beside him, Captain Gideon drew his saber and made his way to the courtyard where the squad in reserve awaited, rolling their shoulders and swinging their swords with anticipation. The squad followed Gideon across the courtyard and up the stone stairs leading to the top of the wall.

As the captain cut through his first infected, a few snarls off to Peter's right made his ear twitch. He turned to the southern wall, where a head slowly rose from its far side. The darkened face of the infected stared at him and growled as it climbed up. He quickly looked around in search of who to warn or who could help.

There's no one else. Only me. He started toward the southern wall, swallowing dryly as he wiped his sweating palms against the leather of his armor. The infected finally stood up on the stone. Its head twitched violently from side to side as it snarled.

Releasing a primal growl of his own, Peter threw himself into the air from the balcony, colliding with the body of the plague victim. They both plummeted to the ground on the other side of the wall.

He groaned as he stood and looked down at the wheezing, twitching body. A pair of solid black eyes glared at him in a face of rotting skin the shade of curdled milk. The open mouth revealed fangs rather than teeth; dried blood painted its chin and neck. The flesh along the fingers of the infected had rotted away, leaving pointed bones like an eagles talons.

This used to be a person. It really is a monster.

He spun around as more snarls and groans caught his attention. A pile of moving bodies extended from the ground up to the top of the wall. The infected wrestled and writhed over one another like a ball of snakes. A few toward the base of the fleshy mound turned toward him. Their heads thrashed wildly as they sprinted at him.

He dashed to the left and halted, dodging the first with ease. The second came at him with its grotesque claws ready to tear flesh. The image of the assassin at Lunsera came to mind and he instinctively thrust his boot firmly into its chest, sending it flying backward and flailing in the air. The first infected veered for him again and a few more from the pile darted for him. On his toes, he dashed between them like dribbling a soccer ball between cones during his practices in high school. With his speed, they couldn't touch him.

He veered away and put some distance between himself and the wall. Feeling more confident, he yelled, "Hey!" The pile of wrestling bodies fell apart, toppling to the ground. Bodies rose one after another, sprinting toward him over the distance he had created.

The southern wall is safe. For now anyway.

He dashed toward the road, turning around the corner of the wall. An army of infected stood at the base of the fortress, pushing one another against the stone of the eastern wall and the wooden doors of the gatehouse.

There has to be more than two hundred! he realized as he ran, assessing the siege at hand. He sprinted behind the last line of plague victims. "Over here!" he called out, gaining the attention of a few small groups at a time. *This should help everyone out!* He ran away from the walls, chased by scores of the monsters. The army that had attacked the fortress began to break apart as more and more chased after the boy from Virginia.

It's working! Along the battlements, the men killed the last of the infected that had climbed up. As Peter ran, he could hear their cheers as they fought with renewed vigor. The muskets fired off rapidly as never before. Behind Peter, the enormous group of infected slimmed in number as they were shot to the ground.

Finally, once the size of the mob had been reduced to about forty, he turned back toward the fortress and leapt into the air. The wall and the cheering men passed underneath him and he collided clumsily with the stone of the high tower, falling into the mud of the courtyard with a thud. As he remained on his back, panting and unharmed from the fall, he found himself smiling and laughing even as the mud soaked the back of his head.

He sighed with pleasure as the soldiers finished off the last of the infected.

* * * * * * *

The warm light from the bonfire illuminated the inner walls of the fort. The smell of freshly cooked meat filled his nose as his ears rang with the laughter and songs of the soldiers who celebrated victory. From the balcony above the celebration, Peter looked over the southern wall. A light glimmered in the distance where the corpses of the infected were burning.

Captain Gideon slowly ascended the stairs with two wooden mugs in hand. Peter graciously accepted one of the tankards. The dark liquid inside smelled strange yet enticing, and bore the obvious scent of alcohol.

"The lieutenant had a barrel of ale stashed away," Captain Gideon said, gently tapping his tankard against Peter's before taking a sip. Peter hesitatingly took his first gulp. It was strong and bitter, with a flat consistency that left much to be desired, but after considering the events of the day he took another gulp that tasted better than the first.

"Today was..."

“Yes, Lord?”

“Easy. Easier than I thought it would be. For so long I’ve been so worried about seeing the plague. I've been haunted by it. But now. . .” He chuckled and took another drink. “. . .I'm not so worried anymore.”

“You ran circles around them,” Gideon laughed. “Never in my life have I seen someone move so quickly. I often heard stories of the first Lionheart and how fast he ran, but to see your power, Lord. . .I am thankful, as is my wife. I'll write to her in the morning, I think.”

Write, Peter thought.

“Maybe. . .maybe I should write to Helen and Aurora. Should I?”

“It would be a notion well received, coming from the Lionheart himself.”

“Separate letters. I think a letter to Aurora will be easy enough. But Helen. . .maybe I should apologize, or just not send one at all.” He took another drink. “I don't know.”

“If you don't mind me asking, Lord, how did you slight the Lady of the Rock?”

The confession rolled off his tongue. “I kissed her.”

Gideon spat his drink out into the air in front of them, dowsing a few men below.

“Oi!” two soldiers called out.

Gideon waved at them. “Drink!” he ordered, before turning to Peter and whispering, “You kissed *the* Helen Moonwey?” He paused before asking excitedly, “Did she kiss you back, Lad?”

Peter shook his head. “Doesn't really matter, because she slapped me afterward. It was so stupid of me. I completely misread the situation.”

The captain grimaced. “Then a sincere apology may accomplish what you want. To make amends.”

Suddenly a few men on the far side of the bonfire screamed and fell onto the ground in surprise as an unfamiliar person walked up to them from a dark section of the wall.

"Infected!" one of the men exclaimed.

The captain dropped his tankard and drew his sword, bolting down the stairs as Peter jumped over the railing and landed near the group of alerted soldiers. They all drew their weapons and pointed them at the walking corpse of an old woman. Her oily eyes gleamed hauntingly. She stopped and stared at the men.

Her black eyes then rested on Peter, and her arm raised, pointing toward him with a twitching claw. Her head twitched violently from side to side, and a rumble of two voices emerged from her throat: "Leave."

A chill rushed down his spine. The men all glanced over at Peter and the infected spoke again. "Leave!" she growled, before sprinting through the fire toward him.

The glowing lumber parted as the old woman thrashed through the flames and their fuel. A gleam of silver flashed in front of Peter as the old woman came close, and her head tumbled to the ground. Blood and some oily substance spewed from the severed neck.

The captain cleaned off his saber as he kicked the body into the mud.

The eyes of all the men in the fortress found Peter as he stared at the severed head of the infected woman.

* * * * * * *

It was afternoon when a squad of riders approached the front gate, riding past the mounds of bodies that remained from a second attack that morning. Peter's hour-long episode of introspection had finally ended and he rose from his cot. He was constantly thinking about the talking infected woman from the night, even when he had fought during the second skirmish of the dawn.

He walked onto the balcony as the riders entered the gate. As the first sergeant walked over to greet the men, the golden-armored rider at the head of the group spoke.

“We are here for the Lionheart,” he stated. The sergeant pointed toward the balcony where Peter stood, and the golden rider removed his helmet, revealing long hair as blond as his own. “Lord. We are here on Lord Rulfin's direct commands. He requests that you depart with us for Carvalel immediately.”

Captain Gideon stepped next to Peter. “What news do you bring?”

“Carvalel was attacked this morning before the sun arose.”

“By the horde?”

“Indeed, half of it. The defenses held and the garrison survived.” Cheers erupted from the men throughout the fortress. “What's more, that was not the entire horde, merely half; the remainder will fall upon the city tonight. Also, the garrison at Low Tower was overrun in the night and the infected now travel directly for the city as well. Carvalel will be attacked on several fronts. The Lionheart is needed there.”

Peter turned to Gideon, who simply smiled and stretched out his hand. “It's been an honor, Lord. I'll tell my children, and someday my grandchildren, about my adventures with the Lionheart.”

Peter gently shook his hand. “I hope I see you again, Gideon. Thanks for everything.”

“Likewise, Lord. And don't forget the letters.” He winked. Reluctantly, Peter released his hand and made his way to the courtyard, where a horse was quickly prepped for him. Before climbing into the saddle, he looked up to the blond man in silver armor.

“I'm Peter, by the way. And you?”

A brilliant smile formed on the man's face. “Sir Titus Turner, my Lord.”

“You're a knight?”

“Correct, Lord. I am a knight like Sir Hector.”

After considering the man's name he asked, "Turner?"

"Indeed. The Turner family of Barrington. You may already be acquainted with my cousin Ian Turner, the current Lord of Barrington."

Chapter 15

The Lion's Legacy

Cold sprinkles of rain pelted his face as they rode, and chill bumps formed along the back of his neck. Ahead of them, a vast blanket of gray clouds loomed over the fields of grass. *It's all so green,* Peter thought.

It seemed like it had been hours since they had departed High Tower, yet no man had uttered a single word. He looked over at the knight riding beside him. The man's sharp gaze remained focused ahead, his long strands of blond hair flowing behind him like golden streamers in the wind.

The Lord of Barrington has a cousin and he's a knight. . .like William.

A nearby willow tree overlooked a pond where they stopped to water their horses. As Peter's black mare took heavy gulps, he looked over to the knight again and met a pair of focused gray eyes.

"Is there something you wish to inquire, Lord?" Sir Titus asked.

“I don’t know that much about knights, but I’m curious, what’s the difference between a knight like you and one from Bastille?”

“The Order of Bastille was the first guild of knights in Arden, that is true. However, the order has a long history of isolation. Few times in Arden's early history did they set forth to do the good deeds they were meant to. Because of that, many guilds began to form at the behest of noble families. While there are several guilds, there are two that stand above the rest: the Eastern Swords of Barrington and the Knight’s Guild of New London. I was knighted by my own uncle when I was but thirteen, the youngest knight in the history of the Eastern Swords guild.”

“Your uncle? The Duke?”

The knight grinned faintly. “Indeed. My uncle George Turner, the Duke of Barrington. The one to reclaim and the one to fail. It was his actions that stripped our family of much we were meant to have. . .such as my father.”

“What do you mean? What happened?”

Sir Titus' face hardened. “To my father? He was slain during the siege of Arden City. By your kinsman.”

“What?”

“The first Lionheart killed my father. Your uncle befriended the Moonwey’s and made war with the Turner’s.” The knight paused, staring solemnly at the boy from Virginia. “What of you, my Lord? It is said that you have fallen into favor with the sisters of Lunar Rock as your uncle did with their father. Will you do the same with our family? Has the time come that we make amends? After all, we bear kindred blood, do we not?”

“I'm really sorry about everything, Titus. I wish it never had to come down to that, and I’m sure Jack felt the same.” He paused and stroked the large neck of the horse. “I met your cousin in Arden City. He seemed really polite. I heard that the assassin group is really after him.”

“And for good cause. My cousin has worked tirelessly to repair the damage his father wrought. We are not the villains many paint us as, I assure you. Soon. . .soon I hope our former glory may be restored and the title of Duke reclaimed."

"What's so important about the title?"

Sir Titus stared off into the distance and smiled. "It is an exclusive title. The Duke is the Lord of Barrington, the count of Von Isla, and the thirteenth member of the Arden City council."

"Wow. . .I didn't really understand why it was so important until now. The thirteenth member of the city council. . ."

"Indeed." The Knight groaned as he climbed into his saddle. The other men did the same. "When you are prepared, Lord, we shall depart."

* * * * * * *

He grew increasingly uncomfortable with each passing hour as they rode. Rain showers fell from the dark clouds above, creating pools of mud along the road. Completely soaked, Peter shivered constantly, and the wind that rolled over the pockets of flat land only heightened his misery. His stomach growled, yearning for nourishment.

Why did I ever agree to this? he kept scolding himself. At times during the ride, he would think about Helen and Aurora, clean, dry, and warm in their beds as the sun was beginning to set.

His ears twitched when he heard a few soft thuds in the distance, like a hammer beating against wood far away.

"Cannons!" one of the men said, and the entire party slowed. "Carvalel must be under attack!"

Sir Titus kicked his heels and his steed rushed forward, forcing Peter and the other five riders to hasten after. The road ascended onto a wide hill, and as they came to its peak, they halted their horses and gazed into the distance.

A walled city stood alone in the sea of fields. The wooden towers spaced out along the wall nearly touched the low-hanging clouds of mist. A few sudden flashes of light occasionally flashed from the towers and along the wall. His ears twitched as he heard the dull percussive bangs a few seconds after each flash.

Just outside the two wooden doors of the gatehouse, an army of people moved over one another to get inside.

Infected! he realized. A horrid shiver descended along his spine. *There have to be thousands! There's no way. . .I don't know if there's anything I can do. . .*

The other riders all looked to the knight. One asked, "What are your orders, Sir?"

Sir Titus grimaced and his eyes wavered as he debated with himself. "There is not much we can do. We must wait until the battle has ended. . .or turned to massacre."

"But..." Peter protested. His eyes remained on the army of monsters outside the gate, beating and scratching against the wood.

What about the men inside? We have to do something! "We can't just stand here getting soaked in the rain and not do anything," he told them.

The knight looked at him and wiped away the soaked strands of hair stuck to his face. "There is little I or my men can do. But you, Lord, What will you do?"

Sir Titus and the five men watched him with the same expectant gaze. He growled as he wrestled with fear and doubt that fought to overtake him. The stares of the men around him weighed heavily.

He stepped down from his horse and swallowed dryly as his heart began to race. The muscles of his legs grew tense and the breaths he took deepened as he paced back and forth in the middle of the road.

Oh, God. I don't know if I can do this. I don't know if I can! The battle at the fort was one thing but this is another! What was I thinking coming here? Why am I even doing all this?

Amidst the frustration, a pair of alluring hazel eyes came to mind like a sudden vision. *Those eyes. Beautiful. But. Why? Why am I doing this? I. . .* The visage of a beautiful young woman appeared around the same pair of eyes that haunted him. He recognized her face and he breathed her name, "...Aurora."

He turned toward the fray in the distance and began walking toward it. His heart raced and his palms grew thick with sweat. The cannons on the walls and in the towers continued to ignite in flashes of light, causing a cacophony of pops to fill the air.

His walk became a jog as rain pelted him in the eyes. The pace and length of his strides increased as he began to run. He eyed the massive crowd of infected at the gate.

Suddenly, the muddy road beneath him betrayed his footing and his momentum carried him forward. He fell and skidded across a field of puddles and grass.

His anger grew and he growled loudly as he stood. Widening his stance, he readied himself and dashed forward. His momentum grew with each step, carrying him across the fields in the rain with speed no animal could match. The city grew larger as he sprinted toward it and he could finally hear the sickening sounds of the infected. The mass of mud- and blood-covered bodies appeared to him in a rush.

Like a bowling ball through pins, he scattered the crowd outside the gate. His momentum carried him down the center of the army, throwing infected bodies aside and into the air. Chalky debris fell behind him as he skidded across the ground and into a few nearby buildings of wood and thatch. He came to a stop on the dusty wooden floor of a house.

He groaned as he stood and dusted himself off. The gaping hole through which he had come acted as a window. Beyond, a path of destruction was revealed. A few houses had fallen into heaps of shattered wood and rubble. A chunk of the city wall was missing, its remnants scattered on the muddy ground.

He began to fear as that he had done more harm than good.

The overwhelming ululation of battle cries, musket shots, and growls outside pulled him from the house. As he stepped onto the street, he saw that the doors of the gatehouse had been opened. A raging battle was underway between the fighting men and the horde.

Now what? he considered. *Do I do something like that again?* As he wrestled with tactics, he noticed a group of people sprinting toward the battle from an adjacent street. *Infected! There have to be about fifty,* he realized, turning his attention toward the fighting men. *They're going to get hit from behind if I don't do something!*

His decision made, he took a deep breath and widened his stance. Pushing off against the mud-soaked earth, he dashed along the street, behind the skirmish at the gate, and down the narrow alley toward the oncoming mob. He raised his arms in front of him and flexed as he collided with the first few bodies. They cracked and crumbled as he plowed through, demolishing the pack.

He stopped and looked back at the narrow street, now littered with broken bodies.

I think I'm getting the hang of this. But how can I help with the army outside?

He jumped onto a nearby building. His boots began to slide against the soaked shingles. Grasping the elevated ridge of the rooftop, he assessed the conflict below.

Beneath the gatehouse, two armies clashed. At the center of the fray, a man in black attire hacked away at any plagued corpse nearby, forming a small clearing around himself with each darkened stroke of his rapier. Alvar sliced through groups of infected like a scythe through tall grass. Little by little, the Blackheart Lord made headway beyond the gate, the fighting men following behind attempting to match his fury.

We can win this! Peter thought as he watched Alvar lead the counterattack into the dark mass of walking corpses. *But there are still so many.*

He scanned the conflict and his eyes settled to the left of the horde where the fighting was thickest.

He jumped from the rooftop, soaring over a series of buildings before landing on the wall of the city. Peering down, he saw hundreds of oily eyes staring up at him as growls erupted from their grotesque mouths. They pressed against the stone, scratching at the wall with claws and fingers that soon lost their nails against the roughness.

Grimacing, he turned to an unmanned cannon. Grasping the metal, he threw it into the dark crowd like a rock into a puddle of mud. Dozens of infected bodies were crushed as the cannon skidded across the ground beyond the wall. He threw another into the horde, and another, until he was left without any more ammunition.

He again assessed the skirmish. The Alvar-led counterattack had completely divided the enemy. Fighting soldiers lashed out on both sides, cutting and roaring with a desperate desire to survive. Nearby, a young man about Peter's age fought three of the monsters. His sword lodged into one's head, but the other two descended upon him, thrusting their claws into his chest and back. His scream of agony carried across the battlefield as their teeth pierced the skin of his neck, taking his life.

"NO!" Peter bellowed as he witnessed the carnage. Fury and agony coursed through him. He leapt toward the two infected that gnawed on the boy's body. With tears in his eyes, Peter fell on the duo and ripped their arms and heads from their bodies with ease. He twisted and lashed out at any snarling body nearby, attacking with wrathful ferocity. The boy's murder had ignited sudden bloodlust within him, and for the remainder of the battle he punched, kicked, and ripped at the monsters who had wrought so much pain.

As the last of the infected were cut down by the fighting men nearby, Peter walked to the boy's mutilated corpse. A pair of lifeless green eyes gazed up at him in a bloody face vacant of expression. He fell to his knees as he pondered who the boy was, where he was from, what his mother was doing at that moment...how she would react when she learned of her son's fate.

A bulge ached in his throat as sadness swelled within him and tears rolled down his cheeks.

* * * * * * *

For two hours he sat alone, listening to the last of the rain pelt against the wooden rooftop, his gaze fixed on the crimson-stained tarp in front of him. He remained still as the corpse underneath the soaked fabric.

Why? he was asking himself. *Why him? Why did this all happen? What am I doing here?*

Adjacent to the canopy under which he sat, two roads converged to form an intersection. Soldiers busied themselves along the routes, carrying weapons or equipment and moving the bodies of the slain.

Muddy rocks crunched as someone approached him and he lifted his gaze.

Alvar's black hair was a mess, tangled with blood. The dried crimson and black substance of the infected was smeared all along his face and clothing. His brown eyes had dark circles beneath them.

The boy from Virginia nodded to the boy beneath the bloody tarp. "Do you know who he was?"

Alvar shook his head. Sympathetically, Alvar extended his hand, saying softly, "Come, my friend."

Peter rose, looking to the ridges along the tarp where the boy's face remained covered. Alvar gently placed his hand on Peter's shoulder and they walked along the road together.

"A somber victory, hmm?"

"Yeah."

"Many good men. Many great men. They died honorably and have earned my appreciation for it. I will not forget them. The horde is gone and our victory all but assured due to their sacrifice." He looked at Peter. "We must not let it go in vain, hmm? Our fallen comrades are most glorified when we are most victorious."

I don't care about glory. I feel awful and dirty. I don't know if I can do this again.

He didn't reply to Alvar but looked around at the bodies of infected and non-infected that still lay around the city.

There is too much pain here to be content with glory.

As they rounded a corner, the sound of a hammer banging against stone began to echo between the buildings as repeated strokes were made. Peter looked over to a ruined building where a man stared at the road with a vacant gaze as he blindly swung a small hammer against pieces of stone.

"Fyraen. . .Fyraen. . ." the older man mumbled.

"Ignore him," Alvar said. "He was found when the army first arrived at the city. Never uttering more than Fyraen or Builds." The old man's vacant stare met Peter's for a moment as they passed him.

"Fyraen...Fyraen. . .Builds...Bui—" He inhaled sharply and dropped the hammer. His old hand pointed toward the two men. Peter and Alvar exchanged a wary glance before continuing along the road. "J-J-J. . .Jack!" the older man called out. "N-N-N...Norfolk!"

Peter stopped and spun around as the older man stumbled toward him.

"What did you say?"

"My friend. . ." he cried. "Jack Loneheart. You're P-P-P-P...Peter!"

"Who are you?"

"Orrick." His arms wrapped around Peter and he cried. "You should...n-n-n. . .not be here. . ." The man's fingers clawed at Peter's torn armor and clothes. "She will use you!" he exclaimed, pain in his voice.

Alvar stepped forward and pushed the old man away, waving his other arm at a squad of nearby soldiers. The men took hold of the man and began to pull him away.

The old man continued to cry profusely as he was dragged, exclaiming, "There were two! There were two, not one! The woman and the one with chains. . .chains like snakes! Chains like snakes! Chains like snakes!" His screams churned Peter's stomach, reminding him of the boy that had been killed earlier that day.

"What was that? Who was that?"

"Pay no attention," Alvar said as he placed his hand on Peter's shoulder. "Come. Lord Rulfin expects us."

But as they walked along the road, Peter continued to look behind him toward where the man had been taken away.

Chapter 16

Northward

He awoke in his own tent and watched as particles of dust hovered about in the beam of morning light that protruded through his tent doorway. He sat up and stretched his aching muscles. Bruises occupied much of the skin along his chest and shoulders beneath his light tunic. He took a deep, slightly painful breath as he struggled to find any happiness in the start of the new day.

This must be what it's like to be an adult.

A soldier poked his head into the tent. "Apologies, Lord." He extended his hand with a letter in his grasp. "Word from Arden City."

The man disappeared as Peter took the rectangular piece of parchment, turning it over to see a silver crescent moon embroidered on the center of the paper. He tore it open and unfolded the letter inside.

Dear Peter,

Helen and I have prayed for your safety every day since you departed.

She remains preoccupied with the parliament—such drudgery I dare not speak of it. To make matters worse, the assassin you subdued from home was found murdered in his prison cell. Despite interrogation, he maintained that he knew nothing.

I remain bored beyond measure, besting every rider in the city that dares challenge me. I long for a proper contest, can you not say the same? Perhaps that is why I write you. Your presence is sorely missed. I frequently wonder what you have discovered about yourself. Perhaps some new abilities or even a sense of humor, I can only hope. Though I am certain that your skills are proving useful, we have received little news of the front. I imagine much will happen before this letter reaches you and I anticipate your reply.

Your friend,

Aurora

P.S: I am certain you have not forgotten my gift!

He read the letter over three more times, and each time his smile widened and he became full with welcome joy. Folding the letter back up, he dressed and looked around his tent for paper to no avail.

Departing his own tent, he walked down the aisle of officers' tents to a courtyard outside the villa where the army's leadership resided. He ascended the steps into the villa. There were two desks flanking the entrance into the manor ahead. Behind the stacks of paper, two clerks focused on their work.

"Can I borrow some paper please?" he asked one of the young men.

"Of course, Lord!" The clerk frantically pawed at a few stacks of paper, finally handing few sheets over.

"Oh!" Peter realized. "And a pencil too, please."

The young man stared, perplexed. "Lord? Ah!" He pointed across the entry patio to a corner of crates varying in size. "Standard supplies in abundance for you, Lord. Just received it all this morning."

"Thanks." He had started across the patio when he saw a group of men in handsome uniforms of black with gold embroidering walking toward him from the villa. The tall man in the center saw Peter and smiled.

"Lord Lionheart," said Lord Rulfin, the commander of the army.

"Good morning," Peter replied, looking up at the man, who stood a head taller than he.

"The storm has finally abated, giving us a beautiful morning sky. Would you care to walk with me, my Lord?"

I guess the letter can wait a little while. He nodded.

"Excellent." The commander said before turning to the men that followed him. "Leave us."

The officers departed and the two began to walk toward the gardens surrounding the villa.

"We spoke briefly during the night, but I must know: how do you fare, my Lord?"

Peter hesitated before answering, "I'm fine; can't say the same for a boy I didn't know."

"Pardon?"

"Nothing."

Lord Rulfin smiled and nodded. "I understand. Lord Blackheart did broach that the battle had a particularly ill effect upon you. My apologies. If there is any way I can ensure your satisfaction, please inform me or my staff. They or I will see to it personally."

"Thank you, Sir. I...actually. There was a man yesterday. He was saying my uncle's name and something about chain snakes."

The commander winced and hesitated. "My apologies, but that man passed in the night."

"He died?"

"Indeed, my Lord. Took his own life, I regret to say. Did you not know who he was?"

Peter shook his head.

"A decade ago, Orrick was a captain from Lunsera during the great war. He relayed messages between your uncle, as he fought in the east, and the late Lord Edward Moonwey."

"Messages?" Peter asked. The path they took was flanked by a few apple trees. The commander reached up and picked two pink fruits, handing one to the boy from Virginia.

"I do not know the nature of the messages, nor could any other than your uncle and Lord Edward. But Captain Orrick was especially fond of your predecessor and was notably loyal to him. It was said that shortly before the siege of Arden City, your uncle sent the captain on a secret mission and he disappeared. Many assumed Orrick had simply fled. We did not know of his fate, not until this morning, when I was informed of the suicide and I recognized the man as a former comrade."

The apple crunched as Peter bit into it. "I wonder what the mission was about. Maybe it has to do with Jack's disappearance?"

"Perhaps." Rulfin took a bite out of his own apple. "Though there was a phrase, or rather a name, that was uttered between the three men that did become public knowledge."

"What?"

"Something known as the *children of the serpent*. Do you know of it?" Peter shook his head and the older man continued. "The few of us that heard it assumed it was merely a cult. We investigated following the war, but nothing more than the same words were discovered."

"The children of the serpent," he muttered. "A cult?"

Rulfin chuckled. "Merely a possibility, presented by our own imaginations through our lack of evidence. Speculation, nothing more. When it was learned that you had first arrived with Lady Helen, those few of us within the city council were hopeful that perhaps you would possess some knowledge of the words."

"Sorry to disappoint."

"No apology is necessary, my Lord. Eventually, all things will come to light."

* * * * * * *

He spent the afternoon relaxing in his tent, eating warm food that bore flavors the meals from the days prior had lacked. He pondered his conversation with Lord Rulfin and what he had learned about Captain Orrick. When he wasn't distracted by unwelcome thoughts, he focused on his letter to Aurora. In his reply, he told her of his actions during the two battles at High Tower, and of how he arrived amidst the siege of Carvalel. Though, he hesitated at first, he wrote about the boy who had died and how it had made him feel. Following the sorrowful words, he wrote of his conversation with Lord Rulfin about Captain Orrick and his uncle Jack. Concluding the letter, he relayed that he felt as if he were truly growing, that he missed hearing her laugh, and that he wouldn't forget her gift no matter what.

A proud smile formed on his face as the ink dried, sealing his unspoken words within the fabric of the parchment. Folding the letter, he enclosed it within an envelope and gave it to one of the clerks at the villa courtyard.

"I'll see that it departs immediately for the capital, Lord," the young man said. Peter stood in silence, pondering the future as the clerk rushed off.

A familiar laugh echoed from behind him, and he turned to see a wide smile behind a thick black beard set below a pair of sapphire-blue eyes.

"Gideon!"

"My Lord Lionheart!" The two embraced one another like long-lost friends. Peter took care to be gentle as he hugged the muscular man, who nonetheless felt like a pillow in his embrace. Though he had only known the captain for a few days, after the two battles they had fought together, Peter felt as if he had known him for years.

They both stepped back and looked each other over. Peter said delightedly, "I'm glad to see you're alright, Gideon."

"Aye. As am I, my Lord." He nodded toward the nearby desk full of papers and weights to hold them down. "Sending a letter, are you?"

"Sure am. I got one this morning from Aurora."

"Replying to your future wife?" He laughed.

Peter smiled and reassured, "No. Just telling my friend what's been going on." A moment of silence passed between them. "So. What are you doing here?"

"Well, with the horde destroyed, it's time to reclaim the west, town by town. Small groups already started riding out to purge."

"So soon?"

"Aye. The northern territories await. The south, however, remains a problem. Another horde is traveling north from New London."

"Another horde?"

"The final. Smaller than those that attacked Carvalel from what I've gathered. Lord Rulfin awaits reinforcements. When they arrive he will personally act as the field commander and destroy the last remaining horde."

"Sounds like a plan. So you're going north?"

"Aye. Northward. Have a few men from High Tower under my command willing to go. Scouting for further additions."

"Further additions, hmm?" a familiar voice purred from the villa. Alvar walked toward them, cleaned and groomed, wearing his typical brimmed hat.

"Lord Blackheart." Gideon inclined his head.

"Captain Gideon of Barrington. Is the offer exclusive to join your troop?"

"Not at all, my Lord. Your presence would be most welcome. But as a vice-commander, would you not be needed at Lord Rulfin's side?"

“There is another vice-commander for that, and yet another to remain in Carvalel. I believe Lord Carlon of Stonewell will take command here after Rulfin's departure. As of a few moments ago, I was given leave to take command of the purging in the northern territories. I must depart on some occasion; why not with yourself?”

“Very well, Lord.”

The two men looked at Peter expectantly.

“What? You want me to go too?”

The captain and Blackheart Lord both grinned and shrugged.

I think it's time to leave this city behind. “So where are we going to exactly?”

“Ilvion itself! The eldest city in the world,” Gideon said.

Alvar chimed in, “Of course, we may take a few detours along the way. To give you the opportunity to bear witness to the western region’s vast beauty.”

Peter couldn’t tell whether Alvar was being sarcastic or not. “Beats staying here,” he told them. “When do we leave?”

Gideon looked to Alvar. “If we depart within the hour, we may arrive at Gareton before nightfall.”

The Blackheart Lord nodded. “Agreed. A fine start. I say we gather in the city square within such time, hmm? Horses readied and watered, with sufficient supplies.”

“Agreed,” Peter and the captain both said. Alvar passed between them and walked along the captain's tents, departing through the front gate of the villa.

Gideon muttered, “Lord Alvar Blackheart, the Lionheart, and the greatest of all, Captain Gideon Wells of the eastern spire. A triumvirate to be remembered.”

“Sure.” Peter rolled his eyes. “Although I can't help but feel pretty excited all of a sudden, especially when you say it like that. . .except the part about you being the greatest of all.”

“As you say,” he chuckled, before turning serious and edging nearer to Peter. “There is something that has remained in my thoughts, Lord. The one that spoke.”

Peter paused, recalling the old infected woman who had told him to leave. “What about it?”

“Has it happened again? And have you told anyone?”

“No.”

The captain scratched his beard. “I see. Merely my own concern, Lord, nothing more.”

* * * * * * *

The large nose of the black horse kept poking at his shoulder.

“What is it?” he asked the animal, gently stroking its large neck as its hair shined in the sunlight. He stood with the animal and one of Lord Rulfin’s staff members near a dried-up courtyard fountain at the heart of Carvalel.

“Finished, Lord,” the boy told him from the saddlebags. “Two wineskins with water and a weeks’ worth of bread, salted beef, and apples.”

“Thanks.” He watched as the young staff member walked away, passing Captain Gideon leading his brown steed on foot between a few soldiers carrying muskets and pikes. Behind the captain were four men leading their own horses.

“Just waiting for Alvar,” Peter told them as they joined him.

The sound of trotting horses caught his attention and he turned toward an alleyway leading to the city center. Alvar rode atop a pale white horse, followed by six hulking figures in full plate armor as dark as the Blackheart Lord’s clothing. Their faces remained concealed by their helms. Great swords and heavy axes clanked against their metal plates with each gallop of their midnight steeds.

"Shall we venture forth?" Alvar called out across the courtyard.

"You have your own bodyguards?" Peter asked when Alvar finally halted beside them.

"I am the commander of the purging forces in the northern territories. It is only proper that I have my own guard."

Peter shrugged and climbed into the saddle. He looked at all of the men on horseback. *Thirteen men. The hordes are gone, but the plague remains.*

"Let's finish it."

Chapter 17

Western Conquest

The sun set behind a wall of orange and pink clouds in the western sky. To the north, a storm system brewed, creeping slowly toward the ghost town ahead. Gareton's small gate was battered and broken. One of the doors yet remained intact; the other lay on the ground next to the road that led into the small town.

Alvar led the charge through the gate on horseback. Peter and Captain Gideon followed and the remainder of the troop trailed behind.

In the center of the town, a few people stood, moaning as they stared out into space. Their oily eyes showed no trace of white.

The heads of the infected townsfolk slowly turned toward Peter and his group before thrashing from side to side violently. The ghost town filled with the horrid echoes of primal snarls and growls.

Over a dozen infected sprinted toward them, spewing blood and black tar as they ran.

Alvar's horse sidestepped and the Blackheart Lord whirled Quickfury in two strokes, decapitating three of the monsters. Captain Gideon bellowed with each stroke of his saber, cutting down one infected after another. The six black riders of Alvar's guard split into two groups of three, riding around the town center along the rectangular formation of buildings.

Peter sat atop his horse as the infected remained occupied with his companions. To his surprise, he was bored. At last, one infected sprinted toward him. Terrifying groans emerged from the old man's mouth. Peter cocked his right arm across his body and as the infected came close enough, delivered a chop to its face. Cracks echoed loudly from the impact, and the broken body skidded across the cobblestone to land about twenty feet away. As the last of the plagued corpses were destroyed, he examined his bloody glove.

I really am getting the hang of this. I don't feel so nervous or afraid anymore. He smiled with pride. *I'm growing, like I hoped I would. If Jack could see me now.*

* * * * * * *

Another grape bounced off of him and fell into the crease between the pages of the book he read. Peter looked up from his story. Across the oak table, Alvar reclined in his chair. He ate a grape before tossing another at Peter, as he had been doing for the last ten minutes. The purple fruit bounced off his shoulder.

"Do you want me to read to you?"

"No need. I am familiar with the tale of Stephen and Avery. I have never been fond of love stories." Another grape soared through the air.

He caught it in midair and tossed it into his mouth. The sweet juice of the fruit serenaded his taste buds with delight. "Why not?"

The Blackheart Lord sighed. "Is it not the same story perpetually retold?"

“I guess. I never really paid that much attention to them.”

“Nor should you. Women are a distraction, nothing more.”

“So you don't date?”

He cocked a dark eyebrow. “I intend to keep all of my interactions with women brief. I recommend you do the same.”

“I don't think I can do that.”

Alvar shook his head, frowning. “Then you will never see your full potential, hmm?”

“What makes you say that?”

“It's quite simple, Little Lion. A man is most dangerous when he retains his essence. I say to you, when you begin to fraternize with one of the Moonwey sisters, if you have not already, you will lose your edge!” Alvar stared off into space as he spoke. “My destiny is too great to be distracted by any woman alive. I have slaved my entire life to attain greatness reserved for me. Such glories await and my reign of triumph is nigh.”

Woah. Peter stared at the Blackheart Lord. At times it was difficult for him to even believe that Alvar was real. He recalled how Helen had always seemed to have an effect on him, and realized that the woman's fabled beauty had never had an effect on Alvar.

“So...you stay away from women? And that's what makes you more dangerous?”

“It does,” Alvar confirmed. “There is a decisive battle within every man, my friend. It is a struggle of impulse that all men are born with and one that few men have ever conquered. It is the weakness of a woman's visage, eyes, lips, legs, whatever it be. To be subject to her will through her greatest and only weapon. . .her beauty. Remove it and what does she possess, hmm? And what of a man? Remove his face and what is he? What can he be? Ah. . .he still may have purpose, I tell you. All men are born with a choice: to be slaves to their impulses or to rise above and find the true purpose that destiny reserves for them, and them alone.”

Peter met Alvar's dark eyes. They were serious, yet compassionate.

Though Peter found the man to be arrogant at times, in that moment he felt bonded to him in brotherhood.

Suddenly, a light flashed outside the large window of the dining room. Jolting thunder shook the manor. A few drops of rain began to pelt the glass in small bursts until a steady heave began to fall in the night.

"Does it always storm so much in the west?"

"Yes," Alvar sighed. "It was most infuriating as a boy. I always abhorred having to remain indoors. I preferred to explore and fight."

"That's right," Peter remembered. "You're from here, aren't you? Hearthelm?"

The Blackheart Lord stroked his mustache. "How do you know of this?"

"Helen *surmised* it during the tournament." They both chuckled.

"Such a clever vixen. If I were a lesser man I would seek to make her my own wife. Fortunately, I bear no interest in wives, as you know, no matter how clever or handsome. But yes, Little Lion, I hail from the hectic streets of Hearthelm."

"What was it like?"

"Hearthelm? Well, a town of pleasure. Brothels, fighting pits, and game houses could be found on every street." He was silent for a moment.

The wooden floor creaked as footsteps sounded from the hallway adjacent to Alvar. Captain Gideon emerged from the doorway holding a dark green bottle.

"My Lords." He inclined his head. "The town is secure, a second group of riders are on approach from Carvalel, and. . .a bottle of sweet red nearly as old as I is in my hand. Shall we?"

"Sure." Peter grinned. They both looked to Alvar.

The Blackheart Lord looked at the window as rain continued to thrash against it in the dark of night. “This storm will break before morning. We shall depart north at sun’s first light.” He rose. “Good evening.” He departed, disappearing down the hallway of the manor.

“A good start, I say,” Gideon said, sitting in the chair to the left of Peter. He wrestled with the wine bottle, grimacing. With a sudden pop, the rich liquid spewed on the table and dripped onto the wooden floor. “First taste?” He held out the bottle and Peter took it, sipping on the sweet and fruity alcohol.

“Woah!” he exclaimed, handing back the wine. “That’s a lot better than the ale.”

The captain took a few gulps and shrugged. “The taste depends on the occasion.”

“I don't know what that means but I’ll take another drink.”

For the next few hours, they passed the bottle back and forth, drinking and talking about their lives. After Gideon procured another bottle, Peter's eyelids grew heavier and his speech began to slur. He began to feel a strong desire to start talking about Aurora.

Why am I thinking about her so much? he would ask himself after telling Gideon about the way she laughed or how she had freckles in the hazel of her eyes.

“They really are beautiful! Especially in the sunlight.”

“Aye. You told me twice already.” He held up three fingers. “Just marry the girl, lad. Apologize to Helen about...you know, and ask for her blessing. It'll be bold but that's what women like!”

“Well, I don't know about marrying. . .”

“You don't think she'd make a fine wife?”

“I'm sure she would, but. . .I’m not ready.”

The captain shook his head and nearly fell out of his chair. “Laddie, I've seen you. You will make a fine husband. You're a man of love.”

Peter stared at the wondering blue eyes that looked back at him.

"I've got it!" he exclaimed, standing for the first time and realizing the manor was on a tilt. He stumbled toward the bookshelf behind his chair and picked up a piece of paper and a quill with ink that splashed all over his hands. "I'll write her a letter and tell her how I feel." He sat back down and hastily began to write his thoughts.

* * * * * * *

He groaned as he awoke. Sunlight shined through the window of the dining room and onto a messy table crowded with papers, spilled ink, grapes, and two empty wine bottles. He raised his head from the table and a piece of paper came with him, fixed to the skin of his cheek. He began to wipe his face before pulling his hands away, realizing he had just smeared black ink all over himself. Peeling the piece of the parchment from his face, he looked over the paper. It was unintelligible. "What the hell did I write?" Wadding the paper into a ball, he threw it over his shoulder and looked over to the captain that lay sprawled on the floor. "Gideon..."

He pushed against the table as he stood. The wood creaked and fell onto the floor with a thud, waking the captain. "Oh! Hey, you're awake."

From the hallway one of the captain's riders appeared. "Morning, Lord. Captain, we are gathering in the town center." He bowed and departed.

For the next ten minutes, Peter washed himself free of the ink and chugged water at the behest of Captain Gideon. He rubbed his aching head as he made his way to the town center, where Alvar and the remainder of the party awaited.

"Jovial celebration?" the Blackheart Lord asked from atop his horse. "Here." He tossed Peter a wrapped loaf of bread.

"Thanks." Peter hoisted himself into his saddle and began to eat.

A morning mist hovered above the fields and rolling hills as they departed the town and proceeded north. During the silent ride, he thought about the night before with confusion. *I remember what I said about Aurora. Do I really feel like that about her? The more I've thought about her, the less I've worried about Helen and the kiss. When I get back to Arden city, I'll apologize to her.*

After the plague is gone, what do I do? Do I keep trying to find Jack and a way back to Norfolk? What about Aurora? I'm starting to feel. . .attached to her, yet I'm so far away from her. He shook his head.

Like his headache and dizziness, the morning fog dissipated as they ventured farther along the wide dirt road north. As the mist unveiled the vast fields flanking them, Peter's eyes lingered on a far-off dark column that extended toward the sky from the ground. The smoky spire moved on its own beneath a series of dark clouds far to their left.

A tornado! he thought, refusing to take his eyes off of the natural wonder. *I wonder if it can actually hurt me. What if I get sucked up by it? It looks big enough. Maybe it'll take me back home.* He laughed abruptly, earning perplexed glances from Alvar and Gideon.

Behind a blanket of clouds, the sun's silhouette sat high in the sky as noon approached and the troop arrived at another town. The wooden buildings of the place lay sprawled out, with no walls like the communities before it. At the center of the township, a stone bastion stood high above a cluster of buildings. The stillness of the ghost town beneath the overcast sent a shiver down his spine.

Despite his own apprehension, he followed Alvar, galloping through the two large buildings that acted as an entry into the main road of the town. A few piles of charred lumber lay scattered around the road and along the encircling thatch buildings. The main road forked around the tall stone spire at the center of the town.

Peter remained on his horse as two of Gideon's riders and two of Alvar's black-plated warriors stepped down to search some nearby houses.

"This is creepy," he muttered to the captain.

"Aye. I didn't realize Oleton had been purged."

Alvar's white steed trotted back and forth in the center of the road. The Blackheart Lord stroked his mustache, his eyes veiled by the long brim of his hat. “This town was not meant to be purged until I arrived to do it myself!” he said.

One of Gideon's riders called out, “Not a single corpse!”

“No bodies?” Peter asked.

“Aye, Lord. Nothing.”

He looked at Gideon. “There have been infected everywhere we’ve gone and now all of a sudden nothing? Something's not ri—”

He keeled over in his saddle as his stomach convulsed. The eerie feeling had returned for the first time since Arden City. He groaned and his horse pranced from side to side, neighing loudly.

“Laddie!” Gideon called out. The captain leapt from his saddle and rushed to Peter’s side. “What is it?”

Something’s wrong! his mind and body agreed. He felt as though he were a small animal, his senses warning him of a predator.

Finally, after a few moments of overwhelming fear and pain, the feeling subsided and he was able to take regular breaths.

The Blackheart Lord's horse galloped over to him and halted. “What ails you?”

He regained his composure. “Nothing. I just. . .it's nothing. Let's go.”

He looked up and met Alvar's gaze beneath the rim of his hat. He stared at the boy from Virginia with cold focus.

“Very well,” Alvar said. “Captain, remain here with your riders. When additional groups arrive, take command and ride for Ilvion. You will remain there until I arrive.”

“Lord?”

“Do as I command. The Lionheart and I will ride for Hearthelm.”

Chapter 18

Hearthelm

They rode after their own shadows as the sun set behind them. On their right, plains of grass stretched to the south. He glanced over to his left where Alvar rode beside him. A vast forest extended along the horizon. Ahead, the Ornian river appeared like a glistening snake dividing the land.

Nestled where the river met the forest, a city awaited them.

Hearthelm, he concluded. As the road brought him closer, he was able to discern the utter size of the community. A wall encircled hundreds of tall buildings of wood and stone. The sound of the steady river against the clanking metal of the six men behind him began to fill his ears. The gatehouse of the city grew larger as they advanced toward it. Dangling from the stone entryway, three black banners flapped in the wind, each bearing a bloody human heart.

Alvar scoffed loudly as they entered the gatehouse, the hooves of their horses echoing with each step on the cobblestones. Peter's apprehension grew with each step his horse took. Though he was growing more comfortable with his abilities, he questioned whether he could combat a small horde even with the help of Alvar and his bodyguards.

The gatehouse opened into a courtyard surrounded by an array of buildings with various designs. Some wooden structures slanted as others more archaic ascended toward the clouds, concerning Peter as they swayed in the wind.

"Hearthelm," he muttered under his breath. "Another ghost town. I don't see any bodies. And it's so quiet...and still. Creepy."

Alvar turned to his bodyguards. "You know why we are here. Go to Heart's Center. We will stay there for the night." The six men galloped away down a nearby street.

Peter looked at the Blackheart Lord. "What's going on?"

"Follow me. I have something I must show you." He kicked his heels and his pale horse raced off down another street.

He seems excited, but why?

Peter grew even more nervous as he spurred his horse forward after the man through the labyrinth of Hearthelm, guiding his horse left and right numerous times down a rapid succession of narrow streets. Alvar's lead took him out of sight as Peter rounded a corner to a fork in a back-alley road bordered by tall shanty buildings.

He pulled back on the reins. "Alvar!"

He heard nothing, not even the beating hooves of the Blackheart Lord's horse. He growled with frustration.

"Are you lost?" a woman's voice said behind him.

He turned. A young woman with long black hair stood in the center of the road. She kept her arms behind her back, veiled by the slender dress she wore, smeared with mud and a black substance.

“Wha...” His surprise robbed him of words. “How are you...”

“Alive?” She smiled and shrugged.

“Are you alright? Is there anyone else here?”

Her dark brown eyes flickered as she strolled gracefully toward him. “Aren't you going to step down from your horse and properly introduce yourself?”

He looked again at the fork in the road, searching for Alvar. With no one in sight, he turned back to the young woman, still walking toward him. He stepped down and tied the reins to a nearby wooden post.

“Ma'am, are you—” he began to ask, turning to where the woman had been standing. He saw no one.

He jumped in surprise as the sound of a loud sniff came from behind him. The woman stood there, her eyes closed, sniffing the air and grinning. She moaned loudly and gazed at him with dilated pupils.

He stepped away from her as she began to pace toward him. “What's going on here?” he asked.

She circled him, looking him up and down. Her hands remained behind her back. “I just wanted a closer a look at you,” she said with two voices that overlapped. “You have both impressed and infuriated me. What is your name?”

His heart began to race as he debated answering. “Who are you?”

“I asked you first.”

“Peter. Peter Loneheart.”

The woman’s two voices chuckled as one. “Loneheart. Another Lion.”

"Another? What are you...you're talking about Jack!"

"Perhaps. Do you want to know the truth?"

"The truth?"

"About the plague, your uncle's fate, and how you will go back to your Norfolk."

Who is she? How does she know so much? he thought. "Tell me. What do you know? Who are you?"

"I can only tell you..." She paused and looked him up and down again with a devious glare. "...if I may kiss you."

"What?"

"Just a kiss. What girl wouldn't want to kiss the boy from Virginia? One kiss and I will reveal the truth to you. All of your questions answered."

He paused and considered it as she slowly walked towards him, licking her lips. *One kiss and I'll know about the cause of the plague, what happened to Jack, and how to get home. Still, it doesn't seem right, it doesn't feel right. Something is wrong!*

As he began to step away and decline, her arms finally revealed themselves. He fought the urge to puke when he saw her hands. The flesh had rotted away at the tips of her fingers, leaving bone-claws. He leapt back a few yards as she continued toward him, raising the bone of her former index finger to her lips to shush him, hissing.

His breath escaped him, "What the hell..."

She stopped suddenly as the sound of beating hooves grew louder behind her. In an instant, she dashed away with blinding speed into the adjacent house. A series of heavy thuds erupted from inside before the street once again grew quiet.

Alvar emerged from the left fork. "What are you doing?" he asked.

"There was a woman!" Peter started towards him, eyeing the house she disappeared into. "She was infected but she—"

“I told you before! I do not care about women! Infected or otherwise. Mount your horse and follow me. I have waited too long for this!”

“Are you serious? This could—”

“I will not be denied! Come.”

And without another word, he turned his horse back down the street.

* * * * * * *

Despite his frequent attempts to tell Alvar what had happened, he was consistently interrupted by the Blackheart Lord and finally silenced as they tied their horses to a tree outside the city. A forest of evergreens stretched from the river to the far west, disappearing in the distance under the evening sky.

“It's going to get dark soon, Alvar. And I don't think we should stay in this town tonight.”

The Blackheart Lord said nothing as he led Peter through a concentration of tall bushes at the border of the forest. Shrubbery smacked Peter in the face as Alvar pressed forward in front of him. The dense bushes came to an end as they entered the forest. The branches above them created a dome and blocked out the sun, leaving a blue light within the woodland. A multitude of flowers populated much of the forest floor.

“Start searching,” Alvar told him before turning left and marching off into the woods.

“What? Search for what?” he called out, but no reply came as his companion disappeared behind a pocket of trees.

He sighed and started forward, gazing at the variety of flowers. *Am I supposed to be picking flowers? There are more important things going on!* His thoughts dwelled on the woman as he walked through the forest. *What's going on? I mean, what is going on?! She had to be infected, but she was talking like a normal person. How? And there were two voices, not one. And her eyes were a little strange, but not like the one that talked at the fort.*

He wove through a cluster of trees, coming upon a clearing with vibrant red flowers. Across the meadow, a series of boulders stood high above the forest floor like slanted buildings of stone. Tiptoeing, he made his way toward the rock formation. An idea came to mind, and he knelt down before the base of the stone, plucking one of the stems from the earth. The petals of the flower glistened as if they had been painted with fresh blood. An exotic scent drifted into his nostrils.

It smells like honeysuckles. He took another whiff.

A twig snapped ahead of him. He looked up from the ground to see a wolf with snow-white fur sitting by the rock formation, staring at him.

"Oh. Hello," he said without fear. On the other side of the boulders, a solid black wolf revealed itself and hesitantly walked toward him. Two more wolves of gray joined the white wolf as another followed the black wolf. Its golden eyes shined brightly against its midnight mask, its head tilted with profound curiosity.

He slowly extended his hand and the tips of his fingers brushed against the soft black fur behind the wolf's ear. Its eyes closed as he scratched the soft patch of fur.

"You're adorable," he said softly. Slowly the other four pack members approached him.

A deep growl echoed throughout the meadow. The black wolf jolted away as the others halted and their snouts turned upward. Peter's gaze followed theirs to the top of the rock formation.

A silver wolf stood glaring down at him.

Larger than a horse, it snarled, displaying enormous teeth. Its eyes glowed in the soft blue air like pools of molten gold. The wolf shifted its stance and licked its teeth as a deep growl emerged from its throat.

It's going to attack! he realized as it crouched down, preparing to pounce. Peter turned and dashed back the way he had come. The ground shook as the wolf jumped after him and gave chase. He passed the cluster of trees nearby and sprinted, weaving to avoid crashing.

He looked back and the wolf snapped at his face. *It's almost as fast as I am!*

He raced harder. The chase continued and the beast kept pace a few yards behind him.

Suddenly, with a forceful thud, Peter collided with a tree. His momentum threw him into the air as the wood exploded into confetti. He fell to the forest floor and the tree crashed to the ground next to him.

He twisted and looked back at the wolf, about to pounce.

"Tobius!" a voice called out.

The wolf stopped in its tracks. Its large ears extended upward and its enormous head turned toward Alvar as he ran towards the fray.

"Alvar, watch out!" Peter said, before realizing his words were useless.

A smile he had never seen before formed on the face of the Blackheart Lord. The silver wolf trotted over to the man, who embraced the canine towering over him. "My friend!" he said, sounding both sad and happy.

The animal whimpered and began to lick at the man with enthusiasm, knocking his hat off his head. Like a little boy with his dog, Alvar laughed loudly, burying his face in the gray and silver fur.

I don't believe it. Staring at the two, Peter stood and dusted off the wood chips and sap. "So this is what we were looking for?"

"Indeed." The muffled reply came from the fur of the wolf's neck. Alvar stepped back and marveled at the animal, continuing to smile. "This is my one and only friend. Tobius."

"A giant wolf. Go figure."

The Blackheart Lord turned toward him. "Does he seem...familiar to you, Lionheart?" Peter shook his head. "No? Is he not from your world?"

"No! I've never seen a wolf that big."

"Hmm." The snout of the canine nudged playfully at Alvar's back. "Well, my old friend, it would appear that you are from a new world entirely."

"You have a giant pet wolf! How?"

"I discovered him as a boy here in this forest, near the northern sea. He was my only solace as I grew. My only friend. And he is not a pet, he is my companion." He looked up to the wolf. "Now, my friend, I have returned to you as I promised. Our age of triumph is nigh. With you and Quickfury by my side, and the people of Arden behind me, destiny will be fulfilled."

As Peter continued to gaze at Alvar and the wolf, he saw a single tear stroll down the man's face.

* * * * * * *

The restless night ended as the sun shined through the window of his bedroom within the capital building of Hearthelm. He rose as tired as he had been when he first lay down. Throughout the night, he had tossed and turned, riddled with visions of the woman from the day before. Multiple times, he had sat up in his dusty bed, expecting to see her standing in the dark corner of the room, her claws scraping against the portions of stone wall not covered with rich tapestry.

As he dressed, he mulled over Alvar and Tobius. The Blackheart Lord had Quickfury, a sword from his own world, and now a giant wolf from another. What's more, both were capable of killing him.

I'm so glad we're going to Ilvion today. It'll be nice to see Gideon again. Before long, I'll head back to Arden City. I'll tell Helen about everything I've seen. Maybe she can make sense of it all. And Aurora. He held up the vibrant scarlet flower from the forest. *Maybe this can be the gift. And who knows what could happen afterward, maybe Gideon is right about everything. It feels right...in a world where everything else feels so wrong.*

Munching on a stale piece of bread, he departed the entrance of the capital building in the city. At the base of the steps, Alvar's six bodyguards awaited with the horses.

“Do you guys ever take your armor off?” he asked. No reply came, only deep breaths through the black helms. Ten silent minutes passed as they waited.

Finally, Alvar strutted down the stone steps, radiating confidence. Behind him, Tobius yawned loudly, flicking his long tongue in the air. As the Blackheart Lord and his companion joined the group at the base of the stairs, the wolf slowly stepped towards Peter, allowing him to touch the soft fur of his large neck.

“You're taller than a horse, Tobius.” Peter giggled like a little boy as the wolf licked him. From his tunic, a wrapped-up piece of cloth fell onto the ground. Alvar reached down and picked up the gray cloth, unveiling the scarlet flower within.

“Ah.” He stroked his mustache.

“It's just a gift for a friend,” Peter assured him.

“No doubt. The Crimson Corpette. A fine gift...for a lover.”

“What?”

“For one of the Moonwey's, hmm? The Corpette was a classic gift of betrothal in the past ages, the Crimson Corpette anyway. It only grows in the north forest outside the city. There is also a Teal Corpette, which grows in the forest south of Barrington.”

Peter hesitated. “Maybe I should find another gift.”

But as Alvar prepared to toss the flower away, Peter stopped him. “I think I'll hold onto it for now.”

He folded it back up and tucked it safely away within his tunic. They all climbed into their saddles and Alvar led them back toward the main gate of Hearthelm. Tobius trotted alongside them, allowing Alvar to occasionally reach over and pet him.

After a while, they turned down a narrow street. An eerie stillness loomed around them, sending a chill down Peter's spine.

The wooden door of a slanted building burst open and a pack of infected spilled out with raised claws. Along the street, a few more doors were thrown open and dozens of rabid humans filled the alleyway. A horrid score of growls and snarls echoed within the corridor of buildings as hundreds of the infected filled the avenue.

As if coordinated, the first group ran as one into Peter's horse. The steed toppled over onto him and the claws of the infected tore into its flesh, killing the animal. Peter rolled onto his back, yanking his uninjured leg from the dead horse and kicking back one plague victim after another.

Bodies were thrown into the air and into the second and third stories of the nearby buildings. Behind him, Alvar and his bodyguards fought the rest of the small horde as Tobius growled loudly, tearing bodies apart with his teeth.

Out of the corner of his eye, he noticed Alvar's horse suddenly dash forward without being attacked. In an instant, the horde that had been attacking Alvar and his men descended on Peter, still flat on his back. He screamed with hopelessness and sheer terror, heart racing. The monsters bit uselessly at his skin, but their teeth seemed to grow sharper after each failure to pierce his flesh.

He punched and kicked and growled until the first pair of filed fangs finally broke his skin.

Pain radiated from his neck and remained as the teeth of the infected broke off within him. Another mouth closed around his hand, piercing his glove and the skin between his thumb and index finger. Over twenty sets of hands clawed at his abdomen and tore away his leather chest plate. Pairs of bone-claws raked the flesh of his stomach, leaving streaks of crimson.

In the chaos, he glanced over and saw Alvar on foot with Quickfury drawn, pacing back and forth in the street as if trying to decide what to do. Out of a nearby building, the woman from the day before emerged.

She strolled over to the Blackheart Lord and spoke, pointing at him with her claws.

Over the symphony of cries and snarls, he heard Alvar reply to her. "Our agreement is at its end, Snake." With a flick of his wrist, the rapier sliced through the woman's neck and her head toppled onto the ground. He sheathed Quickfury and looked at Peter as another pair of fangs pierced his shoulder.

"My destiny is nigh!" Alvar called out over the chaos. "And it cannot be impeded by even the death of the Lionheart. I AM ALVAR, THE SAVIOR OF THIS WORLD!" he bellowed. A few infected ran after him but were cut down by the six bodyguards. "I am the Lion reborn." Alvar turned and departed the city with his wolf and men behind him.

In the center of the alleyway, Peter's life faded as his flesh was ripped away from him bit by bit. He punched at any rotting head his blurring vision could discern. Pain and hopelessness filled him as everything started to go black. A pair of beautiful hazel eyes came to mind and the visage of a woman formed around them.

Aurora, he thought. *I'll never see her again.*

The injustice swelled within him as the boy from Virginia took his last breath.

Chapter 19

Wanderer: The Legend Lives

The road from Bastille was as pleasant as he recalled from his life as a young knight. Though in those days he had preferred to ride toward his beloved city and not away from it. Instead, a metropolis enveloped by sinful deeds revealed itself as he passed over a hill. Arden City sat nestled between the mountains that towered over it and the vast sea that lay behind it.

He sighed and took a deep breath, taking in the salty scent of the ocean.

The road followed the mountain range south along its right flank. As he reached the northern gate, his ears began to ring with the overwhelming discord of celebration from within the city.

William addressed one of the guards. "A lively evening."

The sentry walked over lazily and sighed. "Coming from Bastille?"

"Indeed. What is the cause of such celebration?"

"You live under one of those Christian stones up there?"

He is young, the old knight reminded himself, *and lazy.* His amber eyes glossed over the sentry's attire. His sword remained in its scabbard, leaning up against the stone of the gatehouse with a musket next to it. *He is accustomed to a lack of wholesome work that leaves him lackadaisical.*

William said nothing, but continued to glare at the young man.

Finally, the sentry confessed, "The plague is finished."

"Finished?"

"Aye. A few big battles. Two in Carvalel and one just north of New London. Lord Rulfin, the commander of the army, defeated the infection...but it is said that he fell in the final battle."

Lord Rulfin, dead? This is troubling, even with the plague's demise, he thought. *Also, news travels slowly from the west.* "When did you learn of Lord Rulfin's passing?"

"Yesterday. A vigil was held for those slain during the campaign, but tonight, the celebrations begin."

So soon? And what of Peter? "The Lionheart. What news of him? Did he go with the army?"

"You do live under a stone, don't you? They say he fought in the second battle of Carvalel, I say some weeks ago. Word is he's in Ilvion with Lord Blackheart."

Peter did as I suggested and went west. I am certain he has grown as I have hoped. When he returns, he and I shall discuss a great many things. I am in his debt.

"Thank you. Good evening." William inclined his head and spurred his horse through the gate.

* * * * * * *

The Lion's Den sat in the far corner of a narrow alley. Outside of the pub, two men brawled, grappling on the ground as a few women spectated and giggled. William's nostrils stung from the mixed scents of alcohol and sewage as he trotted down the cobblestone street toward the scuffle. The brawlers ceased their bout and looked up at the Wanderer as he halted his steed. He dismounted, tied off his horse, and strolled past the courtesans without sparing a single glance.

The lively noise of the pub flooded his ears as he opened the door and entered. Laughter and singing echoed throughout Lion's Den, overpowering the lutes played by the small band of musicians in a far corner. Young women danced with graceful precision around the islands of round wooden tables. Though many candles burned within the pub, their lesser flames provided dim lighting.

He strolled toward the bar at the left of the entrance. Waving his hand, he dismissed the barkeep on approach and leaned against the chipped wood. As he surveyed the jovial setting, he caught a flicker of movement behind the bar. He turned and stared into his own amber eyes. The cracked mirror on the wall revealed how old he had truly become. Wrinkles dominated much of the dark brown skin of his face, conjuring nostalgia and regret within him.

I am old now. My body and soul, weary, longing for rest. Yet there is much work still to do.

He shook his head, casting his self-pity aside. His old eyes once again searched the Lion's Den, gazing from one candlelit table to another. In the far corner of the pub, a small bald man raised his tawdry goblet towards him.

William snaked through the crowd and tables toward him.

"The western winds whisper," said the man as William sat across from him.

"And the northern city listens," William replied.

A moment of silence passed between them. Then the bald man chuckled, revealing rows of missing teeth. William leaned forward. "Tell me, friend. What news do you bring?"

"Stories of Serpents, Lions, and Angels. Swords are sharpened in the dark and soon they will strike like snakes from the shadows."

"What do you know?"

The bald man grinned and tapped his finger against the dusty wooden table.

Of course, William thought. He reached beneath his gray robe and removed a palm-sized bag. "Thirty pieces of silver."

The man took it without question and grew serious. "Now. Whispers emerge from both the west and the east."

"The west and east?" William asked.

"Aye. From the west, the infection is thwarted but at a price. Lord Rulfin is dead and his subordinate with him. Half of the army that departed the city now lies beneath the ground. Two vice commanders remain, Carlon of Stonewell and Alvar Blackheart."

"I have heard of the name Blackheart. Continue."

"There is currently a series of rumors that flow from Carvalel, where the army remains. With Lord Rulfin's death, Lord Carlon and Sir Titus Turner bout for command of the army."

"I see. Should Lord Carlon not assume command as one of the appointed vice-commanders? What of Blackheart?"

"Aye. Carlon should be the one to assume command. However, Sir Titus Turner is the cousin of Lord Ian Turner, the Lord of Barrington himself. Barrington has supplied much during the cause to retake the west and now the Turner knight seeks to collect what is owed. Factions are forming within the army stationed in Carvalel and conflict is certain. Blackheart is said to have disappeared after riding north with the Lionheart. Conflicting rumors emerge from the west about him. Some say he commands in Ilvion; others claim he went south to New London after the battle. But a new rumor has recently begun to take flight."

"Yes?"

"They say Lord Blackheart rode through the Ornian ruins some days ago, back toward this city, with a small host behind him."

"A small host?"

"Aye. Some twelve hundred men. He didn't return to Carvalel after going north, just rode straight through the ruins of the old kingdom."

William leaned back and rubbed his temples. "What of the Lionheart?"

"Some say he remained in Ilvion and took command for Lord Blackheart; others say he too disappeared and now rides for the city along with the Blackheart Lord."

"Nothing more?"

The plump-faced man shook his head. "Now. The news you truly seek, I will reveal to you. The truth behind the attacks on the province leaders. What do you know of Milsted?"

"It is a small town along the northern road between Bastille and Arden City," said William.

"A town you rode past on your way here, yes?"

"Yes. What of it? Is the town—"

"—the base of the assassins? Aye." The man's gray eyes shined in the wavering candlelight. "One of the bases, yes. There is yet another in this very city."

"But...the town. It always presented itself as modest and upright."

"A facade, my friend. I have entered its depths on few occasions. A society of its own design dwells beneath it. It started as a small of group of defectors from the past war. Over time, other groups joined; more recently a strange cult has infiltrated its ranks." He looked away from William somberly. "This new group, however, are strange mask wearers, led by one they call the *Angel*."

"The Angel? Is he the leader of the assassins?"

"No. He spoke rarely when I was present, and when he did he spoke with a strange accent I have not heard before. I assume he and his masked followers are the survivors of Somerta. They all disappeared in the night before I fled. I have not heard more word of them since."

"I see. If the Angel and his followers are not the head of this snake then who is?"

"Leadership seemed fickle within the society, I'd say. Each time I ventured into its depths there was a new face issuing commands."

William grimaced as his frustration grew. "I must have details! These attacks must stop."

"Agreed. I feel as if they will conclude soon."

"What do you mean?"

"Consider the attack that occurred at the stadium. A large operation that bore great catastrophe, yes?"

"Indeed. Several province leaders were killed."

"Aye. Yet many still live and the city council survived. Since the attack, the city inquisitors have initiated a full-scale investigation of the capital, with no trace of the assassins remaining other than the few that were killed during the attack at the stadium. This peace that has passed since—merely a calm before the storm, yes?"

"As you say...yet many questions remain."

"I suspect a new attack will happen soon, a greater one than any yet. I do not know the details, as I have said, nor do I know the base within the city, but I do know that certain individuals are preferred targets."

"Whom?"

"Before the attack on the stadium, the first family of Sohn, Lorena Garshin, Alvar Blackheart, Ian Turner of Barrington, and the entire city council. Though it is strange that specific commands were also issued regarding the Lord of Barrington. Both he and Helen Moonwey were ordered to be captured and not harmed."

"This is most disturbing."

"Aye. After the attack, the orders changed. Helen Moonwey has now become the prime target."

"To capture?"

The man shook his head. "To kill."

William shook his head and stood abruptly. Lady Helen was the daughter of his late friend Edward. The thought of her being killed infuriated him. He looked down at the bald man, worried. "We must leave."

"Leave?"

"Indeed. If what you say is true then we must speak with the city council immediately. We shall depart at once for the citadel. It is not far."

The man stood. "You assured me of asylum!"

"Our agreement still stands. You are now under the Order's protection."

The bald man's eyes widened as his gaze shifted over William's shoulder. A force struck the back of his head and neck and he dropped to his knees. He grimaced and peered up toward his informant who raised his hands in defense. Another unseen force hit him and he fell onto the dusty floor of the pub before losing consciousness.

* * * * * * *

A man screeched like a swine being slaughtered. A dull pain throbbed where William had been struck. Above him, the iron links that bound him cut into the skin of his wrists. He slowly opened his eyes.

A dark dungeon surrounded him, a living nightmare made real by the pain he felt, the screams he heard, and the sight of the man being tortured. Across from where William dangled, his informant hung from the ceiling. A blood-covered leather apron hugged the man torturing the informant. His face was veiled by a black mask.

"He's awake," a voice said from the darkest corner of the dungeon.

The tormentor halted his work and stalked towards the open doorway, ascending the stairs William could see there.

From the shadowy corner of the room, the man in the dark spoke again. "What did he tell you, old man?"

The informant cried, "I told him nothing!"

A stone sailed through the air and struck his face.

"Be silent, traitor. I am speaking to the man with no name."

William hesitated, searching the dark corner of the room to no avail. "I am Wanderer." He coughed.

"Wanderer." Another stone was cast from the corner and struck the bloody belly of the informant. "What did you tell this Wanderer, Dusky?"

Dusky? William thought. *An unusual name. He must hail from the west.*

Blood spewed from his mouth as Dusky replied, "I told him nothing."

"So you say."

A series of footsteps echoed from the stairwell and the torturer in the apron appeared. Behind him, a figure in a black robe entered the room.

"Captured a deserter and a Wanderer," the voice from the corner said.

The black hood turned towards William and the shrouded person walked towards him. From the hood, a gruff voice spoke, "Indeed. A wanderer? No! A knight."

I recognize that voice.

"By now, you recognize my voice, do you not, William?"

From the shadowy corner, a young man revealed himself, gasping, "A knight?!"

"Oh yes," replied the familiar voice beneath the hood. "Not just any knight, lad. The knight of knights. The living legend. Sir William of Bastille."

A chuckle escaped William. “Much falls into place as you reveal yourself to me…” He glared into the black pocket beneath the hood and growled, “Rob Grimful!”

A chuckle emanated from beneath the hood before the man pulled it away to reveal his scarred face, one gray eye covered by a leather patch.

William shook his head as he spoke. “The years have not been kind to you, traitor. I recall when your hair flowed like fire behind you as we rode together long ago. Now it is but gray.”

“The years have punished us both, my old friend.”

“I am not your friend, nor comrade, not after you betrayed us to the Duke.”

“What option did I have? You and your—”

“You are an oathbreaker!” William bellowed. “You swore to the Order and betrayed us. Now you fight with assassins, without honor!”

A slap echoed within the dungeon as Grimful's hand swept across the Wanderer's face. “Honor?” he scoffed. “A meaningless construct, devised by fools. It had its uses long ago, but no longer. There are more effective ways to obtain what is desired in life.”

“You never understood. Life is not about desire, it is about sacrifice.”

Grimful chuckled. “Of course. Your nailed God sacrificed himself and you, too, long for such an honor.”

He raised his arm, revealing the shining steel of a dagger, pressing its sharp edge against the skin of William's throat. “I will bestow that upon you. But first,” he said as he stepped back and his gaze darted between the two suspended men, “what have you learned?”

William grasped the chains above him and began to pull. “I have learned enough!” he growled, heaving himself downward.

Grimful and the pair of men with him laughed. "You have become delusional if you think to free yourself. What has befallen you these past years?"

"Suffering. I suffered in the Otherworld for ten years! And that suffering has nourished me with renewed strength." The rusted metal clanked above and the chain fell onto him as he freed himself.

The laughs died out. Grimful turned and sprinted up the stairs. The young man from the shadowy corner lunged at him with a knife.

William dodged the thrust. He threw the chains over the man's wrist and pulled, trapping his arm. Yanking the young man towards him, the Wanderer pivoted, sending his attacker flying over him and onto the ground. He pulled the chains and bones cracked loudly.

The young man on the ground howled in pain, holding his mutilated arm to his chest. William turned to the man in the apron, now dislodging his knife from Dusky's throat. As the Wanderer had skirmished with one foe, the other had killed his informant.

Wrath filled the old knight and he lurched forward with dazzling speed, catching his new opponent off guard. His knuckles smashed into the jaw of the torturer, spilling teeth onto the damp stone floor. The unconscious body followed after.

He looked at the dangling corpse of his informant, desiring to curse loudly, but he ignored the impulse and instead walked over to the moaning man on the floor.

"You will talk!" William ordered, kneeling over him.

Between the sobs, the man spat into the old knight's face.

"Very well. I will find another." A firm punch rocked the man's chin and he slept.

William turned and took flight up the stairs, prepared for whatever might descend toward him. He discerned the frantic sounds of orders barked against the discord of movement. A pair of doors awaited him at the end of the stairwell.

Leading with his shoulder, he collided with the doors, knocking one off its hinges. Sunlight illuminated the room and shined down onto the large wooden table in the center of the chamber. Across the chamber, protected by ten men, Grimful pointed toward him. "Kill him!" he ordered.

A musket shot rang out and William instinctively dropped. The shot pelted against the stone behind him, causing a small explosion of dust on the wall. He looked up to see two swordsmen approaching. The first lunged as the other lingered behind. William twisted as the blade cut through the fabric of his old robe, slicing his leg. He grimaced and pivoted, sending his fist into the young swordsman's face. The warrior flew back a few feet, dropping his sword.

William picked up the piece of steel that had sliced him. The second swordsman grimaced as he swung. The Wanderer struck toward the hilt of his opponent's sword, cutting his hands. The wounded warrior before him turned and fled, cradling his injured hand.

"Take the plans!" Grimful ordered the three men, who began to claw at the sheets of parchment on the table. As others began to follow the injured assailant toward the doorway leading outside, another opponent stepped up to challenge the old knight. Silver flashed left and right as two sabers slashed at William.

This one has skill! he noted as his own skills were pushed to their limits. As he maintained his defense, an opening finally revealed itself. The assailant in black wound his right saber back in anticipation as he lunged forward with his left. *A deception,* William concluded, rushing forward past the lunge and wrapping his arms around the man's chest. He squeezed with his new Otherworld strength and the man dropped his sabers.

The old knight tossed the fighter onto the table, which collapsed beneath him. The room was suddenly silent. "Cowards," he concluded as he surveyed the abandoned chamber. As he walked toward the wreckage in the center of the room, the assailant in black reached for a nearby pistol. William leapt forward and drove his heel into the wrist on the ground. The man screamed.

“You're the assassins that killed the province leaders at the arena,” he told the man. “Correct?”

Some pressure on the trapped wrist and the man confessed. “Yes!”

“Rob Grimful, the fallen knight, is your leader, correct?”

“Yes.”

“But who is your true leader?” He waited but no reply came. He pressed harder.

“T...” The man stopped.

“Who?” The heel of William’s boot dug deeper still.

“Turner!”

Turner? William released the man and stepped back, watching as he cradled his arm. “The Turners of Barrington?”

The man slowly nodded.

“But Ian Turner was targeted by your society!”

His investigation was cut short as three men entered the doorway through which the fallen knight and his men had escaped.

Inquisitors, William noted, seeing their rich black garments.

“Step away, you!” one of the inquisitors ordered.

William ignored the command and said, “Put him in chains and follow me to the citadel.”

“What did you say?” another inquired, as if offended. “Who are you to command us?”

“I am Sir William of Bastille.”

“Impossible. He's dead.”

“No. He yet lives.”

Chapter 20

The Ascension

The morning sun beamed down onto the back alleyway they traveled. The three inquisitors bickered as the five of them rode along. Beside William, the chains binding the assassin rattled with each stride of the horse he had been thrown over.

William considered the three inquisitors. *It is surprising that they believed me so easily. Yet their apprehension remains quite clear.*

"So," one of them said. "You are *the* William? The one who wandered from city to city as a lad in search of quests? The one who slew the Count of Blud in single combat? The one who fought the Lionheart and made him bleed?"

"It was not a fight," William corrected. "Merely a disagreement between two men who had not yet learned to trust one another." He turned to the three men and smiled. "But he did bleed when I struck him."

The trio stared at him with wide eyes.

Half an hour passed before they arrived at the city's center. Standing tall and wide, the citadel was the largest bastion in the metropolis. City guards patrolled on horseback in the courtyard surrounding the massive building.

They trotted to the stone steps outside the entrance and dismounted. William and one of the inquisitors ascended the steps, the other two dragging the chained assassin behind them.

When the large double doors opened, they could hear two men in a heated exchange. Sunlight shined through the window above the doors, gleaming upon the marble floor of the entrance chamber. To the left was a desk, behind which stood two men in silver armor jabbing at one another as they argued.

They turned toward the party as they drew near. "What is this?" one exclaimed, pointing towards the man in chains.

"A man in chains," answered the second guard, rolling his eyes. "What is the meaning of this, is a better question."

"Right...What is the meaning of this?"

William hesitated. "A captured assassin. It is imperative that we speak with the city council."

"Oh? And who are you?"

"Sir William," a feminine voice called out from beyond the entry chamber. All eyes went to the beautiful woman who had spoken. She wore a blue-and-silver dress. Behind her, another woman stood watchfully in leather armor.

"Lady Helen." William bowed, prompting the other men to do the same.

The Lady of Lunar Rock approached them and her guard followed. "What is the meaning of this, Sir William?"

William took a step forward. "There is much to say, my lady, and little time to do so. I must speak with the council immediately."

Her sharp gaze slid over the man in chains and then back to the old knight. “Very well. Follow me.”

* * * * * * *

The Lady of Lunar Rock led them through the double doors and along the corridor, the inquisitors and the woman warrior keeping a watchful eye on the assassin. As they walked, Helen looked over at the knight.

“It has been some time, Sir. You disappeared so suddenly once again.”

“My apologies. There was much work to do. It is important that my return is kept a secret.”

“You returned to Bastille after we last spoke at the arena?” she asked.

“Indeed. The Order has welcomed me home and now awaits my orders. Your cousin is a fine knight, I might add.”

She smiled. “Aaron practically worshipped you as a boy. I am certain he is delighted to serve with you.” They ascended another flight of stairs. “You know of Mr. Loneheart's departure?”

“Yes, my lady.”

“I assume the two of you spoke before he departed with the army.”

“Indeed, we did.”

She smiled. “I am glad for it. He was in need of guidance.”

“I am told he fought in the second battle of Carvalel. Slowly he evolves into the man his uncle long desired him to be.”

“Perhaps. Now that you broach the subject, Sir...” She cast a stern glance at him. “You have much explaining to do. Namely, regarding the fate of Jack Loneheart.”

He hesitated before answering. “I do not know what became of the Lionheart.”

Lady Helen exhaled sharply at the answer. "Your obscure nature is infuriating, Sir William."

They entered a corridor at the end of the stairs.

"My apologies. I departed Arden before his disappearance."

"And you remained in the Otherworld all this time? How did you survive?"

"My faith, Lady Helen."

The corridor opened up to a lounge-like chamber. A series of tables were scattered around the room, each surrounded by small sofas. Bookshelves lined the walls, alternating with windows through which sunlight shined. In the far corner, a few magistrates howled with laughter. Sitting on the table at the center of their attention, a young woman dressed in riding apparel stroked her long hair, which seemed similar to Lady Helen's.

The young woman peered at them as they walked down the center of the room. She brushed her hair back with her left hand and tapped her lower lip with her right index finger. Confused by the display, he glanced at the Lady of Lunar Rock, who nodded as if acknowledging what the woman was signaling.

They passed through another pair of double doors to a new corridor.

"My sister," Helen said. "Aurora."

"I see. I was aware that Lord Edward had fathered another daughter besides yourself, but I have not met her."

"I am certain the opportunity will arise, Sir William."

The corridor ended and another lounge appeared. A younger magistrate approached them. The light from the adjacent window illuminated his maroon robe.

He bowed to the party as they halted. "Lady Helen." His eyes lingered on the chain-bound man.

"Please inform Lord Ornwell that I request an audience. It is of paramount importance," she told him.

"At once, my lady. Please wait until I return." He bowed again before making his way past a pair of city guards and through the double doors they flanked. The Lady of Lunsera strolled over to the window and peered outside.

"The army returns. So sudden," she muttered as the old knight joined her. Far below in the courtyard, crowds descended upon the mass of soldiers as they dismounted from their horses.

"I was informed recently that Alvar Blackheart rode for the city. He passed the Ornian some days past. Perhaps it is he?"

She sighed, shaking her head. "Likely. His boldness knows no bounds. I surmise he intends to present himself before the council in Lord Rulfin's stead."

"A tragedy," William said solemnly. "Lord Rulfin was a former comrade of your father's and mine. His sacrifice will not be forgotten."

A moment of silence passed between them.

"I must admit that I am quite curious to see how he has grown."

"My lady?"

"Mr. Loneheart, of course. He has much been in my thoughts."

William peered behind them and leaned closer to her, muttering, "Are the two of you..."

"No. That is a bold thought indeed, Sir William. It is his wellbeing that I have considered so often since he departed," she stated. "When we last spoke, I was...somewhat cruel, but with purpose. Mr. Loneheart possesses tremendous potential, it is obvious, but he has been sheltered from challenge his entire life and thus has never understood his limits."

"I see. You have grown to care for him."

"Yes."

"After what you have spoken to me, I must know: what are your intentions with Peter?"

"When he first arrived in Lunsera, a thought occurred to me as I observed him. I recalled his predecessor and my own desires when I knew him. As I spoke with Mr. Loneheart, I began to consider how I might make him a part of my legacy, my father's legacy. To make the Lionheart a part of Lunsera. The answer I searched for came in the form of my sister."

The old knight considered what she was saying. "Peter and your sister?"

Her index finger tapped her lower lip. "I was never quite certain until I witnessed them together and knew fate had smiled upon my province. I requested that he protect her. If he could become the man his uncle desired, my sister would gain a man who loves her, and my province a powerful protector. After all, the women of our family do possess a fondness for the Lions of the Otherworld." Her face reddened and she turned away.

The doors to the council chamber opened and the magistrate appeared. "They are prepared for you."

* * * * * * *

Round and ostentatious, the council chamber was the biggest room in the citadel. Stone columns were spaced along the wall; between every set of pillars, large windows allowed the sunlight to shine onto the marble floor, revealing elegant designs. In the center of the room, a table in the shape of a crescent moon extended across half of the floor. Twelve chairs were evenly spaced on the far side of the table. Only one was unoccupied.

The footsteps of the party echoed throughout the chamber as they approached the center of the room. The chains of the bound assassin rattled abruptly as he was forced onto his knees before the council.

At the center of the table, a short man in an elegant black jacket stood. "Lady Helen." said the council leader. "What is this?"

"Lord Ornwell. May I present Sir William of Bastille." William stepped forward and nodded his head as a series of whispers passed among the council.

Ornwell stared at him, astounded. "Sir William? How can this be? Is it truly you?"

"Indeed, it is I. I have returned to Arden from the Otherworld, bringing grave news, but also a degree of hope."

"The Otherworld..." Ornwell muttered. "How did you—how did you depart to such a place?"

"I continue to question that as well," the old knight said. "But there are more pressing matters to discuss." He looked down at the man in chains. "Since I returned to Arden, I have remained in the shadows, revealing myself only to the order. I conducted an investigation when I learned of the province leaders being targeted by a group of assassins. In the night past, my investigation took me to the Lion's Den, where I met with my informant. He and I were both captured and taken to the base of operations for the assassins within the city. What's more, I have learned that it is a secret society and that another base lies beneath Milsted itself along the northern road."

"Milsted?" repeated Ornwell.

"Indeed. This morning I escaped the confines of their base within this city and I have learned the identity of their leader: the fallen knight Rob Grimful."

A barrage of frantic whispers erupted from behind the table.

"During the skirmish this morning, Rob Grimful escaped with some of his followers in tow, except this one and a few more I injured, who I am sure have fled by now. When I inquired about the identity of the true leader of the operations, this one gave me one name. Turner."

Whispers and gasps filled the chamber. Helen tapped her lower lip with her finger as she watched him with a concerned gaze.

The elder woman next to Lord Ornwell spoke. "You refer to the Turners of Barrington."

William looked down at the man in chains and all eyes followed. "Speak."

Perspiration appeared along the pale skin of the assassin's forehead, his gaze fixed upon the marble floor.

"Ro—" He cleared his throat. "Rob directed operations in the city...Ian Turner supplied us with arms and ammunitions."

Curses were suddenly spewed along the crescent table. The elder council woman looked up at Lord Ornwell, whose hard gaze wavered before he collapsed into his chair.

"Honorable council," William said. "I believe this is sufficient evidence. Further evidence can be discovered within the coming days, but for now I believe it would be wise to arrest Ian Turner of Barrington as he remains in the city. A bold action, required to preserve the peace and discern the truth."

"Agreed," Ornwell said. "However, there is an issue. Lord Turner departed the city some hours ago. He rode for Barrington with a haste that many of us questioned until now."

Grimful, William concluded. "The fallen knight must have warned him after he eluded me."

Behind the doors at the entrance of the chamber, a commotion attracted William's attention. He turned as the double doors were opened abruptly by a man in filthy black attire. Stains covered his pristine jacket, which matched the darkness of his brimmed hat. The young man strolled forward across the floor as the doors closed behind him. At his hip, a rapier hung within an unusually slim scabbard.

"Lord Blackheart," Ornwell muttered in surprise.

The man in black cast a quick series of glances over William's party before he disregarded them and inserted himself between the old knight and the council.

He removed his hat and inclined his mess of black hair. "My Lords and ladies!" he hummed.

Beside William, Helen's brows furrowed and her finger hovered beneath her small nose. "You present yourself to the council in such a state?"

Blackheart lifted his arm and sniffed the stained fabric of his midnight jacket. "Indeed, Lady Helen. Does the scent of my victory offend you?"

"It leaves much to be desired."

William took a step toward the man as he began to chuckle at the retort. "Blackheart, did the Lionheart return with you?"

The man looked the Wanderer up and down, eyes dark. "It is Lord Alvar Blackheart to you, and who might you even be to approach me with such a question?"

Helen spoke for him. "Alvar, this is Sir William of Bastille."

Alvar's eyes suddenly shined like those of a little boy as he jolted forward and took William's hand, shaking it with enthusiasm. "Truly? You are *the* William? The living legend? You defeated the Count of Blud in single combat! You made the Lion bleed! Your tales inspired me as a boy, I must admit. Forgive me, my friend."

The old knight gently placed his hand on the man's shoulder. "There is nothing to forgive. It is fortunate that you have returned. Much has come to light and I suspect the people of Arden will once again require your services. But again I must inquire: did Peter not return with you?"

Blackheart's gleaming dark eyes wavered as he hesitated. "The Lionheart elected to remain in the west for the time being. He commands in Ilvion."

A smile formed on the Wanderer's face. "I see." *Well done, Peter. Your uncle would be proud of your initiative.*

"Now." Alvar turned to the council. "What are these new developments?"

Ornwell spoke. “The nature of the assassin group has been revealed. A secret society under the command of the fallen knight Rob Grimful. It is backed by Lord Turner of Barrington.”

“Indeed.” Blackheart combed his mustache with his fingers. “Has he been arrested?”

“He has fled the city. This council will initiate a new commission. You will command what forces we have to ride for Barrington and bring the Lord here for court.”

“You seek to make war with Barrington? With so few to command, you expect me to arrest him? That is certain suicide.”

“This council is confident in your abilities, Lord Alvar. As it stands, we are familiar with your history and know of your affinity for daring quests. This is one such quest.”

The Blackheart Lord’s smile seemed forced. “Daring quests welcome rewards and I have not yet received what was promised to me.”

“This council reserves the right to delay its rewards or to dispense with them entirely if it so wishes. You remain in our service, do you not?”

Alvar's teeth ground loud enough for William to hear as the Blackheart Lord began to pace back and forth. “My service is now in question.”

“Your pardon?”

William's heart began to race as he watched tension build between Alvar and the council. The warrior in black muttered to himself as he paced.

“Your pardon!” Ornwell repeated. “Might I remind you that you only proceed through our good graces.”

Alvar stopped and growled. “I am not your pup! I will have what is owed to me for I have waited too long and labored too diligently for anything else!”

He has the temperament of a little boy, William noted. *What is this promise made by the council? Why such tension?*

As Lord Ornwell began to speak, Alvar raised his index finger to silence him and a sharp whistle escaped his lips.

William turned as the double doors once again opened. Gasps and shrieks erupted within the chamber as the large snout of a dog appeared. The sunlight shined upon the silver and gray fur of the enormous wolf as it began walking across the floor toward them. A deep growl echoed from its throat as it glared at the city council.

Helen's female guard inserted herself between the beast and the petrified Lady of Lunar Rock. The three inquisitors backed away from the center of the room as a puddle appeared beneath the man in chains. William slowly stepped away, watching as the wolf, which stood taller than a horse, joined Alvar and continued to glare at the fearful council.

Alvar spoke with renewed confidence. "My services are in question, I say."

Ornwell's face hardened. "Who...*who*...do you think you are?"

No, William thought. *Do not make this situation worse, you fool!*

"I am Alvar Blackheart, you plebs! It is time this council recognize my glorious presence in this world. I am its savior! I have accomplished feats not even the Lionheart could muster."

The faces of the council members ranged from terrified to offended. The elder woman next to Ornwell spoke. "You...you are no savior if you bring this...this...monster here to threaten us!"

Alvar patted the glaring wolf. "Tobius is hardly a monster, I assure you, my lady. But I would not antagonize him if I were you."

"Antagonize?" Ornwell scoffed. "You deranged bastard! If you remove this beast then we may very well forgive you for your erratic behavior which we have already endured for quite some time!"

"Oh?" Alvar's gaze hardened. "Is that a threat? To depose me as your savior?"

"You are no savior," Ornwell corrected. "You are merely the son of a harlot with no father! We are the council of Ard—"

"FEAST, TOBIUS!" Alvar bellowed. A thunderous growl filled the chamber and with a powerful leap, the wolf pounced on Ornwell. Snarls and then screams of agony filled the room as the wolf tore into the man before turning on the nearby council members.

"Vera!" Helen cried as the elder woman on the council was torn into two pieces. The three inquisitors drew their sabers and rushed Alvar. The Blackheart Lord sidestepped the first and drew his rapier. The blade whistled and blurred into a series of dark movements and three bloody corpses collapsed around Alvar moments later.

The last of the council members were caught by the wolf and torn apart in the pit of blood and body parts behind the table.

"I must admit that I did not plan on this," Alvar said calmly as he walked toward William. He sheathed his rapier and patted the face of the awestruck assassin in chains as he passed him.

"Have you lost your mind?" the old knight demanded.

Before Alvar could retort, Helen stalked toward them and sank her fist into the Blackheart Lord's face. The female guard pulled her back as Alvar stumbled.

The doors of the chamber once again opened and six hulking figures in plate armor trotted inside. Blood trickled from their great swords and heavy axes, dripping onto the floor.

Alvar rubbed his chin, blood trailing from his mouth. "Such ferocity, my lady."

Tears rolled down her cheeks. "You monster! What do you hope to accomplish!? You will suffer for this."

"Perhaps. If there was a city council to punish me for such an action." He peered at the vacant table. "But it would appear that one no longer exists."

William stood between Alvar and the two women. "This was unwise. You have made a mistake, Alvar."

“You may be correct, Sir William. But recent events have demonstrated the importance of my ascension. There must be sacrifices if I am to fulfill my destiny.”

“Your destiny?”

“I am the savior, as I said. It is my destiny to vanquish the remnants of Norvok. I will not deny my purpose any longer.”

He is delusional. He is but a delusional boy with a sword and a monstrous wolf!

“How do you hope to endure what is to come?” Helen asked bitterly as the six armored warriors surrounded them.

“What is to come,” he repeated. “I must ascend and take her head, there is no doubt about that. Until such time, I will need assistance. I require the two of you.” His dark eyes shifted between the old knight and the Lady of Lunar Rock as he extended his hand towards them both. “I want you both to join me. It is fate, is it not? The people already worship me, that is clear, but I am not so vain that I fail to see I am in need of assistance.”

Slowly, Helen stepped towards him. “You are in need of more than that.” she stated before glancing at William. “Flee!”

Her fist sailed through the air and into Alvar's mouth. A blur of dark movement surrounded William as the six men in armor rushed forward. Two of the armored men subdued the female warrior as another grabbed the Lady of Lunar Rock. William dodged the attempts the remaining three made to restrain him and dashed away toward the entrance of the chamber.

Helen called out to him, “Find my sister! Get her out of the city! Find Pet—” A black glove covered her mouth.

As William reached the doorway, he glanced over his shoulder. Alvar stood with his six bodyguards and the two captured women as the blood-soaked wolf hovered over them. They watched as the old knight fled.

Chapter 21

Finding Hope

His mind raced with his body as he descended the last flight of stairs. *This is madness! The council, slain by a monster, controlled by an overgrown boy. But the way he killed the inquisitors—he possesses skill beyond his years. I am not yet prepared to combat such ferocity. Where is she?* Frantic, he searched every inch of the citadel as he made his way to the entry chamber. The double doors remained wide open, allowing the light to beam onto the two guards in conversation there.

William stopped at the top of the stone steps. The courtyard was filled with Alvar's soldiers and the crowds of citizens that surrounded them.

They are Blackheart's men; they will remain loyal to him, I assume. His eyes darted from face to face until he saw her at the base of the steps. The younger Moonwey sister sat alone on a bench, appearing bored, with her head in her hands. The old knight skipped down the steps.

"Aurora Moonwey."

She looked up at him and squinted. “Possibly.”

“You must come with me immediately.”

“Is this...is this a joke? Did Helen goad you into this?”

“Your sister has been taken captive by Alvar Blackheart.”

She cocked an eyebrow as several people nearby began to point at them and whisper. “Who are you?”

“Sir William. You witnessed me with Lady Helen when we passed through the magistrate's lounge.”

“Indeed. I did.” The truth dawned on her and she stood. “Helen,” she muttered, starting up the steps.

He grabbed her arm. “No, my lady. Your sister ordered that I remove you from the city at once.”

She began to pull away. “I am not going to abandon my sister!”

At the top of the stairs, a hulking figure in black armor emerged from the doorway.

“There is no time. You must depart with me at once.”

The young woman’s pained face shifted between the old knight and the man in black descending toward them. “Lead on.”

He led her to a pair of nearby horses. To his surprise, the young woman leapt into the saddle with graceful precision as he slowly hoisted himself into his own. The crowd parted before them. He had started down a nearby street when she called out behind him, “Aren’t we going north? To Bastille? I thought you were the head of the Order. My cousin is there!”

“That road is no longer safe.”

They galloped down a few more streets and along the road that led out the western gate.

“Then what is your plan exactly, Sir William?”

The gate passed over them as they galloped along the prince's road, entering the forest. “There are other routes through the mountains near Stonewell. We will travel that way to my home.”

“That could take days!” she exclaimed. “And after?”

“I will confer with the Order and we will consider the best possible actions to take. Another thing is certain: we will require the Lionheart if we are to end this madness.”

“But I have heard nothing of Peter. I received a letter from him a few days ago but since I have been told nothing of him.”

“It is said that he commands in Ilvion.”

“Peter's in Ilvion?” She hesitated. “Then I will ride for Ilvion.”

“That could take weeks! And you will not go unguarded.”

“You are free to accompany me, Sir William.” Her steed suddenly sped up. “If you can keep up.”

* * * * * * *

The woman rode exceedingly well along the western route. William's horse strained to keep her in his sight as she pressed ahead. Hours passed and the sky's mood slowly changed. The sun began to set ahead of them on a wall of western clouds. He rode blinded by the light as he followed after her through the forest. Behind them, the summit of the solitary peak receded over the treetops.

“Masterstown,” he heard her call out. A few moments later the small community revealed itself, encased by a wall and the forest. They passed beneath the gate. The trotting of their steeds echoed along the cobblestone courtyard. In the center of the town, a poorly dressed man strummed a lute beneath the statue of Toven Ornian. The few people that walked near him fled as he began to sing at them.

“We arrived relatively quickly,” Aurora noted as they dismounted and led their horses to the nearby stables. The animals bent their heads to the tub of water at the entrance.

“So too should we depart.”

"And kill our stolen steeds?" She stroked the amber hair of her horse. "They exhaust easier than you know."

"Indeed, my lady." He sighed and eased himself into a nearby chair, finally relaxing his own exhausted body. He reached to rub his aching head where the blood had dried.

"So. Sir William. It is said that you died ten years ago, yet you stand...or rather, sit here now. Where have you been?"

"The Otherworld."

"Truly?"

"Indeed. I am the one responsible for Peter's arrival in Arden."

"You passed between worlds. How, might I inquire? Peter and his uncle came to our world along with the twelve, but they did not leave, yet you were able to leave and return. How?"

He stared somberly at the hay on the floor of the stable, recalling the day. "My final day in Arden was the day of the siege. The sea called to me. Since I awoke that morning it called my name. My body felt anew, as if I were someone else. An impulse overtook me as day became night, becoming something I could not ignore. I allowed it to take hold and it brought me to the spire over the ocean. I looked down into the abyss of the sea and I saw it. I saw the doorway to another world."

"So you say," she muttered. "And that is also how you returned with Peter?"

"Yes. On that day in the Otherworld, I awoke with the same impulse and the sea called to me. Fortune smiled upon me and frowned upon Peter, as on that very same day, he too was on the beach with his class."

"Class?"

He shook his head, dismissing the question. "Standing on that beach, I knew I would soon return to my world, but I decided that I would not return alone. I tricked him into following me and thus pulled him from his world into my own."

"But why? Why did you do that to him?"

"It was a feeling."

"The impulse?"

"Indeed. The impulse. I am the cause of his plight and I am prepared to receive his hatred until I draw my last breath."

"I suppose I understand." She rested her head on the gently heaving flank of the horse. "Some weeks ago his eyes just came to mind. I was racing and like a vision, I saw those blue eyes staring at me. A feeling like yours, I suppose. Ever since, he has ever been in my thoughts, plaguing me." She laughed. "But I don't mind. It's quite pleasant actually."

Her words brought a smile to the old knight's face. He had dedicated his entire life to the Order. He had never known romance nor cared to as his oath called against such things. But he was filled with delight at the idea of love between the young couple. Lady Helen's words about Peter and Aurora came to mind and he began to laugh.

"What are you cackling about?" she inquired, hiding her face.

He shook his head. *There is yet light in this dark hour, even in the smallest of ways.*

* * * * * * *

A faint light peeked over the eastern sky, warming their backs as the sun slowly revealed itself. Dark clouds of blue and gray occupied the entire western horizon. A cool gust of wind propelled their trot along the road. The young woman yawned loudly, rubbing her eyes as they ascended yet another hill. William glanced over to Aurora as she bobbed up and down with each trot. Her half-closed gaze met his, displaying her discontent with the last few days of brief rests and little food.

Remain strong, little one, he thought before turning back to the path ahead. As they reached the top of the next hill, the Ornian ruins came into view. The ghost city sat nestled in the center of the river that snaked north and south, dividing the vast plains of the old kingdom.

As they stopped to gaze upon history's beautiful disaster, Aurora exhaled loudly.

"This is your first time bearing witness to the ruins?" he asked.

She slowly nodded. "It's...magnificent, yet so dreadful."

Silence followed and her stomach growled loudly next to him, causing his own to do the same.

The road continued through a sea of fields bearing grass nearly as tall as the old knight. As they neared the old city, the steady flow of water soothed William's ears before he began to detect the sound of unseen townsfolk. To his surprise, as they entered, he saw that a small encampment lay sprawled along the main street of the city. Groups of men worked as women washed garments in tubs of water from the river. *Civilians. In the ruins so soon?*

They halted their horses in the center of the bustling encampment. A man approached. His clothing was golden and eccentric. He was of smaller stature, and husky. His head shined, bald like William's own, but he bore a distinct gray goatee. His smile seemed everlasting.

"Morning, friend. Traveling west?"

"Indeed," William replied. "I had not thought the western regions would be resettled so soon."

"Not yet. They're only allowing civilians into Carvalel and in few numbers as of now. The plague still exists but only in small towns that haven't been cleared. Is that where you're off to, if you don't mind my asking?"

"Yes. Carvalel. What do you know of the situation there, other than the few civilians they allow to enter? Who is in command?"

"Seems as if it changes from day to day. One day it's Lord Carlon and the day after it's Sir Titus. The lot of us arrived just as Lord Alvar was departing the ruins. He gave us his blessing to remain here until further word was received from the west. We—" The man's gaze shifted to Aurora. William's eyes followed to see the young woman snoring as she lay over the neck of her horse. “Does she need a respite?” the man asked.

William hesitated. “I believe that would be prudent; she has more than earned it. Do you have room to spare for a few hours so that she may rest?”

The smiling man bowed. “We do indeed. Food as well that you are both welcome to.”

Relief washed over the Wanderer, bringing a smile to his face. “You are most kind.”

Chapter 22

The Vile One

The morning sun shined through his bedroom window. He stretched his little muscles beneath the sheets of the bed, listening to the music. The classic rock song was one of many that Jack liked to listen to on repeat. The words echoed from the hallway and into his bedroom.

Slowly, the boy opened his eyes and rose, yawning as he stood. A whiff of fried bacon rushed into his nostrils, spurring his steps toward the door of the bedroom. He quickly tapped his soccer ball on the way out into the hallway, taking a shot into the open doorway near the staircase. The ball soared into the darkness of the room as he descended the steps, passing the silent family room.

He stopped as he entered the hallway at the base of the stairs. The open door to the left allowed the classic rock song to pervade the home unabated. He peeked inside his uncle Jack's office. The desk in front of the open window featured a few stacks of papers that took flight and scattered in a gust of wind. In the left corner of the room, the black record rotated and the music continued. To the right of the room, a large American flag took up the entire wall, hovering over a table that featured dozens of awards, medals, and photographs.

The scent of smoked meat grasped his attention once again and he turned, running down the hallway to the kitchen. He stopped in his tracks as he entered. Sitting at the far side of the kitchen table, his grandmother stared at him with oily black eyes, showing no trace of white or blue. The flesh along the tips of her fingers had rotted away, leaving bone-claws holding her coffee mug. His nine-year-old body froze, paralyzed by fear.

The old woman smiled. A tar-like substance oozed between her filed yellow teeth. His grandmother spoke with a voice that was not her own. "Good morning, Peter."

He looked to his left, where his mother stood in front of the stove. She turned to him with the same black eyes. Her claws held a frying pan containing a chunk of human skin that sizzled in oil.

"Good morning, Peter," its vile womanly voice said through his mother.

His mouth refused to move; his legs were like jelly, refusing to run.

"Good morning, Peter," the voice said through both women. "Sit!"

His body betrayed him and walked on its own to the nearby chair, across from his grandmother. The midnight pits glared at him from across the table as he sat and his mother moved to stand behind him. The frying pan plummeted to the tile floor as the woman behind him leaned forward and nuzzled his ear, sending chill-bumps all along his body.

She pressed her lips to his ear, the tar dripping from her mouth onto his neck, and hissed, "Bruise his heel."

The voice spoke through both women again, muttering, "Bruise his heel. Bruise his heel. Bruise his heel. Bruise his heel."

* * * * * * *

"Will this deluge ever end?" the woman asked beneath her hood. "It has been raining since we departed the ruins."

William guided his horse around a puddle taking up half the road before he answered, "Eventually, My Lady."

The steady thrashing of the rain against the muddy road and the grass from the fields soothed the old knight. He glanced from left to right, marveling at the vast fields and rolling hills flanking the road that carried on ahead beneath the low-hanging clouds. "Carvalel," he said upon noticing the walled city in the distance, thought it was not yet larger than his thumbnail.

"Carvalel, you say? Thank Fyraen. We may find shelter and sufficient food."

"That may not be all. We may encounter enemies here, that is yet to be discerned. I am certain, though, that we are the first to arrive west from the capital since the council's massacre. Still, at this time Alvar's madness is not the only threat. Sir Titus Turner is the cousin of Ian Turner. If Barrington has turned against us, then it is likely the knight has done so as well. It would be prudent to find Carlon of Stonewell and explain the situation to him. He may be our only ally for now until we find Peter and I inform the Order."

The old knight's apprehension grew as their steeds galloped forth under the rain shower. Slowly, the city grew in size as they approached. The towers spaced along the wall that encircled the city extended towards the sky, promising to touch the low clouds with banners that streamed in the wind. In a field to the south of the city, three piles of charred and indiscernible debris sat nearly as high the wall. His gaze shifted from the piles to the gatehouse as the doors crept open for them.

The doors closed behind them as they entered a small courtyard, surrounded by buildings of wood, stone, and brick. A few streets opened between some of the buildings, and the main road of the city lay ahead of them, leading to the city center. From the brick house adjacent to the gate, a guard strolled towards them. The rain pelted against his leather helm as he looked up to William.

"You from the Ornian?" he asked them.

"Arden City. Who is in command here?"

The guard hesitated. "Depends."

"Depends? Where is Lord Carlon?"

"Who are you to ask?"

Before the knight could answer, Aurora's horse edged forward and poked at the guard with his nose, knocking him off balance for a moment. She removed her hood, allowing the rain to soak her hair and drip along her face. "You will inform Lord Carlon of our arrival!" she told him. As the guard began to retort, she extended her index finger towards him and glared.

The guard glanced over to his comrades in the window of the brick house, who then fled from view. He hesitated before asking, "Who are you?"

"Aurora, daughter of Lord Edward Moonwey. I am accompanied by Sir William of Bastille."

The eyes beneath the helm widened, shifting between the two people on horseback. "We will show you to him, my lady." He bowed before turning and departing.

William looked at her. "Perhaps that was impetuous."

"So you say, but at least we won't have to remain in the rain for much longer," she said, as another guard climbed into the saddle of a nearby horse and trotted toward them, beckoning them to follow.

The three followed the main road of the city. Laughter emanated from numerous houses that they passed. A few soldiers trotted past the trio as they rode through the city center, which bore a fountain with dirty water. The guard led them to a fenced estate where a large villa stood, surrounded by a garden and a city of tents.

All of these tents are vacant, William noted as they arrived at the entrance of the villa. A few vacant desks stood to the left under the stone canopy of the patio. A series of crates occupied the space to the right. After dismounting, they continued along the path to the front doors of the manor.

Once inside the entry room, a man in an expensive white shirt and black vest approached. His brown hair was tied neatly back with a ribbon. He seemed to be in his late twenties.

"Good afternoon." He inclined his head. "I am Lord Carlon. I was informed that word had been received from the council and that it was Sir William and Lady Moonwey that delivered it."

William nodded. "Indeed it is. There is much to discuss, Lord Carlon, and we have little time."

"Forgive me for my skepticism. How do I know that you are in fact the legendary knight? After all, he has been dead for a decade."

Aurora chimed in, "I can vouch for him."

"Of course, Lady Moonwey," Carlon murmured. "I only met Lady Helen on one occasion, so you must be her sister. Aurora, correct?"

Water dripped onto the stone floor as she twisted her soaked hair with her hands. "Indeed. I am in need of a change in wardrobe, and food."

The man chuckled. "Of course. My staff will see that you are made comfortable and then we will speak."

William ate little and changed into a new robe before entering the commander's office. A desk stood in front of the window. Rain poured onto the gardens beyond. On the two walls flanking the desk, bookshelves were filled with various colors and sizes of bindings. The old knight sat in one of the chairs in front of the desk as Carlon eased himself into the seat behind it and smiled.

"So, Sir William. What news do you bring?"

The Wanderer hesitated before answering. "The city council is dead. Massacred by Alvar Blackheart."

The man behind the desk cocked an eyebrow and grinned faintly. "Did I hear you correctly?"

"I am afraid so. He and his wolf murdered every member of the council. He has taken Lady Helen captive and by now the other province leaders who have not allied with him."

After a moment of silence, the man covered his mouth in despair. "This cannot be."

"It is. And there is more, I am afraid."

For the next ten minutes, William explained the events behind Alvar's treachery as well as the details of the assassin group.

"The Turners of Barrington?" Carlon asked in shock.

"Indeed. I was hesitant to approach Carvalel when I learned of the instability of command, not to insult."

"The situation is indeed precarious, Sir William. The command should have fallen to me after Lord Rulfin's unfortunate passing. However, most of the officers hail from Barrington, as well as most of the Fighting knights. Sir Hector of New London was an exception, but he too fell during the skirmish north of his home city. Now most of the forces in the city declare themselves for Sir Titus, stationed in the Marsh Villa in the northern district. Things have been...civil, but moments of tension do indeed arise."

"How could this happen? Such instability. What is the Turner knight intending?"

"I was questioning that myself, sir, until now. If what you say is true about his cousin backing the assassins, the situation will surely worsen."

William rubbed his temples. "We will need assistance if this madness is to end!"

"I agree with you, Sir William. What do you propose? Will your order finally step forth to end the bloodshed?"

"In time. For now I am bound to travel north for the Lionheart himself. The Lady Aurora is quite intent upon the quest."

A flicker of excitement flashed across Carlon's face. "Of course! However...none have seen His Lordship for some time."

"What do you mean?"

"The Lionheart has not been seen for over a week, sir. Lord Alvar claimed that he remained in Ilvion, but Captain Gideon commands there and no other."

A dreadful realization descended upon him and William's head fell into his hands. *No...No! Lord, please no. Where is Peter? What has become of him? This cannot be.* He looked up to the Commander. "Where was he last seen?"

"Captain Gideon said that he last saw the Lionheart with Lord Blackheart in Olton before he was commanded to travel for Ilvion."

"Olton..." He struggled to recall the western cities and towns. "North of Gareton?"

"Indeed, sir. Gareton offers the option of continuing north for Olton or west for the coastal road to Ilvion. The northern road splits once it reaches Olton, I believe. Continue to Ilvion or east for Hearthelm."

"I will conduct my own investigation on this matter. However, I am hindered by the Lady Aurora. Taking her north would be unwise and leaving her in the city in its current state is unsettling. Her protests to ride for Bastille continually confound me."

"I could spare a few of my own men to assist you north," Carlon proposed.

"I cannot rob you of what few men you have. I will depart in the morning with the Lady. The current storm system will have passed and we will proceed north."

"As you say, sir."

"If only Rulfin had not fallen."

"Agreed. It is unsettling in itself, though."

William cocked an eyebrow. “What do you mean?”

“After the second battle for the city, the infected began to attack...differently. Almost in an organized fashion. When I received the report of the battle north of New London, I was confused and quite frankly baffled at what I was told. They said that when Lord Rulfin was acting as the field commander during the battle, the horde began to shift and go directly after His Lordship. The frontlines were quickly overwhelmed, as well as the commander’s guards. The horde descended on Lord Rulfin as if it knew he was the commander. Following his death, the army fell into disarray until suddenly the infected just stopped.”

“They stopped?”

“Indeed, sir. As if they lost interest. Every single infected person ceased any movement.”

William sunk into his chair, his mind racing. “What is happening?”

Chapter 23

Black As Midnight

The cool morning air soothed the old knight as he stood alone in the garden of the villa. The pink and orange eastern sky slowly brightened as the leaves of the trees around him gently rustled in the breeze. *Tranquility*. He smiled, closing his eyes. *These moments of peace are so few, it is sad to say.* His thoughts drifted away into distant memories. He recalled being a boy of twelve, a Wanderer roaming from New London and camping beneath a few bushes along the road as night descended upon him. He remembered laying on his back beneath his home of shrubbery, staring through a hole in the bushes, into the countless stars above. A vast cosmic ocean created by someone and he had to know who. Who was his creator? Who would love him above all else?

"William," someone said. He opened his eyes and turned to see Aurora. She seemed refreshed and wore new riding attire, consisting of fitted trousers tucked into polished riding boots and a leather vest over her black tunic. "Whenever you are prepared to depart, sir."

They stood in the road outside the villa with their saddled horses. As two of Carlon's aides placed food and wineskins into the saddlebags, William shook hands with the commander. "You have my gratitude," he told the younger man. "I pray that the situation will not worsen as we depart. Once we find the Lionheart, we will return to assist in easing the tension."

"And for that, Sir William, you have my gratitude." He inclined his head as William climbed into the saddle. Beside him, Aurora leapt into hers and eased a pistol into its holster beside her.

William sighed. "Is that...?"

"Why yes, Sir William, it is."

"Please do not shoot me," he said, and she chuckled.

William and Carlon nodded to one another and the old knight started forth, followed by the young woman. They trotted along the road to the city center, silent and void of movement. They rode through the northern gate as the guards watched, whispering to one another.

Hours passed as they continued along the northern road. The sun traveled slowly across the blue sky, a rarity in the west, William knew. He looked from left to right, rolling hills extending as far he could see. On the horizon ahead of them, a small town appeared. As they approached, he heard the sounds of construction: hammers beating against wood and stones being chiseled.

They passed beneath the gatehouse into a cobblestone courtyard surrounded by wooden structures. A few soldiers walked forward with no armor, each sweating from their work.

"Afternoon. Welcome to Gareton," one greeted. Stains lingered on the white fabric of his shirt beneath his arms. "You bring word from Carvalel?"

"Is the Lionheart present?" William called out in the town center. The men in front of them looked to one another and shrugged.

"Not here, mister. Who are you to ask?"

William shook his head and kicked his heels into the steed's flanks, bounding forth through the town and out the northern gate, with Aurora threatening to ride ahead.

* * * * * * *

The wind howled dreadfully through the empty streets of Olton. A single stone bastion at the center of the town towered over the buildings that clustered around it. Their horses paced uneasily in the center of the road as William considered which route to take—left or right.

Aurora spoke first. "I think we should travel for Ilvion."

"I disagree. I feel Hearthelm is where we must go."

She glared at him. "Is that so? Is it the impulse? Has it returned to you?" she mocked. Before he could answer, she continued, "Well I feel we should ride for Ilvion. I am pulled to it by a feeling...like the one I felt when I kept seeing Peter's eyes." She dug her heels into her horse and flew down the left road.

William struggled to follow as she raced ahead. Olton receded behind them and in the evening sky, a series of gray clouds formed to the north. The pressure in the air surrounding them began to shift and the old knight grew nervous. Aside from the sea, the destructive power of western storms was the only other thing that terrified him.

An hour passed as the sun disappeared over the horizon. As they rode, the ocean came into view to their left. The glittering sea grew as dark as the sky and the storm clouds ahead of them.

"Riders!" Aurora called back, slowing her pace to join him. William's focus had been so directed at the clouds overhead that he hadn't noticed the three soldiers galloping toward them in the blue air. William and Aurora slowed, finally halting as the three men did the same, and both parties met in the middle of the road.

"Evening," William said to them.

"What do you want?" the soldier in the center demanded.

"We ride for Ilvion in search of the Lionheart."

The three soldiers looked to one another and drew their pistols.

"Turn around and ride back!" the superior said.

William hesitated, debating why they were reacting in such a way. *Are they following Alvar's commands?* he wondered.

Aurora edged forward and spoke. "Please. We're looking for Peter. It's important that we find him."

One of the soldiers whispered to another, "You think that's her?"

"Shhh!" the superior ordered, turning back to her. "What is your name?"

"Aurora. Aurora Moonwey."

The superior nodded and put his pistol away. "You should accompany us, my lady," he said softly and almost apologetically.

The three soldiers rode ahead of them along the dirt path they had taken from the main road. A few trees flanking their path swayed in the breeze. At the end of the rural trail, a few lights glowed from the windows of a country house.

The five of them halted their horses after crossing the fence of the property. To the right, an old barn creaked, threatening to collapse in a single gust. The manor of the property seemed as old as the barn, standing two stories of wood and brick.

They dismounted as a muscular man strolled out of the front door. His black hair and beard were as dark as the night itself. He wore simple trousers and an old maroon tunic with a weapons belt fastened around the waist, allowing his saber to remain at one side, his pistol on the other.

The leading soldier joined the man on the porch. "It's her, Captain," he told him.

"So," he said gruffly. "You are *the* Aurora?"

She walked forward. "I am. Who are you?"

"Captain Gideon, my lady." He inclined his head.

"Captain, where is Peter?" she asked, her voice strained.

Even in the night, William could see the captain waver.

"This way, my lady." He indicated the open door and they all entered.

William's nerves became unbearable as they passed the family room of the manor and ascended the creaky wooden steps. His heart raced; he feared the worst, remembering the little boy Peter had been when he had watched him in Norfolk. A smiling young boy full of radiant love.

They entered the hallway at the top of the stairs and stepped into the master bedroom. Candles flickered from the tables flanking the bed where the body lay. Peter's once-blonde hair was gray and pink, dyed with his own blood. The outlines of his bones pressed against his pale skin where his body had atrophied at an unusual rate. Along the length of his naked torso, dozens of bite marks and scratches turned the knight's stomach. A chunk of the boy's flesh had been torn from his neck. Peter's face was still and dead.

The air escaped Aurora loudly as she laid eyes on him. Her hands covered her mouth as her shoulders began to heave and tears streamed from her eyes. She stumbled forward and knelt over the bed, grasping the scarred hand of the dead boy. "What has this world done to you, Peter?" she cried.

William's own breath escaped him as his heart skipped and he fell to the floor. He felt as if his own son had just died before his eyes.

Next to him, Gideon cleared his throat as he wiped his own tears, struggling to speak. "We found him in Hearthelm a few days ago, surrounded by scores of infected bodies that he had died fighting."

The old knight's eyes stung, his throat constricted. He looked up to the captain. "What happened?"

The man shook his head. "We don't know. He departed for Hearthelm with Lord Alvar when we were ordered for Ilvion. A day later, Alvar came to the city briefly before departing again. He didn't say where. I thought it strange that the lad didn't come by to visit me, so I got curious. I rode for Hearthelm and found him like that.

"Afterward, I didn't know who to tell or who I could trust, so I brought him here with some of my men from Hightower, men I can trust to stand vigil for him." He paused. "I couldn't believe it when I saw him lying like that in a pool of blood, surrounded by the bodies. We cleaned him the best we could and I've been considering how best to bury him." The dark brows of the man furrowed.

William stood and placed a gentle hand on the captain's shoulder. He slowly walked to the far side of the bed to kneel and watch as the woman across from him gently trailed her fingers along the dead boy's still face. The old knight's head fell into his hands as he berated himself, hearing nothing but the young woman's sobs.

This is my doing. Peter is dead because of me.

* * * * * * *

Alone in the darkness, he remained. Between everything and nothing. Between life and death. Between what was and what could not be. He remained.

He remembered. He remembered what he had been before. His name had been Peter. But it meant little now. Without form, his consciousness drifted on the sea of oblivion.

And there she was. There *it* was. Her. The darkness that pervaded, corrupted, and destroyed; it surrounded and filled him. She was the one. The one behind the plagues. Who was she? What was she?

"Fade," her vile voice whispered.

He attempted to speak, to retort, but he possessed no lips to form words.

Words. They were power, a power that he had not fully realized he had possessed until now, when he no longer had it. Void of his human power, he instead listened and waited. She was angry, he knew. The vile one who surrounded him was furious. He suspected why.

"You are nothing. You are meaningless," she told him. It was a lie. He mattered. He had purpose.

She's a liar. Life isn't meaningless, he thought to himself.

She grew fearful. She was afraid of his thoughts. What if he could speak again? What if he had a body again?

From the darkness, her voice sounded ethereal. "Every day to be had will pass, fade, as all things do. You are not free from time, nor space, nor matter! You are locked in the prison of existence. There is no escape but one: death." Her words were icy, bearing some truth, yet he knew they were incomplete and twisted. She was offering him a solution.

Amidst the sudden tempest of thought, emotion, and debate, he resolved. And he found the words. He found the will to say, "I'm not afraid."

Her fear became manifest and a vision appeared to Peter Loneheart.

It was black and white. There was a walled community. A town that he knew, for he had been there before. Masterstown. The statue of Toven Ornian stood highest above the heads of those that filled the courtyard. A procession was on the move through the town. Dozens of riders on horseback trotted beneath the navy blue and silver crescent moon banner of Lunsera. At the head of the column rode the Lord of the province, Edward Moonwey. He was young and handsome, with long honey-brown hair. He smiled and waved to the crowd.

From the top of an adjacent tower, something moved. Someone jumped and landed on an adjacent rooftop. Little by little, those standing in the courtyard began to look to the one who ran so quickly, jumping from rooftop to rooftop in broad daylight. When it landed in the courtyard, a woman screamed as she saw it. A monster of humanoid appearance.

It eyed the Lord of Lunsera where he sat on horseback. In a blur of crimson movement, it dashed through the panicking crowd. It was an infected person, Peter knew. But it was different from the others. It was mutated and something else.

Edward Moonwey's eyes widened just before it struck him. The Lord's head fell from his body.

Another vision formed.

There was a cave. The floor was littered with snakes, the walls lined with hundreds of infected people. Something tall and powerful was submerged within the cave wall, and a man approached her. The man stopped and tapped on the pommel of his sheathed rapier.

"Perhaps I shall destroy you now then," Alvar threatened with a grin.

The vile presence within the wall began to quiver. Was it anger? Or was it fear?

Another vision formed.

Upon a rocky cliff by the sea, three slabs of stone stood as a doorway. Upon the stones, runes were carved, ignited with the same milky light that lingered between the three slabs. A man's hand protruded, wrapped in silver chains.

"No!" Jack Loneheart exclaimed.

Within the darkness, Peter Loneheart remembered. "Who are you?" he asked the vile one. Before their connection could be severed, she told him. And as one they said her name.

"Verluxia."

* * * * * * *

The day had passed in dreary silence. A steady rain shower had continued through the night, lasting into the afternoon. William sat on the front porch of the manor, alone. He hated himself. He hated the selfish decision he had made to trick Peter into following him that day on the beach. The old knight felt he deserved to suffer for what he had done to the boy, taking him from his own life and into another he had not chosen.

"Sir William," Gideon said from the doorway. The captain held two cups in his hand, and handed one to the old knight.

"Gratitude," William thanked him before sipping on warm tea with honey. "Aurora?"

"The Lady continues to sleep and mourn, as we all do. May I join you, sir?"

He smiled. "Of course." The bearded man sat next to him. The two silently watched the downpour as it created mud all around the property.

"When I was in the Otherworld," William began, "I watched over Peter from afar. He was spirited as a boy and affectionate toward those he loved. As he grew, he withdrew within himself. It seemed as if he was hiding, from what I observed. I longed to meet his inner self and to see the man he would grow to become." He stopped as two riders rode with haste down the road toward the manor.

Gideon stood and walked to the edge of the porch, watching as the riders entered the property. They halted their horses in the mud puddles in front of the house.

"Captain, a troop approaches from Carvalel!"

"What?"

"It's Sir Titus!"

William looked at the captain. *Will he answer to the knight?* His gaze shifted to the far-off road where a dozen riders galloped towards them.

"What do they seek?" Gideon barked at his men.

The soldiers remained quiet.

"Well?"

Finally, one spoke. "Sir William and Lady Moonwey."

Within a few moments, the troop of riders filed into the muddy lot between the barn and manor. A dozen musket-wielding dragoons. A man in gleaming armor trotted forth. The rain that pelted his maroon and gold plates also soaked the long strands of his golden hair. He pointed at William. "Sir William of Bastille?"

The old knight looked to Gideon and then to the man in the rain. "I am."

"Arrest him!" Titus ordered. Four soldiers dismounted and grabbed the Wanderer roughly. "Legend or not, you have no right to murder city council members and slander the Turner name."

Captain Gideon hesitated. "Sir, if I may...what is the meaning of this?"

William was pulled into the rain and tied to a nearby horse. Three other dragoons dismounted and entered the house.

"Word has been received that Alvar Blackheart has murdered the city council with the assistance of Sir William. It has also been learned that the Moonwey family are co-conspirators of the atrocity."

"I...I...but my Lord," Gideon stuttered.

Aurora shrieked from inside the manor and a series of thuds echoed loudly. One soldier limped out the front door, moaning with pain as he held his groin. The other two emerged with the young woman in tow, throwing her into the mud beyond the porch. Fury arose within the old knight as he watched her rise slowly, her hair soaked with mud.

"My Lord," one of the two soldiers said to Sir Titus, "he is here. The Lionheart. His body."

"He's dead?" The knight on horseback glared at Captain Gideon and hissed, "You hid the Lionheart's fate from us all?!" His jaw rotated and he pointed at the captain. "I will deal with you in time! As for now, you will return to Ilvion." He turned back to his men. "Have his body prepared for travel. The Lionheart will go to Barrington where he will be buried with our ancestors."

The three soldiers reentered the manor.

"No!" Aurora cried as she stood, wiping the mud from her face. "Peter is the Lion of Lunsera and he will return to my home, not yours."

"You are mistaken, my lady. The Lionheart and I bear kindred blood, and it is time our families make amends. By the time this is over, your family will be extinct and Lunar Rock a colony of Barrington."

Suddenly, a few screams sounded before silence fell. Slow and steady footsteps echoed from the house. William squinted and wiped away the drops of rain as he saw a silhouette beyond the doorway of the manor.

One of the soldiers emerged from the doorway, but he did not walk. His body levitated in the air until it shifted to the side and Peter's face appeared behind it. His black, infected eyes stared at them all from over the shoulder of the dragoon he held. The body was cast aside like a rag doll and Peter strolled forth onto the porch. Half-naked, skinny and scarred, he was a walking corpse with midnight eyes.

"He's infected," Sir Titus spat. "Kill him!" He raised his musket and Peter disappeared. A blur of blue and black darted from where the corpse stood to the knight's horse. Peter reappeared in the center of everyone, holding the knight by his throat with a single hand. Titus' boots kicked in the air as he was raised up high. The animated corpse that was Peter Loneheart wound his free hand back and the nails of his fingers turned black, extending into onyx daggers.

Peter grinned and spoke. "So, you want to make amends, huh?" His arm thrust forward and his long black nails pierced the knight's chest through his armor. As Titus took his last wheezing breaths, Peter's black eyes shifted between each of the knight's dragoons, half of them clutching their pistols.

"Try me," he said to them.

One by one, muskets and sabers were released, falling into the mud as their horrified wielders raised their hands.

Peter retracted his hand from the dead knight's chest and released his grip so the corpse plummeted into the mud, face down. He turned toward William and Aurora. As the old knight gazed upon the resurrected man in front of him, the darkness in the eyes receded, allowing the white and blue to reemerge.

It was Peter Loneheart again.

His face contorted in agony as he glanced down to the dead knight. Tears filled his eyes.

Before William or Aurora could utter a word, he disappeared in a blur of light blue movement.

Chapter 24

Departure

The Lion of Lunsera stared into the distance at the plains and rolling hills beneath the overcast. The rain had stopped, but the cold remained. Standing at the top of the hill alone, as he had for the last hour, he looked down at his bloody and scarred hands. As he rubbed his fingers together, he focused on the short nails of his right hand. A strange sensation ran along the lengths of his digits and the nails slowly turned black like coal. The black shards extended, growing into dark claws.

"Peter," she said from behind, and he turned. Aurora looked up at him, muddy and concerned. She paced toward him and he took a step back.

"No," he protested.

Her gaze lowered to the black claws of his fingernails before shifting back to his eyes. She smiled. "It's alright," she said, edging forward to take his lethal hand into hers. The claws receded into normal nails as her softness enveloped him.

"I'm sorry," he told her. "I'm so sorry. I...Aurora, I'm scared. I don't know what's happening to me. I feel like me but at the same time, I don't. Titus...I didn't have to kill him. I felt a lifetime's worth of pain and rage in that one moment...it was murder." His eyes stung.

She kissed the knuckles of his hand. "But you're alive, Peter! I feared the worst. I never thought I would see you again and it seemed so unbearable..." She shook her head. "I am thankful that you yet live."

He reached into the pocket of his trousers, removing the gray cloth. She smiled as he handed it to her. The red flower emerged as she unfolded it.

"A crimson corpette?" She held it between them and they both pressed the tips of their noses to the red petals, smelling the honeysuckle-like scent. "So much has happened, Peter. So much has changed."

"You're right." He twirled his fingers in the strands of her hair. "A lot has changed." His gaze fell to her lips. She closed her eyes as they both leaned in.

But when his lids shut, he saw the serpent in the back of his mind. The reptilian eyes glared at him, filled with anger and sinister intent, and he remembered.

He jerked away before their lips could meet. "Dammit!"

Aurora's brows pressed together as she looked away, embarrassed. "What? Did I—"

"No! It's not you. It's her."

"Peter...what are you talking about?"

"I know about the plague. I know what caused it, or rather who caused it...I just don't know what she is."

He took her hand and they descended the hill to find William and Gideon. After a few hugs from his bearded friend and a single fatherly embrace from William, he led them to the dining room of the manor. The four sat at the oak table and he explained what had happened in Hearthelm and what followed with the darkness and the serpent.

"Verluxia," William repeated.

"That's her. I don't know what she really is but she's not human. She created the plague virus and I think...every plague in Arden's history. I saw Jack at one point being pulled into some kind of door by white chains. She knows what happened to Jack, and I think Alvar made a deal with her. I think we should find him and have him tell us everything he knows."

"That won't be difficult," Aurora told him.

Confused, Peter looked around the table, and his eyes found William's. He was told of Barrington's treachery, the massacre of the council, and Alvar's ascension.

Helen, Peter lamented as his head sank into his hands. *I'm so sorry. I'll fix this!*

Aurora's hand stroked his back over the gray blanket he wore. He looked up to William. "So when do we leave?"

"You must rest for now, Peter. It is a miracle that you yet live."

"Rest?" he scoffed. "No. I'm done being passive. I'm not going to stand by anymore. I—" Suddenly his stomach growled loudly. "—I'm also really hungry!" he said, earning laughs from the three at the table.

Continuing to chuckle as he stood, Gideon's eyes shined like sapphires. "I'll have the lads fetch you something special." He inclined his head. "My Lord."

"Gideon," Peter said as the captain began to leave. Gideon turned in the doorway. "Thank you for everything." The man smiled and departed.

"Let us not forget Carvalel," Aurora said to Peter and William. "There was an issue at hand as we departed the city. If you recall, Sir William, Lord Carlon provided us with needed assistance...perhaps we should return the favor."

"Indeed," the knight replied. "With the Turner knight no longer in the city, I must confess myself curious about its current state." He hesitated. "Perhaps that may be an appropriate...test for you, Peter. After you rest, of course."

Though he felt as if he hadn't slept in days nor eaten for as long, Peter's body yearned to fight in a way that both disturbed and excited him. "Tomorrow."

"So soon?"

"I fought in Carvalel once before, William," Peter told him. "I found out that I'm not made of glass." He grinned at the young woman beside him.

Aurora squinted at him, half smiling. "Did you...did you just jape?"

William stood. "Are you certain—tomorrow?"

"I'm positive."

"Very well." The knight nodded and allowed his soft gaze to linger. "You have changed, Peter, I see it so clearly. You are no longer the boy from Virginia, but the Lion of Lunsera. Yes, I see it."

As he watched the older man leave, he turned and met Aurora's stare. "What are you staring at?"

"You." She grinned.

"Why?" he asked, pointing to his aged hair and the scars on his neck. "Not much to stare at."

"I disagree. It's your eyes. Beautiful blue again."

"What do you mean?"

"They were black before. When you awakened...they were black like the infected."

He leaned back in his chair, staring at his hands. "Aurora, what am I? What have I become? I'm not infected and I don't feel her influence anymore...but there's this darkness inside me. I don't know if it's always been there, but it's terrifying, and yet so exciting."

She spoke firmly. “The darkness does not define you, Peter. It's what you decide to do with it. I have faith in you and I know that together we can overcome whatever darkness may pervade our lives.” She took his hands. “Together.”

Her touch gave him hope. “Together,” he agreed.

* * * * * * *

A cool morning breeze rushed over the plains, striking William’s face as he trotted along the road. Captain Gideon rode alongside, wearing his chest plate over his maroon tunic. Behind the two, the Turner Knight’s captured dragoons followed, surrounded by Gideon's men.

William turned to see Peter and Aurora trailing behind the caravan. His color had returned to him, his gray hair nearly golden once more. The Lion of Lunsera had told William that he would stay at the rear to keep an eye on the dragoons. If they decided to attack, he would “take care of it.”

Peter, William thought. *You have changed. You are no longer a boy but a man with purpose, it would seem. But I do fear what kind of man will you be.*

The day of riding passed rapidly. It was later in the afternoon when Carvalel came into view under a blanket of clouds. William's apprehension grew as they approached the northern gatehouse. He recalled that it was the northern portion of the city that Titus Turner’s forces occupied. *But how loyal are they? What will they do when they see the dragoons and not Titus? And what when they see Peter?*

The chipped wooden doors opened for them and they entered the courtyard, where about twenty guards eyed their party. They followed the road down the various streets, through the city center, and along the route to the villa. At the entrance to the manor and its grounds, a crowd gathered. Groups of civilians stood around clusters of soldiers talking over one another. At the center of the commotion, Lord Carlon debated with several officers in maroon garments. They were all from Barrington, William assumed.

Before William could ride ahead, Peter's horse sped past him. The old knight and his party halted and looked on as the crowd parted for Peter. He rode his horse up to the officers of Barrington and halted, towering above them all.

The crowd grew silent as Peter spoke to the officer that had been the loudest. "Do you have a problem?" he asked.

The officer hesitated before inquiring, "Who are you?"

"That depends."

"On what?" he chuckled.

"On what you say next." Peter stated flatly, glaring at the officer. On the other side of Peter's horse, beneath the archway, Lord Carlon backed away as he recognized the Lion.

"Who do you think you are?" the officer scoffed. "The Lionheart?"

Peter's gaze turned upward. "How high do you think those clouds are?"

Fear gripped William. *Peter, please don't. Be merciful with your power.* He grimaced, unsure of what to do as the Lion stepped down from his horse. The officer looked to his comrades, half amused and half perplexed. Slowly, Peter strolled forward and grasped the maroon fabric of the officer. The man clawed at Peter's grip and strained to move him to no avail.

"Well?" Peter said as he lifted the man from the ground and held him in the air with a single arm. "How high do you think they are? Better yet, why don't I throw you and you tell me how high when you land...if you can manage it."

"You are the Lionheart!" The officer strained to speak. "Forgive me. I beg you!"

Peter maintained his grip on the man in the air, unwavering as he stared fiercely at him.

"Peter Loneheart!" Aurora shouted at him.

The officer was released and he dropped to his knees before the Lion, who crossed his arms and shifted his glare at the other men in maroon.

The crowd began to disperse as William, Gideon, and Aurora dismounted. The three walked over to where Peter stood, who then extended his hand to the terrified officer he had threatened, helping him to his feet. He then turned to the commander standing in the archway of the villa. “Lord Carlon?”

“Er...yes, my Lord.” The commander bowed hastily and shook Peter’s hand. “You have my gratitude for preventing imminent mutiny.” He turned to the trio. “And I welcome you yet again to Carvalel, Lady Aurora and Sir William.”

“Charmed,” Aurora stated flatly before turning to Peter with her hands on her hips. “What were you thinking?”

Peter rolled his eyes and shrugged. “I wasn't really going to throw him.”

“Well, it was certainly convincing! My heart is racing...”

“I find your lack of faith disturbing.” He grinned and playfully nudged her. She bit her lip and attempted to nudge back, but he dodged in a blue blur of movement, disappearing. She tripped over herself and he reappeared, catching her against his chest.

The two stared at one another for a long moment before William cleared his throat loudly.

“Perhaps we may gather inside to discuss the issues at hand,” the Wanderer proposed.

“Indeed, Sir,” Carlon agreed. They all passed beneath the archway, through the city of empty tents, and into the manor. Once inside the parlor, Lord Carlon offered his own seat behind the desk to Peter, which he declined. After the party of five had all sat down, Lord Carlon spoke.

“So, Sir William?”

William cleared his throat. “This is a dark time for Arden, yes, but in the darkness much has come to light. Peter?”

The Lion explained again to Carlon what had happened in Hearthelm and about the one named Verluxia.

“Verluxia,” the commander repeated. “And she is the one responsible for the plague? You believe that Lord Alvar is in league with this...vile one?”

“Yeah. I saw them both in one of the visions together from what I remember. It all seems hazy now.”

“I see.” Carlon eased back into his chair as his eyes shifted between them all. “What do you propose?”

William spoke. “Alvar is our first priority, as we must free those captured by him and he will lead us to the vile one. But before we further investigate Verluxia...the treachery of Barrington must be dealt with, and swiftly so! It is fortunate that Alvar and Ian Turner are not allied. I learned during my own investigation into the assassins that Lord Alvar was a high priority target.”

“Agreed. But what of Sir Titus? He rode north with some haste after receiving a message from the east.”

Carlon looked to them all before Peter confessed, “I killed him.”

“I see.” A sullen silence lingered. “I am certain that you had no other option. If his cousin is the individual responsible for the assassins, then it is likely Sir Titus knew as well. One less enemy, I suppose.”

“In our absence, have you received any further news from the east?” William asked.

“It is as you said, sir, but the council is said to have betrayed Arden City to the Turners, and Lord Alvar is the one who saved the city from their treachery, or so the people sing in the streets. Many magistrates have sworn to him and he commands a small army of battle-hardened warriors. If you seek to remove him from power...I am afraid that I cannot assist you. I do not possess the numbers to march on the capital against a man of my own status. My orders remain. I am the commander of the western forces. Thus, it is my duty to remain."

"What about Rulfin?" Peter inquired.

"It is with great regret that I be the one to inform you of his passing. He perished during the battle north of New London. From every report following the battle, it is said that the entire horde moved as one and fell upon him."

"They went directly after Rulfin?"

"Indeed, my Lord."

"It was her," Peter concluded. "She had all of the infected go after Rulfin...but why? Maybe...maybe he knew. Or at least he seemed to know something...that's right. Rulfin and I talked about a man named Orrick."

"Orrick?" Aurora asked. "I believe my father had a captain in his service by that name."

"That's right. He was a captain who relayed personal messages between your dad and my uncle during the war ten years ago. I saw him when I first got to Carvalel but he kept saying weird things about chain snakes and there being two not one...he was talking about her! There were two, a woman and one with chains like snakes."

"Are you saying there is another like this Verluxia?" William asked fearfully.

"There could be, but I don't know enough yet. That's where Alvar comes in. If we get Alvar to confess, then we might get all the answers we need."

"It would seem our priorities have asserted themselves."

"What do you mean?"

William stood. "First, we infiltrate Arden City. We will peacefully resolve this conflict with Alvar and free those that have been imprisoned."

"Helen," Aurora muttered.

"Indeed. Freeing your sister is vital."

"You just assume Alvar is going to surrender to us?" Peter asked.

"I am optimistic that he and I will come to an understanding rather than an impasse. If he does not...then a fight is unavoidable."

"Okay. So we get Alvar to confess what he knows about Verluxia, we go after Ian Turner and then Verluxia. Hopefully after all that, we find Jack."

"My thoughts precisely."

Lord Carlon cleared his throat. "With respect, gentlemen. Ian Turner and this...Verluxia aside, Alvar Blackheart is not to be underestimated. After this most recent campaign, most are convinced that he is the savior and cannot be killed. I urge extreme caution."

"Indeed, my Lord." William nodded in agreement. "I have witnessed his skill, his enchanted blade, and the beast at his command. If we do fight, I am convinced that I may not survive."

"No," Peter stated. "Not by yourself. But if I go with you, we have a better chance."

The old knight hesitated. Visions of the past flashed across his mind. He recalled Peter as a young boy with a tender heart...but there was too much at stake. He needed the Lionheart. "Very well. But I think we will require even more assistance."

"Who?" Peter asked.

"Knights. My Knights. The Order of Bastille."

* * * * * * *

His new steed galloped with haste, tossing dirt into the air behind them. In the setting sun, William chased his shadow as he entered the enormous gate of the Ornian ruins.

Three days, he thought to himself. *We will meet at the Inn in Masterstown that the captain vouched for. We will then plot to infiltrate the city together.*

He rode over the wide river via the numerous bridges that still stood, passing an abandoned camp on an island in the center of the old metropolis. As he entered the eastern side of the city on the bank of the river, a gust of wind struck the back of his neck, catching his attention. He glanced back at the entrance of the courtyard he rode through. It was silent and still.

Suddenly another gust of wind struck him from the side, along with the brief sound of rustling fabric that disappeared as quickly as the breeze had. He looked forward at the street. A sudden blur of gray dashed across the archway ahead.

Pulling back on his reins, he halted, listening, but heard only the sound of his steed's heavy breaths.

That was...did Peter follow me?

From the darkness of the old structures flanking the street, many still faces appeared, a pale mask in every doorway around him. Each person, wearing the same white mask, now emerged. *What is this? Who are they? There must be at least fifty of them...mask wearers...*

From the archway, the lone unmasked man walked toward him. He smiled kindly at the old knight. His eyes seemed to be closed. "Good evening, friend," the kind man greeted as he had before, when William had first ridden through the ruins with Aurora.

"I remember you," William admitted. "I must pass, please."

"Of course you must. But first, might I inquire why?"

"What do you mean? It is my business. Now please, allow me to pass."

The smiling man shook his head. "You must answer first and answer honestly."

"And If I do not answer correctly?"

A laugh erupted from the smiling man. “Why, Sir William...do not be frightened, not of us.”

William hesitated, realizing there was no point in lying. “You know who I am?”

The smiling man nodded. “Indeed. I have been bidden to inquire: will you kill Alvar Blackheart?”

“Only if he leaves me no other choice.”

A loud clapping erupted within the ruined metropolis. Somewhere, someone was applauding his response.

“Sufficient.” The smiling man stepped aside, bowing.

Hesitant at first, William glanced around at the mask wearers around him before tapping his horse’s flanks and dashing forward. The archway passed over him and the buildings blurred past in rapid succession as he navigated the streets of the dead city.

Finally, he rode through the encampment along the main road of the ruins. He departed the eastern gate with haste, as the sky ahead of him was dark and the one behind faint with last light.

As the ruins receded behind him, he looked back at the destroyed city. Something caught his eye. He glanced up at a tower that loomed above all others. At the top of the structure, the silhouette of a man stood against the twilight sky. As William galloped away, he could feel the man's gaze upon him.

Chapter 25

The Agents of Alvar

From the moment he had awoken on the morning they were to depart, Peter's thoughts had remained fixed upon confronting Alvar and rescuing Helen. Even with Gideon and Aurora flanking him as they rode, and the seven soldiers he had fought beside at Hightower behind him, the Lion of Lunsera said little to anyone as he raced his steed across the land of Arden.

For two days and two nights, they camped along the Prince's Road, riding under the golden light of day and sleeping beneath the silver hue of night. As the familiar road they traveled began to twist around fewer hills and more pockets of trees, Peter knew Masterstown was close.

Finally, beneath evening light and surrounded by the thick sage forest, the walled community of Masterstown lay before them. As Peter halted his steed, Aurora to his right and Gideon to his left, he gazed upon the peaceful town. Houses of wood, thatch, and brick could be numbered in the small hundreds. The peaks of each home protruded above the stone wall. At the center of the community where he knew the town square to be, a single stone building stood above all the others and the sea of trees beyond. It was the capital building of Masterstown, he knew. And draping from its highest points, black banners flapped in the evening breeze.

"Alvar's standard," Gideon breathed. "The town has declared for him, it would seem."

Aurora scoffed. "Fitting. A red lion on a field of midnight black. It appears as if a child drew it." The comment forced a chuckle from Peter and he looked over to her. Their eyes connected, and potent, confusing feelings bombarded him. He was grateful to have her with him, but he still yet wished that she would have stayed behind in Carvalel. Despite his attempts to convince her to remain in the west, she had not conceded. She refused to leave his side.

"I wonder if William is here already," Peter said, looking back to the town.

"He may very well be," Gideon replied as he scratched his beard. "I think we should be more concerned about the guards in the town, lad."

"Agreed," Aurora said. "When I departed Arden City with Sir William, Alvar ordered for me to be captured. It would do us well to assume that is a standing order. Are there any secret entrances to the tavern?"

The captain smiled. "Aye, my lady."

* * * * * * *

He was surrounded by silence. From the exquisitely designed window, daylight beamed into the old knight's chamber. His knees ached, but he remained there on the cold floor, humble and hopeful.

William's gaze lifted as he finally came to his feet, removing his robe and resting his eyes on the gleaming silver armor in front of him. White designs were woven with fluid elegance on the chest plate, pauldrons, and vambraces. His fingers traced along the smooth metal until he found the cross at the center of the chest plate, woven in gold.

A knock at the door behind him grasped his attention. He turned as the door opened and a handsome young knight entered the room. *The cousin of the Moonwey sisters.* His face appeared stoic and graceful. He inclined his head of long silver hair, a trademark of his Moonwey lineage.

"Sir Aaron," William warmly greeted.

"Our brothers are prepared, sir," the young knight told him.

William nodded as he turned back to the armor before him. "I last wore armor when I departed this world for the other. There on the beach of Norfolk, Virginia, I cast it aside. It is past time that I don the cape of my brethren and my home."

With each piece of armor that he fitted onto himself, the Wanderer faded and the fabled knight of old reemerged. After the last piece had been fastened, Sir Aaron honored the old knight by securing the pale cloak of Bastille to his shoulders.

Together, the two men descended the stairs from his chamber and entered the cathedral, bypassing the sanctuary. There, standing before the two large doors of the entrance, five of his knights awaited him, each wearing the same gleaming silver armor that he and Sir Aaron wore.

The clinking of metal plates ceased as he and Aaron joined their brethren.

"Thank you," William said warmly as he looked to each man. "Thank you for joining me on this quest as it is of the utmost importance. Arden requires us. The Order. Each of you. As you know, Alvar Blackheart has murdered the council of Arden City and taken some province leaders into custody. He has proceeded to claim the city and this land for his own. Let me be clear: we are not going to war with

Arden City, hence I have not summoned the army of Bastille. I selected each of you for your resolve and zeal. Our purpose is not to fight but to bring justice and peace through negotiation. If Alvar refuses to see reason, then we will show the Blackheart Lord what Knights of Bastille are truly capable of."

The stone walls rebounded with cheers from his six knights. They exited the cathedral and took to the saddles of their horses before departing Bastille through the mountain pass to Masterstown.

* * * * * * *

In a gentle rhythm, one cool breeze after the next flowed through the open window and struck Peter's face as he awoke. He opened his eyes and yawned, remaining still to watch as the dusty curtains flapped with each gust of wind sent forth from the dark clouds of the morning sky. From outside the window of the tavern he heard the leaves rustle in the surrounding forest. Based on the sudden cold wind and the dark clouds of the dawn, he knew it would storm that day.

He rose, washed his face, and put on his riding attire, which matched Aurora's: black trousers and a fitted leather jacket to match the tall boots. He departed his room on the second floor of the tavern and made his way downstairs. The wooden planks beneath him squeaked with each step until he halted at the base.

Standing alone and in silence, he looked around the first floor of the tavern. There were five round tables spaced out, a few chairs around each one. Near the door, the bar featured a wooden top, plagued with chips, stains, and inscriptions from drunk patrons of the past. He strolled to the closest table and eased into a chair, remaining in the stillness and silence of the morning as the world still slept.

Footsteps echoed from the hallway of the second floor and continued down the vocal steps of the stairs. Yawning, Aurora looked at him and smiled.

"Morning," he said to her as she joined him. "How did you sleep?"

She rested her head on the table and watched him with sleep still in her eyes. "As well as can be expected. I long for my own bed."

"Back in Lunsera? Tired of traveling?"

She smiled. "I think I've had sufficient excitement."

"I never thought I'd hear you say something like that."

"Now you have. I want nothing more than to rescue Helen and return home. Can you not say the same?"

"Yeah. I want all of this to be over, to find Jack, maybe go home."

"—to Lunsera. You're returning home with us, are you not?"

He paused just as the floorboards of the stairs announced Captain Gideon's arrival.

"We might have a problem," Gideon said to them both.

"What's wrong?"

"I looked out the window to see an entire battalion of Alvar's troops enter the town."

"Oh no," Peter muttered before he and Aurora followed Gideon up to the second floor to peek out the window of the hallway.

As the town continued to sleep, squads of soldiers in black patrolled the streets of the township.

"They're Alvar's men, no doubt," Gideon said. "Why they suddenly arrived this morning when the town was already garrisoned..."

"They must know we're here," Aurora said. "But how?"

"Doesn't matter now," Peter stated from behind her. "We aren't safe here. You're not safe here. If they start searching houses, sooner or later they'll find us. It might be best to leave."

She leaned back against him to rest her head. "It would seem our devious plot to dethrone Alvar has been thwarted. And so soon."

"It's likely the road to Arden City is being patrolled as well," Gideon said. "I think it wise to wait for now, see how they patrol the town, and depart for Bastille when an opportunity presents itself."

"Bastille?" Aurora asked.

"Indeed, my lady. We don't want Sir William walking into a trap either."

"I agree," Peter said. "We should wait until we can slip out without them seeing us, then follow the same road William took to Bastille."

Hours passed as Peter and his company waited and watched as the Blackheart Lord's troops patrolled in pairs. His apprehension grew throughout the day, his imagination conjuring whatever could possibly go wrong. Could he beat Alvar? Would he be able to save Helen? What if William had already been captured? What would happen if Aurora was captured as well?

He stood abruptly from the table of the inn, startling every member of his party.

"I can't take this anymore. All this waiting. I'm going to go insane if we don't do something."

"Agreed," Aurora said, standing beside him.

Gideon began to protest, but Peter said quickly, "It'll be fine. Aurora and I can go first. I'll jump the entire town with her on my back if I have to."

"Lad, give it a bit more time."

"I can't. We'll go first, and you guys can follow after. We'll meet up in the woods outside of town."

Before the captain could argue, Peter and Aurora darted for the cellar door, putting on their cloaks as they descended the stairs into the basement of the inn. "Maybe...maybe he's right," he began to mutter.

"What do you mean?" Aurora asked as she reached to him and pulled his hood up to keep his face concealed. He did the same with hers.

"Nothing. Just being indecisive."

"Peter." She stared up at him, focused yet with a softness in her gaze. "You're the Lion of Lunsera now. You of all people cannot be indecisive. Many are depending on us, on you."

"I guess you're right."

"Of course I am." She grinned.

They followed the secret corridor under the streets of the town. The light of the inn's basement faded as each step took them further into the darkness of the tunnel. Ahead of them, a new light grew brighter until they came to the door from which it shined beneath and above in small pockets.

They opened the door and light spilled into the tunnel, overtaking their sight for a few moments as they stepped outside. They stood in a forgotten courtyard, littered with rubble and overtaken by vegetation.

Concealed by their hooded cloaks, the pair acted as mice within the walls of a home, making their way from alleyway to alleyway in silence. They rounded a corner as a familiar street appeared to them. At the end of the street stood the inn in which Gideon and his men remained.

And in several columns facing the inn, Alvar's troops awaited.

"No!" Peter hissed under his breath. *There has to be a hundred.*

"Well, we departed at the right time, it would seem," Aurora said next to him. "But the captain..."

"I can't leave him."

"Peter!" she hissed at him.

He turned to her. "What?"

She simply stared at him.

He was confused. "But you said my name."

She shook her head and he dismissed it, turning back to the issue at hand. How could he help Gideon and the men from Hightower? "Maybe they took the passage behind us."

“Shall we go back?” she asked.

He hesitated, glancing toward the formation of soldiers in black, all with muskets and sabers at the ready. “Yeah. Let’s head back towards the tunnel.” He ushered her forward and she had begun to jog when a voice hissed his name.

“Peter!” she said.

He halted as the vile voice spoke from within him.

It’s her, he realized.

“Yes,” she answered.

You. You’re her. Verluxia.

“Yessss,” she hissed.

As if a thousand knives had been plunged into his abdomen at once, he fell to his knees as her influence invaded his being. “Feel me,” she said to him as his eyes began to burn and his vision darkened. “Come to me.” She beckoned as his nails turned black and his fingers dug into the cracked cobblestone.

He looked up from the ground to see Aurora stop and turn back towards him. Suddenly two figures in black appeared behind her in the alley. They were Alvar’s agents, he knew. The young woman screamed as they attempted to subdue her, punching and grappling frantically until a bag was thrown over her head and she was forced off her feet and out of sight.

“No,” Peter groaned as the sight of her being taken, and the pain that subdued him, furthered his agony. He roared in fury, his heart bursting with heat as his muscles grew stronger than ever before. The pain subsided.

“Yesss,” Verluxia hissed with obvious delight from within him. “Go. Kill. Find me!”

As he stood, his shrouded vision narrowed. He turned the corner from where Aurora had been taken. In the adjacent street nearby, twelve men in black jumped into the saddles of their horses.

Though each man wore a rich black jacket with golden embroideries, in Peter's vision, they all seemed to radiate with the same crimson hue just as Sir Titus Turner had before he had been killed.

Thrown over the saddle of one of Alvar's agents, Aurora remained motionless with a bag over her head. The dozen riders followed one after the other, hooves echoing against the cobblestone. They rode beneath the gate, departing the town toward Arden City.

Chapter 26

Knives & Nails

It began to rain as William and his knights approached Masterstown. The gray clouds that had loomed about all day had finally begun to deliver the precipitation promised. Despite the circling storm clouds, the sky to the west remained warm in color as the sun set behind the atmospheric veil. As they followed the Prince's Road and rounded the last hill, they saw the walled community before them, surrounded by a sea of trees. A gust of wind rolled over the town from the darkened sky of the east, carrying the scent of roast chicken. The old knight's stomach growled.

"Sir William," Aaron Moonwey said next to him, pointing toward the gatehouse.

The old knight winced. "The banner of Alvar Blackheart. Just as I feared."

"Shall we proceed, sir?" Sir Logan asked.

William nodded and tapped his steed's flanks, leading his six knights along the road and through the open gate. Clad in black, the musketmen atop the gatehouse watched the old knight, adding to his apprehension. As they entered the courtyard of the town, they were greeted by the tall statue of Toven Ornian standing above the formation of troops in black. There were at least two hundred men in various organized columns facing William and his knights.

They were prepared for us, William concluded. *But how? What of Peter?*

The wooden doors of the gate slammed shut behind him as a squad of guards filled in behind the group of knights, trapping them within the courtyard. There was no point in fighting, he knew. He and his noble men were dangerously outnumbered and surrounded.

There was silence as the seven Knights of Bastille remained still, surrounded by the small army sent by Alvar, and the guards behind them. Down the center of the formation of troops, an officer on horseback trotted forward towards William. He halted at the head of the first line of men. He was young and fair, with feathery brown hair. His jacket was black and gold like the Blackheart Lord's own.

"Welcome, fine knights of the northern city," Alvar's officer said. "I am Lieutenant Horris, commissioned by Lord Alvar himself to bring peace and justice to our land. I bring you divine news, my friends. The rumors that you have heard are true. Our Lord has ascended to claim his destiny. He is the lion reborn, passenger of light and shadow, ordained by Fyraen, the redeemer, the heir of Tobius, the champion of Arden City and the common folk, and the one to slay the serpent. He is the savior of this world."

Cheers rang out from the army behind Lieutenant Horris following his charismatic speech.

Before William could retort, Sir Logan's horse stepped forward and neighed loudly before the hot-headed knight proclaimed, "You fools stand before the greatest knight in history! This is Sir William of Bastille! He who hath slain countless foes upon the field of battle, not walking corpses, but living men of great and renown skill. It was Sir William who slew the count of Blud in single combat, who passed between worlds, the man that can make the lion bleed and then befriend him!"

Silence followed the younger knight's words, and one by one, the eyes of every young man within Alvar's small army wavered, turning to one another as if they were uncertain as to whom deserved their loyalty.

"Indeed," the lieutenant said across from the knights, nodding respectfully. "None can question the honorable service of such a noble and great knight. However, I ask you: to what end? To what end will Sir William continue to serve the false lions? They are false! They hail from another world, not our own. What do they know of our suffering? They cannot fathom the struggle, the pain, the humiliation that our people have endured since the age of silver and stars! It is written that it will be one from our own land who will bring the justice, peace, and glory promised to us since Fyraen spoke our world into existence! Turn from these false idols! The Lionheart's are dead, their legacy not our own! Sir William, I beseech you..." Tears streamed from the young officer's eyes. "Come to Lord Alvar. He will welcome you with open arms, forgive you, and with you by his side, the idols of yesterday will fall and a new kingdom shall arise. No provinces warring with one another. Instead, one kingdom. The kingdom of Arden!"

The army behind him shouted in wondrous cheers, "For Arden! For Arden! For Arden!"

Horris wiped away his tears and waved his hand to silence the cheering men. "What say you, Sir William?"

The evening wind howled as it rolled through the silent courtyard, whistling as it passed each musket, spear, and drawn saber. As the army of two hundred men watched him, so too did the citizens of the town who spectated from the windows of their homes. *Alvar chose his officers well. Most charismatic and persuasive.*

William briefly turned back to his knights and then faced Horris. "May Arden endure," the old knight told them all, conceding.

Or so he led them to believe.

* * * * * * *

The atmosphere turned blue and cold as he ran, but Peter burned with hatred. Alvar's agents continually glanced back at him as they rode. The closer he came, the more often they turned back to him, sometimes firing off muskets towards him, missing every shot as the day's last light faded.

The horses were at a full sprint, but he gained on them in the dark. He eyed the rider trailing behind. As he caught up to him, he reached forward and yanked the man from his horse, tossing the agent in black over his shoulder and into the air. The man's scream receded as Peter eyed the next one. The rider's head turned towards him and he shouted to warn the others as he aimed his musket. He fired and the shot pelted against Peter's hip, digging into his skin—a minor irritation. Peter grimaced and growled, ignoring the pain to reach after the one who shot him. The man howled in pain as Peter's black nails found him and crushed his ribs before pulling him from his racing steed.

Two riders pointed muskets at him and both fired off. His ear twitched as the first whizzed past his head. The second dug into the skin of his chest.

"Peter!" Aurora's muffled scream reached him from the front of the pack of riders.

"Kill them!" Verluxia's vile voice told him from within.

Using his claws, he severed the legs of two horses and the animals toppled onto their riders. He swiped his claws again through another rider's midsection as he ran past. The top half of his body fell behind as the lower half continued riding.

He slashed at another rider and his claws tore through the flesh of both horse and man. The rider screamed in agony, fueling his bloodlust. As the animal slowed, he swiped his nails across the rider's neck and the head rolled to the ground.

He looked to the next racing horse, where a bound person was draped in front of the rider. A hood concealed her face, but she screamed and kicked.

Just as Peter prepared to jump after the rider, the two agents flanking him fired their muskets in unison. One of the shots struck the side of his neck, the other his collarbone, pinging loudly. The well-placed shots distracted him with sudden pain. He lost his footing. The intense speed he had generated betrayed him and he plunged forward face-first into the dirt of the road, skidding across the ground with a mouthful of grass and dirt. As he finally halted, the sound of beating hooves died out.

With a growl, he stood and started forward along the road after them, ignoring the pain of the musket shots that would have killed any other man. Peter chased after Alvar's agents once again as night finally descended, yet he found no sign of the riders.

He halted as he found the mutilated corpses of the two horses and the riders that had shot him. His beating heart and raging breath pierced the night air as he looked upon the massacre. Further down the road, the silhouette of another dead horse lay over its mutilated rider.

All of Alvar's agents had been killed by someone else, or rather something else.

"Aurora!" he yelled at the top of his lungs, spewing desperation and confusion into the night. "Aurora?" he cried. *Where is she?*

He turned into the nearest tree at the edge of the forest. In a single movement, he plunged his claws into the wood and pulled it from the earth, casting it into the air behind him. Peter turned to the next tree, ripping it from the ground as the one before it. "Aurora!" he cried out after her as he tore through the forest in the night.

* * * * * * *

Be clever as serpents, William continually told himself as his horse galloped along the road. His knights followed behind him, a squad of Alvar's soldiers flanking both sides. Sympathizing with his enemy was the wisest choice he could have made, he knew. And now he would follow through with his plans, to confront Alvar and seek a peaceful resolution. However, a problem remained. *Where is Peter? What of Aurora, and the captain? This plan has gone awry, and for the worse. I yet hope that Alvar will see reason.*

"Oi!" one of the Blackheart soldiers called out, halting his steed, and William and the others did as well. William glanced around, straining to see what it was within the minuscule light of night that had alerted one of the soldiers.

The old knight's horse neighed loudly beneath him and his own gaze fell onto the shadowy scene of carnage. From the mutilated corpse of a horse and its rider in front of him, his eyes followed the road to several more bodies of those that had been slain in the night, fleeing from something.

The realization dawned on the old knight. *Peter, what have you done?*

He turned to the soldier that was leading the party, but before he could utter a word, the soldier ordered, "Ride for the city! Do not stop!"

Alvar's soldiers charged forth as William and his knights did the same, weaving around the corpses as they rode. After a short duration, a few small lights appeared further down the road.

Torchlight, he observed. The party once again slowed their pace as the four torches illuminated the surrounding area with warm light, including the masked men that held them. There were ten of them, each wearing the same pale mask, void of any design or human imitation. From the midst of the group that blocked the road, one man stepped toward William and his group with no mask, but a seemingly everlasting smile.

“You,” William said, recognizing him as the one who had greeted him on both occasions he had passed through the Ornian ruins.

“We meet again, Sir William.” The smiling man politely bowed his bald head. “I see you have your knights accompanying you, but these men...” He indicated to the Blackheart Lord’s troops. “I’m afraid that they were not spoken for.”

“What do you mean?” William asked.

The mysterious man maintained his smile as a rustle of fabric quickly passed behind the knight's party. There was a flurry of gray movement to their right and then to their left as something moved in the dark around them.

It was fast, impossibly fast. There was a series of sudden cracks as the head of the soldier to William’s right turned to face the terrified troops behind him, yet his body remained still. His neck had been broken in an instant. His twitching body slid from the saddle just as the soldier to William’s left briefly yelped before meeting the same fate. His head, too, had been completely twisted around to face his horrified comrades behind him. It happened again, and again. One by one, each of the troops from Masterstown was killed, even as they drew their sabers or pointed their muskets toward the darkness surrounding them. As the last of the Blackheart Lord’s troops were murdered, William saw it as it took the young man’s life. A mask. It was silver with golden embroideries, appearing for one second in the air behind the man, and disappearing as the soldier met the same fate as his comrades.

William and his knights remained untouched by the unknown force as the last body fell to the ground, and one by one, the horses of the slain soldiers began to wander off.

“You have been shown mercy.” The smiling man said to them. “Go, Sir William. Alvar Blackheart has caused quite the commotion. He is your responsibility.”

The wall of pale and still faces parted, allowing the knights to pass.

Without sparing a single glance to his brothers of the Order, William kicked the flanks of his horse. The beast neighed and dug its hooves into the earth, tossing soil into the night as it sprinted forward. William's knights followed after. The seven men rode through the dark, the torches fading behind them, and the old knight considered what had happened, how easily the Blackheart soldiers had been killed, and the silver mask that had murdered them.

Casting its roaring light into the dome of night and blotting out the stars, Arden City soon revealed itself to them. The nocturnal proclivities of the metropolis howled in elemental fragments, causing the knight to long for the somber nights of his own city.

As they approached the gate, William and his knights were not surprised by the Blackheart banner that hung from the stone walls and towers, but they were by the escort of Alvar's agents that awaited them.

Chapter 27

Alvar Blackheart

Through the streets of Arden City, they rode single file, flanked by the young men loyal to Alvar. William rode at the head of the column. Beside him trotted the lieutenant of Alvar's agents, a noble-looking man much like the officer he had encountered at Masterstown. He too was young, probably just twenty years of age. The agent often glanced over to the old knight.

"My apologies," the lieutenant confessed after William caught his stare. "It is merely that...I cannot believe I ride beside *the* Sir William of Bastille. I only wish that I had met you under different circumstances, sir."

“Agreed.” The knight inclined his head and they pressed on down the road. Few people stood at the edges of the streets in the hours of the night. The shops were closed and vacant of light or life, but the numerous taverns and inns throughout the district bustled with music and laughter, bearing the unmistakable scent of alcohol. The young lieutenant and the agents that accompanied him all turned their heads towards the lively events as they passed. *How simple it would be to gain the advantage and escape. However, we are not here to fight unless we must. We are here to talk and to make peace if it can be so. Far too many lives have already been lost this night. What was it that killed the troops from Masterstown?*

The street they followed ended as the courtyard of the citadel opened up to them, a clearing surrounding the wide and tall bastion towering above all other buildings in the district. Even in the night, the stone of the citadel seemed to glow with milky light. As they rode toward the base of the steps outside the entrance, fourteen men in armor descended from the double doors. Leading them was another of Alvar’s young officers, wearing the same distinct black jacket. He halted the men in armor that followed him at the base of the steps and walked towards the lieutenant's horse.

“Well struck, Arious,” he said with a grin. “ Lord Alvar has been expecting them. We shall escort from here, I think.”

“As you say,” Arious the agent acknowledged before turning to William and nodding in respect. The old knight dismounted and his six brothers of the Order followed after. Surrounded by men in darkened armor, the seven Knights of Bastille ascended the steps and entered the citadel. Upon entering the double doors, two guards at the desk to the left caught William's eye. It was the pair that had continually argued with one another the last time he had entered the central building of the city. The duo stared at the knight in his silver-plated armor and their jaws dropped as their shared gaze found the golden woven cross on his chest. He simply smiled at the two and nodded.

The captain of the Blackheart guards led them up the numerous flights of stairs and through the various corridors of the citadel. Finally, they came to the waiting lobby before the double doors of the council chamber. The officer halted the procession and turned to them. "I will inform my Lord of your arrival, sir." He bowed and departed through the doors.

The old knight turned back to his men, surrounded by the guards. He nodded to them and faintly smiled in reassurance as his own nerves grew restless.

I feel as if I am once again a young knight. My nerves betray me. Closing his eyes, he took slow and deep methodical breaths as he lay his worries at the feet of his God.

His meditation was disrupted as the doors opened and the young agent reemerged. Bowing, he said, "My Lord welcomes you and your knights, Sir William. This way."

William took a final deep breath and exhaled slowly, regaining his focus before entering the council chamber. His gaze fell upon the action at the center of the room. There, clad in his typical black attire, Alvar wielded a silver rapier, slashing and jabbing at his female opponent. The woman known as Barda grimaced and groaned as she struggled to defend against his advances. On her sweating arms, fresh cuts bled as a result of her failures in defense.

Watching from behind the council table, Lady Helen gazed emotionlessly at the Blackheart Lord. Behind her, six men in large suits of armor stood, a wall of black, their longswords and greataxes at the ready. Flanking the table, two separate groups stood watching the bout. They were hopefuls, William knew. Sycophants. Magistrates who now feigned loyalty to Alvar to further their own political agenda.

From behind one of the pillars that encircled the room, the monstrous wolf stalked about, taking slow steps as its fierce golden eyes rested on William and his knights.

"Come, Barda the Bold!" Alvar exclaimed as he advanced towards her again. He twisted his blade in a silver blur and disarmed the woman. The longsword she used skidded against the marble floor toward the crescent table.

Alvar turned to face the knight and his men. "Sir William! You return to me." He smiled and tossed the bloodied silver blade over his shoulder. The rapier crashed loudly against the floor as he made his way over to the knights.

"Alvar." William inclined his head before the young man took his hand and shook it with the same enthusiasm as before.

"Let us not stand on ceremony, Sir William. I am most pleased that you have returned. You departed so quickly last we spoke." He waved towards the others in attendance. "We have been awaiting you for some time. Barda the Bold has proved adequate at keeping me entertained." They both looked to the panting woman. Alvar waved his hand toward her. Three of the guards grasped hold of the warrior woman and removed her from the chamber.

"Now. I see you have brought forth some fine knights with you, sir." Alvar strolled by him and looked each of the six knights up and down. "They will be a fine addition to my personal guard, and you as their captain under my command. After you swear your oaths, of course."

Presumptuous, and impetuous. His mentality has not changed. William sighed. "Alvar, we did not come to swear oaths."

"Hmm?"

"You know why we are here."

The Blackheart Lord smirked faintly. "Walk with me, Sir William."

Hesitant, William slowly followed the younger man past a group of onlooking magistrates and walked along the walls of the room. "The last you and I spoke, sir, you departed with such haste that I was not given sufficient time to explain what I had done."

William spoke softly but firmly. "You and your wolf murdered the council, Alvar."

"Er...indeed." He chuckled. "As I said before, I did not plan for such a thing. Ornwell left me little choice, you understand."

"No, Alvar, I do not." A moment of silence passed between them.

“Well,” the younger man scoffed. “The world is a better place without them! You know as well as I that they were corrupt beyond measure.”

“The council did have their share of shortcomings, yes, but do you not think your...reaction was extreme? Not to mention you arrested three province leaders and held them captive. And what is this I hear of a new kingdom with no provinces? Why have you chosen to exalt yourself as a king?”

Alvar halted and stared up at the knight. “Is it I that tout myself as a king? No, Sir William. It is the people that have chosen me to be their champion.”

They began to walk again.

“And I have no interest in being a king. My sacred duty is my only desiree. It is I that will slay the serpent of old.”

“Verluxia,” William said flatly as they continued along the pillars, earning a perplexed look from the young warrior. “The one you speak of. Verluxia, the serpent. The one who created the plagues of Arden.”

“So that is her name!” Alvar exclaimed excitedly.

“You did not know?”

“Of her name? No. She refused to reveal it to me.”

“But you did meet with her.”

“Indeed. Quite the monster, but she knew that I was to be feared.”

“Your reasons for meeting with her aside, why did you not slay her when given the opportunity, Alvar?”

“I have undertaken many suicide missions on behalf of the late council. On one such occasion, I even hunted a monster in the hills of Blud. It was a menacing beast with a screech that could paralyze a man. With the help of Tobius, I ended its wretched existence. This serpent, however, is something more. I knew that if she and I clashed that both of us would fall. But no matter. Her head will be mine in time.”

"Where is she, Alvar? It is imperative that I know."

"Do not be careless, sir. She would destroy you if you faced her without me."

"We believe that she may know the whereabouts of the Lionheart. Jack Loneheart."

Alvar shook his head as they stopped again in front of one of the large windows of the chamber. "Why do you love these Lions from the Otherworld so? Why not I? You and I are of the same world, Sir William. I beseech you, place your faith in me. The Lions played their role. It is time that I play mine."

"Alv—"

"Enough! I will not be denied. You and your knights will swear your new oaths. Here and now!"

"Knights of Bastille do not swear oaths outside of the Order."

They continued again along the pillars of the room. "Then it is time for new traditions. Let the old ways fade."

"That cannot be done. It is the law."

"Hmm? But there are older and more ancient laws also, are there not? What of the first laws of the world? The law of what was promised? Alvasar, the great lion, did slay Norvok, the ancient serpent, and its venom did kill the lion as the stories told. It is true. And it is also true that the great Lion has been reborn." Alvar smiled and extended his arms as they walked. "I have known in my heart the divine truth. It has plagued me since boyhood. I am the Lion. I will save Arden. Fight with me, Sir William, I beseech you. Together, we will honor the ancient laws and slay the serpent, and finally bring peace to our world."

The Blackheart Lord's dark eyes, full of hope, remained fixed on the old knight as he thought. *How can I reason with him? He is so convinced. I do not want to fight him, not of fear for myself, but out of fear of not knowing how it would end.*

William continued to debate with himself until they had completely walked around the chamber, halting where they had begun. All eyes in the room were upon them.

“Now,” Alvar announced. “It is time. I beg of you, Sir William, recognize my destiny, have you and your knights swear a new oath to fight with me. We will bring the Turners of Barrington to justice, and we will destroy the serpent, together.”

“It is as I told you, Alvar, we do not swear oaths to those outside the Order. It is the law, it has always been and will always be. Now I beseech you! Lay down your arms and command your men to do the same. If you comply then you will be given a fair trial for your crimes. It is more than generous! Please!” William pleaded.

The Blackheart Lord frowned. “I thought I had made myself clear on this matter, sir. I will never surrender. My destiny is too great to be ignored.”

“So be it,” William muttered, reaching for his sword as his six knights did the same. The guards surrounding them also reached for their weapons as the six warriors in armor behind Helen shifted their stances.

“Hold!” Alvar commanded everyone. William and his knights remained still with their hands on the handles of their sheathed swords. The room remained still and quiet as the standoff ensued. “Are you so determined to die for such a foolish cause, Sir William? To have your knights follow you in death?”

“There is no need for anyone else to die this night. You speak of the ancient laws, Alvar. Then let us honor them properly. I challenge you to single combat.” The words departed the old knight's mouth reluctantly.

The Blackheart Lord’s brimmed hat inclined, hiding his face as his shoulders seemingly heaved. Alvar chuckled before revealing his face and the few tears that trickled from his dark eyes. “I weep for you, Sir William. But I think the contest would hardly be fair at all. I could defeat you and all your knights. Singlehandedly.” He tapped on the pommel of his sheathed rapier.

William wavered as Alvar spoke with utter conviction.

Suddenly, from behind him, the hot-headed knight stepped forth. "The words of a coward!" Sir Logan exclaimed. "Why not duel?"

Beside the younger Knight of Bastille, Sir Aaron Moonwey spoke up. "Why would any follow you and fight for you, Alvar, if you will not duel for them?" the silver-haired knight asked.

From the table where she sat, Helen Moonwey stared thoughtfully at her cousin.

"Fight us!" Sir Logan said. "Prove to us all that you can fight the lot of us at once as you claim you can. Prove that you are the Lion reborn. Prove that you are not some upstart bastard from Hearthelm, as Ornwell hath said!"

The warmth that William had seen in Alvar's eyes had abated and turned cold as he looked from the six knights to the six hulking figures in black armor behind the Lady of Lunsera.

"So be it, knight," Alvar spat. He waved his hand and the black-plated warriors trudged from behind the table with each heavy step, facing off with the six knights. "Let us see a new contest," Alvar announced. "Those of humble origin against those of privilege. As Sir William and I are also of a humble start, we will not partake in this bout."

"This was not a part of the proposed contest!" Logan called out.

Alvar chuckled. "Afraid of a challenge, hmm? Some Knight you are."

The hot-headed knight scoffed and said, "So be it." Sir Logan unsheathed his longsword and the five knights with him did the same as they squared off with the six mysterious men in black armor.

William turned to Alvar in an attempt to protest the contest, but Alvar halted him, saying, "Come now, Sir William. Let us spectate."

Alvar raised his hand and dropped it lazily. The fight commenced and steel beat against steel, filling the chamber with the chiming and chipping of metal. Twelve men hacked and slashed at one another in the center of the room, six figures in silver against their foes in black.

At the center of the fray, Sir Aaron's silver hair flowed behind him as he struck blow after blow at his armored enemy. To Aaron's right, the knight beside him faltered and his opponent's greataxe swung through the air and cleaved through the silver armor. The knight howled in agony before dropping onto the marble floor, twitching as he took his last breaths.

The Moonwey knight roared as he slashed the greatsword from his opponent's hands and twisted, thrusting the tip of his blade through the black armor. Removing the bloodied blade, he turned to face the armored foe that had slain his comrade.

William grimaced as he watched, clutching his own sword tightly. He looked to Sir Logan as he advanced on his opponent, unleashing strike after strike. The young knight's skill proved true as, after a decisive combination of movements, he thrust his sword into his opponent's chest. As Sir Logan removed his blade, another knight was struck down by a greatsword nearby. Sir Logan turned and descended upon the foe in black that had killed his comrade.

Two more knights were killed and another foe in black joined them in death, leaving Sir Aaron dueling against an opponent as Sir Logan struggled against two. As Logan parried an incoming thrust from an opponent, he spun to defend against his second foe. Suddenly the first man in black armor revealed a knife. The blade was plunged into Logan's side just as the knight defeated the second foe.

Sir Logan groaned in pain and grasped the gauntlet of the warrior that had stabbed him, holding him in place as Sir Aaron finished off his own adversary. The Moonwey knight turned and thrust his sword through the back of the armored foe that had stabbed Sir Logan.

As the final enemy in black fell onto the floor, the two knights stood as the survivors of the skirmish. The Knights of Bastille had won.

William peered at Alvar. The Blackheart Lord stood with crossed arms, tapping his boot as he stared at the aftermath, disappointed at the result. "I did not plan on this happening," he muttered through clenched teeth.

The old knight turned to face Alvar. "The contest is concluded. Surrender, Alvar."

"I think not." Alvar grinned and turned to the dozen guards that had escorted William and his knights. "Take them away. Let us give these knights more time to consider new oaths as they wait in a cell."

The chair behind the table screeched against the marble floor as Helen stood abruptly. "How dare you not honor a contest that you proposed!" she called out. "Have you no honor, Alvar? Are you not the savior of Arden?"

The floor and walls rumbled as if an earthquake had struck the building. A moment later, the double doors of the room were thrown open and torn from the hinges, skidding across the marble floor.

Slowly, the Lion of Lunsera strolled into the chamber. His eyes remained fixed upon Alvar. They were black like the infected. Black as midnight.

* * * * * * *

The walls and floor were dull, appearing gray to Peter. He saw the numerous bodies on the floor in front of him, beneath the two knights still standing. The guards nearby backed away as Peter took a few more steps into the chamber. To the left, William stood with his sword at the ready as he faced Alvar. The Blackheart Lord turned toward Peter and his eyes wavered as he looked the Lion up and down. From behind the table, Helen stood, watching Peter as he entered the room. Her gaze rested on him for a moment, appearing painful before she looked back at Alvar and grinned. "This evening is not going the way that you had planned, I think?" she said.

"Quite right, my lady." Alvar laughed. "But it is what you cannot plan for that is often the most entertaining!"

Just as Alvar was going to speak again, Peter bellowed, "Where is she!?" All in the room flinched except the Blackheart Lord. The question had been running through Peter's mind as he had torn through the forest in search of her. "Where. Is. She," he said coldly.

Alvar hesitated. "You should know, Little Lion. It seems as if you are under her influence. Most unusual, hmm? You have traded one woman's influence for another. Your new eyes are a testament to that!"

From within him, Verluxia's vile voice hissed at him. "Kill him, Peter!" He wanted to oblige the serpent, yet as he hesitated he felt her own feelings as if they were his own. As she saw the Blackheart Lord through the Lion of Lunsera's eyes, she was afraid and embarrassed.

To both Alvar and Verluxia, Peter said, "Aurora. Where is she?"

"Perhaps you are the one to answer that very question," Alvar said. "You have become quite the monster. How you have evolved since we first met. Would you not agree, Lady Helen?"

"Your men were the ones that kidnapped her!" Peter retorted.

"Yes. I gave strict orders for the lady to be brought here. For protection. Now she and my subordinates have disappeared, just as you stand here before us stained with fresh blood. Are you certain that you were not the one to harm her, hmm?"

"I didn't. I would never."

"But how can you be so certain? You are under the influence of the serpent! I say to you all and to all of Arden," the Blackheart Lord announced, "look upon the infected eyes of the Lionheart before you. Is this your gallant protector? Is it, Sir William? Your Lion of Lunsera, Lady Helen? This boy who hails from a world not our own has allied with the serpent and by extension has become it. But fear not!" Alvar grinned as he paced forward, and in a single fluid movement, he unsheathed Quickfury, the thin rapier from the Otherworld. "I will remove it from this world. I am the Lion. I am Alvar, the savior of Arden."

Peter shook his head. "You left me to die in Hearthelm and you took Aurora away from me. At one point I really thought you were some kind of savior, Alvar, but now I know that you aren't. You're just some overgrown boy who thinks he's a hero."

The Blackheart Lord threw his brimmed hat aside, his brown eyes blazing with passion and focus. He grinned as he twirled his rapier in a blur of dark movement and pointed it toward Peter. "Come then, Little Lion. Let us see who is right."

With his midnight claws ready to kill, Peter started forward, prepared to dash ahead and take the head of the Blackheart Lord. Alvar stood in a ready stance, elegant, deadly, and poised to strike. Peter became a blur of black movement as he raised his claws. Alvar wound Quickfury back as Peter reached him, but before Peter could make contact, a thundering growl echoed as Tobius the great wolf slammed into him, digging its teeth into the flesh of Peter's back and shoulders.

Peter and the wolf collided with the wall. Tobius continued to snarl as its teeth retracted and once again dug into Peter's flesh. A series of primitive growls escaped the Lion of Lunsera as he became the wolf's new chew toy. With the canine's teeth digging into the flesh of his back and chest, the beast's hot breath washed over him, its large paws pushing him harder against the floor. Desperate to escape, Peter reached toward Tobius' head and raked his nails across the fur and flesh of its face. The wolf instantly whined like a pup and released him, backing away to allow Peter to stand.

As he stood, Tobius growled and snapped, licking the blood from its snout. The two groups of magistrates fled the room behind the squad of guards. The clash of steel on steel echoed from the center of the room. Peter's gaze shifted from the aggravated wolf and over the pit of bodies and blood to where two knights fought Alvar. One of the men in silver armor had long silver hair, the other short brown locks. Both were younger than William and older than Peter.

Watching the fight from the side, William stood with his sword in his hand, seemingly unsure of what to do. Alvar simply grinned as he defended against each attack from the two knights with relative ease.

"Kill him, Peter!" the serpent's voice told him from within.

"Get out of my head!" he growled, starting toward Alvar but stopping just short as the giant wolf barked and inserted itself between the Lion of Lunsera and the duel at hand. "Move, Tobius."

The gray wolf refused, staring fiercely. Peter didn't want to kill the wolf, but it stood in his way. It had to be removed.

He anticipated another bite from Tobius. When the wolf snapped toward him again, he punched, striking its nose with his fist. The wolf jumped back for a moment, sneezing abruptly before refocusing on him with an animalistic gaze before pouncing. To defend, Peter raised his arm as a shield. New, yet familiar pain pierced his left forearm as Tobius' mouth closed around it, sinking its teeth into his flesh. Any normal person would be dead at that point, he knew. The entire weight of the animal bore down upon him and he collapsed onto his back. With its head so close to his body, he didn't have to reach far to dig his black nails into the gray fur and the flesh of its neck. Again, it whimpered like a pup and released him. As the wolf backed away, Peter glanced over at William. The old knight continually shifted his gaze from the duel between his knights and Alvar, to Peter's own fight.

Another growl from Tobius grasped Peter's attention. Before it could attack again, he pounced. They scratched and bit at one another as they crashed through one of the marble pillars, sending shards and rubble scattering across the floor. Peter raked at the thick coat of fur with his black claws, and Tobius tore at his skin with its teeth.

The wolf pinned him up against another pillar. With his back against the hard surface, he dug his nails into the wolf and roared like a lion as he tossed it to the side, slamming its body into the next pillar nearby. The glossy surface of the marble cracked from the impact and shattered as the wolf collapsed beneath it.

With shaking legs, Peter leaned back against the marble column where he had been pinned. His hands shook. The bite marks on his back, chest, and arm all ached with the same dull and yet sharp pain as warm blood spilled from the wounds. As he caught his breath, he watched the duel across the room. Helen had departed the table and taken refuge behind one of the many pillars. She, too, watched as the two knights strained, striving to land a single hit on the Blackheart Lord, who seemed only amused by their efforts. Alvar danced around their strokes with graceful precision. He countered with an abrupt thrust into the shoulder of the silver-haired knight and then slashed at the wrist of the other warrior, following with a thrust toward his throat. Before the tip of the dark rapier could strike the skin, it had been knocked aside by William's.

The old knight stood over his two knights with his longsword locked against Alvar's Quickfury. There was a strange and surreal silence in the large chamber as the two renowned warriors faced off. Though their duel was on the other side of the room, Peter could discern the focus and strain upon William's face, and the look of wonder upon Alvar's.

"As you wish, Sir William," Alvar said.

The living legend, Sir William of Bastille, faced off against Alvar Blackheart, the apparent savior of Arden.

The Blackheart Lord retracted his blade and twirled it in a blur as William's steel was thrust forward. They clashed, again and again, and then paused. The two men aimed their blades at one another, their tips nearly touching as they both assessed the other, remaining poised to strike. Again, they clashed.

Shards of marble dropped onto the floor, drawing Peter's attention. He turned to where he had thrown the wolf. Pools of molten gold stared back at him. Much of its gray fur was soaked with its own blood. He looked upon Tobius in its tattered condition, and suddenly the anger that he had felt since Masterstown abated. His eyes no longer itched or burned. The influence that he had felt from Verluxia had vanished. He no longer hated Alvar or Tobius. Instead, he felt ashamed.

The wolf growled and snapped at him again, lashing its tongue and baring its teeth.

"No," he muttered. "Tobius, please. Don't..."

The great wolf ignored his pleas. Driven by devotion to the Blackheart Lord, it pounced again onto Peter. Before its jaws could once again clamp down onto him, he grasped both the snout of the wolf and the tip of its lower jaw. With his back on the floor, he maintained his grips to prevent Tobius from biting him, holding its mouth open. The wolf struggled, twisting in every direction to either free itself or devour him.

Peter anticipated its struggling movements and twisted at the exact moment Tobius shifted its weight. A few cracks echoed from the neck of the animal, turning Peter's stomach. It whined and collapsed immediately. He released his grips to allow the injured animal to fall onto him. It attempted to stand, but could not, simply whimpering and falling back down.

Peter eased himself from underneath the beast. He crouched over it as it dared not move, continually whimpering as its chest heaved. Its neck was broken, he knew, although it had been unintentional. He stared painfully at the state of the great wolf.

His gaze lifted as the symphony of clanking steel ended. Alvar stood with his rapier in hand, surrounded by the three knights he had begun to duel simultaneously. The three men in silver armor all bore their share of cuts. The steel of their longswords was chipped, and one of the blades had been completely cut in half. They were all exhausted.

From across the room, Alvar's eyes wavered as he looked upon Tobius and Peter. "Tobius..." he muttered. He jogged past the knights. As the silver-haired knight attempted to strike at him, his sword was knocked aside by a blind strike from Alvar, who didn't spare him a single glance.

"Alvar," Peter pleaded. The dark eyes of the Blackheart Lord turned passionate with anger. When he came close enough, his sword arm became a blur of dark movement as he thrust downward with all his might. In an instant, Quickfury was plunged through Peter's leg where he had crouched. The tip of the blade stabbed through his muscle and into the surface of the marble floor as well.

An unintentional yelp escaped him as the pain in his leg overrode everything else. His hands trembled as his fingers brushed the hilt of the rapier against his trousers. He cried in agony as the dark blade was then removed and he fell back onto the floor, holding his new wound. Alvar stood over him and glowered before turning toward the defeated wolf. The rapier dropped to the floor and Alvar to his knees as he attempted to console his dying wolf.

Peter studied the Blackheart Lord. Alvar's gaze, filled with hate moments before, was somber. His shaking hands gently touched Tobius as he hummed, "Tobius...my friend."

A final whimper escaped the great wolf before its eyes rolled upward and its chest ceased movement.

The council chamber was quiet save for Alvar's sobs. He wiped his tears on his sleeve, grasped his rapier and stood, turning to Peter with a cold gaze. "You pathetic pleb. I knew you to be a less-than-adequate fool when we first met. Get up. Face me."

Peter remained still, holding his leg that bled as he stared up at Alvar.

"Get up!" he ordered again. "Meet your fate with some honor, will you?"

After taking a few breaths, Peter groaned as he struggled to stand. Leaning onto his uninjured leg, he faced Alvar.

"Alvar!" William called out. The old knight and his two comrades stood with the remnants of their swords in their hands. The Blackheart Lord turned to them as they rushed forward. Peter reached for Alvar's back, hoping to pin him.

As if guided by instincts, Alvar twisted as Peter's fingertips touched his black jacket. Peter's own momentum betrayed him and he collapsed forward as a new duel ensued between the three knights and Alvar.

William and Alvar briefly exchanged strikes before the Blackheart Lord pulled back and then rolled over Peter to meet the advance of the silver-haired knight. They too briefly dueled before Alvar turned onto the third knight. The brown-haired knight roared as he threw strike after strike. Peter reached after Alvar's boot, barely caressing it with his fingers to distract the Blackheart Lord. The brown-haired knight's chipped longsword pierced Alvar's shoulder.

The Blackheart Lord roared as he launched a furious counterattack, slicing completely through the longsword that had pierced him.

He twirled Quickfury, cutting Peter's back and drawing a line through the silver chest plate of the third knight.

Unable to endure the wounds he had received from both Alvar and Tobius, Peter collapsed and remained still against the blood-soaked floor. His vision blurred. Though he was still, the room wavered.

He heard footsteps—Helen. She lowered herself as he struggled to sit up, placing her hands firmly against the fresh wound in his leg. He grimaced and their eyes met. Painted with his own blood, she gently placed her hand to his cheek and spoke with motherly warmth. "You have done beautifully, Peter. I'm so proud of you."

"Peter?" he muttered. "That's the first time...you've called me Peter."

Before she could reply, a yelp caught their attention. The brown-haired knight had been grievously wounded. The silver-haired knight rushed at Alvar to avenge his comrade but was disarmed, suffering a slash across his back, then a firm punch to his jaw, knocking him out.

"Aaron!" Helen said. That was the name of the silver-haired knight, Peter thought. With Sir Aaron and the other knight out of the fight, William fought with Alvar alone, doomed to lose. The Blackheart Lord's skill shined through strongly, like a golden sun through a thin blanket of clouds. He truly was the greatest duelist in Arden's history. *No single person can stand against him, not even the Lionheart,* Peter thought.

Out of the corner of his eye, Peter glimpsed one of the large battle-axes nearby, still in the grip of one of the Blackheart Lord's bodyguards. He reached for it, but halted as the pain along his body restricted his movement.

Helen reached for the large weapon, straining to drag it across the floor. She placed the wooden handle into his open hand.

"Get back," he told her. She obliged.

Peter eyed Alvar as he dominated the fight, landing strike after strike upon William's armor and sword. When the old knight tripped and fell onto his back, exhausted, Peter grasped the ax with all his strength and wound his arm back. With a desperate growl, he tossed the weapon like a Frisbee. It soared over the ground and struck the heel of the Blackheart Lord. Bones shattered, cracking loudly within the chamber.

Alvar yelped and dropped to one knee. Grimacing, he turned his gaze toward Peter and Helen. His dark eyes were sad as he shook his head. "You...are no Lion," he said between heavy breaths. "I am...the only one willing to die for my people. My destiny will not be denied!"

Using Quickfury as a cane, he stood, straining and growling. Peter and Helen stared in disbelief as he limped towards them. He finally halted as he stood over them both and wound his sword arm back, preparing to make the final thrust that would end Peter's life.

Suddenly, a chipped longsword appeared through the chest of the Blackheart Lord. He gasped loudly and dropped Quickfury. The sword that had stabbed him was removed and crashed against the marble floor as it was dropped. Alvar turned to William, and their eyes met before he collapsed. The old knight caught the great duelist and eased him down.

Alvar's eyes filled with tears as he clawed at the man who had stabbed him, staring up at him as if he were a little boy in his father's arms, begging for the pain to end.

With tears in his own eyes, William spoke. "Why didn't you just surrender?"

Blood dripped from Alvar's mouth as he smiled. "...I am Alvar," he answered. "The savior...of...Arden. I am."

Then, Alvar Blackheart died in William's arms, and the world wept for him.

Chapter 28

Bastille

Peter awoke in a strange bed. It was small like the room that it was in, appearing gray and dour as rain pelted against the stained glass of the window to his right. The atmosphere was cold and he was alone, straining to peer around the simple and empty chamber.

His ear twitched and a chill ran along his spine when he heard the first gurgle beneath his bed. There was something underneath him, in the dark and on the cold stone floor. It moved around and the same disturbing gurgle sounded. It called out again and another voice added to it. In a perverse and chilling act, they both hummed together.

The voices began to snarl and wail like rabid animals, or rather, as infected humans.

A hand appeared over the edge of the bed as if from the murky depths of the sea. Yellow, dirty, and festered, its bone-claws tore through the simple blanket. Another hand followed, and another, and then another, until dozens of infected hands surrounded him in his bed, weaving their skeletal talons further into the blanket, strapping him down. Suddenly, they went still, unmoving as the snarling and gurgling ceased. The room was quiet and dreadful.

As one, the infected revealed themselves. Their festered and rotten heads appeared, each bearing the same set of eyes as if dipped in the blackest of oil.

Panic ensued and they descended upon him. He screamed and desperately attempted to push them all away, even as the morning light began to shine into the bedroom.

Then he heard her voice.

"Peter!" Aurora said.

She was there, but he could not see her, only the dozen infected humans that surrounded his bed. But one by one, they all disappeared. The dour and gray color of the room abated as the rays of the sun brightened, shining through the stained window. And there by his bedside, she watched him with a pained gaze. As he calmed himself, she eased onto the bed. "It was only a nightmare," she reassured him.

"Aurora," he breathed, relaxing his body before the dull pain struck him. The muscles and flesh of his chest, back, shoulders, and left arm ached. His left leg, however, burned with a certain pain and irritation. All injuries as a result of his most recent battle.

And then he remembered. He looked up to her from his pillow. "Alvar. Tobius," he said.

"Alvar Blackheart is dead," she told him gently, "and his wolf with him."

Peter paused, saying nothing as he recalled Alvar's last stand. The Blackheart Lord had fought William, two of his knights, and the Lion of Lunsera himself and still had managed to dominate most of the fight. Yet he was dead. In all his glory and splendor, he was dead, slain by William the Wanderer. His last words, the smile on his face as he died, and the death of his companion Tobius, all suddenly weighed heavily upon Peter. As his eyes stung and his throat ached, he shook his head, refusing to cry for the man that had become his enemy.

Instead, he looked back to the young woman. His friend. She appeared more beautiful than the day that they had first met. The sunlight kissed the exposed skin of her neck and face.

Her honey-brown hair flowed freely. She wore a long and fitted jacket. A belt hugged her thin waist. Beneath the jacket, there was a long navy blue tunic bearing silver designs. She was dressed to combat the cold.

"Aurora," he said. "Is this real?"

"Of course." She smiled. "I'm here."

"But where were you? What happened after the agents took you? I looked everywhere."

She hesitated and her smile faded. "You should speak with William when you are able."

"What? Tell me. What's going on?"

"Peter..." Again, she hesitated before uttering the words. "We believe that there may be someone else in Arden like you."

The words took his breath away and his heart skipped a beat. "Someone else from my world?"

She nodded. "But don't be concerned with that for now!" she commanded gently. "You will rest! You were recently the chew toy of a giant wolf."

"But how can I not be concerned? There's anoth—"

"Shhhh!" She pressed her index finger to his lips, silencing him with a grin. "Don't. Be. Concerned. And besides, I suspect you'll be pleasantly distracted by the change of scenery." She pulled back her hand.

"Okay. Where are we by the way?"

"Bastille," said a man's soft voice. Peter and Aurora both looked to the open doorway of the chamber, where a man in a gray robe stood. His hair was silver and long. His face, handsome, appearing to Peter as what he thought all knights should look like.

"Cousin," Aurora greeted.

"You," Peter noted. "You fought against Alvar with William. I remember you."

"And I was soundly defeated, my friend." The man smiled. "I am Aaron. Aaron Moonwey. Helen and Aurora are my cousins. On my mother's part."

As the young knight entered the room, the Lion struggled to rise in his bed to greet him. "I'm Peter. Peter Lone...gah!" He winced as the pain in his leg flamed.

"Take care, my friend," Aaron hummed, rushing to the other side of his bed. "You have endured much since you arrived in Arden, and on behalf of my own family. For that, I am most grateful. Although..." He peered across the bed at Aurora. "This one you could have just left on the rock. A joker she is. Always has been. And mischievous. She always forced me to assist her in teasing Helen when we were children."

Aurora gasped and grinned. "You! Don't listen to his folly, Peter."

"You know it to be true. Teasing Helen was your favorite activity as I recall. Still is."

"I recall your favorite activity: pretending sticks were swords."

"Many boys did, and still do!"

"How many continued to do it until the age of thir—"

"Shhh!"

Despite the pain he felt, Peter laughed for a few moments. It was a welcome joy. "So. Helen. Is she okay?"

Aurora answered, "She's well. Stressed, of course. There's a new council in Arden City. She's assisting it however she can. She wrote us a letter, saying that she looks forward to seeing us and that when you recover, we will depart for the rock immediately."

"Go back to Lunsera? To Lunar Rock?"

"The war is over, Peter. We did what we came here to do. The plague is gone."

"But the Turners of Barrington. The assassins. The other...me." He paused with dread. "And her. Verluxia. What about them?"

"Don't you want to return home with us?" Her brows furrowed, her voice brittle.

He hesitated before deciding to change the subject. "So how come we aren't in Arden City? And how long have I been asleep?"

Aurora' s eyes narrowed before she answered. "Well, after Alvar's downfall, the population of the city quickly heard of his demise. They blamed you. Helen ordered William to take you from the city for your safety. You lost an extensive amount of blood and you were unconscious after the fight. You have been in a most unusual state for four days."

"What do you mean?"

"Your eyes were black again. I suppose your new abilities aided you as you healed."

He sighed. "Right. What about Gideon?"

"The good captain returned to Barrington."

"What? Why?"

"Because he has a wife with children there, Peter. I honestly don't know how the guard of the eastern spire will react upon his return. He may very well be imprisoned, tortured, or executed. But that all depends on what he tells of his exploits during the war."

On whether he helped the Lionheart murder the Lord of Barrington's cousin or not, Peter thought. He looked back to Aurora. "And you still haven't answered my question. Where were you after Masterstown? I was terrified that something happened to you."

She sighed. "Let us see William first. Then I will tell you."

"He is in his office at this very moment, I believe," Aaron said. "Shall we go?"

They both looked at him. Aurora grinned. “Well, can you manage, Lion of Lunsera?”

He flexed his leg. There was initial pain, but it turned to mild soreness. He grinned. “Indeed...my lady.”

Delight filled him as she smiled at his words and she moved to assist him as his feet touched the cold stone floor. Aaron moved to Peter’s other side to further support him, and the two Moonwey’s assisted him in walking out of the room and into the hallway. The three proceeded slowly down the corridor, where light shined into the hallway from the numerous open doors along the right side.

“I must confess myself curious about your...abilities, Peter,” Aaron told him. “I know little of the plague that ravaged the west and I possess no experience in combating the infected, but I am informed that you fought in the western campaign and you gained new powers from it. Did you develop them on your own?”

“Er...I was bitten by infected. A lot of them.” He chuckled.

Aaron winced. “I see. But you did not change as the countless ones before you did. I am certain it is due to the power of your heritage.”

“Maybe, or I was just lucky. Regardless, I'm not the same as I used to be.”

“But that is not so unfortunate,” Aurora said, tickling his side.

He looked over at Aaron. “Did William tell you about what I told him? About the one that made the plague and the ones before it?”

“Verluxia is her name?”

“Yeah.”

“An unusual name to be sure. And you were connected to her after you were bitten?”

“That's right. It's all kind of hazy now, but I remember some visions I saw as if I were in the body of other people that she had infected. I don’t how she's done it or what she is but she's old, really old.”

“Indeed. Sir William confirmed that Alvar was in league with her but still planned to kill her himself. Unfortunately, he did not disclose where she dwells.”

Peter sighed. “Something else to dread. What about the assassins? And Barrington? Any updates?”

“Barrington bolsters with more forces as the days pass. It is certain that Ian Turner will march on the capital soon enough. We have dispatched word to Sohn, and to Lord Carlon in Carvalel for aid.”

“Jadiel,” Peter concluded. “I hope he's doing well and that he'll come. What about Lord Carlon?”

“From what we have been told, his command has been most successful. He remains in Carvalel, consolidating and overlooking the efforts to resettle. Returning to our current theater, Milsted yet remains an issue.”

“Milsted?”

“A town between this city and the capital. It lies at the foot of the mountains. It is the base of the assassins and their secret society.”

“So what's the plan? Do we go after Barrington or Milsted first?”

“Milsted, after you recover.”

Aurora cocked an eyebrow. “What? No. Peter has fought enough!”

“Of course,” Aaron quickly added. “It is your choice if you wish to accompany us when we depart. But with you by our side, it is more likely the group will surrender without a fight. Too many have already died since this war began.”

Peter looked to Aurora. “I'll have to give it some thought, Aaron.”

“Of course.”

They exited the hallway and entered a cathedral. Rows of benches faced the altar, behind which a large wooden cross hung on the stone wall. Opposite of the cross, in the back of the enormous room, a large window above a balcony allowed sunlight to shine into the church. On top the balcony he could see a piano.

“A piano.”

“Indeed,” Aaron said. “Do you play?”

“No. Jack did. He used to play after we would eat dinner. But whenever he was alone, he played a lot of Chopin.”

Aaron frowned. “I see. I have never heard it played as it should be. I was rather hoping you would know. I do weave a few melodies myself through the harp.”

Aurora chimed in. “Do you still sing?”

“Indeed.” A sharp smile formed on the young knight's face and he looked to Peter. “I could play for you if you like.”

Aurora chuckled. “Spare him further agony, cousin.”

He sighed. “Indeed. But if you decide you wish to hear, I shall be ready to serenade.”

The three followed a series of hallways from the cathedral. At the end of the final corridor, there was a closed door. Aaron knocked and a reply came from the other side. The silver-haired knight pushed the door open and there William sat, behind a large desk of dark wood. There was a window behind him and two bookshelves that flanked it. Across from the old knight, there were two chairs.

In the one to the right, a woman turned to greet them. She wore a dress of black and gray. Her brown and gray hair was neatly fixed into a single braid that fell over her right shoulder. She peered at Peter through large, cat-like eyes. The woman had to be two decades older than him and emanated a strange allure that he couldn’t ignore.

William stood from behind his desk as the three entered. “Peter,” he hummed, and he looked upon the young Lion with glee in his eyes. “You are well?”

“Yeah. Getting there.”

The knight smiled. “This is Madam Rosa.”

“Hello, ma’am,” Peter greeted, gently grasping her hand before he was assisted by the Moonwey’s into the empty chair.

“A pleasure, my Lord Lionheart,” her voice sang as she smiled.

William introduced the two Moonwey’s before he sat back into his chair. Aaron stood behind the older knight as Aurora remained standing beside Peter.

“Peter, Madam Rosa has come to Bastille at my invitation,” the old knight said. “She possesses information on who Alvar was.”

Spurred by genuine interest, Peter and the two Moonwey’s gazed at the woman as she spoke. “I knew Alvar Blackheart when he went by a different name. I knew him as a young boy by the name of Til.”

“Til?” Peter repeated. “What kind of name is that?”

“A cruel one,” William answered. “The word comes from the ancient river tribes. In the elder tongue of the people, it means flea.”

“Flea? Why would someone name a kid that?”

“Because,” Madam Rosa said, “Til’s mother was a lady of the night as I once was.”

“Lady of the night?” Peter asked. Aurora cocked an eyebrow as she cleared her throat, giving him an expectant glare that prompted the realization. “Oh! I got it. Sorry.”

“No apology is necessary,” the woman giggled. “Ezala was her name. She was quite young when she gave birth to him, and she hated him. The boy was raised in the house we worked in. He was a sweet and shy boy, always eager to help any of the girls that worked the house however he could.” Rosa swallowed. “Despite all this, Ezala frequently beat him.”

“She beat him?”

“Yes, my Lord. She truly hated him and we didn’t understand why. He was such a gallant boy. He loved to wrestle with the other boys in the street and always won despite his size. He loved stories as well, often helping me with many of my chores if I would tell him any of the old legends before he would go off to sleep at night. I obliged, of course." She looked back to William. "Your own adventures were among his favorites."

The old knight smiled, but despite his expression, Peter could see an all-too-familiar sadness within his gaze. It was a sadness that he himself felt: regret.

"Although he was never fond of romance," Madam Rosa continued. Peter chuckled, earning stares from both Aaron and Aurora. "His favorite was the legend of legends. The first tale of them all. The tale of Fyraen, Alvasar, and Norvok. When I would finish that story and tell him of the savior that would come, and that his name would be Alvar, he would repeat the name until he finally slept. And then I would listen to his little breaths as he dreamed."

"If I may," William said. "Who was his father?"

"I'm afraid that I never knew, nor did he know, but that didn't seem to bother him. Ezala died when he was thirteen, during the war. He changed when she did. Perhaps it was the stories of the new hero from the Otherworld that inspired him, but he left the home and began to work for a few merchants, and tradesmen, protecting their stock. Soon enough, Lyle Heart, the last Baron of Hearthelm, took Til into his own service to protect his family as he fought in the western skirmishes of the war. When the war ended, Til seemed to have disappeared for a while. I think he spent some time in the north forest alone. He then briefly visited home before he departed for Ilvion. He worked there for some time before returning to Hearthelm. When he returned, he began to work with six other boys his age. They called themselves the black barons, acting as...mercenaries, quite simply.

"Eventually, they all disappeared and I didn't see Til again until he was twenty, in Arden City. We met by accident after I had moved there. He told me that he had acquired a new occupation due to his new connections within the government of the city, often performing a few obscure tasks that he would not share with me. But he would send me many gifts from his adventures, many of those gifts worth small fortunes. Due to his generosity, I was able to live a better life, as I still do because of him." The woman paused again, staring into the desk, lost in thoughts of the past.

"Madam," Sir Aaron said. "The sword that he wielded. It was powerful enough to break the skin of the Lionheart himself. Where did he obtain it?"

"The one he called Quickfury? The last we saw one another, he did have a sword with him that was impossibly thin. Perhaps it may be the one you refer to. He told me that he swam to the bottom of the Ornian river and pulled it from the heart of the world. Quite the embellished tale. I had no idea that he was this...Alvar Blackheart, though I had heard the name incessantly preached in the city." She looked at William. "And you were...the one that did it? You were the one to kill him?"

"It was I, Madam. Not a moment has passed since that I do not regret it. My heart aches as if I had lost my own son."

Her gaze was cold upon him. "I pray that he rests at peace with Fyraen. And I pray too that it will haunt you for the remainder of your days." The woman stood and departed the old knight's office, leaving silence in her wake.

It was Aurora who spoke first. "That was a dramatic conclusion." A few moments passed as she waited for the three men to speak. Peter's own thoughts dwelled on the boyhood story of the man who would become Alvar.

Aurora threw up her hands. "Honestly! What has possessed the three of you? I understand Peter to be of the brooding sort and it adds to his charm, but all of you mourning that man?"

"Cousin—" Aaron began.

"—he tried to kill all of you! Not to mention he massacred the council, arrested Helen, and abducted me."

"Perhaps," William said.

Peter flexed his leg. Wincing, he stared at the gray fabric that covered the injury the Blackheart Lord had left. “This doesn’t change anything,” he said to them all. “Til doesn’t matter to me. Alvar. If anyone deserves that name it's him. His name was Alvar. Alvar Blackheart. Let's not talk about him anymore.” His eyes met William’s and the older man nodded.

“So,” Peter began again, “I hear you think there’s someone else from my world here in Arden.”

“With all my heart, Peter,” the old knight answered. “Why he has remained in the shadows for so long, I do not know. But I am certain that he wears a mask.”

“A mask? What else?”

“I saw him, Peter,” Aurora told him. “When the agents took me from Masterstown and you followed, it was the masked man that killed them. He took me. He was strong and fast much like yourself. I was brought to a cave, well-lit and furnished. There were other mask wearers as well. It must have been some sort of base for them. They gave me water and a blanket. I saw the smiling man there as well. He was the only one who did not wear a mask. He departed shortly after with a few of the others.

“The masked man followed soon after, but not before I was able to watch him for some time. He wore a strange coat of some sort. When he removed it, his body was covered in bandages, every spot. There was no skin to be seen. And he was thin, like a skeleton, and taller than William. After he left, I escaped when the others who were supposed to remain vigilant over me decided to either play a game or fall asleep,” she proclaimed proudly.

Peter smiled. “Of course you did. So is he on our side, do you think?”

William spoke. “It is fair to say that he and Alvar were not in league with one another. The smiling man did inquire both times that I encountered him whether I would kill Alvar. I believe they wanted him dead. I also believe this group to be made up of the same mask wearers who infiltrated the secret society of assassins that has targeted the province leaders these recent months. And I believe this other to be the one they call the Angel."

"Okay."

"There is more. Over the course of the days since Alvar's demise, there have been reports of mask wearers appearing in several towns and other cities, including Barrington itself. Often they appear in pairs. The day before yesterday there were two in the streets of this very city. They scouted, I believe, and then departed."

"Scouted for what?"

"You, I think."

"Me? But why?"

"It is impossible to know what he wants for certain. Whether he seeks you as an ally, we simply cannot say as of yet."

"Or if he wants me out of the way...like Alvar. Maybe he wanted us to kill each other. Maybe that's why he's stayed behind the scenes for so long. But why? What does he want?"

"In time all things will be revealed," William answered. "For now, I want you to take a respite. Relax, Peter. Enjoy my city."

"Relax?"

"Yes. All of us who fought were injured and we must recover before our next objective. We will gain intelligence as we rest. It is the best strategy."

Before he could utter another word, Aurora moved behind him and placed her hands on his shoulders. "Come along, Peter. Aren't you famished?"

His stomach growled loudly for all to hear. "Looks that way."

They all laughed as he stood, and the two Moonwey's assisted him in departing the room.

* * * * * * *

The door closed and heavy silence lingered as William sat behind his desk. His hands remained locked before his mouth as he thought.

Alvar was dead, and at the old knight's very hands. The Angel and his masked followers were obviously scheming, but to what end? Ian Turner was said to have been mustering more and more forces to Barrington. Would he strike Arden City as his father once did? Rob Grimful was still at large as well—were he and his followers still in Milsted, or in Barrington?

And Verluxia. *The vile one that is responsible for the plagues.* What was she? What was her precise nature? Where was she hiding?

All of the questions and problems at hand could have been better contended with if Alvar had simply surrendered. If the Blackheart Lord had decided to lay down his arms, he would have been able to assist the old knight and the Lion of Lunsera in answering those questions and ending all the conflict.

Such a waste, William thought to himself. *Such a waste of what more he could have been. Til. Alvar. Savior of Arden. How you have fallen. To what end? For what purpose? Was it your pride? Were you truly so delusional? To come from such a humble and foul beginning, and to arise from it through pure strength of will...*

William's heart skipped a beat. He closed his eyes as tears welled within them. The fatherless son of a harlot, who came from nothing, had been able to shake the entire world to its core.

Be at peace, Savior of Arden.

* * * * * * *

With Aurora to his left and Aaron to his right, Peter limped along the stone corridor. The cousins pushed the doors at the end of the hallway open, allowing the light to blind him as he heard the sounds of laughing children coupled with familiar sounds of the cityscape. When his eyes adjusted, a courtyard lay in front of him, surrounded by the buildings of a small city, a mountain range looming to the right of where they stood.

"Welcome to Bastille, the northern city," Aaron said as they walked out and approached the stone stairs leading down to the cobblestone courtyard, in the center of which a single tree bore large pink apples.

Peter took a deep breath, taking in the scent of freshly baked bread. "It's peaceful here."

A pack of children rushed past the base of the stairs, laughing as they chased one another with sticks in hand. Far across the clearing, a few smiths beat molten steel. Adjacent to the smiths, the doors of a baker's shop remained open, allowing the fresh scent to attract a few men and women.

"It does possess a certain charm," Aurora confessed.

"Let's sit down," Peter said. They made their way over to the top of the stairs, where he and Aurora sat with Aaron standing over them.

The young knight smiled. "Perhaps the splendor of the city will aid in your recovery. And of course, the Moonbow is upon us. Tonight and the night after, it will be at its most vivid."

"The moonbow?"

"Indeed. There is a path that leads into the mountains behind the city. At the end of the path is a lagoon and waterfall. When the moon is at its fullest, it forms an array of light through the mist of the water. Many come here to witness its beauty."

Peter looked up to the sky. "Great. We'll check it out. Hopefully Carraas doesn't—" Words escaped him as he saw what remained of the silver planet that typically loomed in the blue sky above. It appeared torn in half, split down the center, remnants of it scattered around. "What happened?" he asked.

"No one knows," Aurora told him. "It happened last night. The planet just...split in two. Many were crying in the streets as it occurred."

An eerie feeling descended upon him as he looked back up to the remains of the silver world hovering so far away.

What's happening? Why is there so much destruction? His head sank into his hands. He felt Aurora rubbing his back.

"Do not fret, Peter," Aaron told him. "Though there is much evil and destruction, it will not prevail. Love will triumph. I take my leave. Enjoy the city and the moonbow, my friend." He bowed and then departed back into the cathedral, leaving the couple alone on the steps, taking in the scenery of the city.

"So," Aurora said to him. "What shall we do first?"

He paused as he thought. The group of children that had been laughing as they chased once another once again took flight across the courtyard. Their wooden swords thrust toward one another as they all claimed which hero they pretended to be.

"I'm Sir William!" one exclaimed.

"I'm the Baron of Hearthelm!" said another.

"I'll be the Lionheart, the greatest of all!" claimed a third boy.

As they advanced past Peter and Aurora, a smaller boy followed the others with a mutt trailing behind him. "...and I'm Alvar Blackheart! Come, Tobius."

To Peter, it sounded as if it were Alvar's voice that had said the words. An icy breeze robbed him of the cool breath he had taken. The group of boys disappeared and he looked back to the sky. The ruins of a planet lingered there.

Out of the corner of his eye, he caught Aurora's stare. "What?" he asked. She maintained a satisfied grin whilst her eyes looked him up and down, stopping at the crown of his head. She reached forward and began to comb his hair. "Ow!"

"It's tangled, see?" she giggled as she combed her fingers through the locks, each stroke becoming more pleasant than the last. "Your radiance has finally returned since we found you with Gideon. And it's grown so much since we first met. Golden, and thick. There." She stood and took a step back, placing her hands on her hips and staring proudly at his head.

“Finished?”

“Indeed. Let us scour for food.”

Together, they crossed the courtyard to the bakery, where the delightful aroma of freshly baked goods filled his nose and watered his mouth. He stood outside the brick building as Aurora dashed through the door. Taking a deep breath, he looked around the city, from the apple tree in the center of the courtyard to the cathedral that towered over every other building.

“Here,” she said as she joined him, thrusting a hand-sized wheel of bread into his grasp.

“Woah.” He smiled. “It's still warm!”

They both took a bite of their baked goods, moaning in unison as the sweet, creamy, and yet salty cooked dough tickled their tongues. “Bread is easily one of my favorite foods. It's so simple. Pizza is the best. There's no debate.”

She tilted her head. “Peace...sah?

He laughed. “No. Pizza. It's basically bread with tomato sauce and cheese. You would like it.”

“It sounds delightful. I wonder...” But she shook her head. “No. Never mind.”

“What?”

She hesitated. “I wonder what it would be like to go to your world. I wonder what your mother would think if you brought me.”

“She'd like you. I can tell,” he reassured her with a playful nudge.

“Truly? Then if it were at all possible, I would be delighted to go.”

“If it were possible,” he muttered to himself. “But...” How would he get home? What about Jack? The questions that had plagued him since he had first arrived in Arden had resurfaced to haunt him again. The stressful reality of the world slowly began to weigh upon him.

He suddenly thought of the battle at Carvalel, when the army of infected had smashed against the gate. He remembered how Alvar had led the counterattack, slashing through the undead with hundreds of fighting men following his assault. The boy that had been torn apart in front of Peter during the fighting came to mind. He had been younger than the Lion of Lunsera, and probably far from his home when he died, away from his mother and those that cared for him. The boy Peter didn't know had died in the mud, in a puddle of his own blood. He remembered staring at those lifeless green eyes after the battle.

How the boy had felt as he was being devoured alive—Peter knew that as well. Hearthelm. When the Blackheart Lord had left him in the street of that ruined town beneath a score of infected.

His body reacted on its own just before she screamed. The thoughts that had played like a scene in a movie had ended, and he stood over what remained of the tree in the center of the courtyard. Every person nearby stared at him. He removed his hands from the splintered bark and backed away before looking to her. On the ground nearby, Aurora stared up at him, horrified.

The single tree that had stood in the courtyard now lay across the cobblestone, broken, chipped, and shattered. What had happened? What had he done? He had been irritated, but by what? One moment he had been with her, enjoying a peaceful moment. But within an instant, memories had flooded his mind and driven out any peaceful thought. Now he stood surrounded by the destruction that he had wrought without knowing.

His eyes met hers and he saw the fear within them. He was a monster.

Before she could speak, he turned and limped across the courtyard, up the stairs, and into the cathedral to hide away.

Chapter 29

Moonlight, Midnight

"I know of his affliction," William told them. The old knight sat behind his desk, gazing between Sir Aaron and Lady Aurora. "It is not uncommon among even the most experienced of warriors. They return home from war, yet a scar remains upon them. It is a scar within the mind, easily festered and torn. Peter is young and has endured much in so brief a time. This change within him, it is the result of his near-death experiences. It is disconcerting. And the fault is mine."

"But for how long?" the lady asked. "How long will it affect him?"

"Regretfully, I do not know, my lady. In some warriors who are afflicted, it abates with time, in others, it simply does not. I am hopeful that Peter will be of the former group."

The young woman scoffed, leaning back into her chair. "Hopeful? Is there no other way that you can aid him? After all, you are the one responsible for all that has befallen him."

“Yes. The fault is mine, but the choice was his, and he relented. Peter made the choice as a man would. I am justly proud of him for his sacrifice—”

“Justly proud—?”

“As his uncle himself would be!” William stated firmly. “He does not suffer alone, my lady. I know his pain, and I suffer with him.”

She stood, her cold gaze upon him. “Good,” she said before turning and departing his office. The door slammed behind her and the chamber fell quiet like the evening air beyond the window.

Softly, Aaron spoke. “Sir, what is your solution to the issue at hand?”

“Peace,” William replied. “Peter is in need of peace. He deserves it.”

Aaron sat back in his own chair. “The Lion threw her aside and destroyed the old tree in an instant. Aurora did say that he had a look within his eyes when he did it. She said that he appeared both fearful and hateful at once. He must have felt in that moment such despair.”

“As if he were still fighting against the infected. The incident at Hearthelm, perhaps.”

“Will you allow him to continue hiding?”

“I have known Peter since he was a child. I watched over him from a distance. There are some known remedies to the trauma.”

“Such as?”

“For him, dogs, I think. He was always fond of them.”

“Sir William, is that wise? After all, he was the one to slay Alvar’s beast. The wolf. Would that fight not still weigh heavily upon him?”

“Perhaps,” William replied. “But for now it is our best choice if we are to aid him.”

* * * * * * *

The golden rays of day seeped through the window as they had all morning. William sat in the quiet recovery chamber, shifting his gaze from the window to the sleeping man in the bed nearby. Sir Logan's breaths were slow and constant, a rhythm amidst the silence as he continued to recover from the wounds he had sustained in the fight against Alvar. The old knight had remained at his bedside for the past hour, watching over him, wishing to speak with him, yet also desiring his full recovery even if it meant they would not speak.

After a few more moments, the old knight stood and departed the chamber. He took slow steps along the corridor, his hands clasped together behind his back as he walked and thought to himself. When he rounded the corner into the next hallway toward the chapel, Sir Aaron stood there awaiting him.

"Did you find Peter?" William asked.

"He walks in the gardens. Alone."

"I see. Ensure the pack finds him," he told the silver-haired knight, who nodded and turned to exit the cathedral as they entered the chapel.

William stopped. He took a moment to gaze around the pulpit, and at the few people dispersed among the benches, all muttering prayers to themselves with their faces in their hands. Lingering for a few moments, he allowed a few prayers for Peter and Sir Logan to pass through his thoughts.

After departing the chapel, he returned to his office. His eyes narrowed at the person sitting in front of his desk. The back of the man's head was bald and his stomach pressed against the orange silk jacket he wore.

"Morning to you," William greeted as he closed the door behind him. The bald man turned and an everlasting smile presented itself to the old knight.

"Sir William," the smiling man greeted as he stroked his goatee.

"You." It was the man from the ruins, from the night upon which Alvar's agents had been killed by the masked man.

As the old knight lingered, unsure, the man before him simply chuckled. "I beg your pardon, sir. I showed myself into your office in hopes to speak with you alone." He indicated to the vacant desk. "Please."

"I remember you," William muttered, remaining by the closed door. "You were there when the agents of Alvar were killed, one by one. You are in service to him. The masked man from the Otherworld."

"You are most perceptive, Sir William the Wanderer."

There was a moment of silence. The old knight finally walked to his desk and eased into the chair behind it, maintaining his gaze upon the small dark eyes of the smiling man.

"Why are you here and who are you?" William asked.

"Esper. Esper Cloud is my name."

"Very well, Esper Cloud. Why are you here? What is it you seek? What of your master? Who is he?"

Esper crossed his legs in a feminine manner. "So many questions, great knight. You have played your part with exquisite effort. I have noted that you are a bit...dogmatic. Personally, I find it endearing. So. Alvar Blackheart is dead. And you were the one to slay him." He gently clapped his hands. "We were overjoyed when we heard the cries from the city. 'The savior of Arden is dead!' It was inevitable, I think. He was vain, was he not? Just hubris." A chuckle escaped the smile.

"How dare you!?" William growled. "How dare you mock the dead? Alvar had his share of faults, but he was a true warrior and died as such. He was no snake such as you and your master."

"Warriors die, Sir William. Snakes are clever. They live."

"Very well," he snapped. "You are a snake. What is it you want, Snake?"

"I am simply here to...assess." The smile remained, but the dark eyes appeared dreadfully cold as the man said, "The Lionheart. Where is he? He is here, is he not?"

William said nothing, but continued to glare at the man.

"Of course you would never betray the Lions of the Otherworld, sir. But when I entered the city this morning, I did notice the catastrophe just outside. That tree in the courtyard. It was not simply chopped down or blown over by the wind, was it not? No. Nearly pulled from the ground it would seem."

"Peter is not here," William lied.

"Peter is his name!" he said excitedly. "We did come by Lady Aurora when I encountered you that night. A clever fox she is. She also stays here with him? Of course."

"Enough of this!" William stood. "Depart from my city or I'll throw you out in chains."

"Most amusing, Sir William. We are fond of you but that endearing quality has its limits. The Angel wants him."

"Return to your master, Esper Cloud. He will not have Peter."

Slowly, the smiling man stood. "He said that you would say something quite like that. He, too, admires you, sir. He also bid me to give you something." Reaching into his orange jacket, he unveiled what appeared to be a playing card. It was stained but still mostly white, bearing a printed sketch of a king with two black hearts on opposite corners. He placed the card onto the desk. As the card left Esper's hand, it cut his flesh and drew a little blood. "Your reward," he said before licking his cut thumb.

"Leave. While you can."

Esper Cloud bowed and departed the chamber.

William looked down to the card on the table. He picked it up and studied it for a moment. It was rigid, more rigid than any card he had ever held before. With the fingers of both hands, he attempted to rip it in two. It resisted as if he were trying to tear an entire book. Halting his effort to tear it, he gazed upon the sketched king.

It is as Alvar's sword. A remnant of the Otherworld, he thought. *Peter.*

With haste, he departed his office and took flight down the hallway. The smiling man was nowhere to be seen. He continued along the next corridor and into the entry chamber. The doors of the main entrance into the cathedral had already been left open, allowing the autumn air to strike his face as he ran outside. He turned to his left and followed the stone path along the side of the cathedral and into the labyrinth of trees.

He had rounded a corner when he heard laughing. It was Peter laughing, he knew. Halting, he observed the scene at hand.

Peter lay on his back in the grass as three pups converged on him. They were shepherds. wolf-like. One nibbled at his clothes as he held another on his chest. The third bit at his hair. He smiled and laughed.

The old knight began to back away, seeing the Lion at peace. Peter looked at him and waved.

"You are well?" William asked.

"Feeling great." Peter smiled. "I was just going for a walk and then these guys came out of nowhere."

"Most fortunate," the old knight said before he sat at the base of the stairs. One of the pups ran over to him and began to chew on the tips of his gray robe. It tugged and growled. "Cease that!" he told it.

"So what's up?" Peter asked.

William simply extended his hand and the card that Esper had given him. Peter's brow furrowed before he took it, bending it with his fingers.

"It's just a playing card. Looks old. Really old. King of hearts. Black hearts."

"It was given to me by the smiling man, the one in service to the Angel."

A sigh escaped Peter. "So what?" He extended it toward William, who shook his head.

"Keep it. I have no use for it and do not want it."

Without a moment to spare, Peter ripped it as if it were a normal card, casting the two torn pieces aside. Two of the puppies converged upon the remnants and began to chew.

"He said that it was a reward from the Angel. For defeating Alvar, I suspect."

"You think he came all the way here to give you a card?"

"A few days ago two mask wearers entered the city. Now the smiling man has. They were searching for you. The Angel wants you, Peter. I feel in my heart that he is a threat."

The Lion gazed toward the sky as the puppies wrestled on his chest. "So what do I do? I'm a monster. I kill and destroy. I killed men and Tobius. I hurt the girl I care about."

William spoke softly. "The fault is not yours. You are not the first to experience what ails you now. Jack himself did. I did. We all did. You will overcome it."

He shook his head. "She hates me. She has to. I'm just...messed up now. How could she ever love someone like me? Someone broken like me? She should just leave and be with someone else."

"No," William said to him. "I do not want that for you, Peter. You are dear to me. And no matter how many battles you win, or mountains you jump, to me you will always remain the little boy from Norfolk, Virginia. The little boy who scored that game-winning goal when I first watched him play all those years ago. You are a champion. Now. I want you to rise and be the champion I know you to be. Not just for yourself, but for those closest to you."

The old knight watched the Lion of Lunsera as he stared sullenly into the sky. One puppy remained on his chest. It was the darkest of the pack, appearing almost black. It rested its head on his chest and, like the Wanderer, it stared at Peter expectantly.

"Maybe..." Peter said. "Maybe you're right. There's this darkness that's hanging over me like a cloud that just won't move on. But I feel like the sun is going to break through it soon enough. I just know it."

The dark pup that lay on his chest barked in approval. Peter looked at it. "You think so too?"

It howled and he gently scratched behind its ear. "I think I'll keep you." He smiled. "If that's fine with you, William."

The knight smiled. "Of course, Peter. What will you name him?"

Peter's blue eyes flickered as he thought. He turned to the fragments of the nearby card and then back to the pup that stared at him. "Ace," he said.

The pup licked him in approval.

* * * * * * *

Peter sat in the grass most of the day, playing with his pack. Ace remained in his lap as the others ran around him. The dark canine slept often as Peter talked with William. He had stayed away from Aurora as much as possible since the incident the day before, to avoid any possible risk of hurting her again.

When the first star began to shine, William finally stood, groaning like an old man. "I'll see to it that your friends are tended to."

"Thanks. Oh. And I'm sorry about the tree by the way."

"If I am to be sincere, I was never fond of it." Peter chuckled before William spoke again. "The Lady Aurora. She and I spoke yesterday. She was...passionate in her defense of you. I think it would be wise if you talked with her. The Moonbow is upon us again this evening. It will be a clear sky. Take her to the lagoon in the mountains. Forget all that has happened and be a teenager for an evening."

The knight didn't give him any chance to refuse as he quickly scooped two of the dogs up, leaving Ace with Peter, and departed with them. In silence, Peter sat looking at the pup in his lap. It looked back up at him and tilted its head.

"Well. What do I say to her? Maybe, sorry? Of course. I'm an idiot either way." He stood and the pup stood with him. They both stretched at the same time and yawned. He took a deep breath. "Alright. Let's find her."

From the garden to the entrance of the cathedral, he walked slowly as a result of his still-healing leg. Ace stayed by his side, always on his left. He stood at the top of the stairs, the entrance to the cathedral at his back, and looked over the courtyard as the last of the tree was removed. Small flames flickered from the lamps being lit along the streets, and from the candles in the windows of each house. A cool autumn breeze passed over the bakery, carrying the scent of fresh bread into his nostrils. He ignored it, continuing to look around for her.

"Pete!" someone called from behind. He turned to the entrance of the cathedral. Sir Aaron stood in the open doors. The breeze tossed his glowing silver hair as he walked over to Peter, glancing down at the pup by his side.

"Oh. This is Ace."

"Charmed."

"Aaron...your...your hair is glowing."

The young knight chuckled. "A family trait of the Moonwey's. I trust you are familiar with the tale of Lady Lunsera?"

"Yeah. Of course. Aurora told me about it. Speaking of which, you haven't seen her around have you?"

He smiled and indicated an adjacent street. It led to the base of the mountains, where a path was lit by lanterns, ascending toward where Peter knew the moonbow to be. "If you are to make the journey, may I accompany you?"

"Er...sure." Peter bent down and picked up Ace, cradling him as they walked along the street and then started up the trail to the lagoon. "So. You're from New London," Peter prompted.

"Indeed. My mother departed Lunsera and married my father, a noble and guild master. A year after their marriage, I was born."

"How was New London? I keep hearing about it."

"It was an intriguing city to be sure. Large. Outsized only by Arden City and Ilvion. My boyhood consisted of incessant lessons in academics. After all, my uncle was Lord Edward Moonwey, and my mother was intent upon education. My father, however, cared little for it. He became distracted in life by gambling and drinking, and slowly my inheritance was squandered away through his lack of self-control."

"I'm sorry to hear that."

"And your father?"

"That's not important."

"Apologies. I did not intend to pry."

"It's fine." Peter smiled to reassure him.

"Aurora and her mother visited us often when I was but a boy. Helen, however, always remained by her father's side, his pupil in many ways. They visited some and we visited Lunar Rock little, I regret to say. I do miss it. Enchanting."

"I agree. I look forward to going back."

"So you will return to Lunsera after all. Helen and Aurora both seem to enjoy your company."

He sighed. "Maybe not after recent events." He hoped he was wrong.

After a while of ascending the snaking path, he heard the water crashing close by.

Aaron stopped. "I think it best if I take my leave here. I wish you good fortune, my friend."

Peter waited and watched as the knight descended the path before placing his pup on the ground and continuing to the lagoon as it revealed itself. Its mist hovered above the water and through it, a pale rainbow appeared for all the onlookers to see. Dozens of people from the city gazed at the scene at hand. And just as he turned his gaze from the moonbow, he saw her standing there near the water. The mist sprayed her, the moon's radiance illuminated several strands of her hair, and Aurora stood alone with crossed arms.

He made his way toward her, feeling greater guilt with each step. Just as he halted to turn back, she looked to him and smiled faintly.

"Hey," he said to her as he joined her.

She simply smiled and then looked down to the pup with him. "Who is this?"

"His name is Ace. William gave him to me."

"Charmed," she said before looking back to him. "How do you feel?"

"Don't worry about me. How are you?"

She simply shrugged. "Seeing the spectacle before I depart."

"You're leaving?"

"In the morning. For Arden City. There's no purpose in staying here."

"What makes you say that?"

"Helen wants me to return with her. And after your efforts to elude me, I see your desire to be alone. So I'll leave you alone."

He shook his head. "Are you mad at me?"

"No," she said flatly.

"Then why are you leaving?"

"To give you time alone, since that's what you want."

"So you are angry at me."

"No," she said flatly again.

He looked around, unsure of what to say before she spoke again.

"I have helped you, Peter. Ever since we first met I have helped you, and never have I requested anything from you. All I have ever wanted was to be your friend, your partner, to face all of this together. But you don't want that."

"Aurora—"

She extended her index finger and silenced him. Suddenly she seemed more like Helen than the woman he knew her for. "I detest being alone," she told him. "But you must love it. Every time something ill-fated happens to you, you shut yourself away and sulk. I try to be the light to your darkness, but I don't think you want that." She paused, looking into his soul, her own on display through her soft gaze. "I will leave you to your darkness then since you value it so much more than me. Goodbye, Peter."

She turned from him and walked away.

"Aurora. Wait," he said, expecting her to keep walking. She stopped but did not turn.

"About the other day, I'm sorry. I don't know what happened to me, but I hate myself for it. That's why I've stayed away from you. Because I don't trust myself, that I won't hurt you again." His gaze remained on her back and she started to walk away again. "Please," he told her and she stopped but again did not turn. "Aurora, look, I...I can't promise that I'll change, because I still don't know who or what I am. Despite how much has happened, I know in my heart that there's still so much more. And when it does happen I don't want to face it alone. I need a partner. I need someone that I can help, someone that will help me, someone that I can face life with, and grow with. Maybe you are the light to my darkness."

He shrugged as the sincerest words he had ever uttered flowed from his lips. "I'm seventeen years old, Aurora. I just graduated high school not long ago. I should be in my own world, focused on...college and soccer. But I'm not. My life hasn't gone the way I wanted it to at all. I've killed men, Aurora. I've killed men for you." He shook his head as his eyes began to sting. "And I'll kill again for you. I'd die for you. And being alone isn't what I want. I just want you." He paused. "But if you want to leave, then go. Leave me."

Please don't leave me, he thought as he watched her back.

She turned, smiled, and shook her head. "You're impossible," she told him, slowly walking back.

She stopped in front of him as her arms remained crossed. “So what—” she began to say before he grabbed her waist and pulled her body against his.

Her breath escaped her as she looked into his eyes. She reached around his neck as they leaned into one another and their warm breath mingled. He closed his eyes as his lips met hers. Both went weak at the knees and nearly collapsed where they stood, forcing them to break contact. He watched her as her eyes remained closed and she bit her lip, smiling.

“That was nice,” she told him. “And long overdue, I think.”

“My timing has never been the best.”

“Well,” she said, tracing her finger along his lips. “We shall endeavor to remedy that.”

His reply was simply another kiss.

Chapter 30

The Fall

The mountain morning cold struck William when he stepped foot outside the cathedral. Though he wore his armor and his pale cloak shielded his back against the elements, it did little to thwart the chill he felt. He stood at the top of the stairs overlooking the courtyard before him and the army that had assembled. There were men saying goodbye to their families, and men who had none to bid farewell to. The latter felt the morning cold as the old knight did, without tears to distract them from it.

William glanced to his right, where the commander and his officers stood. They all wore gray jackets with golden embroideries, each bearing the same cross of the northern city woven on the chest. To his left were the brothers of the Order. Merely five knights, including Sir Aaron Moonwey. Both groups joined him at the top of the stairs as the entire might of Bastille was mustered.

An hour passed quickly, and as the sun's light began to peek over the roofs of homes, the army was fully accounted for. Five-hundred men in total. Half wielded pikes and spears; half bore rifles slung over their shoulders. As the horses for William and his staff were brought toward the cathedral, Peter arrived. He was dressed in typical riding attire, fitting of Lady Aurora, with whom he was hand in hand.

"Watch my pups for me while I'm gone?" he asked her as they walked toward the group of knights and officers.

"Of course. I will watch over your beloved canines until you return." She halted and he stopped to look at her. "And after...we depart for Arden City as we agreed."

"I promise," he told her with a smile. Their gazes held and they stood like statues for a moment before coming together for a brief public display of affection.

William spoke. "When you are prepared, Lionheart."

Reluctantly, Peter left Aurora and joined William and his staff. All the knights and officers nodded to the Lionheart. He nodded in turn before looking to William, who held his gaze.

"What?" Peter asked him.

William could feel a smile form on his face. "You are noticeably different. At peace, it would seem."

"I've figured some things out over the last few days. There's still a lot to figure out, but I'm making progress."

"I am relieved to hear it. Your decision?"

"I'll go with you today to Milsted, for the assassins. But that's it. After we're finished today I'm leaving with Aurora. We're going back to Arden City to meet up with Helen."

"And then?"

"We'll see."

"As you say, Peter. It is your decision to make. But the Angel. What of him?"

The Lion simply shrugged. "Haven't seen him yet, have we? I can't do anything about a shadow, William."

"As you say."

Without another word between them, they turned and descended the stairs of the cathedral, followed by the knights and officers. William and his party stepped into the saddles of their steeds, and as the army looked upon him and silence set in around the courtyard, he spoke.

"Justice," he announced to the army in front of him, and his party on horseback behind him. "Justice will be delivered today upon those that scheme in the shadows. For weeks we have known that Milsted is the base of operations for the assassins. For those who have slain several province leaders, their families, and countless others in this unjust ploy for terror and power. We are Bastille! We will not bring terror upon them as they have done. We will bring Justice. Now. Ride with me!"

Hundreds of spears and pikes were thrust into the air. The voice of the army roared as one against the surrounding rock of the mountains. William spurred his horse forward, his party following behind, and the army itself behind them.

As the old knight rode with Peter by his side down the road, he looked back to his city and a feeling made itself known to him. A feeling that he would never return to it.

As noon approached, the march began to come to an end as they turned onto a road leading into a small valley formed by mountains. Though the rocky hills still hid it from them, William knew the base of the assassins was nestled there. The road curved around a few hills, and as they passed over another, the town came into view. It was small and modest, consisting of buildings made from wood and thatch with few stone structures standing. As they halted, William noted that there was no sign of life, no movement within the town beneath the shadows of the mountains.

The commander rode up next to him. “Shall I send a squad forth, Sir William?”

He hesitated as he scanned the ghost town. His eyes caught movement in the town center, where what appeared to be a few men in black climbed onto horses led from a stable. Four riders galloped from the town toward them.

“Peter. Aaron. With me.” He kicked the flanks of his steed and galloped along the road with the Lion of Lunsera on his right and the Moonwey knight on his left.

It is him, he assumed as they raced along the road toward the riders. The distance closed quickly between them and finally, both parties halted in the center of the road, staring one another down. “It is you,” William concluded.

One of the riders in black came forward and removed his hood. It was Rob Grimful, the fallen Knight, easily recognizable by his red and gray hair as well as the eye patch he wore over his right socket. “William,” he called gruffly. “You bring friends and an army. To force me into submission?” His single gray eye looked to Sir Aaron, and then to Peter. “Story is, you murdered Alvar Blackheart.”

“Believe what you want,” Peter replied.

“Belief.” He chuckled. “Your Christian friends can tell you all about that. Worshiping your sky father. Your nailed god. You should worry little—”

“You should really worry about you right now.” Peter snapped coldly.

Grimful chuckled and pointed at Peter. “I like this one, William. There’s darkness in him. Aye. He’ll make a fine tyrant, if he lives to become one.”

“Enough, Grimful!” the old knight spat. “I have tolerated you for far too long. You understand why we are here. You will surrender, and be tried in Arden City for your crimes.”

“Is that what is to become of me?” he laughed before turning serious. “No. No. No! Still, you cannot see it. The end is near. You do not see it, Turner doesn't see it, the Savior of Arden did not either. It's all over."

"What is this madness you speak of?"

The fallen Knight stepped down from his horse and unsheathed his sword. "Fight me," he said. "I will not rot in a dungeon cell."

William hesitated. To his right, Peter began to stir. "No," he told the young man. "He is a former brother. It is my responsibility to end this if that is what he so desires." He stepped down from his horse and reached across his body. With a single movement, he unsheathed his longsword.

Between the two parties of men on horseback, the two knights on foot approached one another. Grimful roared as he swung his blade overhead towards William. The old knight parried the strike to the side and spun, following with a slash to his former comrade's unprotected hamstring. The man grimaced and groaned from the slice as he turned toward William. Steel sang as William advanced and pressed the attack during most of the bout. Grimful struggled to keep up with the newly acquired strength that William had earned during his ten years in the Otherworld.

After a few minutes of fighting, both men paused and stared at one another, panting as sweat rolled down their foreheads. "Your skills are mediocre," William told him. "You have grown lazy. It is little wonder you fled when we last saw one another."

"Self-preservation," the fallen Knight muttered. "But it matters little, whether you win or I, it does not matter. Soon this world will see its end."

"Why do you say such things? I have allowed this fight to continue in hopes you would tell me."

As William focused on the panting warrior in front of him, something finally caught his eye far beyond Grimful and the men on horseback. On the top of the mountain that stood above the town, a blur of gray movement dashed around a jagged peak.

* * * * * * *

From his horse, Peter watched in suspense, longing for William to finish the fight as soon as possible so he could get back to Aurora. After the brief exchange between the two knights, William suddenly seemed distracted. The one-eyed warrior he fought turned also toward the town. "What is that..." he muttered gruffly.

Peter glanced around the town and the base of the mountain until he found what both men were staring at. A single figure stood on the top of the mountain overlooking the town. And the realization dawned upon him. It was him. It was the masked man.

The lone figure at the peak remained fixed for a moment, like a gargoyle. Suddenly, he jumped from the mountain, plummeting through the air like a meteor. As he landed in the center of the town, a crater formed beneath him as all of the buildings around him were utterly destroyed by the force generated from his fall. A small shock wave reached them from the impact, spooking Peter's horse.

In awe, they watched as the man walked through the debris and fresh fires toward them. The silver mask shined brighter with each step. The three black riders that had accompanied the fallen Knight spurred their horses with haste around Peter and Aaron, fleeing what was to come.

Grimful looked between William and the man that approached. He stepped toward the older knight as they both focused on the masked man. Peter dismounted and strolled forward past the two, his eyes upon the man ahead. The silver mask shined against the sun, becoming larger with each ominous step. Finally, when both were close enough, the two men halted, facing off with a gap between them.

The masked man was tall, taller than William, and thin, reminding Peter of a cowboy from some old western that his grandfather would watch on a Sunday afternoon. The mask itself was silver with golden embroideries, with lips forming a wicked grin. Within the sockets, burned and scarred flesh surrounded the man's icy gaze. His eyes were gray, emanating emptiness and cruelty.

Suddenly, one of the masked man's hands revealed itself. Outstretched and bandaged without any skin to see, he offered his hand to shake. "Angel," his gritty, cold, American accent said from behind the mask. "Angel Harlow."

Peter remained still, looking down at the hand, inexplicably recalling how the Blackheart Lord had never shaken his hand when they had first met. His gaze turned back to the cold eyes within the mask as he simply said, "Peter. Peter Loneheart."

Angel's empty hand disappeared as he looked Peter up and down. "You're a Virginia boy?"

"I am."

"I am," he mocked. With his hands clasped behind his back, he began to pace around. "You come here alone?"

"What?"

"Did you get here on your own? Arden."

"I came here with William. He brought me. You?"

"Just me. You've been having a fine time, ain't ya?" A moment passed. Peter didn't reply. "You don't have to tell me, son. I know about you, and your friends. You and your posse have been making a ruckus. But I'm glad for it. Kept me where I wanted to be."

"What are you doing here?" Peter asked blatantly. "And what do you want?"

Angel stopped pacing. The cold eyes behind the mask watched Peter, and no reply came. A few moments passed. Then the gray eyes looked beyond him.

"Ginger's still alive?" A brief chuckle echoed from behind the mask. At first, Peter felt the need to look behind himself at the fallen Knight. Instead, he watched Angel, keeping his guard up.

In an instant, the mask and the man within it became a blur of gray. Peter turned in time to see Angel reappear in between William and the one-eyed warrior he had fought. The masked man grasped the fallen Knight by the throat and lifted him into the air with a single hand. Without effort, Angel walked in a circle around William, displaying the suffocating man he held for the army of Bastille to see. He then skipped forward and pitched the man he held through the air, over Peter, and over the ruined town. The screams of Rob Grimful receded before he collided with the side of the mountain overlooking what had been Milsted. His lifeless body rolled down from afar, appearing a speck in the distance.

Peter turned back as William and Angel looked each other over. With growing concern after what he had seen, he dashed forward himself, becoming a blue blur and stopping next to William.

The gray eyes looked from the old knight to Peter. "Hope you don't mind me gettin' rid of him."

"You did us a favor," Peter replied.

"I take issue," William breathed as sweat rolled from the dark skin of his head. "He was not meant to die here. He was to return to Arden City, to see justice done."

"Easy, Wanderer," Angel chuckled. "Don't get your dander up. I ain't here to piss on your day."

"No? Then why are you here? Why have you remained in the shadows for so long?"

Angel's gaze appeared no more than amused. "Spectating," he muttered.

"Spectating?" William hissed. "As if the crisis of this world were a game?"

The eyes behind the mask squinted as if Angel were smiling a wicked smile that they could not see. "You talked to Esper," he noted. "He gave you the gift?"

"I had no use for such a thing."

"Well. You deserved it. Gettin' rid of Blackheart. He was one of three that had to go. And honestly, I didn't know if I could have put him down myself." He applauded.

"One of three?" William asked.

Angel nodded.

"Alvar was one? And whom are the others?"

The cold eyes widened with hatred as they looked to Peter, and he knew.

Angel suddenly lurched forward, catching him off guard. Angel's fist struck Peter in the left cheek full-force, throwing him from where he stood to about a hundred feet away. He collided with the side of a hill, tossing up grass and forming a crater in the dirt. Groaning, he shook his head and had begun to stand when the silver mask appeared over him in an instant. Angel delivered another punch, pressing him further into the dirt before he grabbed Peter and tossed him back toward the road. He flew over William and Aaron, plummeting into the ground about fifty away from them on the opposite side.

He had again begun to stand when Angel came at him once more. Another punch from the masked man sent him flying, skidding across the grass like a flat stone skipping across a pond of water. Again, he came to a stop on the ground, spitting out grass, groaning with pain as anger brewed. He looked up as he remained low, watching as the silver mask darted straight for him with rapid speed. His eyes began to itch and he could feel his nails sharpen and extend into claws on both hands. Like a sprinter in a crouched starting position, he pressed against the earth, flying forward and colliding head-on with his foe. The impact sent a small shock wave along the grass around them as their momentum sent each flying backward. Upon recovering, he stood, and Angel collided with him, throwing him back again into the wall of rock at the base of a mountain. His body rattled and ached as he fell to the ground.

"Ain't nothing personal, son," Angel said as he stood over him. Peter's reply came in the form of a sudden slash from his right claw, cutting through the black trench coat but missing his target's body.

He followed with his left hand, forming a fist as his claws receded, and hitting home in Angel's sternum. A sharp groan emanated from the mask as the man inside of it was thrown back from the impact. His body rolled back along the ground. Peter followed, dashing forward and driving his knee into the man as he stood. Another groan from the masked man ignited his bloodlust. The darkness within him was prepared to take over, he knew, and he could feel Verluxia's power growing within him. His heart began to grow warm as he watched Angel stand, and he prepared to continue his attack.

But as he dove forward with his claws ready to kill, Angel rushed at him and grabbed the wrists of both hands, bringing him to an abrupt stop. They stood face to face, struggling with one another as Peter glared deep into the gray eyes behind the mask.

The eyes squinted as if Angel were smirking and suddenly horrid pain radiated from Peter's groin as Angel's knee made contact between his legs.

Before the power of the impact could send him flying backward, Angel's grip on his wrists tightened and Peter was pulled back down as the masked man gave another knee but into the Lion's sternum.

Angel released his grip and Peter fell to the ground, unable to breathe amidst the worst pain he had ever felt radiating from his groin and stomach. He puked where he lay in the grass.

“That hurts, don't it?” Angel mused.

Continuing to hold his agonized body, Peter coughed, tasting the bitterness of his vomit. Angel grasped the back of his neck and dragged him along the ground toward the nearby flow of water. Peter peered up. It was a river leading between two of the mountains, nowhere near as wide as the Ornian but still deep, he knew. “You know, I was warned to stay away from the sea,” Angel said. “Still, I think we should put the theory to the test.” Peter was raised to eye level with the mask. Surrounded by the burned and scarred flesh, the gray eyes glared at him bitterly.

“Adios, Amigo,” Angel said before he tossed Peter into the flowing water.

The bitter cold consumed him and coupled with his pain to further his misery as he began to sink straight to the bottom. Despite the pain, he kicked his legs and glared at the sun that hovered above the surface. The water carried him away and he flailed as he sunk, desperate for air and desperate to return to Aurora. In the water above him, a playing card had been thrown into the water after him. It floated around, following after as he sunk to the bottom. It was an Ace.

* * * * * * *

The captains issued the orders William had given them. The sergeants barked loudly and incessantly, forming new ranks as they prepared to fight. His gaze remained upon the tops of the hills the two men had disappeared over. The sounds of their impacts had rolled over the earth and grasped his attention multiple times. Next to him, Sir Aaron and the other knights formed up behind him as the army of five hundred men struck a new formation, facing the direction in which Peter had disappeared.

"Sir William," Aaron said to him.

He was about to reply, but something caught his attention. Across the grassy field and few hills, a figure walked towards them. The sight of the silver mask and black trench coat sank the old knight's heart and drew the eyes of every man with him. As the Angel marched towards them, he suddenly halted. The silver mask turned from one end of the five-hundred-man army to the other.

As the army and the masked man faced off in an eerie stillness, William heard only the gulps of his men and the cocking of hammers from muskets as they prepared for the inevitable. The stillness lingered as if for eternity.

Suddenly the silver mask appeared rapidly and larger as the Angel dashed towards them. Muskets rang out and men roared over one another as the masked man crashed into the line of men on William's right flank, where the formation was heaviest with rifles. Bodies were thrown into the air from the impact. At least fifty men were dead already, he knew.

Screams filled his ears as he saw the Angel punch into men, destroying their bodies with a single movement if they weren't thrown into the air or into a nearby group of their comrades. Bodies dropped lifelessly onto the ground as a blur of gray movement dashed around the battlefield. Two captains were killed simultaneously, each with a single strike before the man in the mask grabbed their pistols and twirled them in an unusual but proficient way with his index fingers. The two pistols were aimed and fired off, killing two more of William's men beside him. The knight and his fellow brethren of the Order charged forth into the tornado of movement on the battlefield. As he focused, at times he could discern the silhouette of the masked man as he ran. Anticipating his path, William rushed forth and swung his longsword through the air in hopes his enemy's own movement would be his undoing.

The sword collided with the forearm of his foe, who stopped and glared at the old knight. The Angel punched into his breastplate, instantly knocking the air out of him and sending him flying backward fifty feet.

William landed on his back and stared into the sky above as he struggled for air, seeing stars, and hearing the screams of his men. Never before had he been hit so hard, he knew. He struggled to rise, studying the dent in the silver plate that protected his chest. His gaze turned upward toward the fray. His knights were being disposed of one after the other, tossed into the air or struck down never to rise again. He charged forth a second time with his sword at the ready to thrust into his adversary's chest.

The silver mask turned toward him after killing off another knight. William roared as he sprinted forward, aiming the tip of his blade towards the man. His movement ended abruptly as the hand of the Angel grasped the blade of his sword. Distracted by William's attack, the masked man was struck across the back of the neck by Sir Aaron's furious stroke. The sword bounced off the masked man as he groaned with both fury and pain. William's sword was pulled upward and he was thrown along with it into the air as his foe punched Sir Aaron's chest plate, sending him flying backward.

William collided with the dirt. The last hundred men were being killed off in droves as the Angel dashed through them, tackling and swinging his fist with deadly precision.

The old knight spat blood, and the last of the screams died out as everything went black.

Chapter 31

The Serpent's Kiss

He was asleep, he knew, but his slumber ended abruptly as he heard the deep but soft voice of his uncle calling his name. "Pete," Jack said.

As he returned to consciousness, he first smelled an odious stench that reminded him of a landfill. His feeling returned, reminding him how badly his groin hurt. Beneath him, he felt sticky, cold dirt, and slowly something slithered across his hand. Opening his eyes, he saw that it was dark and dirty where he lay. A brown and black snake slithered off of his hand and he jerked it away before looking up to see a body standing over him. As he scanned the person, his eyes halted on the sight of the bone-claws the body had instead of hands.

His gaze turned upward and he met the oily-black eyes of the infected man that glared down at him. It didn't move, but it watched him. Behind it, a wall of infected people stared at him with the same black gaze. He slowly rose and turned, following the dense line of plague victims that lined the cave, surrounding him.

There must be hundreds.

"I continue to marvel at you, Peter."

Her deep and sinister voice echoed through the cave. He whirled around to the wall of the rocky cavern from whence the words had issued. Through the darkness, there was a faint light on the wall and an unnaturally tall silhouette of a person against it. Standing below the silhouette, a single infected stood and glared at him. It was different from the others, he knew. Its face had mutated over the centuries it had been infected. There was only one black eye and another yellow. The gray and scarlet clothing along its body had grown into its flesh.

"Step forward, Peter dear," the silhouette told him. Her voice was elegant, seductive, ethereal, but no less demonic. Slowly, he stepped over the snakes that slithered around his boots and toward the silhouette on the wall. The mutated infected at the base glared at him with intelligent eyes as he approached. As he came close enough, he turned his gaze to the tall silhouette behind it, to the source of her voice.

His pulse quickened as he saw her. She was twelve feet tall, her gray flesh submerged in the dirt and rock of the cave wall. Her hair, as long as the length of his body, was black and tattered like old yarn. Her visage was seemingly perfect, though it housed pale lips and slits that acted as a nose. Like a crocodile, she stared at him through reptilian eyes, obviously thoughtful. "Finally," she said, flicking her long tongue like a snake. "We meet."

"Verluxia." he breathed.

A deep, disturbing chuckle emanated from her. "I am." she mocked.

He fell short of words as he watched her, for there was no single word that could be used to describe her. She was both beautiful and haunting. Powerful and ethereal. As he looked deep into the sage pools of her eyes, he knew that she was old, archaic, ancient even. He became sure that songs of terror and marvel had been written about her in some histories of distant worlds.

"You continue to marvel at my presence," she said with obvious delight. "You are not the first."

"What are you?" he breathed.

She smiled. "I have never once allowed a human to ask me such a question and live." He stiffened, and she smiled. "But you are no mere human, are you? For never has my influence been thwarted by a creature, not once since the first word was spoken. You...you are special to me, Peter. Ask anything you would like."

He shook his head, unsure and uncertain. "Okay. Same question. What are you?"

She smiled again. "I am...serpent. Draconi. Ilfonti. Khadra. Dragon, even. Merely a few of the many names attributed to me by the many peoples of the many worlds."

"Worlds you destroyed? Like what you've been doing to Arden? All the plagues, they're your doing, aren't they? You were the black morning."

"I am that I am."

Her answer infuriated him. "That's not an answer or an excuse! You've killed countless people."

"And I saved you. When the Angel cast you into the water, it was I who pulled you out. But it was not the first time I have saved you. My power is in you. My blood flows through your veins."

"I'm still infected," he spat. "Every time the darkness takes over I hear you, your voice in my head. It's like I'm not me anymore."

"Nor will you ever be again," she assured. "You...are evolution, Peter. Be proud knowing that you and I have become something *more* together."

"So you infect people, that's your power. Why?"

"It is...my function. Just as you eat food, drink water, and breathe air, it is what I do." The rock of the wall along the right side of her body cracked and her long arm revealed itself.

The infected body of a young girl stepped past Peter and stopped short of Verluxia. The long arm reached forward and the black nail from her index finger touched the crown of the girls once-red hair. The girl's body trembled, her head thrashing violently from side to side as her figure changed and mutated. The bones of her body suddenly protruded from her receding skin. Verluxia's arm retracted and the mutated body of the girl spun around towards Peter. It was no longer a girl, but a genuine humanoid monster bearing sharp fangs. It crouched and scuttled across the cave floor away from them. "...I corrupt the image."

He ground his teeth. "You're a monster."

"As are you!" She suddenly grew bitter. "What of the ones you have killed, my lion?"

"I had to."

"Did you? Did you have to kill all the ones that you did? Surely you didn't. Surely you could have shown mercy. If you had, perhaps they would have returned to their families who now weep for them. See, you are just as much a monster as I. How can you ever forgive yourself? Would you ever truly deserve it?"

"I...I don't..."

"Would *she* ever forgive you?"

"Leave her out of this!"

"You think she waits for you now? No, Peter. You and I both know that she will replace you. After all, what do you care for her? Is she really the one you wanted when you first arrived in Arden? No. It was the other...Helen. Why else did you lust after her so? And is she even the one you truly want? The one you truly need?" Her tone reverted to elegant and charming. "Accept it, Peter."

"Accept what?"

"You and I belong together."

"No." he protested.

"You know it to be true. You will use my power again, and again, and again until it takes you."

"That's not what I want!"

"It is. How else will you defeat the Angel, or save the ones you love?"

He fell silent, unsure.

"Use the power I have given you. Become the Entity. And then you and I shall make anew—"

"No! All of this is your fault to begin with. I wouldn't be the way I am if it wasn't for you."

"Oh, Peter. Those are the words of a boy. I expected more. Very well. Blame me for destroying this world and forging you into the glorious being you are now. But would you still blame me for bringing you to Arden, away from your home? Would you blame me for your loss at the Angel's hands? Will you blame me because of your weakness for those confounded sisters? You need me! You will use my power to defeat the Angel, and to defeat Alvar."

Peter paused. "What? Alvar? But he's..."

"A wretched villain!" she hissed. Her composure had abated. Fury departed her vile lips. "Kill the Savior of Arden, Peter! Bruise his heel. Bruise his heel. Bruise his heel. Destroy our enemies, Peter! Kill Alvar."

To his surprise, amidst her panic and fury, he chuckled and began to laugh. "...You don't know?"

"What?" she hissed.

His laughter faded as he told her, "Obviously you've been living under a rock. Alvar Blackheart is dead."

Her eyes widened as he had never expected. "Alvar? He's dead?"

As surely as the wicked smile formed on her face, sudden regret weighed down upon him, exacerbated by the vile laugh that passed through her lips, filling the cave. A tremor of twitches passed along the line of the hundreds of infected. It was a victorious laugh. “Did you kill him, Peter? Was it you?” she asked with frantic glee.

“No. It was William. But I was there.” He paused. “You...you and Alvar teamed up, didn’t you? I remember a vision where he threatened you. He was standing here where I’m standing now. He figured it out, didn’t he? Of course he did. Alvar loved the old legends of Arden. He pieced it all together that you were the black morning, the second to last calamity, just before the twelve came to Arden from my world.”

“It is of little consequence now,” she said coldly. “The wretch is dead. Now is the time.” Another tremor of twitches passed along the dense line of infected that surrounded him. “Arden’s time has come, for it no longer has a savior.”

Peter shook his head. “No. You can’t. you’re done! The plague that you created has been destroyed and I won’t give you enough time to make another.” His nails turned black and extended into claws. His heart raced as he prepared to fight, unsure if he could beat her.

She simply smiled and said, “Very well.”

The lone mutated infected in scarlet suddenly jetted towards him. It was fast. Like Peter and Angel, it became a blur of movement as it ran towards him, a crimson blur. It tackled him, knocking out his air as they both tumbled back from where he stood.

Peter held his breath as he stood to gain control of his paralyzed diaphragm. As he looked to his left where the scarlet infected had landed, it again dashed toward him. He countered, punching its mutated face as it came close enough and sending it flying through the dark air toward Verluxia herself. It crashed to the ground just short of her and stood again.

“Edward’s Bane, I call it.” She referred to the lone infected. “It was the one. The one that I used to kill Edward Moonwey, the father of those wretched sisters.”

Peter said nothing at first, but watched it and studied the old garments embedded in its skin. “It’s like me and Angel. It's from my world.”

"It once was, yes."

"There were thirteen," he concluded. "There weren't twelve founders of Arden from my world, there were thirteen. You found him, didn't you? And you infected him. He's been your slave since."

"Right again. So smart, when you choose to be. The offer still stands. Fight for me, Peter. I will give you all that you desire. I will tell you the fate of Jack Loneheart, I will tell you of the doorways between worlds, and I will give you the woman of your dreams. Use my power."

He hesitated as he lingered on her offer over his uncle, and the doorways between worlds.

But before he could utter a word, a voice spoke from within. "Flee," it told him. Was it Jack? Or was it Alvar? He could not tell, but he listened and turned, digging his boots into the moist dirt. He dashed forward, knocking aside a few infected standing nearby. The hairs on the back of his neck stood. A strange, heavy cold descended upon him as he rushed out of the cave and into a tunnel of darkness. He trusted his instincts to guide him as he ran desperately.

He detected movement ahead and stopped.

Verluxia's voice echoed throughout the cavern around him. "Not that way, darling."

One by one, torches were lit. Countless infected were before him, mutated like the little girl from before. They watched with the same black eyes, all appearing more reptilian than human.

It was an army. An army of thousands that she had been saving, he knew.

Out of the horde before him, Verluxia spoke through every infected monster. "Their savior is dead. My time has come."

Abruptly, the thousands of infected began to laugh at him. Horrified, he turned and dashed through the tunnel, leaving them behind. His eyes caught light ahead and he followed it. The ending to the tunnel stood directly ahead.

He emerged onto the cliff of a mountain. The first stars of night began to gleam in the sky over the vast, calm ocean that lay before him. To his right, beneath a canopy of rock next to the entrance of the tunnel, there was a strange archway made of three stone tablets, each bearing unusual ruins. He had seen the doorway-like structure before, he knew, in a vision. It was tall, large enough to act as a doorway for Verluxia herself, yet it was hollow, bearing none of the silver light he had seen before.

His eyes lingered on the odd structure until he heard the infected snarls from the tunnel. He turned and jogged to the cliff on the opposite side. A forest lay below, stretching across the earth until it met a city on the coast. Arden City was ablaze with lights in the night.

"Peter, my love," she called through the tunnel. He looked one last time at the archway of three stones before jumping from the top of the solitary peak.

* * * * * * *

It was the iron-like taste of blood he first experienced as he awoke. There were several voices shouting, and he heard scuffling, as well as steel clattering against steel. There was a fight.

As William lay on the cobblestone, he groaned as he struggled to open his eyes. The rough stone, cut into his left cheek as his blurred vision revealed a familiar courtyard at an unfamiliar angle. He spat out blood and lifted his head, attempting to move his arms to no avail. They were bound with iron behind his back.

He rose to his knees, watching as a crowd of citizens encircled the courtyard of the citadel under the night sky. There was a fight in the center of the mob, and several bodies on the ground. They were mask wearers, each with the same pale mask concealing their faces. Musket shots rang out in the evening air as more mask wearers were killed off by those clad in familiar black attire. They were agents of Alvar, or at least those that remained after his death. The Blackheart Lord's loyal followers now fought against the mysterious group that followed the Angel, clashing over the fate of Arden City it seemed.

Clad in chains next to him, Sir Aaron slowly turned his head toward the old knight, revealing his bloodied eye and missing teeth.

William was about to speak to the young knight when across the courtyard, a certain sight ensnared his attention.

Like himself and his last living knight, there was another group bound by chains, on their knees in a line before the steps of the citadel, facing the battle at hand. Among the newly elected city council was the Lady of Lunsera herself. Though bound by iron like those beside her, Helen Moonwey assessed the situation with a calculating glare. Her eyes rested on her wounded cousin next to the old knight, and then on William himself. She spoke with concern written upon her face. Due to the ruckus, he heard nothing that she had said, but he knew. She was inquiring about Peter and her sister's fate. The old knight cleared his throat...and then thunder shook the foundation of Arden City itself.

In a blur of gray movement, the Angel appeared.

One of his hands was wrapped around the wrist of a young woman. It was Aurora in his grasp, punching uselessly at him as she cried. The masked face looked over the fight before tossing the woman aside onto the ground without a care. A familiar face stepped forth from the battle, wearing a black jacket similar to that Alvar himself had once worn. It was the lieutenant from Masterstown who had once spoken so poetically about the Blackheart Lord.

The Angel and lieutenant Horris faced off. The young officer pointed his pistol toward his masked adversary. The shot rang out as he pulled the trigger and the fighting stopped. The remaining agents and mask wearers gazed upon the same sight that the citizens of the city did.

Angel held the young officer up high in his grasp for all to see, just as he had done with Grimful. The silver mask turned toward the captured city council and slowly, he walked to them, stopping in front of Lady Helen. Her fierce gaze remained unyielding as she stared up at the man behind the mask. There was a crack, and the young lieutenant ceased his movements before his body was cast aside, effortlessly.

Though many watching gasped in horror, Lady Helen grinned as she stared up at the Angel. "I surmise that you are the one responsible for the destruction of Somerta. You've lingered in the shadows for quite some time. I suspect...you were afraid. Of course you were." She rolled her eyes as she said, "Alvar Blackheart. Frightens all, it would seem."

Angel squatted down, coming face to face with her. "You got some fire to you," he said. "I can see why he liked you."

From behind, Aurora approached him with a knife in her hand.

"Liked you both," he said before twisting around in a blur. The knife fell to the cobblestones as he forcefully took Aurora's wrist and threw her back down.

"Bold man!" Helen snapped at him. "Throwing a woman to the ground."

He waved his hand at the younger Moonwey sister and two of his masked subordinates grasped her, struggling to put her hands behind her back to be clasped in iron. She was forced onto the ground next to her older sister.

Esper Cloud appeared in the entrance to the citadel in his usual orange jacket. He bore his everlasting smile as he descended the stairs with two objects in his hands. He stopped behind the Moonwey sisters and handed over the first object he held. Angel took it, unsheathing the thin and dark blade from its scabbard.

"The sword of Blackheart," he said, looking it up and down before he reached over and took the brimmed hat that Esper handed him. "Not too bad," he said, spinning it around with his bandaged index finger. He looked back to Helen, extending the hat into her face. "I'll keep the sword, you take the hat."

She flinched as he pulled the hat away. "It's putrid, and belongs in the crypt of the one who wore it."

Regardless, he placed the hat on her head, kneeling to face her. "You must be burnt up bad about now," he mused. "Despite everything you try to do, you just keep losing."

"I see your scarred flesh. Is it any wonder you hide behind a mask? You must be intimately familiar with losing."

Angel chuckled. "Ain't no woman ever spoke to me the way you do. Even now, without Blackheart or Lionheart to help you." He shook his head and rose, stepping back as Esper Cloud began to speak for all to hear.

"Behold the Angel," Esper announced. "The one to bring down the tyranny of monarchs and corrupt politicians alike. He is the herald of a new republic."

There were no cheers from the crowd, only whispers. "He's a cheat!" a young man yelled from somewhere in the crowd of citizens.

"Why didn't he fight the plague?" a woman yelled out before others spoke.

"What is he to us?"

"A fake!"

"He's no Lionheart!"

"The Lionheart is dead, as is Alvar Blackheart," Esper snapped back at the crowd. The forces of Barrington draw nearer to take this city, to enslave you! There is no protector, save for the one before you. Who else will thwart the Lord of the eastern spire who comes for your homes and your lives?"

"Lady Helen!" a boy shouted.

Esper maintained his smile. "Lady Helen? The one who conspired to murder Lord Ornwell and the council of Arden City? Do not forget that she, along with Sir William, played her part in murdering the late council. But most importantly, do not forget that it was the same party along with the Lionheart himself that murdered our beloved savior, Alvar Blackheart."

The crowd's whispers turned to robust arguments as the mob of citizens separated into opposing groups. Some continued to argue with the accusations made by the smiling man as others called for Lady Helen's head.

This is madness, William thought. *These people. All the sacrifice, all the burden and strain to protect them, and they turn so quickly.*

He eyed Angel, standing motionless in the center of the courtyard. *This villain! All of this is his doing.* His thoughts shifted, stealing his breath. *Peter. Peter, forgive me. I have failed to protect you and to protect those dear to you.*

The crowd went silent and all looked to the old knight as he roared, "Fight me!"

Slowly, the silver mask turned towards him.

"Duel me, you coward!" William said.

Beside William, Sir Aaron's wheezing slowed to a disturbing rhythm as he uttered, "Sir...Will...iam."

The old knight turned to the young knight beside him as his bloodied lids closed and he collapsed forward onto his face, taking his last breath.

A dreadful groan escaped him as the last of his knights died before his eyes.

"Aaron!" Aurora Moonwey called out with tears flowing. Beside her, Helen's jaw flexed.

"What do you expect to happen?" the Lady of Lunsera inquired. "What is it you want?"

The masked man did not reply, but simply watched her. The smiling man standing behind her answered. "Revolution, my lady."

"What you want is of little concern to me," she told Esper without looking away from Angel. "It is what *he* wants that concerns me so."

Esper's smile faded at last as he retorted, "As it has me. For even I do not know."

Angel's mask shifted towards Esper, and the smile returned as he stiffened.

"Peter will stop you!" Aurora told them through her sobs.

Angel chuckled. "You think so?" He paced towards her. "No. Not where he's at now."

"What did you do? Where is he?"

"Bottom of a river," he answered.

No words came from her, only a roar of fury and agony.

Angel ignored her and looked back to Helen. "That's two down. Blackheart, and the Virginia Boy. One more to go. Can you guess who it is?"

"I have no idea," Helen replied coldly.

"Take a gander."

"I will not."

"You sure?"

"I am certain."

"Fine then." He reached into his black coat, revealing the deck of cards. He removed one card and put the others back within his coat. "This. This one's for you." He gently tucked the card under the shoulder of her dress. William discerned a red heart on the card and the queen.

The realization must have donned on Helen as flickers of emotion flashed across her face. "What is it you want?" she asked Angel one last time.

Moments passed without a reply as Angel stared down at her, silence surrounding them, even with the crowd that watched.

In a blur of gray movement, he thrust Alvar Blackheart's sword forward, piercing her heart. The Lady of Lunsera gasped before the blood spewed from her lips, soaking her navy blue dress. There were cries from the crowd. William roared. Aurora screamed for her sister. And a horrifying yell thundered.

The old knight turned to see a blur of black movement. Peter had appeared within the courtyard, his eyes black as midnight, claws ready to kill as he tackled Angel. The two men were thrown through a series of nearby homes, battling, destroying the metropolis, with each strike like a cannon firing off in the distance.

Ignoring the ache of his body, William stood and rushed across the courtyard with his hands still bound behind him. The sight of Peter had turned the crowd to panic, sending most running away in all directions just as the mask wearers too had fled. The Lady of Lunsera had collapsed, her face in a puddle of her own blood as her sister cried next to her, struggling with her restraints.

As William approached, he looked to the few agents of Alvar that remained. "Help her! Remove the restraints. I beseech you!" he begged the warriors in black.

Hesitant at first, the Blackheart Lord's loyal followers closed in around those in chains, removing Aurora's first and allowing her to wrap her arms around her sister.

In a blur of blue and black, Peter appeared beside William, panting as the blood dripped from his claws. The Lion of Lunsera dropped to his knees as he looked upon the sight of the slain Lady of Lunsera, with tears in his eyes and defeat upon his face.

Chapter 32

A Final Mourning

For hours that day, Peter had stared at her heaving shoulders. Within the temple, the gray walls of stone cradled the dour and dark atmosphere. Before them both, Helen lay on a table of stone with a Lunsera flag covering her body, save for her head. Peter shifted his gaze to the dead woman. Her face was just as beautiful as it had been the moment he had first seen her, yet it was hauntingly still and cold. He would never see Helen's smile again, nor hear her fabled words spoken. He looked back to Aurora. He wanted to hold her, to tell her that everything would be alright. But he didn't know if that was true.

I hate this, he thought. *There's so much pain. And I'm powerless to stop it. No word exists that I can say to her, nor is there anything I can do to take the pain away.*

Across the temple, William lingered by the double doors with his hands clasped before him, head bowed as it had been for the past hour.

There was a low knock at the doors and one creaked open. William turned to those outside, briefly conferring before the doors closed again. A sigh escaped the old knight as he made his way toward the pair, each step echoing against the walls. He halted on the opposite side of the table where the Lady of Lunsera lay.

"Forgive me," William said. "There is much we must discuss, Peter."

"Give us time, William," he replied.

"Peter. There is no more time." William's dire gaze told him enough.

With a deep breath, Peter reached for Aurora. As his fingertips caressed her arm, she pulled away, saying nothing.

"I...I'll be back," he said to her. "I promise."

He followed the old knight, exiting the temple and stepping out into the light, where he was met by a familiar set of blue eyes and a black beard.

"Gideon."

"Lad," the captain from Barrington said solemnly, wrapping his arms around Peter. "My condolences. I am sorry, lad. The Lady Aurora?"

"She mourns," William said. "As we all do. But we shall mourn later. Good captain, what news do you bring?"

"As you know, I returned to Barrington to see my family. All are well." He smiled briefly. "But the rumors are true about Ian Turner. He has the entire might of Barrington ready for war. He and his army are on their way here. He wants the city."

“He’s not the only one,” Peter said. “Verluxia. I was in her lair in the solitary peak.” The three men looked over the sea of rooftops to the peak in the west. “She has another army of infected. Thousands. Another horde that’s been mutated. I think she’s been saving it for the right time, and the time is now.”

For a moment, he thought the eerie words had caused his own legs to shake, but to his surprise, the two men next to him also shook as did the ground beneath them.

“What in Fyraen’s name!” Gideon exclaimed.

“Earthquake.” William noted. The quake ceased and the last of the dust fell from the nearby buildings.

“It really is the end of the world,” the captain said. “The army of Barrington comes from the east, and a new horde comes from the west. What are our options, Sir William? Do we flee and allow Lord Turner to fight this horde for the fate of the city?”

The old knight descended the stone steps of the temple and began to pace back and forth by the street, thinking.

Peter watched him. He had known William long enough to know his most defining qualities. The old knight was dogmatic, stubborn, and honorable.

“William,” Peter said, moving to stop the older man. “I know what you’re going to do. Ten years ago you defended this city, but you didn’t do it alone.” He joined the old knight. “I’ll fight with you, just like Jack did. After all, Angel got away from me. He’s still out there. I’m the only one who can stop him if he comes back. I’ll fight with you, but as soon as I see Angel...” He ground his teeth and clenched his fists. “I’m going after him.”

William’s eyes shined and he extended his hand. “I would most welcome it, Lionheart.” They shook, and both looked up to the captain expectantly.

“Well...” Gideon sighed. “My girls are safe. If I don’t fight now when the Lionheart needs me most then I’m not worthy of them.” He smiled, stepping down to join them.

The three turned as twelve men approached, each wearing the same black jacket. Agents of Alvar.

"Sir William," the leader said, "there is much talk among the city guard. It is said that the Lord of Barrington and his host ride for the city."

"You are correct." The old knight paused. "But another force comes from the west. A new and final horde will fall from the solitary peak. It will roll over the forest, and this city. And when this city falls, all of Arden will follow."

The young officer turned back to his comrades. "We spoke with those in the citadel that desired to defend against the forces from Barrington. The security council seeks your guidance." The man's jaw flexed. "As do we. Let me be clear, Sir William. You and the Lionheart robbed us of our Lord. You robbed this city of its champion. We cannot forgive you."

William glanced over to Peter. "The Lion of Lunsera and I do not seek forgiveness for what transpired. But know this: that we do regret with all heart and soul what happened. He and I both wish that Alvar were still here, that he might fight alongside us as we defend this city. As we defend *his* city. Can you accept that? Will you fight with us?"

The twelve men in black nodded to one another. "It is what our Lord would have sought as well," the leader said. "We will fight beside you."

William and the twelve men spoke for a few moments before the old knight departed with them. Peter lingered at the steps of the temple with Gideon. Both turned as a young boy wearing a dirty dark tunic ran toward them. He stopped and panted briefly before looking at Peter.

"My Lord Lionheart?"

"I am."

The boy smiled. "There are rumors that there will be a great battle!"

"You're an apprentice," Gideon noted. "You ought to leave the city while you can, lad. Or will the engineers assist in the defenses?"

"Don't know, sir. I work for Gyle Waters, the greatest blacksmith in the world."

"Good for you, lad. What does Gyle the Blacksmith need with the Lionheart?"

"A standing order for his Lordship was finished just this morning!"

"Standing order? For what?"

"Armor. Armor designed, and bespoke for the Lionheart himself."

Peter stepped forward. "I didn't order armor. Who did?"

"It was Lady Helen, Lord. Some weeks ago...I think...the day after the army departed the city for the west."

"Helen...had armor made for me?" He took a deep breath and looked up to the sky. Fractured, split, and hovering with dread stillness, Carraas lingered in the blue sky above. Not too far away from the destroyed planet, the moon could be seen.

She had it made for me the day after I left for the war. For when I came back a man, and not a boy anymore.

He turned to Gideon, but the captain spoke before he could. "I know, lad. I'll remain here and look after the lady for you."

"Thanks, Gideon."

Before leaving with the apprentice, Peter turned to the woman in the adjacent ally. He paced towards her alone. There in the darkness, Barda sat with her head in her hands, defeated. He stopped, towering over her.

"I failed," she said. "She trusted me and I failed her." Her strained voice and the words spoken stung his eyes.

"So did I," he told her. "We both failed her."

"Twice. Twice I was captured. Rendered useless, and unable to protect my friend."

A few moments passed as he attempted to control his own grief. He cleared his voice and spoke firmly. "You and I have never seen eye to eye. That's fine. I can't wait around to coddle you, because I'm going to do something about all this chaos. I'm going to fight. I'm going to avenge. What about you?"

With that, Peter turned and along with the apprentice departed to the shop where his armor was kept. The beating of iron grew louder with each step. As they entered the main building of the complex, a middle-aged man paced back and forth. His leather apron was blackened with the same substance smeared on his salt-and-pepper beard.

"Mr. Waters," the apprentice said beside Peter. "The Lord Lionheart."

"This way," Gyles said, ushering them into the next room. Peter's breath escaped him when he beheld the gleaming suit in front of him as he entered. The sun's light shined through the window and onto the silver suit on the stand. There was a helmet, a large breastplate that would also cover his shoulders, and gauntlets, all of shining silver. The remainder of the armor appeared to be leather with traces of navy blue fabric and some of the same silver spaced throughout the body.

"It's...unbelievable," Peter said, tracing his fingers along the woven silver designs of the chest. "A Lion. It's amazing. It's...gorgeous."

"The metalwork is a blend. A unique blend," Gyles said behind him. "Rold steel from Stonewell, the best steel in the world. And Lunarite, it's a silver that's not from this world. We were able to blend them, mold them, and forge a new steel. This is the strongest armor in the world, my Lord. Exactly what the Lady ordered."

Peter pulled away from the armor. "Helen," he said somberly, staring at it until he heard the bells in the distance. "Aurora," he said, reaching forward and taking up his armor to defend what, and who, he loved.

* * * * * * *

William stood in a familiar stance behind an unfamiliar desk, looking over a map of the city. Surrounding the desk were the commander of the city security forces and his three captains.

"Your pardon, Sir William," Colonel Tavington said from across the desk. "You would see that the eastern wall is nearly defenseless? Why post most of our fighting men on the western wall? Along with all of our artillery?"

The old knight cleared his throat. "Because the force that attacks from the west cannot be reasoned with. Ian Turner is but a man who hails from an esteemed family. He can be reasoned with. It is my hope that he will fight with us against the real enemy when he arrives."

"And if he does not?"

A good question, William thought before answering. "Send word to Sohn."

"Word has already been sent, sir," one of the captains said.

Colonel Tavington spoke. "It is Jadiel, the first son of Sohn, who is its current leader. Since the incident at the arena following the tournament, he has remained there, licking his wounds. Can you trust a boy of seventeen to come to our aid?"

William looked to the colonel, clad in his gold jacket. "I remember you, Tavington. You were a lieutenant when I last defended this city against the duke. You, too, were young like the boy Jadiel. You were incompetent then. Are you now?"

The colonel averted his gaze and cleared his throat. "My apologies if I have spoken out of turn, Sir William."

William smiled to reassure the man. "There is nothing to forgive. Go now and see that the final preparations are done."

Tavington and his captains turned and departed the office into the bustling hallway outside. Just as William looked back to the map, the door closed, catching his attention. The tall person who had closed the door wore a black cloak, hiding his face.

“Your pardon,” William said as he watched the person grasp the nearby bookshelf and, without effort, place it in front of the door before turning to the old knight.

William drew his sword when he saw the silver mask.

“Security around here ain’t so great,” Angel said.

His blade aimed at the masked man, William said, “You villain! Why have you come?”

Angel’s bandaged hands remained raised before he made his way over to the nearby sofa and sat. “Where’s the Virginia boy?”

“If it is a fight you seek, then you and I shall bout.”

Angel chuckled. “Simmer down. I’ve always liked you, Wanderer. And with your new position...it would be a real shame to take away the army’s general. I just came to talk for a minute or two.”

“You destroyed my army. You eradicated my Order. And you murdered Lady Helen. I seek no words with you.”

“What do you know about this...mutant horde?” Angel asked, but William did not reply. “I’ve been hearin’ talk around the city. They say this one came outta nowhere. What do you know about it?”

“What is it to you?” William hissed.

“I didn’t plan on another horde happening. But oh well...” The gray eyes filled with sudden malice. “Just what the hell is behind this plague anyway? You know it, I can tell. And how is it the boy almost beat me? What does he have to do with it?”

“What of your Esper Cloud? You appear before me and inquire yourself.”

“The bootlicker’s run for it. Tell me the truth about this plague.”

“Linger for another day and you will discover that for yourself, villain.”

Angel stood abruptly. “I ain’t playin’ around anymore. Tell the boy I’ll be waiting for him. Top of this building at sunset.”

“I will relay no such thing on your behalf.”

“Now that’s where you're wrong. You will. And you’ll do it because if you don’t, I’ll hunt down his girlfriend, that’s right the one that’s still alive. Then I’ll find the boy and give him her head. And then I’ll watch while he’s overcome with rage and he tears this world apart. I ain’t kidding.”

The old knight grimaced as his sword lowered. He glowered at the monster. “What is it you want?”

Without an answer, Angel turned, effortlessly pushed the bookshelf aside, and left. William collapsed into the chair behind the desk as the captain of Alvar’s agents entered.

“Sir William.”

“Send word to Peter,” the old knight told him. “..The Lionheart.”

Chapter 33

The Siege of Arden City

Bells tolled throughout the metropolis as William and his staff departed the stairwell and climbed onto the rooftop of the bastion. As he paced along the top of the structure, he scanned the entire length of the western wall before him. Sergeants barked orders from below as squads of men carrying muskets and sabers hurried along the wall. Slowly, each section between the evenly spaced towers was garrisoned with cannons and squads of men. From the coastline to the mountain, the towers displayed the muzzles of muskets as the riflemen posted there awaited the assault.

As the bells began to cease their ringing, a coastal breeze struck his face and brought with it the sounds of hysteria in the distance as citizens fled the city by ship. Ahead of him, beyond the wall of the city, the vast forest darkened as twilight descended behind the solitary peak. As the last of the squads were posted and the orders of sergeants began to die out, silence followed.

From the forest, a woman screamed.

She was joined by another and then a dozen more. On the wall ahead of William, many of the young men began to look at one another fearfully before glancing at their nearby sergeants. The cries and screams from the forest grew in number until what sounded like hundreds screeched in a dread cacophony.

Verluxia, he thought. *She seeks to frighten us with such wretched sounds. So be it.* He looked to the captain on his right. "Drums."

The captain nodded and yelled the order. "DRUMS!" The lieutenants along the wall relayed the order and their sergeants did the same.

The percussive instruments began to beat in a thundering rhythm. He looked back to the same young soldiers on the walls in front of him. They rolled their shoulders and nodded to one another, occasionally nudging the shoulder of a comrade nearby. Their own music had provided the desired effect.

William eyed the leafy branches as the drums and snarls of the infected filled the air. From the gatehouse adjacent to the bastion where he commanded, a lieutenant issued orders and one of the soldiers waved a flag of black and red. The lieutenant looked up at William.

"Cannons. Make ready," the old knight ordered. The captains relayed the order and the sergeants on the walls bellowed profanities at their squads as the cannons were prepped and loaded.

A stillness set in along the wall.

Treetops began to shake in waves. The snarls and growls grew louder as thousands of infected overpowered their drums. William nodded to the captain and the order was relayed along the wall. "FIRE!" The first cannon fired off, causing William to jump slightly even as he anticipated it. The others fired off. Puffs of smoke appeared all along the wall as paths of destruction were carved through the forest in explosions of chipped wood.

Entire trees were cut in half and smoke rose from the wall as all thirty cannons ignited one after the other. Even atop the bastion, William's ears began to ache. He pitied the young men on the walls, who might very well lose their ability to hear if they didn't lose their lives in what was to come. From the tops of the towers along the wall, muskets began to fire off with discreet pops compared to the thundering artillery. The muzzles pointed downward at the base of the wall as the infected smashed into it. They no longer resembled humans. They all lacked hair and took the form of humanoid monsters with protruding bones. They scurried on all fours across the ground and over one another to reach the top of the stone wall.

In the courtyard below, fifty men in the heaviest of armors rushed into two formations. The wooden doors of the western gate began to shake violently as the men on top of it frantically used every weapon at their disposal to defend their post. The two formations of heavily armored warriors marched toward the gate and chanted fiercely, sending chills along the skin of William's neck and arms.

The old knight frequently shifted his gaze around the battle, from the towers where rifles fired one after the other to the walls where the cannons ignited, sending masses of metal into the trees and the army of infected. As the sky darkened and stars began to shine, his eyes lingered on a shape in a demolished area of the forest. There, in the path of destruction, an unusually large silhouette stood above the thousands of infected around it. Slowly, it walked forward toward the wall.

* * * * * * *

The battle raged for a few hours. Cannons and muskets fired off over one another far away in the night. Peter stood alone on the top of the citadel, the evening breeze his only companion. He watched the western wall ignite with explosions, tearing the forest beyond it to shreds. He felt as if he were a conductor overseeing a symphony. *Requiem for Arden City*.

There was a gust of wind and he turned to face the silver mask and the man within. Angel no longer wore a coat or cloak, revealing how thin his body was beneath its tightly bound bandaging.

"Handsome armor," Angel mused.

"It was a gift," Peter said as they faced off. He looked over the silver gauntlets he wore. "From Helen. It's only fitting that I wear it when I kill you."

A laugh escaped the mask. "I'm surprised, son. That's rare. I was certain I killed you that day by the river. You came back, and with those eyes, blacker than oil. You're a real piece of work."

"Are you trying to flatter me? It won't save you, not from me, not after what you've done." The nails of his fingers turned to black claws.

"Spooky," Angel chuckled.

A few moments passed as they silently watched one another, the stars above them and the battle for the fate of Arden around them.

"It's time," Angel said.

Peter didn't reply but charged forth in a blur of blue. Like a meteor hurtling from space, they fell from the highest building in the entire district, slamming into the citadel courtyard to form a massive crater. Both men stood immediately, ignoring the same pain as the adrenaline coursed through them. They clashed, throwing each other into nearby buildings as they fought their own battle.

* * * * * * *

The tempo of the cannons slowed as the battle for the western wall continued. William's ears rang, overwhelmed by the orchestra of battle. Though his hearing began to diminish, he now began to detect heavy impacts far behind him within the city. He turned to look behind the flagmen and idle lieutenants standing with him on the bastion. Over the city, clouds of chalky debris hovered in a path leading from the citadel toward the mountains north of the city.

Peter fights the Angel, he realized. His gaze lingered until the captain that had been relaying his orders called for his attention.

"Sir William!" The officer indicated the nearest section of the wall, where a pack of mutated infected climbed over, their skeleton-like heads appearing over the edge.

The soldiers nearest were taken by surprise as the monsters dug their claws into their legs before pulling them over the edge onto the far side, out of sight. The pack of infected took to the wall and began attacking more men, piercing their flesh with bone-claws and fangs. Sergeants barked new commands and even grabbed the troops nearest them, forming fresh squads that then slammed into the infected on the wall, hacking at the monsters with sabers that gleamed in the torchlight.

As the situation on the wall was dealt with, William looked to the adjacent courtyard below, where the unit of fifty men in heavy armor continued to standby in formation. In front of them, the large wooden doors of the gate quaked and splintered in various areas. William realized that it would soon burst open.

His gaze shifted back to the wall, where infected began to climb onto the vast stone structure in various places. No doubt they climbed over one another on the far side where he could not see. As they ascended onto the stone garrisons, they were all met with the steel blades of the fighting men. The plagued heads were sent backward off the wall and their mutated bodies followed after into the darkness beyond.

William's eyes turned upward to the scarred forest. Beneath the starlight, though dim, he focused on the large figure of a person slowly moving toward the city. Squinting, he discerned a glossy shine along the vast body, but remained unable to see its face in the night.

"Sir William," the captain said again, pointing to the gate. Toward the top of the wooden doors, chips of various sizes began to fall. He drew his longsword.

"With me!" he ordered. "Draw swords." He departed the bastion with the agents of Alvar in tow, entering the courtyard.

The two formations of heavy-armored warriors parted and faced him in a single movement. The knight and his officers strolled forth toward the gate and the two formations followed behind, forming a wall the entire length of the courtyard.

The officers stopped and he slowly paced forward, halting between the soldiers and the doomed gate. He looked to the weakening doors and then to his men.

"Hear me! You are men. Each of you are made in the image of God himself. Do not falter or flee. Do not know fear, nor accept defeat! Fight! Fight for life!" he called out to them, and the courtyard filled with their roars. They beat on their shields and chanted as they marched forth and joined the old knight.

The doors trembled as never before and abruptly opened. A mob of mutated people growled and spewed black tar as they ran through the gate shoulder to shoulder. Every pair of eyes were as black as oil and their hands were but claws of their own bones. Some sprawled on the ground as others ran forward. The two forces collided in the center of the courtyard.

William's blade cut into one infected body after the next, sending splashes of crimson and black ooze into the air as the men beside him did the same. Their line pushed forward, stomping over the chopped corpses at their feet as they advanced. Though he and his men fought with a ferocity worthy of recognition, slowly, their advance was halted as hundreds of infected flooded through the gate, clawing over one another to taste flesh.

Finally, his fears were made manifest as the line halted. The men that flanked him moved inward and their heavy shields joined together in front of the knight. Grunts and groans sounded from all around him as the men strained against the ever-increasing weight of the infected army flooding through the gate.

The ground trembled and his gaze turned upward in time to see a blurring movement of blue and gray. Peter and the Angel passed over the courtyard like a shooting star, plummeting into the thick of the infected beneath the gate. The impact of their landing sent plagued bodies flying in different directions, broken and mutilated.

He looked over the shields in front of him to see Peter standing beneath the gate. The Lion of Lunsera punched the masked man as he began to stand and the Angel was plunged into the advancing horde, carving a path through the bodies towards the forest. Peter disappeared in a tempest of movement, destroying the nearby infected beneath the gate. The men who witnessed the display of power cheered and chanted, "LIONHEART! LIONHEART!"

The warriors in the courtyard pushed forward with William as they cut down the vile monsters, stepping over their butchered corpses until they reached the gatehouse where Peter pressed on, attacking anything that moved. The men closed the large doors and pushed against them as others followed after with whatever rubble was nearby to secure the gate. Thanks to the Lion of Lunsera, the gatehouse had been cleared.

The gate was sealed again and fixed with planks, aided by the foraged rubble of nearby masonry propped against the doors. Some men cheered as others panted, merely thankful to be alive.

Suddenly, William's breath escaped him as chills erupted all along his body, from his head to his toes within his boots. His muscles tensed and then relaxed as his head began to spin. Air returned to his lungs, and his body felt anew. His ears twitched in anticipation. It was happening again, as it had when he had departed Virginia, and before when he had departed Arden.

To his delight and confusion, a thousand voices uttered his name from the abyss of the sea. "William," they called in unison.

Chapter 34

The Angel & The Lion

The wooden doors abruptly shut behind Peter and he stood beyond the city walls in the center of the battle. On both sides of the gate, the infected climbed over one another frantically to reach the top of the wall. Ahead of him, a path had been cut down the center of the advancing horde where Angel had been thrown. Now, the vile monsters sprinted for him as they growled and spewed tar, parting around the ruined trees of the forest, darting straight for him. He punched at them, shattering their bodies and sending them flying with each powerful strike. On the wall behind him, the men cheered as they watched.

After cutting down a pack of the monsters with his nails, he looked into the ruined forest to see his adversary fighting as he was himself, striking down any infected that ran at him. Finally, the silver mask turned toward him and jolted forward to meet him in the center of the conflict.

Peter swiped his right hand through the air to slice Angel, who dodged and twisted to counter. An impact upon Peter's cheek robbed him of his helmet, which flew into the air. The punch tossed him from where he stood into the nearby wall. The aft of his head bounced against the rocky masonry, sending chips of stone and dust flying around him. He grimaced and looked up in time to see Angel advance again, a blur of gray.

Led by his instincts, Peter shifted his head to his left as Angel's right fist sailed past his face and into the stone, forming a crater amidst a cloud of dust and debris. The Lion sidestepped and punched the masked man before he could react. His adversary was thrown into a pack of infected, mutilating them on impact. Peter raced forward after him, shoulder-checking the few monsters that ran toward him. Ahead, Angel shook his head, stunned, surrounded by the broken bodies.

Peter saw the gray eyes widen with surprise as he began to descend upon the man. Before he could strike, a blur of crimson to his left caught his eye and he was tackled hard into the ground, skidding across bodies with something strong clutching onto him.

He crashed into the base of the stone wall again, forming another crater. With his back to the cracked stone, he saw the monster. Its distorted face featured one gray eye and another yellow, both glaring with intelligence. The mutated infected that had tackled him snapped with filed fangs as its claws dug into his armor. They were the same claws that had beheaded Helen and Aurora's father.

It was the thirteenth. Edward's Bane. Verluxia's favorite tool.

He allowed his own claws to dig into its flesh. Undaunted by his tactic, it pushed him further against the wall and its fangs drew nearer to his neck.

Suddenly, the thirteenth was pulled away as Angel jerked the monster by the remnants of its archaic crimson garments, tearing them in the process. The monster released its grip as the masked man tossed it into the air. The monster flailed and growled as it soared over the edge of the ruined forest beneath the night sky.

The silver mask turned to Peter, and for a moment they stared at one another.

A cannon fired off directly above them, causing them both to flinch. As Peter once again found the gray eyes within the sockets of the mask, he felt a ping of sympathy for the man, which further confounded him.

He remembered Helen's face as the rapier was pulled from her chest. The haunting screams of Aurora as she watched her sister die.

A warm sensation grew within his chest. His eyes itched as never before. The ground beneath him and the battle around him suddenly went black. All he could see was the man in front of him. Again, he felt Verluxia within his mind. Angel's eyes widened as Peter threw himself into the masked man. They grappled for a few hundred meters along the ruined field of bodies and shattered trees.

Destroy him, Peter! Verluxia said from within. He punched at Angel as they rolled over one another. Groans issued from behind the mask with each impact from Peter's fists.

Finally, the masked man managed to get to his feet and disappeared in a blur of gray. Peter followed, dashing toward the gray trail that hovered in the air, snaking around infected and trees alike. Angel fled toward the mountain looming over the city. And the Lion followed.

Angel dashed past the wall and leapt into the air, landing on the rocky hill at the base of the mountain. The man continued to leap in gray blurs of movement, higher and higher, skipping from boulder to boulder.

Like a predator on the prowl, Peter darted for the gray blur of movement ahead of him. He anticipated his prey's next move and leapt forward as the masked man touched down upon the rocky face of the mountain again. Peter crashed into him and raked his black claws along the man's body. An agonizing howl echoed from behind the mask as they both slammed into the side of the mountain.

Angel's elbow struck the top of his head and the two grappled with one another on the rocky perch. Peter growled as Angel groaned, each struggling with one another's strength.

The darkness within the Lion seemed to give him an edge, and he felt his adversary's strength give way little by little. Finally, Peter rolled onto Angel, forcing the thin man's back into the rocky surface before finally placing his fingers around the throat beneath the mask. Angel's hands grasped at his gauntlets as the man struggled to get free.

Suddenly a familiar sharp pain radiated from his groin as Angel's knee made contact between his legs. The hit threw him over the edge of their perch. His body curling from the pain, he rolled off the rocky ledge, finally stopping halfway down the mountain on another rough outcrop.

As he lay on his side gasping for air, bile spewed from his stomach and mouth. The heat in his chest disappeared as the darkness within his sight did the same. Verluxia's presence disappeared.

The sharp pain lingered as he lay, and he heard Angel land behind him, sending a small tremor through the earth. Laying still, he anticipated another hit, but heard only Angel panting through his mask as he stood behind him.

"Quite the sight," the man told him. "Gives you this feeling, you know?"

Peter opened his eyes and looked down at the vast walled city. Far below, the cannons ignited at a slower pace all along the western wall that divided the city from the battlefield. Amidst the dark and destroyed forest, countless shadows continued to overlap each other toward the wall. Beyond the battle and the city, the vast ocean glistened in the starlight. The remnants of Carraas also lingered, bearing a dim light.

A sudden spark of light appeared in the middle of the ocean and a vortex began to form in its place. Another spark of light ignited in the sea and a massive whirlpool followed.

"Well, I'll be..." Angel muttered. "There must be twelve of 'em now. You reckon one could take us back home, or maybe someplace else?"

Peter's own eyes shifted among the dozen vortexes out at sea, chills traversing his body at the mere sight.

"Well, how about it, son?"

He spat out the bitter saliva from his mouth before he spoke. "Don't call me that!" He grimaced as he slowly began to push himself from the rock. On all fours, he looked up at the silver mask.

"You're easier to deal with when your eyes ain't black."

"Lucky for you." He coughed, wincing as another aftershock of pain radiated through his groin and stomach. He waited, allowing the pain to subside. When the pain dulled enough, he lurched upward to uppercut his foe.

Angel grabbed his arm and used the momentum to throw Peter into the side of the mountain again.

Peter's left shoulder hit the rocky surface, chipping and cracking both his armor and the mountain itself. He caught movement in the corner of his eye and sidestepped as Angel rushed forward, plunging his fist into the newly formed crater where Peter stood. The Lion spun and slammed his forearm into the back of his foe's head, planting the silver mask into the rocky wall.

As if he had absorbed Peter's rage, the masked man growled loudly and rushed at him. As he did, Peter noticed the crack that had formed along the left socket of the silver mask. Within, the gray eyes glowered with rage as they both fell from the perch.

* * * * * * *

William had lingered in the courtyard behind the gate for a time before returning to the bastion to resume his command. The heavily armored soldiers in the courtyard continued to focus on the maintenance of the gate as he departed. Peter had surely saved them, he knew. As he and the warriors had sealed the gate, he had heard the loud impacts echoing from beyond the wall as loud as cannon fire.

He had returned to the top of the bastion sometime after the gate had been resealed. From his position, he looked to the northern mountain. Through the nocturnal air, he could see the blurs of gray and blue ascend the mountain and then descend, briefly disappearing and then reappearing again.

“William,” a thousand voices uttered again from the abyss of the sea. His head jerked toward the ocean, where a dozen vortexes lay scattered about the dark surface of the water. His fingertips tingled and his muscles yearned for him to run forth and leap into the ocean.

Why? he wondered. *What is this feeling? Why do I feel this?* As the battle raged on, he asked himself the same questions every time the voices spoke his name from the sea.

Ahead of him, the western sky grew darker than ever before as the eastern horizon behind them began to brighten. Morning dawned. The sun's golden rays shined across the vast sea of buildings behind him, whence came a rider along the road leading into the courtyard. As the last cannon fired off its remaining ammunition, a messenger entered the top of the bastion and nodded to him, panting as he spoke. “Word from the eastern gate, sir.”

“Speak.”

“Barrington has come.”

“Barrington...now?!”

“Yes, Sir William. Lord Turner has also sent terms. He demands the surrender of the city.”

“Was he informed the city is under siege?”

“Yes, sir.”

Before William could continue, a roar echoed loudly over the sound of the ongoing battle. He and the men around him looked to the nearest section of the wall as an infected leapt onto it in a blur of crimson. The torn scarlet garments that hung from it were embedded in its mutated skin. It landed in the center of a squad that defended the wall. The four men charged at it with sabers but were each beheaded in a blur of red. The bodies of the soldiers fell onto the wall after their heads and the nearby soldiers who had witnessed the atrocity halted in fear, staring at the beast before them.

Standing still, the infected looked to the men surrounding it and then toward the bastion where William stood. Its gaze lingered on the old knight, but something further beyond it caught William's attention. He looked out into the destroyed forest beyond the walls. Something large slithered around the ruined trees and smaller infected near it, briefly disappearing.

The large silhouette that he had been seeing all night finally reappeared in a clearing. It stood as tall as the few trees that remained. Long black hair fell to the waist of her slim mottled-brown dress. William fought the urge to puke as he realized it had been made of human skin. He looked back up to the face of the tall creature that wore it. Verluxia's reptilian eyes shined in the distance and a devious smirk formed on her large face.

Suddenly, she stretched her long arms out in both directions and all the remaining infected formed into two hordes, each moving as two separate entities in different directions. Far to the left, one of the hordes collided against the wall and began to climb over one another, flooding over the top. To the far right, the same situation occurred and the men there were overwhelmed.

William looked back to the mutated infected that stood on the wall in front of him. It crouched low, preparing to jump. He drew his sword again and the officers on the bastion did the same.

The old knight readied himself as the monster jumped, sailing through the air towards him.

* * * * * * *

Peter's body ached and moved slowly as he punched at the man he had grown to hate yet did not fully know. Angel's movements had slowed as his had, panting through his mask just as Peter did. Throughout the night they had fought up and down the mountain. Standing on another rocky outcrop, they stared at one another. As dawn broke, Peter squinted, staring at the crack around the left socket of the silver mask.

Angel rushed at him again.

They briefly wrestled with one another as they stood. Angel's arms twisted around his own, breaking free of any grip he attempted to trap him. It was a tactic he had used numerous times during their fight, showing his experience.

Angel grasped Peter by the throat and tackled him, choke-slamming the Lion into the bed of rock. The collision knocked the wind out of him and he lay on his back, the silver mask hovering over him. He tried to push against the man who pinned him, but to no avail.

Holding him in place, Angel spoke between breaths. “You got some endurance.” The mask turned towards the city. “That bastard of Barrington finally got here. Looks like the fight is almost over. This city is as done as a turkey on Thanksgiving. And we have the best seats to see it.”

“No...” Peter groaned, pushing against him. The man's grip remained, but weakly so. “Angel...what do you want?”

No answer came. Angel did a double take at the horizon. “I'll be a son of a...” he breathed.

Peter allowed his head to roll to his left despite Angel’s grip around his throat. His eyes settled on the city below at first and then went to the army outside its eastern wall. Along the coastline, from the south, another army moved toward the one camped outside the city. The rear formations of Barrington's army began to shift to meet it as others of the Turner host began to disperse and flee. His gaze lingered on the new army from the south and he noticed a flag gleaming with topaz delight as the morning sun shined onto the leading columns of riders. Amidst the front lines of the new army was the banner of Sohn.

It's Jadiel, Peter realized, relief washing over him. *Will he be in time to help William? I have to help.* He looked up toward the distracted man that loomed over him. His right leg lay between his adversary’s two, and he decided to take a page from the other man's book.

Abruptly, he thrust his knee into Angel's groin, following through with his little remaining strength to toss the man off of him and completely off the mountain as well. Angel's pained groans receded as he sailed through the air away from him, falling from the mountain and toward the city below.

Aching as he rolled over, Peter crouched at first, watching as his adversary grew smaller as he fell. Then he stood and took a deep breath before his first leap down the mountain.

When he came close enough, he jumped over the northern wall of the city and the series of buildings adjacent to it. He landed clumsily in the center of a cobblestone street, falling onto his face after his boots touched the ground. Lingering for a few moments, he continued to hug the hard surface as he contemplated passing out before reminding himself of the threat that Angel still posed. *He has to die*, he knew. *He's too dangerous and unstable. But so am I...maybe he's right about me...No! I'm not like him, I can't be! I'll prove it...that I'm better.*

He groaned as he pushed himself up from the ground and started to jog down the street toward the temple where Angel had happened to land. The fear of Aurora being hurt by the evil man sped his steps and he dashed down the road, becoming a blur of blue as he navigated the twists and turns until the courtyard in front of the temple opened up to him.

There, in the shadow of the tall stone structure, Angel wavered as he attempted to stand before falling back down to his knees. His right arm hung uselessly, his left hand clutching at the injured shoulder. As Peter watched the masked man shake, hunkered at the base of the stone stairs within his crater, he felt another sting of sympathy for the man.

The silver mask turned towards the Lion of Lunsera and then toward the temple.

With tears still in her eyes and a grimace on her face, Aurora descended the steps toward the man who had killed her sister with the weapon in her hands. The rapier was pointed directly at Angel, its dark tip coming closer with each step.

Angel's shoulders slightly heaved as he chuckled and then coughed. “Here to take to revenge for your sister?”

“I will plunge this wretched blade into that thing you call a heart!”

“Go on. Do it. Ain't gonna bring your sister back.”

Angel’s leg shifted slowly beneath him as his words brought Aurora closer. She raised the sword to strike. Peter pushed off the ground, throwing himself forward as Angel suddenly lurched at the woman standing over him. Just in time, Peter tackled the masked man before he could hit her. They grappled with one another as they crashed into the cobblestone. Angel's deceit was brought to light as his right arm suddenly came to life and he thrust the knuckles of his bandaged hand into Peter's nose.

They came to a stop with Peter again on his back with Angel over him. Warm blood oozed from his nose and Angel gripped his throat. He clawed desperately at the man's hands to no avail and the mask was suddenly pressed against his face. The gray eyes appeared to him closer than ever before, scarred and flaking skin around them.

The man stared at him coldly as Peter slowly suffocated in his grip. Darkness began to narrow his vision until he saw her head appear over Angel's shoulder. There was an abrupt puncturing noise and then Angel's eyes widened as he gasped loudly. The two hands around Peter's throat eased their grip.

He looked to Angel’s stomach, where a dark blade protruded from the red-stained bandages. Stumbling, the masked man stood and backed away, glancing down to his wound as his trembling hands encircled it. He howled in pain as the tip of the blade disappeared.

Barda stood behind him, glowering with the rapier in hand. As he turned to face the warrior woman, she thrust forward, plunging the sword back into the man. It abruptly stopped as its tip punctured his abdomen, and went no further.

The bandages of his hand grew thick with blood where he held the blade in place. Barda struggled against him, attempting to thrust forward to no avail. He slapped her, tossing the warrior across the cobblestone at least twelve feet from where she stood. The darkened sword followed, falling to the ground.

Aurora, the younger sister of the fabled woman Angel had murdered now stepped forth. She picked up the sword and pointed it again toward the man.

Angel's stance shifted as he prepared to strike at her.

The Lion of Lunsera widened his own stance, pivoting his body with full force as he punched Angel. The impact sent the masked man flying over the adjacent buildings. Peter fell onto his face again, unable to catch himself after the sudden momentum. The rapier clanked against the cobblestone as Aurora dropped it and rushed to his side, placing her arms around him to help him stand. He could feel her struggle to help him to his feet, and he could feel her gaze, but he refused to look at her.

He feared he no longer looked the same as he had before, that the hits he had sustained during the fight had mutilated him.

Her hand gently caressed his cheek and guided his face to meet her gleaming eyes. Tears stung his eyes as their lips briefly met.

As he held her to him, she spoke into his chest with soft but firm words. "Go, Peter. Do it. Do it for Helen."

Her face pulled away from his chest with the hint of a smile, a sight he lingered to see before taking a step back to run down the nearby street after Angel, toward the sea.

After turning a corner, Peter came to the straight road that led to the port. There at the end of the road, the sea behind him, the thin body in white and red bandages remained on its knees. The silver mask turned up toward Peter as he approached. The upper right corner of the mask had been chipped away, revealing the scarred skin of the forehead and flesh around the eye. There was a weariness about him, as palpable to Peter as the hatred in Angel's glare.

"So..." Angel coughed at first and then began to chuckle. "This is how the game ends..."

Peter took another step so that he was in range. As he had destroyed so many infected, and the first man he had ever killed in Lunsera, he planted the heel of his right foot into Angel's chest, pushing him away and into the ocean where a dozen vortexes continued to rage. The masked man's body splashed into the sea like a heavy rock. Peter stood on the cobblestone with the sea in front of him and the city behind, watching as the surface of the water settled.

"That was for Helen."

Chapter 34

Lionheart

The monster charged at William again. The knight rolled out of the way, dodging another thrust of crimson that dashed across the bastion top. He stood again and turned as another of his officers was struck down by the beast. Its black nails sliced through the young captain, and his body fell onto the stone like all those killed before him.

The monster turned back toward William. Its one yellow eye seemed to glow, while the other gray reflected sentience. The crooked mouth formed a sinister smile, revealing yellow fangs as it began to pace back and forth as if strutting with confidence.

William maintained a shoulder-width stance, his longsword at the ready to meet the next attack. The monster strutted victoriously, the city a landscape behind it. Behind the old knight, the battle continued.

Only a few muskets could be heard over the sound of yelling and roaring as men hacked away at the two hordes that climbed over the wall.

Again, from the sea, a thousand voices uttered his name from the abyss below. "William." He shook his head and glowered at the monster, refusing to allow it to frighten or intimidate him.

"I am a warrior, you dark creature," he said to it. "Fear will not thwart me, nor will you or any monstrosity your mistress can conjure. I am a knight and I will die as such!" he bellowed. Sprinting forward on the tips of his toes, he raised his longsword to decapitate the monster.

What he thought was his final battle cry escaped him as he descended upon the crimson infected with his sword raised. He swung with all his might, and the blade dug into the flesh of its neck and stopped there, barely breaking the skin. The yellow and gray eyes stared at him and it continued to grin as William pulled his blade free.

He pulled his sword over his head and brought it down again with renewed momentum. His stroke was halted, the monster's hand grasping the blade as if it were a stick rather than a sword. The knight's grip remained as he struggled to pull his blade free, but after a few moments, the sword was completely wrenched from his grasp and thrown from the bastion.

The knight backed away slowly and raised his fists as he heard the steel of his sword clash against the cobblestones far below. The monster before him glowered, taking one eerie step toward him after another.

Once it came close enough, William jabbed at it with his left fist. It felt as if he had punched a wall, but he jabbed again with his left and followed with a right straight into the remnants of the monster's nose. He jabbed again, but his left wrist was caught in the monster's grip. The knight threw another right hook and his remaining arm was trapped.

The crimson beast twisted him around to face the wall and forced him to his knees.

Though the fighting continued, a stillness lingered on the section in front of the bastion where William was restrained. He looked to the adjacent section, littered with bodies of slain men and dismembered infected bodies. Slowly, something rose over the wall on the far side. A head of long black hair appeared.

Verluxia's reptilian eyes seemed to shine like sage pools as she glared at William. Her enormous body was fully displayed upon the wall, standing nearly as tall as the towers that flanked her. The riflemen in the two towers barked new orders, catching her attention. Her long arms rose and sliced through the stone garrisons, collapsing the towers into piles of rubble around her. She turned back to William and grinned.

"William the Wanderer," her voice echoed.

He struggled against the monster that restrained him, but its grip was like steel. "You," he said. "Verluxia."

"So you do know me." Her snakelike tongue flickered. "I have great plans for you."

"There will be no plans. I will die before I succumb to your influence."

"Perhaps."

Then she spoke in an unintelligible hiss to the monster that bound him. She raised her right hand and extended her index finger as the nail turned from a dull gray to an oily black. The infected that restrained him hauled him forward against the edge of the bastion, and her arm began to extend, the outstretched nail growing nearer.

She was going to infect him in some way, he realized.

Suddenly a horn echoed from the city behind him and was joined by a few others. Verluxia's arm halted and the sound of hooves beating against the cobblestone grew louder and louder. To the old knight, it sounded like an entire army. He turned his head to see an array of riders charging down the main road. They wore copper armor that shined with topaz delight, just like the orange banner of Sohn wielded high above them.

William looked back to Verluxia as her grin faded and she glared at the army of Sohn. Her gaze shifted back to the old knight and then to something behind William. Her eyes widened.

Before William could turn, there was a blur of blue, striking the monster that held him and then colliding with Verluxia, knocking her off the wall.

Free from the monster's embrace, William rolled to his feet and his gaze fell on the familiar dark rapier lying on the stone of the bastion. He turned to the wall, where Verluxia was attempting to climb up again, but she was knocked backward as Peter punched her before stumbling. He seemed weak, William noted, before turning his attention back to the crimson infected.

The old knight ran forward and scooped up the rapier of Alvar Blackheart. It was heavier than he expected as he twirled it and sliced through the monster's defending arm. The dark blade cut halfway through its forearm with ease.

The beast snarled and struck at William with the black claws of its other hand. The knight jumped backward, narrowly escaping the deadly stroke. He countered by thrusting the tip of the blade into the gray eye of the monster. It howled and hissed before lunging forward. William was struck harder than he had ever been before and they both flew off of the bastion and landed in the courtyard below.

William remained on his back, wheezing for air before he took as much of a deep breath as he could, holding it until his diaphragm regained its composure. The monster stood over him, growling as blood and tar oozed from its vacant eye socket, its black claws raised to strike, but a barrage of small impacts appeared all along its archaic garments. Muskets rang out and the monster was struck repeatedly by the shots, then by spears thrown by the approaching riders of Sohn.

William's fingers found the rapier. He grasped the handle and swiped it in a dark blur, spilling the rotten guts of the monster. A sharp pain coursed through the knight's chest. A broken rib or two, he knew.

The infected disappeared in a blur of crimson movement and the courtyard filled with the beating hooves of the horses that flooded down the street, into the courtyard, and out the gate that had been opened. William groaned as he struggled to rise, the sharp pain of his few broken ribs impeding him. As he finally stood, he leaned against the base of the bastion, clutching Alvar's rapier and savoring each breath he took.

"Sohn has arrived!" a young man called out from behind him. William turned to meet a group of horsemen as one of them trotted forth. The man on it was about Peter's age, dressed in rich copper armor, and bearing the tanned complexion of the first family. "I am in search of the one in command. I am told it is Sir William, the legendary knight of old, yet I do not see him."

"It is I. And who might you be?"

The dark eyes of the young man began to shine. "Jadiel, Sir William. I am Jadiel, the first son of Sohn," he said with boyish pride.

"Indeed you are. We may continue the niceties later. First, Peter requires our assistance if we are to be victorious."

The young man smiled fiercely as he thrust his halberd upward and yelled, "To the Lionheart!"

* * * * * * *

He felt as if he would pass out at any moment as he slammed into the sickening dress that Verluxia wore again and again, using his force to push her back away from the wall. Her long arms slashed at him, cutting down trees as she missed. She was strong, he knew, stronger than he was.

He glared up at her face as they stood in the ruined landscape of broken bodies and shattered trees. Behind him, a group of riders in copper armor charged out of the gatehouse, followed by a flood of additional warriors from Sohn. The riders separated into two groups, charging after the two hordes that continued to assault the wall.

As Peter and Verluxia faced off, a streak of blue lightning fell from the sky beyond her. It struck the peak of the solitary mountain and the thunder clashed abruptly as the light from the bolt disappeared. The ground itself, shook. *Another earthquake*, he realized. He looked back up to Verluxia's face as she glanced back to where the lighting had struck the mountain, her lair. She turned back to him with a flicker of concern before attacking him again.

Her long arms reached after him and he dodged her attempts again and again, knowing she could easily capture or kill him if she closed her enormous fingers around him. As he continued to evade he assessed that, like himself, she was fatigued. But after dodging another one of her attacks, a powerful force slammed into him from the side, throwing him about fifty meters away from where he had stood.

He landed in a pile of dug-up dirt and sharp wood chips that were unable to penetrate his skin. As he stood, he caught a glimpse of what it was that had blindsided him before the thirteenth turned into a blur of crimson and collided with him again. He braced at the last second and they both tripped backward, skidding across the battlefield.

Rolling onto his feet, Peter crouched instinctively, preparing for the next attack. The one yellow eye of the thirteenth found him, the other now an empty socket of blood. It charged again and he threw himself forward to meet it head-on, leading with his right fist. His knuckles dug into the flesh of the monster's face.

Peter watched as the snarling thirteenth went sailing toward Verluxia, who charged him with frightening speed. Her large body slithered across the ground disconcertingly. To his right, the nearby horde suddenly stopped attacking the wall and the hundreds of remaining infected toppled over one another to fall from the stone garrison and sprint after Peter.

But before the horde could descend upon him, the riders from Sohn slammed into the packs of infected, trampling and hacking at the plagued victims with their spears and sabers.

Verluxia appeared before him faster than he had anticipated and her right hand slammed into him. Her long fingers wrapped around his body and tightened as if he were in the coils of an anaconda.

A disturbing yelp erupted from Verluxia and she released Peter. Looking beyond her, he saw that a group of men hacked at her, the tallest of whom Peter recognized. William slashed at the vile one with Alvar's sword, which trickled with black and red liquid. Standing with the old knight, Jadiel and his guards threw spears towards Verluxia's face uselessly, but they irritated her.

Peter had prepared to jump onto her back with the intent of ripping her head off when the thirteenth appeared once again in a blur of crimson. The monster crashed into him and they sailed through the air away from the skirmish. He landed hard, and what hatred remained within him ignited as he rolled to his feet.

“Enough!” Peter roared as he looked around for the monster. When he saw it, he charged with his black claws ready to tear. The thirteenth growled in defiance as he slammed into it and dug his claws into its flesh. With his onyx daggers, he raked through its decayed flesh, ripping at what he could as they both fell to the ground. He rolled over onto the monster that had slain Helen and Aurora’s father. Pulling his claws away, he wrapped his arm around its neck and pulled.

Peter grimaced and struggled as the body in his hold fought and snarled. Something in its neck popped, but it continued to move, so he applied more force, pulling with all his might. He roared as he pulled a final time, and in rapid succession, a series of pops echoed from its neck.

The snarls died out and the monster’s movements weakened until they became nothing more than minor twitches. He released the corpse and stood, turning to the skirmish at hand to see Verluxia fighting with William, Jadiel, and Jadiel’s guards. As Peter watched, she pulled a man from where he stood and bit him in half.

Peter started toward the fray but tripped and fell onto his face. With his belly against the dug-up ground, he took deep breathes and tried to crawl forward, but his muscles would not obey him. The full night of fighting had finally taken its toll.

The ground began to vibrate once again and he heard what sounded like a train's engines beating, or a trumpet being blown, or even a lion itself roaring. He couldn't discern. As he looked up from the ground, he saw a blur of emerald green movement dash from the forest. The blur of green zoomed around a few packs of infected that charged at William and Jadiel's flank. The infected were thrown into the air, their flailing bodies soaring away. Before Peter could see what it was that was so fast, the snarls of a pack of infected grew louder and the group of mutated monsters descended upon Peter as he lay helpless.

Just as they converged, they were all thrown into the air in an abrupt explosion of emerald green that evaporated as the silhouette of a man appeared over Peter. The morning sun shined into Peter's eyes, keeping him from seeing his savior's face, but he heard a familiar chuckle.

"Is that...is that really you, Pete?" Jack Loneheart asked him. The muscular silhouette loomed over him as he squinted into his uncle's face. A hand was extended to Peter. It was a man's hand, strong and rough, bearing a silver chain-linked bracelet around the wrist with a few small charms in the shapes of crescent moons.

The Lion of Lunsera grasped the hand and its grip grew firm as he was hoisted onto his feet. His weary eyes fell on the vibrant emerald pair that stared back at him. The dark eyebrows were the same shade of black as the long unruly hair that fell down the man's neck. A beard of the same dark shade covered his jawline and met a mustache, which shifted as he smiled with bright white teeth. Jack's eyes gleamed with fresh moisture as he smiled and looked Peter up and down.

A tempest of emotion erupted within Peter. He felt like a child again, staring at the man who had meant so much to him. A rush of nostalgia and sadness brought tears to his eyes as he looked upon his uncle. He reached forward and his trembling fingers brushed the rough hairs of the black beard and the bulky shoulders of solid muscle, just to be sure he was real and not a vision.

Before he could utter a word, Jack's arms wrapped around him in a fatherly embrace, and for the first time since Peter had arrived in Arden, he knew everything was going to be okay. Without a second thought, he allowed himself to feel like a little boy, and he wept.

Jack eased away and looked him up and down again. "You got big, kiddo," he chuckled.

Peter giggled as he wiped away the tears. "But you're still bigger."

Before Jack replied, his head turned toward where the skirmish was at hand. Peter's gaze followed and he saw the last of the infected cut down as the battle was won. At the edge of the ruined forest, William and Jadiel frantically waved at the two Americans and pointed toward the portion of the forest that remained. His gaze followed and he saw her.

Verluxia slithered across the ground and around the broken trees, fleeing with unnatural haste to the mountain and her lair.

"No!" Jack exclaimed as he started after her, but he stopped abruptly as Peter again collapsed. His uncle turned back to him with a hard glare that turned soft. As Jack walked back to him, Peter's eyes looked over the torn trousers the man wore and the various scratches all along his bare chest. Though the wounds were merely papercuts, they were still a glistening red, fresh.

As his uncle helped him to his feet, questions clawed at the inside of his skull until, at last, he asked, "Jack...where have you been?"

Chapter 35

Fate of Arden

"So, ten years, huh?" Jack asked beside him. Peter's arm was slung over his uncle's shoulder for support as they slowly walked across the battlefield toward the wall. In front of the gate, William and Jadiel stood with a score of men cheering in disarray.

Peter nodded. "Ten years. And it was only a few seconds for you?"

"Seems that way." Jack stared solemnly at the city ahead of them as columns of smoke continued to rise along the wall. Peter considered asking again about where Jack had been, but the man told him that it would be best to address the topic when William was with them.

As they approached the group of victorious warriors, William smiled warmly at the two of them and bowed, causing every man nearby and along the walls to do the same. As the knight straightened, Jack stared at him for a long moment before shaking his head. "The stories weren't wrong, you really are a wanderer. Wandering off from battles, that is."

The old knight began to speak, but Jack raised his left hand and gently patted him on the shoulder.

"I'm sure you had your reasons, Will. But that can wait. Let's get to the citadel and rest up a bit so I can fill you all in on what I know and maybe you can make sense of what's going on here." Jack looked around at the battlefield and then back to the solitary peak beyond the forest. He sighed. "If we have enough time."

Side by side, the Lions made their way along the road from the war-torn gate to the citadel. Behind them, Jadiel followed beside William, barraging the old knight with incessant questions, all of which the older man happily answered. The guards of Sohn followed, and along the streets of the city, the citizens of the city reappeared, cheering and applauding. Occasionally, the first son of Sohn would stare at the back of Jack's head as they walked. After an instance in which Peter and Jadiel caught each others eyes, he nudged his uncle.

"You have an admirer."

"You think so?" Jack looked back to the first son of Sohn. "I saw you fighting back there. You got some moves, kiddo." As Jadiel's face lit up like a little boy's, Jack faced his nephew again and grinned.

They entered the courtyard of the citadel and were greeted with thundering applause. Witnessing the mobs of citizens that had appeared after the battle had been won, Peter scoffed loudly, catching his uncle's attention.

"What's up, Pete?"

"These people. They all ran. Last night, almost every one of them just ran away without even considering fighting."

Jack nodded. "I'm sure they had their reasons. I don't hold it against them."

"But still...this isn't even my world or my city and I fought. They could have too."

“How many of them can do what you can, Pete?” His uncle's question halted his response as he mulled it over, knowing his mentor was right. “Let’s hold off on passing judgment, bud,” Jack said softly. “Not everyone has the same capabilities, no matter what you think. So please be patient with them. I think they’ll come around.”

“I guess you're right. As usual.”

Jack led them through the main doors of the citadel. They made their way to the security office, where Jack eased Peter onto one of the leather sofas flanking the desk in the center of the room. William and Jadiel both sat on the sofa across from him as his uncle sat on the edge of the desk. A few staff members of the citadel rushed in and out of the room, tending to Peter’s and William’s wounds to the best of their ability as well as bringing water and platters of fresh fruits.

Peter sat with his shirt off as two physicians cleaned his new cuts with ointment. He complained louder than he had wanted to as a cloth brushed over a fresh cut on his side from his fight with the thirteenth. From the desk, where he was rehydrating, Jack looked over at him. “Got a few new shiners, huh?” he asked with a grin that disappeared as his green eyes caught the numerous scratches and bite marks all over Peter’s body. He jumped to his feet. “Pete! Those scars...those things bit you?”

He nodded. “Back in Hearthelm when I was fighting in the west.”

Jadiel spoke. “And you were not infected as the others?”

“No...” Peter held up his right hand and allowed the nails of his fingers to turn black and extend into dark claws. “And yes. I'm not necessarily infected like the others, but I’m not the same as I used to be.” The claws receded and he looked at his uncle, who bore a serious expression.

“I'm so sorry, Pete,” Jack told him. “It's my fault.”

“No. You weren't here, there was nothing you could do. But it would have helped if you were. And with that, I think you have some explaining to do.”

“Indeed,” William chimed from beside Jadiel.

“Right.” Jack nodded, looking to the physicians. “Would you please excuse us?”

The citadel staff members exited the security office, closing the door and leaving the four men alone.

Jack took a deep breath and sat on the edge of the desk again. “Where to start...”

“I think we would all like to know where you've been all this time.” Peter said.

“Well, I don't know what it really is so, for now, I’ll just call it the void.”

“The void? What are you talking about?”

Jack raised his hands to calm Peter. “Easy, Pete. I'll try to make sense of it the best I can because unfortunately, I still don't know enough.” There was a brief silence as the man collected his thoughts.

“During the war,” he began, “Edward and I had to go our separate ways, but we maintained a correspondence, a runner named—”

“Captain Orrick,” Peter interjected.

“Yeah. You met him?” Jack stood with wide eyes. “Peter, where is he?”

“He's dead. I'm sorry, Jack.”

The Lionheart eased back onto the desk. “That's too bad. He was a good guy when I knew him. But he acted as a runner, delivering messages between myself and Ed. You see, for a long time Edward had been investigating the history of plagues, inspired by the legend of the black morning. Do you know about it?”

Just like Alvar, Peter thought. “Yeah.”

"He knew that they weren't just coincidences, that there was something almost supernatural behind it. Many of his suspicions were confirmed when I washed ashore and met him. Almost as soon as I had arrived in Arden, I got this feeling that something was wrong with this world, like it was infected by something and it was crying for help."

Immediately, Peter and William locked eyes, realizing that they had shared the exact same feeling when they had come to Arden.

"I told Edward how I felt and it added to his theories. When we were separated during the war, while he was out west, he learned about the *Children of the Serpent*, and about an ancient structure that was built as a prison."

"A prison?" As Peter asked the question, an image came to mind of a doorway-like structure of three large slabs of rock bearing runes. He remembered seeing the same structure when he had left Verluxia's lair at the top of the solitary peak. "It's a door," Peter said. "It's outside Verluxia's hideout, isn't it?"

"You've seen it." Jack concluded.

"Yeah. It had old-looking writing on it. So, that's where you've been."

"That's right. In Ed's last message, he told me he had learned about an ancient prison that held something evil within it. It was responsible for the plagues. Before the Duke of Barrington attacked the city, I found out about Ed being assassinated in Masterstown. After the battle, lightning struck the peak of the mountain where he had told me the prison was, and from far off, I could tell that it had been activated. I ran after it, thinking that whoever had killed Edward was there, trying to release whatever was inside. At the top of the mountain, I found Captain Orrick. He had realized the same thing I had. When we arrived, the void had been activated and next to it was that thing. Verluxia.

"We fought and I told Orrick to run for it, but by the look in his eyes, I could tell that he wouldn't be able to deal with what he had seen. Despite all that, I fought her one on one. There was something else in the void, a silhouette of something. I heard chains and then I saw them. Black and white chains wrapped around me, pulling me inside. I was in there for what felt like a few seconds, unable to move, until finally, I could again. I don't know what reactivated the void again, but when I came out, it was day, not night, and I heard a battle in the distance. I assumed it was the same battle still going on but when I showed up...I sure was wrong. I found you."

The three men mulled over what had been said. Peter considered his uncle's story.

"How did it activate?" Peter asked. "Did Verluxia do it? And who built it?"

"I honestly don't know, Pete."

His uncle's answer infuriated him. Yet again, he had more questions and no sufficient answers.

"But," Jack began, "we can probably figure that out together. Verluxia high-tailed it back to her hideout when I got to the fight. She's already back at the void, setting up an ambush for us more than likely."

William chimed in, "You plan to assault her?"

"We have no other choice. We can't let her remain in Arden, or any other world for that matter. She's too dangerous, Will, and I can't beat her on my own."

"You're kidding!" Peter exclaimed, unable to believe it. "I get that she's strong...but you're you! You're Jack Loneheart! The real Lionheart. If anybody can beat her, it's you."

"What you experienced earlier is only a fraction of what she's capable of. When I fought her, I knew that I couldn't beat her. She's so powerful, Pete. I mean really powerful. I fear for this world and any other if we don't stop her."

"What do you propose?" William asked.

The veins along Jack's biceps and forearms enlarged as he stroked his beard. "Creating these plagues costs her a lot of power, and she's been at it for centuries. Today, when she ran, she did it because she knew that against all of us together, she would lose the fight. I say together we go and end it. Before the sun goes down, we go to the solitary peak and kill her."

"So soon?"

"She's only going to get stronger the longer we wait, Will. If we wait too long then she may very well be too strong for us all to fight her."

The old knight sighed. "As you say."

Jack took a deep breath and his face relaxed. "So. Why don't the three of you catch me up on what I've missed over the past ten years? Pete, how exactly did you get here?"

The Lion of Lunsera immediately gave William a stout glare and Jack's gaze followed. "So, Will," he said, "I assume when you disappeared during the battle you went to my world?"

"Indeed. I—" William's head snapped towards the window and he stared off into the distance as if he had heard something.

"You okay, Will?"

"Of course." The knight regained his composure. "I arrived in your world as you have surmised and over the course of the ten years I watched over your successor in your stead. When the time came to return, I chose not to do so alone."

"So you brought Pete along with you." Jack's dark brows furrowed. "I wonder how you knew those portals would open."

"I agree," Peter confirmed. "That's a good question and one that he hasn't been able to answer clearly...kind of like you, Jack."

His uncle chuckled. "Everything is so shrouded in mystery. So what happened afterward?"

“After being brought to Arden against my will? Well, I washed ashore in Lunsera and I met Helen.”

“Oh!” Jack smiled. “Little Helen. You already met her, did you? She’s a clever young woman. With ten years...I bet she's gorgeous. Probably married with beautiful kids of her own. How is she, Pete?”

His gaze fell to the floor with his sinking heart and silence filled the room. “I...”

“Pete.” Jack's sudden enthusiasm died out and his voice deepened with seriousness. “What is it? What happened?”

* * * * * * *

In the silent temple, Peter stood beside Aurora, facing the body of the late Lady of Lunsera. Across from them, Jack was a statue, looming over Helen's body with a soft gaze. “And the one who did this?” he asked them.

It was Aurora who answered. “At the bottom of the sea, where he belongs.”

Jack nodded. “I am sorry for your loss,” he said, looking down to Helen one last time. “I've never known a woman as fierce, beautiful, or intelligent.”

He turned and departed the temple, leaving Peter alone with the younger sister.

“Aurora,” he said. The word echoed against the stone walls. He raised his hand to touch her shoulder before halting his advance and dropping his arm altogether. “Aurora, I...”

His words disappeared as he gazed upon the beautiful woman who wore her heart on her sleeve. Her shattered soul was visible through her eyes. It was pain that Peter wished he could take away, but he knew that no such power existed, and he cursed himself for his inadequacy as he had done so many times before. “Aurora, I...I'm going to leave again, not because I want to but because I have to. Jack needs me and I’m going to help him. When...or if I come back, I’ll explain it all to you and I’ll never leave you. Never again if that’s what you want.”

He lingered for a few moments, waiting for her reply, but she said nothing. He turned, and after looking upon Helen one last time, he began to depart the temple.

When he was halfway toward the door, she finally spoke to him. “Peter. I...”

He turned to her. “Aurora,” he said, “It might be a little forward of me to say it, but I feel in my heart it's true. I just want you to know that...I love you.”

He waited again, watching her gleaming eyes from afar. Then he turned and walked once more toward the doors. As he reached the entrance of the temple, he heard footsteps as she ran after him. He stopped and felt her arms wrap around him as she hugged him from behind.

“Peter,” her muffled voice said. “Return to me, will you?”

He twisted in her embrace and took her face in his hands. “I promise to.” he said, and sealed his promise with an affectionate kiss.

Every step he took away from the temple strained his body and heart, taking him further away from the woman he loved. In the courtyard, Jack stood with Captain Gideon. The two men appeared to be having a serious discussion that was cut short as Peter joined them.

“Gideon,” Peter said. “Thanks for everything.”

“Oi! Don't be hasty now, lad. You know I'm going with you to the mountain.”

“No. Please, Gideon. We don't know for certain what we're getting into. If things go bad, I'm counting on you to get Aurora back home.” As he spoke he recalled his promise to return to her. *But I won't let it come to that!*

The captain paused. “You and I have been through a great deal, lad. I trust in you. I believe in you. If you need me here, then I will remain in the city and watch over your bride-to-be.”

“Thanks.”

Jack shook his head. "What? Did I hear that right, Pete? Are you...are you getting married?"

Peter simply smiled and shrugged. "You know what...I hope I get to."

After saying their goodbyes to Gideon, Peter and Jack mounted a pair of horses and traveled back to the citadel. During the ride, he explained to his uncle all that had happened since he had arrived in Arden.

The two deliberately rode slowly so that they could spend as much time together as possible. After Peter had told him about his adventures, Jack exhaled loudly. "Woah. Better story than mine, Pete. So, Alvar...Blackheart?"

"And Tobius. I think Alvar was your biggest fan." As he rode along, he stared off sadly as he thought about the Blackheart Lord and his wolf.

"I can see it still bothers you. That you wish it had gone different with him."

"I do. William and I both do."

"You both admired him?"

Peter nodded. "We did. Jack, with all that's happened, with Alvar, and with Helen...I don't know if I'll ever get over this."

Jack looked ahead of them as they rode, staring thoughtfully into the west. "There will always be a sunset, and there will always be a sunrise. I guess what I'm trying to say is that life throws a lot at a man. A lot of it will knock him down, and keep him down there if he lets it. But life is more than just bad things lurking around the corner, there's plenty of joy too. Life is full of both. You can't have one without the other. That's life, son. That's the reality we live in, and the sooner you can make peace with that," he said, smiling, "the better you'll feel. I promise."

A few moments passed as Peter mulled over what his uncle had told him. He knew it to be true, yet he was unsatisfied.

Again, Jack spoke. "On a lighter note. You and Aurora?"

Peter could feel his cheeks grow hot. "Yeah."

Jack laughed. "Is she your first girlfriend?"

"No." Then he smiled. "It's crazy, but I think she might be my last."

"You're that sure?"

"I am. We've been through so much together. We're partners."

Jack's gaze lingered and he smiled. "I think you might be right, Pete. I hope it works." He paused. "You know, aside from your mother and gram, I miss pizza the most."

"Agreed. I...I wonder how they are. Ever since I got here, I can't think about them without getting homesick. It sucks."

"I know, Pete."

When they entered the courtyard, they found William in new armor at the base of the citadel with Jadiel and his six guardsmen behind him. William's longsword was sheathed in a scabbard that hung from his left hip. On his right hip hung Quickfury. The eight-man squad paced forward as Jack and Peter halted their horses.

Everyone looked to Jack as he spoke. "All of you know exactly what we're going to do," the Lionheart told them. "We're about to fight something that isn't human. She's powerful, more so than anything you can imagine. We're going to stop her. Are you willing to accept that and fight with us?"

William clutched his side, grimacing as he stepped forward. "With you, my friend. With you both. Let us end this. Together."

"Sohn has remained out of the fold for too long," Jadiel announced. "I, the first son of Sohn, shall fight with the legendary Lions and the fabled knight. Together we will end this darkness."

Jack raised his eyebrows and grinned. "That was poetic. Alright then. Let's finish it."

* * * * * * *

The company passed through the ruins of the western gate. Jack and Peter led the final effort, trotting forth with Jadiel and William following behind. An army of Sohnish warriors and the fighting men of Arden City followed. They navigated the war-torn battlefield outside the western wall, passing countless bodies of those mutated and those not. From the desolation, they entered the ruined forest. As they proceeded, the trees became denser as the solitary peak ahead grew closer and the sun began its course to set in the western horizon.

In the forest, a path of flattened grass had been woven, snaking between the trees toward a cave at the base of the mountain. There at the foot of the solitary peak, the squad dismounted as the army halted and began to form columns.

"So," Peter said as he examined Verluxia's path. "Do we really go inside...or do we jump?"

"You and I would be the only ones who could make that," Jack said. "And for good reason."

"Are you seriously saying that we split up? That's the kind of stuff from a horror movie."

As the two stared up at the faraway peak, William stepped forward. "Perhaps...those of us who cannot make the jump enter into the mountain through the cave before us."

"That sounds like a recipe for disaster," Jack said before Peter could. "I would much rather carry you all to the top myself."

"As you said yourself, it would prove tedious and not the least bit tactical."

"Will, I don't know if you've ever spent a lot of time in caves, but they're dark, I mean really dark. A grown man can easily lose his mind inside a labyrinth with no light."

Before William could respond, the ground trembled again as it had earlier that day.

"Earthquake," Peter noted. Next to him, William suddenly glared at the ocean again as if he had heard something everyone else had not. A pained expression occupied the old knight's face as his body tensed beside Peter. "Are you okay?"

The knight nodded. "I am well. Let us be rid of this evil. And soon. Enough debate. Jadiel and I shall enter the base as the pair of you attack from the peak."

Jack stepped forward. "That's a terrible idea, Will! We've been over this."

"An army will follow us!" The knight grimaced as his body trembled. "We cannot stall any longer! The witch must be defeated here and now!"

He started forth, walking toward the cave opening. Jadiel's guards lit torches, following the fabled knight as column after column of the army approached the cave as well.

"That fool!" Jack scoffed. "After ten years, he's still stubborn as a mule, and impetuous to boot."

"Jack...did you notice his body?" Peter asked. "It was vibrating."

"I noticed it." He sighed. "But he is right about one thing. This has to end."

His uncle eyed the rocky spire above them and lowered his body before disappearing in a blur of green. Jack grabbed a rocky ledge far above, about a hundred feet higher than where he had jumped. Peter widened his stance too, and pushed against the ground, soaring against gravity. He came short of his uncle and grasped a rocky ledge about thirty feet below him.

As he looked up, Jack leapt higher and higher, creeping up the mountainside. Peter used his hands and feet to follow his uncle, slowly pursuing. After another leap, he looked up again and Jack was nowhere to be seen. Ready to catch up to his uncle, he leapt upward two more times, finally landing on a familiar ledge.

Ahead of him, Jack stood in a ready stance with his feet about shoulder width apart, looking from side to side of the clearing in which they stood. Beyond Jack was the opening to Verluxia's cave through which Peter had escaped. To the left of was the void. A pale light lingered between the three large slabs of stone.

As Peter approached, Jack lifted his hand to bar his path. "Careful, Pete. Keep your distance from it."

"Got it," he acknowledged, and scanned the void from a distance. A few of the runes along the three slabs glowed with the same milky light as the illumination within the void. Suddenly one of the rune letters lost its light, giving Peter an idea. "Jack...do you think it's on a timed delay?"

"It could very well be. But still, what activated it in the first place? Who made it? What's its exact purpose?"

From the shadows of the cave, Verluxia's vile voice answered. "To imprison that which is divine."

The ground rumbled, and a moment later, she emerged as a snake from a hole. She wore no sickening dress as she had before, revealing a pattern of gray and green scales all along her body.

While Peter flinched at her arrival, Jack remained still and immovable. "Well," his uncle said to her. "We thought you'd just hide away. You're making this easy for us."

She seemed almost amused by his words. "You speak as if victory is already yours, wretched man," she hissed.

"Vile witch," he retorted. "Where's the other one? That one with chains that blindsided me before."

She ignored him and shifted her gaze. "Peter, dear." Her eyes rested on him, appearing more sincere and less feral. Her scales shimmered and shifted, causing her to appear more human than ever before. "You know the truth of my power. I can give you anything you want. I can send you back to your own world. Both of you. You can leave this world and all the suffering it has inflicted upon you behind."

He felt Jack glance over to him.

"At what cost?" Peter asked.

"Nothing more to you or your family."

"Alright." he feigned.

"Pete!" Jack grimaced.

"You, and us! That's what I ask. Send us back to Norfolk, and you leave too. Leave Arden. Go to a different world. I don't care what you do to it, just leave this one." He briefly looked over to his uncle, who shook his head, clearly disappointed. Peter looked back to Verluxia. "What do you say?"

"That is a fair request. Very well. The three of us shall leave Arden to its own fate."

"Really? You'd agree just like that?"

"For you, Peter, I would agree to anything."

"Okay? Alright. So how do we do it?"

With a grin, she waved her arm toward the sea. Nothing appeared to have changed about the dozen ever-churning cyclones. "The portal nearest will take you both home. The one beside it will take me to a new, *golden* opportunity."

"You really have power over them?"

"And more."

He paused, thinking about everything that had happened up until that point. Then he smiled. "You never should have come to Arden in the first place."

He dashed forward and prepared to dig his claws into her in any way he could. Before he could get close enough, her long arms animated and one struck him, casting him back toward the edge of the cliff. As he landed, he looked up as Jack raced forward to meet Verluxia's advance. Jack's muscular arms bulged as he caught her enormous hands and pushed against her.

She grimaced as she returned his force, but gained no ground. Jack roared, taking a step forward.

As the two remained locked together, Peter rolled to his feet and became a blur of blue as he leapt into the air, landing on Verluxia's shoulders. He twisted around and dug his claws into the scaly flesh beneath her chin. With the notion of ripping her head off, he pulled. As he struggled, he realized Jack was right: she was a lot stronger than before. His uncle's veins pulsed, his teeth clenched so hard that Peter feared they would shatter.

The head in his grasp suddenly thrashed from side to side and he lost his grip. Two of his black nails broke off and he winced before falling onto the ground. His back against the stone, he looked up and saw a large clawed foot hovering over him. Verluxia stomped just as he rolled out of the way. As Peter stood, Jack pressed forward and tackled her, slamming her into the wall of rock next to the cave entrance.

Wrenching one of her hands free, she slammed a fist into Peter as he approached to help Jack. The powerful blow knocked the wind from him and tossed him back toward the edge of the cliff. He landed and rolled, falling over the precipice, but his fingers found rock and held, his body dangling over the side.

It was obvious to him that Verluxia was trying to keep him from the fight, so he pulled himself up quickly to see her standing over Jack, pinning him to the ground with both of her freakish hands. Peter was infuriated by the sight, and a warm sensation flooded his chest as his eyes began to itch. He dashed forward, leaving behind a trail of black and blue vapor, and tackled her, knocking her onto her back and releasing Jack.

As he stood over her, he felt her influence again and he knew that his eyes were turning black. New fearful ideas came to mind: could she control him? Would she turn him against his uncle?

Claws ready, Peter slashed her again and again, tossing her black blood into the air as she cried out. Her left arm retracted and her hand reached over to grab him but she was thwarted as Jack landed on it with a thud and held it in place so that Peter could work.

Her right arm suddenly slithered as if it had no bone structure. She clutched Peter and tossed him from where he had her pinned. Flying through the air, he collided with one of the stone slabs of the void. As he fell onto the ground, panic ensued.

From the ethereal, milky light of the doorway, bright chains of light began to protrude from the surface before animating and wrapping around his body.

He struggled against the silver chains, but gained no ground, and just as they began to pull him toward the light, he did the only thing he could. "Jack!" he cried out.

The true Lionheart punched Verluxia, knocking her back before he became a blur of emerald movement. Jack reappeared in front of Peter, grasping his hand and pulling him further from the light. One by one the chains fell from him as others attempted to wrap around Jack himself.

Peering over Jack's shoulder, he saw Verluxia turn with a foul shriek. From the entrance of her lair, William led Jadiel and at least two dozen men. They had made their way through the mountain itself. At first glance, it appeared as if they had fought some concoctions that Verluxia had conjured, whatever they might have been.

In a blur of dark movement, William's rapier sliced through her, causing her to cry out again. Jadiel and the warriors of Arden City and Sohn fired off muskets, threw javelins, and thrust their spears into her, all with little effect.

A growl escaped her as she reached forward into the group of men and plucked Jadiel from where he stood. His halberd fell and terror filled his eyes.

The sight ignited fury within Peter and the darkness overtook him. In an instant, his eyes no longer itched, and he felt her influence. It was different than before, he knew. There were no longer thousands of others that she controlled. All of her power focused on him and he became hers. His worst fear had manifested.

Let us even the odds, Peter, she said from within him. Her will gave the order and his body reacted. He turned to his uncle, standing next to him. Jack's green eyes widened as he peered back into Peter's own midnight black. Peter's fist struck his uncle's chest, knocking him toward the light of the void. The chains animated once again, wrapping around his uncle, who struggled to avoid the same fate for the second time.

Verluxia howled in pain again. He looked as William struck at her with the rapier, forcing her to release the first son of Sohn. In a blur of black movement, she forced him forward. He stopped in front of William, grasping the wrist that held the dark blade as well as his throat. The old knight released the blade and groaned as Peter raised him from the ground by his throat.

Do it! she told him. He stared into the older man's eyes. He knew them. He knew him. The old man he had seen around his city as a young boy. The one who had watched him during his soccer games. The one who had stolen his future, taking him from his own world and bringing him to a new one, and a new life.

With his free hand wound back and his claws ready to decapitate the fabled knight of legend, there was another voice from within.

Of all the women, this one has overtaken you, Little Lion? Alvar asked him. *You are not worthy of the title of Lionheart if you give in to such meager darkness so easily. Pathetic pleb.*

Another voice arose from within. *Fight, Mr. Loneheart,* Helen said, bringing tears to his midnight eyes. *Fight for Lunsera. You are my living hope for my home, for my people, for my love. My sister waits for you.*

In a tempest of passion, duty, and destiny, Helen and Alvar's voices overlapped. *Fight! End Arden's Crisis!*

From a place deep within his chest, Peter roared like a lion. He released William and turned on her. Before he charged, he dropped low and grasped the sword William had dropped. In a blur of blue and black movement, he dashed forward and sliced through her with the fabled sword of Alvar Blackheart. The severed arm fell to the ground beside her.

After his stroke, Peter landed and prepared to attack again. Verluxia shrieked in pain and fury, slashing at him with her remaining arm, catching him by the chest and throwing him against the rocky wall near the void. The rapier fell from his hand and onto the ground between he and the vile one. He dashed forward again, reaching to pick up Quickfury as he passed it. Before he could, he was struck hard and forced to the ground.

As he looked up, the rapier was thrust into his abdomen, pinning him to the ground. The darkness from within, and her influence, immediately disappeared. The pain worsened and his fingertips found the hilt of Alvar's sword. Through his chipped armor, the clothing surrounding the hilt grew warm and red as he coughed up the first bits of blood.

"No!" Jack yelled before he was pulled back into the void. A single hand remained outside, clawing at the dirt. Peter's body convulsed and his vision began to blur. Behind Verluxia, the warriors they had brought reared back in terror, unsure. But William roared as he charged at her, thrusting his longsword uselessly. The blade bounced off her scales and she picked him up in her remaining hand.

"Good riddance!" she screeched before throwing the old knight through the air and from the mountain completely, toward the sea.

"No," Peter breathed as he saw William vanish over the edge, flailing as he fell. Again, he coughed up blood. A new pain radiated from his abdomen as Verluxia yanked the sword free. Her fingers wrapped around his body and he was raised to her eye level. He coughed and spit his blood into her face. "Do your worst....bitch."

With a horrifying grin, her mouth opened enough to fit his entire body, revealing the long and sharp rows of fangs that would be his end. He regretted that the last thing he would experience would be her hot and stinking breath.

Just as her mouth surrounded his head, he heard the clinking of chains and a milky light filled his vision as Verluxia was suddenly pulled away.

He fell back onto the ground, watching as Verluxia struggled with the silver chain that had been lassoed around her mouth and head. On the other end of the chain, Jack pulled, half his body out of the light of the void. He pulled, again, and again, bringing her into the light with him. Peter's vision blurred more and more. The last thing he saw was Verluxia being pulled fully into the void, and Jack's heavy gaze upon him as he heard his uncle's last words.

"I love you, kid," Jack told him.

Everything went black.

Chapter 36

The Lion Of Lunsera

Peter awoke in the middle of the night. It was the waves he first heard, crashing against the rock of the island outside the balcony. Slowly, he opened his eyes, listening to the sea on his left and the woman snoring to his right. He glanced over at his wife as she slept. The moonlight that radiated through the balcony shined on her serene face and illuminated numerous strands of her tousled hair, making them appear silver.

He sat up carefully, trying not to wake Aurora, as she had been sick the past week. His bare feet touched the cold stone floor, conjuring a wave of chills that rolled from his ankles to his neck. Standing, he walked from the bed to the balcony and was met by a cool coastal breeze that kissed the skin of his bare chest, neck, and face. He leaned forward against the stone railing, gazing at the full moon over the shifting night sea ahead of him.

Alone with only the night and the sea as his company, Peter contemplated. *I'm the Lord of Lunsera. I'm the blood of the Lionheart. I'm the Lion of Lunsera. What do I have to be nervous about? Well...public speaking never really was my strong suit, but it's a part of the job. A part of this life.* He sighed. *Alliances with other provinces, trade agreements, holding court like Helen did when I first met her. It's...not what I imagined my life would be like.* He peered back to his sleeping wife. *But she's worth it.*

He looked back out to sea and the dark sky above it. *This is worth it. No matter all the pain I've endured, and all that I've lost*. He smiled. *It's been a life worth living.*

He nearly jumped at her first touch. From behind him, Aurora's arms wrapped around his toned midsection and he felt her head rest against his back.

"Gah!" he winced. "you're like a ninja. You were asleep like literally a second ago."

"Nervous?" she mused.

"Me? Nervous? I fought hordes of zombies, giant wolves, and the black morning itself. What do I have to be nervous about?"

"Why else would you be awake so early?"

He shook his head. "Just a dream."

"A dream?"

"A dream."

"The same dream?" she inquired.

He sighed. "Yeah. It's been over a year, and I keep seeing Jack's face as he's pulled into that light, with her."

"Peter, I love you, but you cannot continue to sulk over this. The void has been closed since the fight. And William has never been found. None of this was your fault. You did all that you could. You must make peace with this." Her fingers brushed against the scar where Alvar's sword had punctured him. "It is yet a miracle you lived. Can we simply be grateful for that alone?"

"You're right." He smiled. "As usual, you're right."

"Quite right," she giggled as she tickled his sides and he turned towards her, taking her in his arms.

"I can't keep letting the past get to me like this. Regret. It confounds me."

"You're quite the philosopher this morning," she mused. Just as he began to speak, she pressed her finger to his lips. "Hush."

* * * * * * *

The day's light passed through the balcony. Along with it came a coastal breeze and the sounds of Lunar Rock. Waves crashed against the island, women laughed, children played, hammers beat against iron as the seagulls sang their morning song.

Peter sat in his chair, eating breakfast at the table in their chamber. Aurora had finished, having eaten little that day. She now paced to and from the wardrobe as well as the desk near their bed. Stacks of books and documents lay on the desk, which had once been Helen's, as had the room itself. The Lady of Lunsera now dressed and styled her hair in a similar fashion to that of her late sister's.

"You really should dress soon," she told him from the desk. "Quite pressed for time."

"It'll be fine," he replied, reaching over to Ace, now fully grown. He massaged his dog's ears. Lying on their bed, Bruce, the solid black shepherd, watched Aurora as she sighed loudly. Just as the Lady of Lunsera turned away from the desk with books in hand, their third dog, Clark, trotted in front of her. She nearly tripped over the solid white shepherd.

Aurora stomped her foot one time and groaned. "Peter! These canines will be the death of me!" As she passed the bed, she gently pet the black dog there. "All but you, Bruce."

He was her favorite, Peter knew. Bruce remained poised and silent as Ace and Clark barked when the knock at the door came.

"Enter." Aurora said.

The door opened and Tom appeared. The thirteen-year-old boy entered the chamber, briefly petting Clark before turning to Aurora. "The physician is prepared, My Lady."

"Indeed," she sighed. "Dress soon, will you?" she asked Peter as she passed the table before departing the chamber.

"How do you fare this morning, my Lord?" Thomas asked.

"Feeling fine, Tom."

The boy looked over to the desk and its stacks of contents. "The remnants of Lady Helen's work?"

"Yeah." Peter stood, walking over to the desk. "There's a lot to keep up with. More than I thought." His hands brushed against a stack of books and they fell, leaving only one remaining. It was bound by navy blue leather, bearing a silver crescent moon at its center. "What's this?" he muttered, flipping through the pages of carefully written notes and what appeared to be letters in neat writing.

"My Lord," Tom said as he pointed to the letter that had fallen from the book.

"You can go, Tom," Peter told him after picking up the letter and unfolding it to see his name upon it. The boy departed the chamber and in the silence, Peter read.

Only when a tear struck the page did he begin to feel the stinging of his eyes and the aching of his throat. He folded the letter and held it for a moment. It had been Helen, he knew. She had written it and left it in Lunar Rock before they had left so long ago. But had she ever intended for him to read it?

Regardless, he shook his head and placed it inside the pocket of his navy blue jacket as he put it on. Before, he had dressed as a boy from Virginia. Now he dressed as the Lion of Lunsera.

He departed the chamber with his head held high. As he walked down the hallway, he smiled as he readied to do one of his favorite activities. Dashing forward, he jumped from the window at the highest part of his home.

The courtyard appeared beneath him, filled with his people. They looked up at him as he shouted with glee. Cheers erupted as he landed in the middle of the market. He was greeted by a crowd, shaking hands as gently as he could while scores of others clawed at him.

In the blink of an eye, the woman in front of him suddenly appeared no longer human. Her eyes were black as midnight and she spewed a black tar through her filed fangs. Peter's heart fluttered as a vile voice manifested through hers. "Morning, Lord. Today is the day."

He pulled away, unable to take in air despite his dramatic breaths. Just as he fell to one knee he heard a familiar voice.

"Make way!" a man called out. The crowd around him was pushed back as the squad of men ushered them away. The Lionsguard. Each warrior clad in shining silver had been hand chosen by Peter and Aurora when they returned to Lunsera and toured the four islands of the province. They were the best fighters in Lunsera, and they were devoted to the Lion, and his Lioness. The silver warriors formed a circle around Peter as their captain assisted him to his feet. "A bit nervous today, lad?" Gideon whispered.

"Of all the days, Gideon, I'm having trouble today. The mental kind."

There was a brief stare from the black-bearded man. "To the keep!" he ordered his men.

"No," Peter told him. "Let's get some air...away from everyone.

* * * * * * *

They reached the road outside the gatehouse, the same road on which he had first tested his speed when he first came to Arden. His guards stayed behind as he and Gideon paced along the coastal road, flanked by cliffs.

"Today is the day," Peter repeated what the woman had said, and what he knew to be true.

"The summit. Word is that the new overseer of Emerald Island is expected shortly."

"Arliss. Lady Garshin's little cousin. And her last living relative. He's only thirteen."

"And now the Lord of a province."

"How are Kara and the girls?" Peter asked his friend.

"Well." The captain paused. "They love it here, lad," he chuckled. "A fine life. A good life. It's perfect for my girls. I am grateful for meeting you, and for the new opportunity."

"I'm glad I could be useful. Anything new from the mainland?"

"Since last you asked?" Gideon smiled, shaking his head. "Esper Cloud remains at large."

"Barda is still on the hunt then."

"Aye. The new Arden City Council seems to prove adequate in their new posts, as does the Governor of Barrington that they've appointed."

"The Turners' replacement," Peter noted. "The Duke, and his son Ian. They both made the same mistake and look at where it got them. Play stupid games, win stupid prizes."

The captain laughed. "Very good, lad."

"Still though. Think about all the people who would still be alive if neither had done it. Stupid! It's all such a waste."

"The ancient squabbles for power. With so few noble families remaining it's not likely that we will ever again see a war of reclamation. That is fortunate, and even more so, I happen to be fond of the families that remain."

As he listened, Peter stared off at the distant horizons while they continued to walk together.

Gideon placed a hand on his shoulder and laughed. "Smile, lad! It's a new day."

A smile formed on his face as he listened to his friend's laughter.

"What are the two of you going on about?" Aurora asked from behind. Peter turned to his wife. She placed her hand on his shoulder. "Are you well? I was informed that you were ill."

"I'm fine," he reassured her gently.

"Perhaps you should visit the physician as well."

"And how did that go for you? Are you okay?"

She looked at Gideon. "Good captain, forgive me if I appropriate my husband." She slipped her arm through Peter's arm and guided him away.

The two followed the road to the adjacent stone stairs that led to the beach. As their feet met the sand, she spoke. " Do you remember this place?"

He looked around the beach and the cliff overlooking it. "Of course. It's the beach where I first came to Arden. Just over there." He pointed and she playfully pushed his arm away.

"Quite right. How do you feel at the moment? Is there a rush of nostalgia? A poetic moment that transcends all of time?" she mused, and they giggled together.

"I guess so. Honestly, I try not to linger on the past so much. You know."

"So you're determined to look to the future, and the possibilities it holds for us."

He nodded and waited for her reply. She hesitated as if she knew what she wanted to say, yet was unsure how to word it. "What? What's wrong?" he asked.

"I am relieved to hear that you feel so. The possibilities of the future. So much could happen. Such new titles that you could soon earn aside from Lionheart, or Lord of Lunsera. Perhaps...father."

He stopped in his tracks and spun around to face her. "What?"

She said nothing more but took his hand in hers and gently guided his fingers to her lower stomach. The moment that he peered into her tearing eyes, the realization dawned on him. A flood of emotion followed. He was bewildered, confused, unsure, afraid, and yet happy.

They held one another, allowing their tears to fall together as they smiled and laughed in a moment that Peter Loneheart never imagined that he would know.

The shimmering light out at sea finally caught his attention. He had been so focused on her and the news she had brought that he hadn't seen it sooner. Far from the beach, above the surface of the water, a glowing sphere hovered about. He looked at it. The hovering sphere of light began to glow brighter and the water beneath it began to part.

"Peter, what is that?" his wife sobbed.

Dread filled him as he knew not what it was, yet his instincts assured him of its nature. A few grains of sand around them began to rise and fly towards the glowing orb.

"No," Peter muttered.

Suddenly his body felt weightless, as it had once before. He looked to his wife. Her tearful and fearful eyes mirrored his own. An unseen force plucked him from where he stood, yet his wife remained, untouched. She screamed after him as he sailed through the air, weightless, toward the glowing sphere.

Why? he asked. *Why me?*

His legs were the first to be sucked into its crushing power and light. He saw nothing, but he heard. There was chanting, like an arena full of spectators. He turned back toward the beach, now far away. "Aurora!" he cried out for her before he was taken from Arden.

Epilogue

He was thrown through the waves by an unknown force, onto the beach as before. After hugging the wet sand beneath him, he slowly rose, taking deep and welcome breaths. He turned to look at the water of the ocean behind him as it settled beneath a twilight sky.

"Finally!" a voice called from the beach ahead. He looked up as a man in a brown robe approached him with outstretched arms as if to hug him. The man had long white hair, but he was young, in his twenties. He had one blue eye and one green. The man smiled and wrapped his arms around him as he stood. "William, the Wanderer. Finally, you arrive!"

"Wha...who are you?" The old knight pulled away, stepping back into the water. "Peter!" he realized, turning back to the sea. "I must go back. My friends..."

"The fight is over, William," the mysterious man said.

“What?” William turned back to face him. “So soon?”

“For you, William, the fight was but a few moments ago. But for I, and the others, a year has passed since you fell.”

“That is not possible!”

“It is. You have encountered another before who has fallen through time. The Angel.”

“But my friends...what...what has become of them?”

The man hesitated before he answered. “Your friends were victorious, but at a cost. Verluxia was sealed within Fyraen's contraption along with your friend Jack Loneheart. Peter Loneheart barely survived, but he did. Unfortunately, something has just happened to him.”

“What do you mean?”

“Peter has passed beyond my sight, William. He is no longer in Arden, nor is he on his homeworld. I suspect those that attempted to abduct you succeeded in doing so with Peter.”

William could form no words.

“My name is Lorien. And I watched your fight with the serpent. When you were thrown into the vortex, I attempted to summon you here. But there were others observing the decisive battle as well, and they also attempted to summon you. This resulted in you falling through time.”

The old knight shook his head. “This is too much. This cannot be!”

“I am afraid it is, William,” Lorien said as he looked out to sea somberly. “You and I are similar vessels. Adrift in the cosmic sea of obscurity. I was once a man given great purpose, and I fulfilled that purpose. It left me a cripple, dependent upon this world for survival, alone in this sanctuary. But we are never truly alone, are we, William? We are never truly adrift on our own for too long.” He smiled. “It is true. Because here you are now. My time has passed and now your journey truly begins, Wanderer.”

"What is this you speak of?"

Lorien's finger tapped his ear to hear. "Quiet, my friend. Listen."

With a cocked eyebrow, William obeyed, allowing the coastal ambiance around him to reign supreme. The wind howled as it passed him, and the water frothed as it converged around them. The hairs on the back of his neck stood when he heard it from the sea. A thousand voices whispered his name from the abyss below. "William," they said before uttering something new. "Wander."

Suddenly the old knight's body felt anew once more. Every molecule within him began to vibrate and light caught his eye. His gaze fell to his own left hand. In his palm, a radiant sphere of light shined brightly.

"Lorien!" he called out. "What is this?!"

"This power is yours, William! Follow your instincts!"

The knight diverted his attention back to the glowing light. It was ready, he knew. Amidst the thoughts that flashed across his mind, he lingered on a familiar image: the solitary peak near Arden City, where they had fought Verluxia.

There was a flash and a snap. His body felt weightless, and then he felt a sudden constriction before he reappeared.

The coastal wind howled as it struck him. He peered up from where he stood on the mountain top. It was the solitary peak. The void stood there next to Verluxia's cave. It was inactive, with no pale light. Lorien was no longer with him. Instead, ten musketmen called out in alarm as they saw him, pointing their rifles toward him. Just as the first shot fired off, his body again quivered, the bright sphere appeared within his grasp, and he remembered the beach where Lorien stood.

There was a flash, and a snap. He disappeared from Arden and reappeared on the beach of Lorien's sanctuary.

He looked over at Lorien just as the man began to clap. "What a gift! William, you are truly blessed."

Before William could reply, his muscles gave out beneath him. He felt as though he had just run dozens of miles.

Lorien rushed over to him, maintaining a smile. "Such a power exacts a heavy toll, it would seem."

The old knight's eyes fluttered. The sudden drain of energy, along with his bruised and broken body from the battle, all weighed upon him. He could feel himself falling asleep. "What...what is the purpose of such...power?"

"You are the Wanderer, just as I was once the Magician. Rest assured, William, I will help you with this power of yours. I will help guide you before you go."

"Go where?" his lids grew heavier. "And...for what...purpose?"

"William, you faced the Distorter. Soon you must face another like her. The Deceiver, the one to take many forms."

As the eerie warning was spoken, William peered past Lorien with his wavering eyes. There, far beyond the beach, was a city. The tall buildings of unique design featured no movement and no life. They were ruins, a city dead for centuries. A city that was not his own.

The story will continue…

New Horizon

The force from the vortex carried him onto the beach. Its salty bite burned his wounds. He lay on the wet sand as the sizzling water receded behind him. The soiled bandages around his fingers blocked the feeling he knew to be coarse. The sand. It had been so long since he had felt something pleasant. But he knew pain. Who better than he?

His stomach hardened as the remainder of the salty and bitter water spewed from his lungs and stomach. It filled his mask, dripping away. He remained there for a while, allowing the pain of his wounds to simmer as he thought of the ones who had done this to him. The two women, and the boy from Virginia.

Angel looked up from where he lay to see what appeared to be mountains of rubble. Heaps of trash, consisting of objects he knew and things he knew not. Beneath his mask, he smiled as he saw the people there on the mounds. He chuckled. There had been *three*. There were always *three*. And there would always be *three*.

"Let's try this again."

www.ingramcontent.com/pod-product-compliance
Lightning Source LLC
Chambersburg PA
CBHW030429310726
48979CB00009B/1679/J

* 9 7 8 1 7 3 4 4 9 4 2 0 4 *